## Advance Praise for *The Five O'Clock Follies*

"A freelance writer struggles to find her place among hard-nosed newsmen covering the Vietnam War in this depiction of wartime journalists.

In her debut, former Associated Press editor Tuohy describes the Vietnam War through a journalist's lens. Freelance writer Angela Martinelli arrives in Saigon in 1968, wearing her 'greenness' in the form of high-heeled shoes and a gorgeous mane of red hair. As one of the few women correspondents in a war zone, Angela is greeted with misogyny, skepticism or disdain by her male colleagues, except for Nick, who works for a Chicago newspaper and gives her the benefit of the doubt. She soon proves her merit and bravery in the middle of a covert operation in Cambodia, surviving capture by the Viet Cong, living in a bunker during a siege and chasing truths that the military denies and her fellow reporters doubt. Angela also finds romance in the midst of this chaos; eventually she must choose: her career or love. Angela's determination is commendable as she forges ahead in spite of incredible dangers and an unconscionable lack of professional support. She's a model for young women seeking equality in male-dominated professions. Some portions of the book are slow, but they accurately reflect the downtime journalists endure between scoops—hanging out at bars, drinking Scotch, swapping gossip and waiting for the next gig. The story picks up steam when Tuohy describes pivotal moments of the war: the Tet offensive, the siege of Khe Sanh, soldiers on the line and the horrific injuries they sustained, even the psychological torment of walking endlessly through the jungle. The action is riveting and the writing is clear, detailed and highly readable.

An engrossing portrait of a woman among men in wartime."

—Kirkus

"Theasa Tuohy's gripping novel immerses us in the chaotic world of war reporters. In the late sixties in steamy Saigon, correspondents find that their everyday experiences of street explosions, hospitals, and helicopter crashes conflict with the stories spun by the politicians and military brass at the official press conferences, soon dubbed the 'five o'clock follies' by the skeptical journalists. Stateside problems of racism, sexism, and political divisions about the war haven't been left behind. We follow three reporters—successful, well-connected Ford, savvy loner Nick, and talented rookie Angela—as they try to make sense of the war and of their personal yearnings for home, for adventure, for truth, and yes, for bylines. Tuohy's deep knowledge of reporters, editors, sources, and the pitfalls of reporting from foreign lands enriches every page of *The Five O'Clock Follies*."

— P. M. CARLSON, author of
*Murder in the Dog Days*

# The Five O'Clock Follies

# THE FIVE O'CLOCK FOLLIES

## What's a *Woman* Doing Here, Anyway?

A Novel

### Theasa Tuohy

Calliope Press
NEW YORK

This is a work of fiction. Names, characters, places, and incidents are either the product of the author's imagination or are used fictitiously, and any resemblance to actual persons living or dead, business establishments, events, or locales, is entirely coincidental.

Copyright © 2012 by Theasa Tuohy.

All rights reserved. No part of this book may be used or reproduced in any manner without written permission except in the case of brief quotations embodied in critical articles or reviews.

Published by Calliope Press. For information, contact Calliope Press, Post Office Box 2408, New York, NY 10108-2408; phone (212) 564-5068; fax (212) 563-7859.

All photos used by permission of the Associated Press.

"My Funny Valentine" music by Richard Rodgers, lyric by Lorenz Hart
Copyright © 1937 (Renewed) by Williamson Music and WB Music Corp.
MY FUNNY VALENTINE (FROM "BABES IN ARMS")
Words by LORENZ HART Music by RICHARD RODGERS
Copyright © 1937 (Renewed) CHAPPELL & CO., INC.
All Rights for the Extended Renewal Term in the U.S.
Controlled by WB MUSIC CORP. and WILLIAMSON MUSIC CO
All Rights Reserved   Used by Permission.

"Little Boxes" words and music by Malvina Reynolds
Copyright 1962 Schroder Music Co. (ASCAP) Renewed 1990
Used by permission. All rights reserved.

Library of Congress Cataloging-in-Publication Data

Tuohy, Theasa, 1935-
The five o'clock follies : what's a woman doing here, anyway? : a novel / by Theasa Tuohy.—1st ed.
    p. cm.
ISBN 978-0-9847799-1-8 (alk. paper)
    1. Women journalists—Fiction. 2. Americans—Vietnam—Fiction. 3. Vietnam War, 1961-1975—Press Coverage—Fiction. I. Title.

PS3620.U59F58 2012
813'.6—dc23
                    2012001339

www.CalliopePress.com
Printed in the United States on acid free paper
9 8 7 6 5 4 3 2 1
FIRST EDITION

Interior Design by C. Linda Dingler

# Acknowledgments

This Is Not Your Ordinary Rock Band: Kaylie and the Group

Hats off to Kaylie, a world class teacher/mentor, and the group who pushed, tugged and got me through: Al, Pat, Stacy and Bob. With a special nod to Jerri, and a big thanks and hug for Kay Williams.

It was a long time ago, this war. Many of us remember it through the veil of memory, many are too young to know it other than history. A few words or phrases stand out, regardless of the age divide on which we rest: The Viet Cong, who fought the Americans, were the progeny of the Viet Minh, who defeated the French at Dien Bien Phu in 1954. The Ho Chi Minh Trail was the jungle supply route named for the revolutionary leader who sought to unite the country, which had been divided north from south following the defeat of the colonizing French. The United States came thereafter in fits and starts with the aim of "containing Communism." This eventuality was brilliantly foreshadowed with a laser of truth that only fiction can provide by Graham Greene in his novel, "The Quiet American," published in 1955, a mere year after the French defeat. In a special irony, the same Vietnamese military leader, Gen. Vo Nguyan Giap, who had routed the French at Dien Bien Phu, commanded North Vietnam's armies until the Americans left.

# 1

## Bird Watching

It was the sounds of the camera that caught Nick's attention. Bo Parks, his photographer for the assignment, must have spotted her as soon as she appeared in the plane doorway. From the shots Nick saw later, Parks' camera was clicking away the moment her foot touched down on the top ramp of the metal stair rolled up to the DC-10. At the other end of the field, a little Army Huey rose straight up, its double dragonfly rotors sucking more dust and gravel into the already opaque air. But it was that urgent clicking-whirr of the Nikon that made Nick look away from the congressional delegation that had just deplaned and was moving like a mirage through the shimmering heat. Nick O'Brien's assignment that blistering day—when Ho Chi Minh City was still called Saigon—was The Honorable Representative from Chicago. Nick had been trying to single out the politician from the rest of the pack.

Swiveling in the direction of the camera, Nick saw her just as Parks let out a pent-up sigh of breath that formed the words, "What a bird!"

The tall redhead moved like an oiled machine. A classier person might use a word like grace, Nick thought, but that wasn't really it.

She was fluid, her back straight, her head high, but nothing rigid—she flowed. Her legs were long and slim and firm, smooth pistons, down then up, as she negotiated those steps wearing the closest thing Nick'd ever seen to high-heeled bikini shoes. Just a thin strip of leather across the back of her heel and another across her bare toes and that was it. The movement dappled the hem of her light summer dress, which was already starting to glue to her body in the sudden rush of Saigon's sludge-like heat. She clutched the brim of a giant saucer of a sunhat, and a Leica on a Swiss-embroidered strap hung over her shoulder.

Parks was gyrating like a fashion snapper out of Antonioni's "Blow-Up." It was whirr-click, whirr-click, down on one knee, up again, right hip out, hip in, camera straight up, camera sideways, all in a blur of motion that would produce a score of shots in the matter of seconds it took Parks' bird to descend the stairs.

Nick's congressman was proceeding across the tarmac toward the low-slung Quonset terminal of Tan Son Nhut, and Nick had to snap his own mind back to business. Shit, he thought, the city desk back in Chicago would have his ass if he let their prey get away while he was bird-watching. He usually worked for the foreign editor, better known as Harry "the Arse" Bodowsky. But this time, the local desk needed some inane hometown comment from The Chicago Honorable on the earth-shattering significance of his junket into a war zone to assess the U.S. "effort" in Vietnam. Nick had brought Parks along to catch the political mouth in motion.

He jabbed Parks with an elbow. The combat photographer was a scarecrow with a doper's ever-present, vacant grin. A London street kid, Parks had never been in a dentist's chair and his teeth were a mass of rotting stumps. Limp, greasy hair hung to his skinny shoulders except for a shock of cornsilk that stood straight up over his right eye.

"Get the lead out, Limey," Nick ordered as he jerked his head toward the terminal and then headed in that direction at a trot.

# 2

# And All That Jazz

SHE STEPPED from the refrigerated cool of the Pan Am interior onto the sizzling metal ramp that burned through the thin soles of her high-heeled sandals. Her eyes smarted in the haze, squinting into the blast furnace of sunlight that was Saigon. The heat literally took her breath away. Stomach knots rose up to greet the stagnant air blasting its way down, a collision course that made her heart race, then thud, then flip-flop. What an embarrassing place for a coronary, she thought, right here at the top of the stair. The Quonset terminal flashed fast forward, out of control, a photographer on the tarmac took flight, sailing past, then reversed himself and flew backwards like a Mexican road runner in a stop action shot from a childhood cartoon. Dizzy, she shook her head and tried to clear jet lag and yesterday from her brain as she started down the stairs to her new life.

She had come out of the bright sunlight of Broadway less than 36 hours before, down those steps in her high heels, into darkness and the smell of marijuana that hung sweet in the thick cabaret air. The horns of the yellow streams of taxis feeding into New York's Times Square were muting behind her as a soft, high screech hit like a rush of adrenaline. Coltrane was playing! She hesitated, trying to adjust her eyes to the blue haze layered over the dim light. Coltrane, that sax that could wail like an agonized bird. Had Jackson known The Trane was playing when he picked this place to meet to say goodbye?

She took a deep breath to calm herself, but all she got was a lungful of smoke—it hadn't been an easy day. Stepping off that elevator on the fourth floor of The Associated Press, asking for the foreign editor, hearing him warn her Saigon was a mess, nothing would be easy from here on. That was a big move in her life. This was a little one, just a few stairs down into one of the last joints left on 52nd Street, legendary land of jazz, a trip back into her past. But only for the evening, just for a little while. Then off to work, the one thing you could count on. No family second-guessing, no betrayals. An enemy on the battlefield, straightforward as that. Off to the land of Vietnam with a camera handed her by the editor, no strings attached. Just send them war pictures, and they'd pay $15 to $25 for each usable shot. You make your own way. No strings, how nice. Nothing to tie, nothing to bind.

And no one to care.

The man taking admissions at the bottom of the stairs said Jackson had paid and pointed her way to his table. Through the haze, she could make out the rapture in his posture, tilted as his long bulky body was toward the musicians on the slightly raised stage. She thought he wouldn't notice, wouldn't see her coming, but he did. Yet there was no sign of acknowledgment as he watched her move through the red-checkered tablecloths, making her way toward him, the house-painter's son in the undertaker's suit, with no expression on his face.

"Hi, my lady." He didn't smile or get up. He didn't straighten from his slouch as she bent down to brush her lips against his cheek.

"It's been four years, Jackson," she said. "You act like it was yesterday."

"I know, my lady," he said.

"Too cool to be forgotten," she said.

He looked surprised. "Who, you or me?" he asked with a grin, the first emotion to touch his angular, pockmarked face since she'd walked in.

"I'm not cool, Jackson, I never was. The gremlins are always there."

"*Au contraire.* You're the metaphor for cool, lady."

Back at square one. Why was she always the one accused of being distant? "I got it," she said, changing the subject. She patted the Leica, putting it on the tiny table between them. "This is my passport to Vietnam."

"Peter?" he asked.

"It's over," she said.

"Oh?" The question was as light as the touch of his horn blower's fingers, which he was playing across the ridges of her newly won camera.

"I wasn't much of a wife."

"I thought he *liked* to do the cooking." He grinned his wicked grin, and bent forward to his absent horn, his slicked-back shoe-polish hair falling forward on each side of his 1940s center part. He played a phantom riff on his imaginary sax as he duplicated the forward sway of the on-stage Coltrane. Only the song he mouthed to her across the drinks on the tiny table was different. "But then, again, it's not for me to say."

"I guess no one wants to carry someone else forever," she said, moving to pick up her Scotch to avoid the intensity of his stare.

"You get around without much help, Valentine. But I would've carried you, if that's what you want." Again she was reading his lips, their faces so close, the music so loud, in the small space.

"You weren't taking either of us any place, Jackson. We parted over that long before I met Peter. We had no home life, remember? Booze and drugs and one-night stands."

"I wasn't drugged."

"Everyone else was."

"So? That wasn't me. I'm a musician, for Christ sake. That's the way I pay my freight. And don't lay on any of that old crap. I earn my bread, good bread."

She smiled to herself. Peter had made bread, too. Real bread in the kitchen, punching down dough, his hands floured, white handprints on his big canvas apron. A husband who had created a nest, who was a shelter.

"Jacks, I don't know what's wrong with me," she said.

"I do. You're a class act, my Valentine, but you'll never outgrow Doctor Mom's expectations. Always one more river to cross." His horn blower's cheeks puffed air through his nose. "Harvard and all that, you know."

"You haven't changed," she said with a grin, hearing Coltrane on the stage and Coltrane in her mind, the first time she'd heard "Olé," that familiar opening vibration: plunk, plunk, plunk of the bass strings and then the straining to hear, worrying the record player wasn't working quite right, the first off-stage, nearly inaudible notes from the arriving piano. Coltrane's sax so soprano it sounded like a flute, a trilling Arabic bird, then there really was a flute. Where did one end and the other begin? Maybe there really was a bird. A down-home country viola, fiddlestick backwards, wood on wood, where was the right key?

Atonal, yes, but wow she'd grooved on it. Jackson had been amazed, and impressed, when he'd noticed her fascination with the record at an off-campus party in San Francisco's Haight-Ashbury. "Very sophisticated taste," he'd said. For someone who knew nothing about jazz, he'd left unsaid. But modern jazz was the cutting edge. Few knew it, much less understood. It was exotic, spelled danger. When someone in her high school class had gotten busted on a pot charge just before graduation, most of the kids didn't know what marijuana was. "What happened?" they had whispered, gathered in clusters around their hall lockers. It was the jazz, they said, he played the trumpet, fell in with THOSE MUSICIANS, the ones who played around midnight, in dingy basement clubs, their heads poking through the circles of smoke like Washington out of Mount Rushmore.

"Everyone else was into Elvis," she said out loud to Jackson, lost in his own reverie of "A Love Supreme" moaning out of Coltrane's horn on the stage.

"Yeah," he said, "you always were out of step. Too bad you can't live with yourself that way."

"Too bad," she said.

Da da deda da da, he tapped flatfooted like a drummer, his black, no-nonsense, clergyman's shoe, marking the atonal passage from the wailing horn, a pedal back and forth, slapping the floor with his giant's foot.

"I got a pad in the Village. Can you stay in town for a few days," he paused, "with me?" he asked, still looking at the stage.

"I can't, Jackson. I have to go. I wanted to say goodbye."

"In case you get killed?"

"I just want to get good at something, have something to show for myself," she said, her voice coming out too shrill, stuck high in her throat. "But no one thinks a woman should cover a war. There's so much in the way."

"I wasn't."

"Yeah, you were always off at some gig."

"Doing my work, while you were doing your work. One of these years you're gonna have to make up your mind, Valentine, do you want yourself, or do you want all this togetherness horseshit."

She shook her head to clear yesterday from her mind as she descended the stairs into the Saigon heat.

# 3

# The Five O'Clock Follies

NICK O'BRIEN slumped in the plush movie-theater seat in a back row of Saigon's Joint U.S. Press Assistance auditorium, his 6-foot-4-inches balanced on his tailbone, his knees lodged against the metal back of the chair in front. His posture was awful, not quite 28 years old and a widow's hump was already starting to sprout at the top of his broad shoulders—the result of too many years of hunching over a beat-up portable pounding away with the two-finger jab.

He sat up straight, suddenly snapped out of his reverie and boredom. The bird from the airport yesterday! She was making her way past him down the aisle to a seat in the auditorium's front row.

For a moment, his mouth literally dropped open.

Fortunately for him, there was only the usual deadwood at the afternoon military briefing, so no one of any consequence was witness to his momentary lapse from the reportorial pose of cool detachment. Besides, the rest of those duffers who weren't in total torpor had their own mouths open wide enough to catch flies themselves.

As one might expect, this phase almost instantly gave way to snickers. How else could cool detachment express itself except as sneers for anything so untoward as this imperious beauty in her nude shoes walking up there and trying to present *press* credentials to the information officer at General William Westmoreland's Saigon headquarters?

The young Army captain on stage running the MACV show didn't even try to keep a straight face. Captain Smart-Ass Lasky made an exaggerated show of being helpful to the beautiful bird. He told her she would have to go to another part of the building—this was not the time or place to pick up her MACV press card. "Military assistance command, Viet Nam," he explained, making "Nam" rhyme with "command" and articulating the words slowly and mouthing them, as though she were deaf.

Jeez, still wearing those bikini stilts, Nick noticed with amusement, but at least she'd jettisoned the picture hat and the voile dress. She had on some kind of a WAC skirt that was tight and hit her just about at the knees, but those sure were no regulation Army shoes.

"Tell me, miss," Lasky said, the smirk still so wide his mouth reminded Nick of Donald Duck, "what paper do you represent?"

"I'm freelance," she said. "But I have a letter from my hometown paper in North Carolina, and the AP has given me a camera."

"How impressive," said Lasky. "Come by the office tomorrow, and I'll give you a *Bao Chi* tag. That's Vietnamese for journalist. I guess you're as qualified as half the hippies running around here."

Before picking up his pointer and turning to his map with its moveable cardboard bombs that indicated U.S. air strikes, Lasky explained there was a briefing there at 1700 every afternoon. "Briefings, my ass," Nick chuckled to himself.

"The Five O'Clock Follies," that was their official title as far as reporters were concerned. But the military insisted on referring to them as "briefings." That wasn't altogether inaccurate since there was scant information and only brief interludes of candor. But hell, Nick thought, it was hardly a help telling the woman about the so-called briefings; obviously she knew about them or she wouldn't be here, right? At last, dumb Lasky could finally feel at one with the press guys by sniggering at a mutual target. It was rare in this crazy war for the military and the press to be on the same side.

Then the bird really stepped in it.

"Tell me, Captain," she asked, "are you the one I make arrangements with to spend some time with troops?"

Oh, sweet Jesus, Nick swore under his breath, a letter from her hometown paper. And she's asking Lasky to *arrange* for her to interview some troops. He slumped back down in his seat expecting an explosion of guffaws from the assembled reporters, but there was a conspiracy of silence. You could look around the auditorium and see guys biting the insides of their lips to hold in the laughter.

Shitheels, thought Nick. But hell, what's a woman doing here, anyway?

He grinned at his thought. Hardly original. That tough broad Dickey Chapelle wrote a book about her days as a combat photographer and called it "What's a Woman Doing Here?" But look where Dickey landed: Stepped on a land mine and she and the foot went to kingdom come. But everyone said you couldn't tell Dickey from a grunt. The grunts even said it—for her obits.

Well, the few broads back in the cityroom in Chicago would probably call that sexist, let 'em. Nick laughed to himself. His reputed fiancée, Mary Alice Ordinary, or his stepmother wouldn't. Neither of them even knew what sexist meant. But they didn't know very many words, period. Come to think of it, they didn't seem to know much of anything. Most broads didn't.

He wasn't so sure the new bird did, either. She was a looker, all right. And she certainly was doing her part to perpetuate the notion of a dumb blonde, even if she was a redhead. Jesus! Wonder if she's Irish, all that red hair. Naw, too aristocratic looking. Imperial. She carries herself like a queen. Never can tell, though. People rarely guessed Nick was Irish, curly black hair—it's like they'd never heard of the black Irish, never heard of the Spanish Armada beaching on the Ole Sod. Thought he was a fucking Greek.

So, the looker wants to be a war correspondent. And she's on her own, with the barest—Nick grinned at his pun—of credentials. She must be pretty dumb not to know you don't command any respect that way. Can't expect sources to give you the time of day, if they know you haven't a network or a wire service or a solid outfit behind you. Here Nick was representing one of the largest papers in the Midwest, still he was made to feel pretty much of a greenhorn when he first got in-country last month. But you gotta expect that, it was his first overseas assignment.

Take Bo Parks, for example. In a way, he's a special case since he's a certifiable crazy. But Parks had no credentials of any kind when he arrived in Saigon on his motor scooter, riding all the way from London with nothing but a camera and a backpack. And Parks never was able to get exactly what you'd call respect during his Saigon days. There was

## 10 THE FIVE O'CLOCK FOLLIES

Dickey Chapelle receiving last rites, November, 1965

a certain something—you might call it awe—for the bucks that kid got paid and the play his pictures got in big-time publications. Anyone who would literally get his butt shot off for a picture deserves a kind of professional status, not STATUS status, but a certain acknowledgment. And crazy Parks had indeed gotten his butt shot—twice so far. The first time, he had shrapnel wounds that were pretty superficial, but on the second go-round, he lost a piece of his ass, along with other things. And he just didn't seem to give a damn. In a few weeks, he was right back out looking for more, riding his mini-motor scooter headlong into battle like some daredevil Evel Knievel. If you're the underbelly of a mortar shell with a camera strapped to your chest, you can't help but get action shots. And, one supposes, it does make you a journalist, begrudged or otherwise.

As Captain Lasky used his pointer on the blackboard to mark the latest spot where a ton of American bombs had fallen from a B-52, Nick doodled on the information office handout and wondered who had given the bird the bum steer to show up here on her first full day on the job. She obviously hadn't taken the trouble to ask around before she left home about how to hit this town running so she could look like she knew what she was doing. That's the first thing guys had told Nick back at the Anchor Bar in Chicago when they heard he'd weaseled a promise out of the foreign editor that he could have the next rotation assignment budgeted for Vietnam: "Don't go to the Follies unless you're desperate, you're more likely to pick up clap off the seats than find a decent story there."

Nick'd had it all set up weeks ahead—you didn't just need visas and shots and shit like that. He'd arranged through a friend of a friend to get the room at the Caravelle of a guy being rotated back and was already lined up with a Medevac unit to get a lift in with them on their first trip of the day so he'd have a story to file as soon as possible after he got here. You took three or four days messing around getting your bearings and the paper'd yank you home before you got mud on your boots.

Nick turned over the handout he was doodling on and grimaced as he read about the alleged number of enemy dead euphemistically called body counts, the tonnage of TNT and the bullshit about no American casualties. The girl was a freelancer. How could she write a story that would sell based on this pap? Even if it weren't fiction, as it so often was, it was about as thrilling as reading an ordinance manual.

He looked over and saw that sure enough, Joe Fried of the New York Daily News was in his usual seat. Joe was a fixture at the Follies, and his presence was a protection for absent reporters in the unlikely event that some real news actually came out of one of these briefings. But the Daily News had several men in their bureau, and they could spare someone to sit there every day to make sure they didn't miss anything from the official line. The News was also typical in that its editors back home weren't much interested in stories that strayed far from the government line. This is, indeed, some goofy war, Nick thought. Besides the battles between the U.S. and the Cong, there were also the wars between the press and the military, the war of the young correspondents versus the old-timers who thought Vietnam should be covered just like World War II and, saddest of all, the internecine warfare between the reporters on the line and their state-side editors who were riding the barricades of the hawk-dove split over the war raging back home.

Never mind which side you were on in the correspondents' war; few guys of any consequence bothered much with these Follies briefings, unless they were looking for something specific or for someone to get drunk or play cards with. Nick was here this time because he was keeping tabs on The Honorable while he was in The Nam. You get an assignment, you give 'em what they ask for.

The Honorable claimed he was here in his official capacity. Ha! He mistakenly thought since it was called a "press" briefing that the media—i.e., cameras—would be there. Politicians thrive on reporters and cameras. Absolutely love 'em. Nick always got pissed at critics saying presence of the media triggers events, especially violent ones. Causes them to happen. It's true, sometimes. But why blame the recorders? Why not blame the performers, the assholes who were showing off? But the girl, she'd just get chicken leavings trying to work from one of these press handouts.

She picked up right away, though, from the smart-ass captain's tone that they were doing a number on her—she blushed a little, then her jaw line got real rigid and squared out, as though she were clamping hard on her back teeth.

Nick slid still lower in his seat. He was remembering fall hazing at the ATO house at Northwestern that was only a little less subtle than this. He felt sorry for the girl. But no one in his right mind would've gone to her rescue. In fact, there's no such thing as rescue in situations where proving yourself is all that counts. This was a tough place, and a worse profession. If she can't take the heat, Nick thought, she belongs back in the office taking obits. Besides, no man could speak up in defense of a broad—especially one who looked like that—in front of this bunch of oglers. You'd never hear the end of it.

But Nick liked her, she looked gutsy and scared. He felt a wave of protectiveness. It was clear to him (and maybe to her, all of a sudden) that she wasn't going to have an easy life here.

Nick was never to see those wondrous shoes again, but he knew he would never forget them, especially the way they were an extension of those strong, bare legs.

As things progressed, her footwear became increasingly sensible, and it wasn't long before few in Saigon ever saw her in anything but jungle boots. Like that old epithet, "your mother wears Army shoes," that's the story of Angela—Army boots and how she grew to fit them.

# 4

# Doing the Continental

Word got around she was staying at the Continental, a main press hangout in the center of town. As Nick walked up the hotel's terrace steps, the clatter of traffic on the broad tree-lined Tu Do deafening behind him, he was startled by how equally clamorous and packed the terrace bar was.

Surely, he thought, all these dudes couldn't already have heard of the beautiful bird at the Five-O'Clock briefing—it was barely sunset.

Still, the place looked as though someone at least as important as Westmoreland had called a press conference. There were an awful lot of familiar guys lolling around who looked like they'd just shaved. The lobby bar was jammed as well.

Maybe it was just what the shrinks call projection. Maybe Nick was just feeling guilty about the feature story he'd been struggling with, and figured everybody else had something they ought to be doing too. His piece on that so-called U.S. agriculture representative, Kevin Leahey, was a bitch. The guy was hard to put your finger on. Or maybe Nick'd just never noticed that the Continental was always crowded. God knows, he thought, the sameness of life in Saigon got boring if you weren't on deadline—and sometimes, even then. Most people think war is adventure. Maybe so, but it can also be deadly dull. You're not part of the culture, you don't speak the language, so you hang out with each other, primarily in bars. And you don't see a lot of white women, good looking or otherwise. Even the ones in battle fatigues and helmets that look like grunts start looking pretty good. The cleaning women begin to take on the shape of Natalie Wood. Anyway, there were an awful lot of guys in clean safari jackets lounging around the Continental that night.

But Nick was out of luck. He did a quick turn around the potted palms of the lobby and passed through its standup bar. The redhead wasn't around. Shit, he thought as he headed back for the terrace, he should have known that if the woman showed her face in this den of hustlers, some fast mover would long since have moved her out to a quieter place with the promise of showing her how to cover the Vietnam war in one easy lesson.

"Who you looking for, Boyo?" a burly, gray-curly-haired Irishman named Ray Corrigan asked as Nick eased himself into a wicker chair, trying to find a place for his long legs under the low-slung table on the cramped terrace. Corrigan spoke in the thick brogue he'd never lost even though he'd been with Reuters, the British wire service, since he'd distinguished himself with dispatches from Spain when Madrid fell to Franco in '39.

"That tobacco stinks," Nick retorted to Corrigan, whose grin came off like a sneer, skewed as it was by the effort of talking and smiling while gripping a Sherlock Holmes pipe between his teeth. "Can't you find something better to burn than seaweed?"

The inquisitive Corrigan was the one person who knew how to get under Nick's skin. Nick really looked up to the old guy, so was constantly defensive when Corrigan razzed him so much. When Nick wasn't losing his Irish temper, he vaguely understood that the Reuters guy liked him, too, and was trying to toughen Nick up since this was his first overseas assignment.

Nick stuck around with Corrigan and his Fleet Street pals long enough to polish off a BaBa beer, then got up to leave, saying he had to find a guy so he could double-check some figures on the U.S. pacification program for a Sunday story he was writing on Leahey.

"That CIA asshole? Why are you doing a story about him, fer Christ sake?" Corrigan boomed.

"Get off it," Nick said, turning red. "Tough shit, if you don't like this war."

"Bloody American war," said one of Corrigan's marbles-in-the-mouth pals.

"Yeah, so?" Nick said. "A break for you. Gives you something to do. Now you don't have to write a story every time the Queen takes a leak."

Corrigan laughed. Marbles didn't look too happy.

"We got a war," Nick went on. "It's our war. And if we're working for a U.S. paper, we've got to cover the U.S. pacification program. I'm doing a piece on how it works."

"Or doesn't work," shot back Marbles.

"Listen, Boyo, just watch yourself," Corrigan warned, so serious for once he momentarily took his pipe from his mouth. "You can't trust Leahey. Everyone's convinced he's CIA. The very blokes who fomented this damned war in the first place."

"Quite," said Marbles. "And those spooks are still skulking around a decade later, claiming they've got legitimate jobs. Whilst all they're really doing is stirring up additional trouble."

"Whilst? Jesus," Nick said with a grimace at the offending Brit. "I'm getting out of here. The party's getting too literary for me."

As he lifted himself up out of his chair, he turned for a parting shot. "I know something's fishy about Leahey. I guess you're all too drunk to remember that this conversation started out with my saying I was going to check the figures out with this other dude."

"Right," Corrigan said with a grin. "It just seems a bit late in the evening for that."

Nick headed back to the interior bar and ordered another BaBa. It didn't take longer than a couple more beers to get the story about the redhead. In the process, Nick had to listen to a long-winded tale about the zillion retakes some network camera guy had to do with a fresh-blood standup who'd just arrived from the real world and had never before covered anything more newsworthy than a fire in Cincinnati. But with some selective eavesdropping and a few direct questions of an AP guy too drunk to ever remember Nick had asked, he got the all-too-predictable details. The redhead had gone to the roof of the Caravelle Hotel to watch the fireworks.

When Nick would shoot the shit years later, drinking and telling old war stories in new hot spots like Tunis or San Salvador, he recalled that time in Vietnam as the fall or maybe winter of '67. The war was heating up on its way to winding down and encroaching by fits and starts on Saigon. For a lot of the press, entertainment of an evening was watching that war over hamburgers and drinks from the Caravelle's rooftop club—firefights in living color with the sky as a wide screen.

Guys used to bring dates, or their wives if they were in-country, and it was an ideal place to show off the redhead and let her meet the folks.

Nick had just slid his empty BaBa bottle down the glossy teakwood surface to signal the bartender he needed a refill when he heard the familiar raspy brogue at his elbow.

"So now, Boyo, why didn't ya say it was the redhead's itinerary that interested ya? I heard you quizzing those other blokes. I could have saved ya all the sleuthin.'" Ray Corrigan shoved in and put the glass of Scotch and milk he was carrying down on the bar.

"Ah, Jesus, Corrigan," Nick said, "what're you talking about?"

"Nuthing, Boyo. Nuthing," the big Irishman said with a sly grin. "But in case you're interested, the lady's name is Angela Martinelli, although how a bonnie redhead could end up with a name like that. Come to think on it, maybe the same way you ended up a Greek."

"Damn it, Corrigan, I'm sick of your joke. You know I'm not a Greek," Nick sputtered, grabbing his fresh beer and taking a long swig. "No wonder British papers are such rags. You can't get your facts straight."

"Easy, kid, easy." Corrigan laughed. "Why so touchy? I must've hit a nerve."

Nick's only response was to stare at his beer.

"All right, so here's the bulletin, kid," Corrigan said, lowering his voice conspiratorially and winking at the Vietnamese bartender as he grabbed a handful of peanuts with his thick fingers.

"The lady left here with some dandy from United Press, but she hadn't been at the Caravelle roof anytime before she left again with—you'll never guess who."

"So who, you old buzzard. Are you going to tell this story or not?" Nick groused. "But it would be nice if you'd finish chewing your peanuts first."

"Braeford Curtis," Corrigan said with a flourish, sending a fine spray of spittle and nuts in Nick's direction.

"Curtis," Nick grimaced, taking longer than he needed to wipe nut bits from his shirtfront as he tried to evade Corrigan's penetrating gaze.

"Hmm," Nick finally said. "I guess she's not going to waste any time with us peons. But Curtis will clue her in to not waste any more time at the Follies."

"How'd you know she was there?" Corrigan asked, his bushy eyebrows making a huge shift skyward.

"That jerk politician from Chicago was there and I had to keep tabs on him."

"Ah ha, so you saw today's performance," Corrigan said.

"Lasky acted like a prick. It wasn't her fault she didn't know the procedure," Nick retorted.

"I see," Corrigan said, a smile slowly lighting up his eyes. "I hope, my young black Irish friend, that you're not foolish enough to set yourself up against Curtis. That guy's been in this business nearly as long as I have, and he is truly a heavyweight. You're not such a greenhorn you don't know that?" Corrigan said, putting it as a question as he drained the last of his Scotch.

"Christ, I know who Curtis is. I also know he's married," Nick snapped.

Nick knew Curtis didn't have the longevity stature in Vietnam of someone like Bill Tuohy from the LA Times or AP's Peter Arnett. But Curtis had cut his teeth in Korea and had been bureau chief for the old Herald Tribune in London, Moscow, you name it. Rumor was he was being groomed now for big things back home in New York. Six months in Saigon would give him an added edge over his competitors in the political in-fighting that goes on in the base camps surrounding every managing editor's office in every city room in the U.S. of A.

Corrigan slid his empty Scotch glass down the bar, cutting into Nick's reverie.

"So what were you doing with crazy Parks, and what's his interest in all this?" he asked.

"I dunno. I just had him at the airport to take pictures when we discovered her," Nick told the older man.

"Discovered? That sounds proprietary. She could have a formidable ally if that fearless lunatic, Parks, decided to take her in tow. Curtis would be worthless, he doesn't have any sources in Nam that he didn't go to Harvard with. And they're all running the CIA."

It didn't take Nick more than a few days to realize that, as usual, Corrigan was right.

# 5

# They Meet

SHE HAD been sitting on this barstool for nearly an hour listening to the UPI guy, Bill Whatshisname, tell her what a great guy he was. As Angela nodded, and smiled politely, she inspected the crowd in some detail. It was men, jammed with men. A few were business-looking types, and most of those were Asian. The rest were a motley crew. Open neck, short-sleeved shirts (God, even a few of them were those loud Hawaiian things), safari jackets, lots of photographers' vests with their oodles of little pockets and cubbyholes filled with pens, pencils, light meters, notebooks, cigarettes, no doubt condoms, and, on occasion, even film. No one looked too sober, and everyone seemed to be smoking. One older guy sitting across the huge circular bar looked British, or at least his salt and pepper hair did, cut longish like a Bond Street banker. He seemed strangely apart, even though lots of people had stopped and spoken to him over the last hour. The very few women in the place, well scrubbed and sedate looking, were most likely correspondents' wives or girlfriends. At least, according to Bill.

Not a lot of good information from Bill. He seemed taken aback and a bit miffed when she had insisted upon paying for her own drinks. She had hoped to get some ideas of how one went about being a war correspondent without letting on to him she didn't know what the hell she was doing. But other than finding out there was a so-called "op shack" at the airport where one signed up for military flights to whatever battle you wanted to get to, she had learned little. Par for the course. That's pretty much the same deal with being a reporter any place, she thought.

She'd at least learned that much, being a police beat intern in Chicago and at that dinky upstate Gazette before Peter dumped her. You have to figure out the ropes for yourself. Sure, the city editor sometimes calls you over and says go here or go there. But if you have a beat, it's up to you to figure out where and what the stories are.

So she'd quit her job, done a couple of months modeling for quick money and assigned herself to Vietnam. And fought off family, friends and acquaintances who'd said she was nuts. No job for a woman. Too dangerous, too foreign, thankless, pointless. She was too inexperienced. That she couldn't argue with—she'd had only the two newspaper jobs, both of which were cut short by Peter, one way or another. Being top notch in journalism school was just that, *school*. Too raw from a recent divorce, that's the one everybody had harped on. But she had to get on with life, couldn't wait for the "year adjustment period" that everyone talked about. Funny, no one suggested she was too young. Naive, maybe. Idealistic. But of an age where if she didn't start having babies pretty soon, she would miss some kind of boat that she wasn't sure she wanted to catch. So here she was. Now she only had to answer to her stomach and her pocketbook. If you don't sell freelance, you starve or go home. But where was home?

"So," Bill said, "I, uh, bunk at the UPI office just down the street here. So, uh, you're staying on your own at the Continental?"

"Yes, I am, Bill. It seems very centrally located," she replied with a serious, thoughtful frown. "We only had to come across the square to get to this great bar. Able to just look out the window and see the war going on. I guess the UPI office must be central, too, if it's near here."

"Lot a guys there," he said.

"Gosh, that's handy for everyone," she said.

Yikes, she thought, how do I get out of here?

She had assumed Bill would be a good way to meet people. Forget it. They were surrounded by guys sitting, standing, jostling around the bar, sucking in smoke and booze, but it felt like most of them were pretending she wasn't there, even though they were all talking too loud and shooting sideways glances in her direction. When she finally decided on a momentary getaway to the ladies room, she had to shove her way through the crowd even though at five-foot-nine she was certainly tall enough for them to see her coming. She was clearly being studiously ignored and studied at the same time. But she had a plan as she circled around the bar heading for the john. She'd left a swallow of Chivas in her glass. That way when she got back she could slug down the rest of her drink, say she was paralyzed from jet lag, blah, blah, thanks for a lovely evening, and split.

The minute she stepped out of the ladies in its little setback off the huge terrace room and began heading back, she spotted the guy with the British haircut now turned full around on his stool, with his back to the bar, watching her approach. She got a slice of a view as he shoved away from the bar and started toward her. Tall, huge man. Strangely, with all the milling people, the first thing she noticed were his shoes—black wingtips. She giggled. Stockbrokers' shoes. A banker's haircut and stockbroker shoes. Otherwise, he looked like a correspondent. Safari jacket. Nice shirt underneath. Both jacket and shirt looked like they had been pressed within the last half hour. Must be some kind of network executive or something, she thought.

Two long strides and there he was, sticking out his hand. "Ford Curtis. You're new, aren't you? Haven't seen you around."

"Just arrived yesterday," she said, shaking his hand. "I recognize your byline. Last I noticed you were in Moscow."

"That was a while ago. Let me buy you a drink. Chivas, I think. Saw you from across the bar, and noticed what the bartender poured. So I know your taste in Scotch, but not your name."

"Oh, gosh. Sorry," she said, flustered. "Angela Martinelli."

Before she quite realized what had happened he had maneuvered her by her elbow onto the only vacant stool—the one he'd occupied—and he, of course, insisted on standing. So everyone else tries to pretend they don't notice a new woman in town, and this guy goes out of his way to meet her. Older, smoother, more mature.

"A Chivas and another martini, Ling," he said, raising his hand to the bartender, who was serving someone a couple of stools down.

Angela looked across the expanse of the bar and gave a little finger wave to Bill, who was staring over without a very happy look on his face. Shit, she thought, within 10 minutes, the jungle drums will have moved this bit of gossip all over town. Like the silver dollar on the barroom floor, the lady goes from hand to hand.

"Look, Mr. Curtis," she said, "I really . . ."

"Ford," he said, "what's this mister stuff?"

"Ford," she said, "I really . . ." and Ling set a tumbler of Scotch in front of her.

She looked at her glass, then shook her head with an I-give-up wisp of a grin.

Ford lifted his martini in a salute, and said, "Just one drink. I won't keep you long. If you just arrived, I'm sure you're exhausted."

Before they had the chance to utter even the smallest of small talk, acquaintances of Curtis began dropping by. To a man, their opening gambit was the Red Sox.

It was the question on many lips: Could Boston win the '67 series, its first in 49 years?

Angela joined in the speculation. She had been a Red Sox fan as a kid, so did have a minor interest in the outcome. But whenever she tried to bring the conversation back to war, she didn't get very far. Eavesdropping on snatches of other conversations, though, it seemed the war was a more popular topic than the series.

Polishing off her drink, she picked up her huge handbag, and got ready to say goodbye, when another tumbler of Scotch appeared.

"Good idea to get out of here," Curtis said, picking up his drink. "I'm tired of baseball, aren't you? Just grab your drink, and come with me for a moment over to this great view. I want you to see it before you leave."

He steered her through the crowd over to a far corner of the rooftop terrace. "Wow," Angela said. The sight was indeed spectacular. The lanterns from hundreds of gently bobbing houseboats played their light in watery patterns over the Saigon River.

"It feels like it's close enough to touch," she said. "How far is it?"

"About three blocks away," he replied.

"It makes me think of Nantucket," she said, a catch in her voice.

Suddenly the background noise was gone, the war disappeared, she was in a quiet zone as they talked of their separate memories of the Massachusetts island. They talked of a time when they each had been happy, and life had seemed simple. Summer neighbors in a sea of strangers. The reminiscences spilled over—supper dances at the ancient Harbor House, cocktails at the Jared Coffin, hot cranberry muffins, The Sunday New York Times or Boston Globe fetched at The Hub.

They had wandered into a minor disagreement over the comparative virtues of the Oceanside beach at Sconset versus the more sheltered Cliff Beach in town, when, with no prelude other than the downing of his third martini, Curtis blurted: "You're so beautiful. I can't believe we never ran into each other in Nantucket or Boston. I wouldn't have forgotten."

The outburst startled Angela in mid-sentence of an exuberant summer reminiscence. She involuntarily leaned toward the pull of the man, but just as quickly jerked herself tall. She felt her jaw tighten, her face shut down.

The jolt brought them back: A foreign place, surrounded by the clink of beer bottles, of ice in correspondents' glasses and by the talk of war.

"I'm sorry, but I can't imagine what I've said to offend you." Curtis was direct, his voice sounded tender. "You are beautiful. You must know that. You're charming, funny. We're from the same world."

"I never really lived in Boston," Angela replied. "My mother's from there. It was my grandfather's house on Nantucket."

Curtis laughed. "That's definitely what a reporter would call an unresponsive answer."

"Then that's probably what I'd call it, too," she said crisply.

"What are you afraid of?" Ford prodded, his voice low and husky.

The question had a soothing effect. Her posture relaxed, her body seemed almost to unfurl.

"Failure, maybe. Perhaps you," she said with a soft smile. "I don't know exactly. I've been wired ever since I stepped off that plane."

And besides, she thought, I don't need to fall for another wrong man. I came here to work, to give myself something to hold on to. Not someone to lose.

# 6

# They Eat

ANGELA WAS startled by the elegance of the restaurant as soon as they walked in, but decided to refrain from commenting. She feared this Curtis guy would take it as a sign of her inexperience. Not green at life, of course, but at combat.

"I can't believe this setting," she wanted to say, as the waiter was leading them to their table. "This is a mighty strange way to fight a war."

Actually, she would have liked to say a lot more than that. She'd come to Vietnam with some kind of expectation. An idea that there was work to be done, important work that she could lose herself in and quit thinking about how she'd messed up her marriage, failed her parents' expectations, broken up with Jackson when Jacks had been the one person to support her no matter what she tried to do. So this was work? This was war? So far her "correspondent's career" had consisted of capturing the two beachheads of a rooftop terrace bar where her C-rations had been Chivas Regal, and now this, one of the most elegant French restaurants she'd ever seen. She'd been ogled and leered at, yet treated like a pariah. She'd totally fucked herself at the Follies, looking precisely like the stupid greenhorn she was. Now all these horny bastards had perfectly good reason to assume she had no business here other than pleasure. Shit, Angela, welcome to war. Your own damned war, she thought. You're obviously going to have to figure out how to make friends with these guys. You're probably going to have to take them on one by one to let them know you don't want to arm wrestle, that a woman in a war zone is not some kind of freak, but that goddammit, you can write and drink with the best of them. Otherwise, this is going to turn out to be the loneliest place in the world.

So here she was, against her better judgment, going to dinner with a guy who'd picked her up in a bar with probably half the Saigon press corps as witnesses. He seemed to have chosen the most expensive restaurant in town. Sophisticated approach. Sexy, nice guy, with the easy grace and charm of her father. And he's probably nearly as old, too. Have to scare him off, squelch his notion he's got the inside track because he's from Boston and you've been to Boston on occasion. We're from the "same world," he'd said.

But instead of blurting out the song of life, the psycho/sexual history of the human race, she smiled across the small round table at her handsome companion, as the waiter shook out the tablecloth-sized damask napkin to place in her lap.

After taking their drink order, the Chinese waiter bowed and offered them a huge, oversized menu, but Curtis suggested they wait a while before ordering dinner.

"I don't mind waiting for dinner," Angela said with a smile, "but I think we ought to move on from Carl Yastrzemski and the Red Sox. At this point, I'm much more interested in the war."

"Right," Curtis said, with a somewhat startled look. "I've asked you more than once this evening just what you're doing here. It seems rather curious to me. But I don't seem to have gotten an answer, other than you're here, that's all."

"I'm here to work," she said, "not this." She waved her arm to encompass the hushed, elegant restaurant with its sterling, its white linen dotted by purple hibiscus floating in crystal bowls at each candle-lit table.

"Of course," he replied.

Angela picked up her Scotch, and finished off her drink.

"You know," Curtis said after a pause, "I'd really like to help you. I really would. It's tough, nearly impossible, this freelance business. You simply must have a major news outlet behind you. Otherwise, how in the world can you make enough to survive?"

She ignored the question and instead brought up the subject of the M-16, although through the carefree abandon of too much Scotch, she knew she was making her move to pick a fight, to push him away.

"The U.S. military brass has a lot to answer for in that debacle," she said with authority.

"I really think that's not an informed opinion," he said.

"It was bureaucratic bungling and you know it, Curtis," Angela shot back. "After that firefight in April, they found dead Marines all over the hills of Khe Sanh with their cleaning rods down their gun barrels. They were trying to dislodge jammed rounds while the Cong mowed them down."

Curtis cleared his throat and called for the wine list. "I'd like something in the way of a claret," he said. He then made a minor ceremony of tasting and choosing one of the oldest and finest bottles the sommelier had in his cellar.

"If you'd simply told him Bordeaux in the first place," Angela said in a mock whisper leaning across the table with a conspiratorial gesture, knowing she was being obnoxious and snotty, yet cringing at the thought that she wanted to make sure this nice guy took her for a jerk, "we'd have had less commotion. Claret is a British word, you know, and we're in a French restaurant in a basically French culture."

Curtis didn't laugh. And it wasn't long before he suggested Angela should turn her hand to a profession for which she was more qualified.

"Like being a doctor?" she asked with sarcasm.

"That didn't exactly leap to mind," he said with a smile. "But when my children were small, I used to think how nice it would be if there were more lady pediatricians."

"My father's a pediatrician," she said.

"How nice. You could follow in his footsteps," Curtis said.

"Or my mother's," said Angela. "She's a surgeon."

He shifted his 195 pounds uneasily on the fragile teak and tufted silk chair.

He's uncomfortable. Good, thought Angela, by the time we get to the peach flambé, this little war should be over. Don't trust myself about this guy. I could lose myself in him, just as I did with Peter. Getting involved with anyone would be a mess. This hotshot would spell real trouble.

Much to her surprise, Curtis didn't take the hint.

"Look," he said, as Angela started to shake hands after they'd made their way around midnight to the lobby of her hotel, "despite my getting off on the wrong foot, I'd like to see you again. You're stimulating company, to say the least."

"I think it's best that we not," Angela replied. "But thank you for a lovely dinner."

She turned and climbed the wide, dark wooden staircase that curved up to her second-floor room.

# 7

## She Frets

IT WAS a funny key, big, brass, old-fashioned. Must be French. Was it night before last? Three nights ago? A New York hotel room with a simpler key. Hotels seemed to be a staple in her life lately. Move on to make room for the new girlfriend. She stumbled over a suitcase before she found the switch on the strange little Oriental bedside lamp with its minuscule bulb. Enough light from the neon outside, she hardly needed to bother. Why bother, indeed? Just drop her clothes on the floor and pull the covers over her head. Switch the lamp off and then she wouldn't have to look at all the unpacked suitcases and detritus of former lives strewn around. Yeah, well, leave it on long enough to locate the pull chains on the overhead fans. God, this heat was relentless. A major pointer for the new life: Don't turn off the fans when you leave the room *no matter how long you think you'll be gone.* But leave the balcony door open? I don't think so! Nothing is safe around here. She'd probably find a Viet Cong, or more likely a drunken correspondent, in her bed when she got back. She opened the louvered shutters, then folded back the metal ones, and so what. There didn't even seem to be enough air moving to catch the stale stuff being shoved around by the ancient, creaking fan blades. Scotch was next. Another major pointer, always keep a bottle in your room. Where had she packed it? When she'd stuck in the flask as a last minute thought, she'd felt a bit silly, pretentious about it. A flask, my dear, for going to war? But she couldn't very well get on a plane lugging a fifth in her handbag.

She pawed through a bunch of underwear and short-sleeved

blouses, just piling them on the floor as she went. What was wrong with her that she couldn't pick herself up and find the energy to put this stuff in a drawer? At least the things she'd already dragged out of the suitcase. Ah ha, here it was. Nice smooth feel, concave, it was sterling, had been her grandfather's. A present from Mother. Not Mom, or Momma, like other people said. But Mother. Well, for once, Mother, you came through. Must drink to that. Switch off the light, ignore the mess, sit down in my new house that's not a home and drink to Mother out of a silver flask. An image of her mother as a young teen on her polo pony, Angela's grandfather grinning at her side, flashed in Angela's head. The picture had forever stood in a silver frame on her mother's desk. Her petite mother, her dark hair hidden by her riding helmet, brimming with confidence and self-assurance, basking in the glow of yet another medal she had won. The photo in the ornate frame was black and white, the contrast between me and Mother, Angela mused. She's dark and petite. I'm big and red, like Pops. So, here I am in my new home, a hotel room in Saigon. A home I am going to have to make for myself, not by relying on Peter.

She'd made her first big home-style decision before she came. Get a room in the Continental on the second floor. She knew the hotel was where all the correspondents hung out. Hoped something might rub off, that it would make it easier to make friends. Fat chance. They all just wanted to hit on her. And she knew from research that the second floor was where Graham Greene had written "The Quiet American." Hoping what would rub off there? Her best shot, probably, was ending up like Fowler, a burned out, lying hack of a newsman. Now wasn't that a romantic notion. But she'd forgotten that since everything was French, what they would call the second floor would really be the third. An extra flight of stairs to climb every day for a romantic notion. Story of her life. Always made it difficult for herself, choosing a path that no one else took, much less wanted. She might as well have joined the French Foreign Legion.

Mother seemed to think that was just about what the prodigal daughter had gotten herself into. "Seems like a low-life profession to me. But if you must do it, it makes sense to go where the big story is, be the best."

That was one bit of motherly advice that was good. She didn't have the experience or connections to land a proper news job. No one wanted a woman in the city room, anyway. How many times had she seen old coots in green eyeshades look up from a copydesk and flinch when she walked in looking for a job. Or how about the guy who said, "If you're a woman, lady, the deal's off," after sending her a note to come in for a tryout. He had responded to a resume from A.A. Martinelli. An age-old, female writers' trick: use initials, not a tell-tale first name. She could have been stuck forever toiling away on the women's pages, proof-reading recipes and covering bridal showers for the little Gazette.

Incredible, the light outside. It's nearly midnight. Neon, neon, neon. The GI bars apparently stay open all night. What a place. Would she ever get used to it? Would she ever fit in? The whisky was good, warmed her throat. Only thing you'd want warm in this weather. But warm in the throat felt good, comforting. Or maybe it was just the glow the whisky gave, made the heebie jeebies, the fear, seem less. So what was she afraid of? Failure? Loneliness? Isolation? She'd faced all that, so what the fuck. Getting shot? That felt pretty remote.

She walked out on her little balcony, overhung by the feathery leaves of a Tamarind tree. You couldn't see much from the room when you were sitting down. Just the balcony railing and through it, glimpses of the Caravelle Hotel across the way. The setting for her coming-out party this evening among the swells of Saigon. But looking down, there were still all sorts of lights and traffic and rickshaws and motor scooters. That bunch of drunks up in the Caravelle rooftop bar were probably still going strong.

"I'll lift my glass to this," she said out loud to the scene below, flashes of colored neon playing across the bare white walls and unpacked luggage of the room behind her. "Let me make a new life. I'm the house I live in."

She threw back her head and laughed at the irony of those wise words of Jackson, the guy whom she had left because she felt they had no home. She needed a home, a place to feel safe. She thought she had found that in Peter—he baked bread, taught her how to plant a tree—before he left her.

# 8

# Parks' Pad

NICK COULD hear Hendrix over the din of petticabs and horns and fishmongers as he rounded the corner of the alleyway where he'd heard Parks had found a crash pad. God, this place stunk in the stifling heavy air and heat! As little as he knew about Cholon, the Chinese quarter, Nick had no trouble following the sound of Jimi Hendrix's guitar to the dirty, smelly apartment above the Chaio Xi fruit and vegetable stand.

The scarecrow photographer was dancing by himself in the middle of the tiny room, its black-painted walls adorned by huge blowups of Mick Jagger, Hendrix and the young Beatles, dressed in black choirboy suits with starched white Eton collars.

Hendrix was blasting his way through "Foxy Lady," but Parks' personal needle was grooving on one line: "I wanna take you home, ya, I wanna take you home, ya, I wanna take you ya, ya, ya, ya, Foxee, troxee, ya, ya, ya, ya, lady, foxee lady, lady, lady, lady, fox ya, ya, ya . . ."

His scarecrow arms flapped out of sync, as his body jerked in time to the music, the ever-present vacant grin on his face. As he stepped across the threshold, Nick noticed the vapor from a bubbling Chinese waterpipe trailing up the wall. As his eyes followed the vapor trail, they saw a shapely leg, a wind-blown skirt, an airline stair, a high-heeled bikini shoe.

"Jesus," he whistled, the series of blowups hanging above the waterpipe were the redheaded woman stepping off the plane at Tan Son Nhut.

"Hey, Limey," he yelled at Parks over the Hendrix twangs, "so that's what you were shooting while I was paying you to snap The Honorable." The photographer stopped moving, his grin altering only slightly as a form of welcome: He rearranged his mouth to display his rotten teeth, and turned down the music.

"You're a dancing wonder, stone freak," Nick said to Parks. "Your body and your arms aren't doing the same tune."

The photographer's only response was a grin.

"Listen, Parks, I got another assignment for you, but you're not that easy to find."

"Yeah, man. Another bird-watching expedition?"

"Afraid not. But you got enough shots for your walls already."

"Nice Lady Bird, woeee, that's a joke, man," and Parks was gone, whirling around in a fit of laughter, dancing through a pile of dirty clothes and old newspapers lying about on the floor.

"Corrigan told me the other night you got some special interest in the bird. Is that so?" Nick asked.

"I dig pretty things," said Parks. "Women is nice. Is she still in-country?"

"Jeez, guy, your internal clock doesn't work too well. She's only been here a few days," Nick said. "Her name's Angela Martinelli. She's a freelancer, but that's rough. If you've got the handicap of being a woman in a war zone, it sure helps to have the clout of a major news organization behind you."

"Right on, mate. Some of those bloody bastards from the 'major news organizations,' as you guys call yourselves, have rubbed my nose in it more than once," Parks said with a wide grin on his face.

"You've still done OK. Guess we'll just have to see if the lady has anything like your guts. I hear she's been on a couple of junkets, following the pack whenever the government sets up a trip for the press to go look at a firefight. But she won't get anything there except what everyone else is getting. And you sure can't sell freelance what's already available for free on the wires."

"Righto. Cheerio. Gotta go on your own. Gotta be all mine, all mine," Parks began to sing Hendrix again. Although Hendrix was singing something else, Parks didn't seem to notice. "You know you're a cute little heartbreaker, sweet little lovemaker, ya, ya, foxee, ya, ya . . . Gotta go on your own, cute little heartbreaker, ya, ya, ya . . .

"Who does she run with?" Parks abruptly asked Nick, focusing again on the reporter.

"Nobody, as far as I can tell. Corrigan said she's seeing the Curtis guy. When I've seen her around, most of the guys act like high school jocks and won't sit next to her on a press bus or take the empty stool next to her in the lobby's mini bar."

"I bet she's lonely," Nick added with a sudden burst of insight. "And she sure can't be making her rent. I wonder how she pays for the Continental? That's steep when you don't have a paper or someone picking up the tab."

NICK MET Parks the next day so the photographer could take some shots for the Sunday story on "pacification" Nick was still struggling to pin down. But Parks nearly broke up the photo-taking session when he called the official, Kevin Leahey, Mr. Kevin CIAster.

"God damn it, Parks," Nick yelled at the photographer as soon as they got out of the Embassy building. "If I'm going to hire you and my paper's going to pay you, you've got to behave halfway civilized. You can't say shit like that right to those guys' faces. You may think he's CIA, but there's no proof."

"Parks has to face the music, yeah, woe, woe. Choo-choo, Chattanooga, pardon me boys," Parks started dancing around Nick as they walked down the Tu Do, and Nick cracked up laughing along with him.

"We'll show those bloody spoke blokes, spook kooks, kook spooks," Parks sang out.

He stopped dancing and jabbed a crooked forefinger at Nick. "I like the bird, mate. She's a bit of all right. She doesn't hang back."

That was Parks' highest compliment, but one that could get you killed traveling with him. He was always way ahead of the pack. And Parks had a simple, child-like approach to life. When he liked someone, he liked them. Inside his drug-scrambled brain, the connectors to feelings or people were straight and direct.

"I think I'll begin to take the red bird with me," Parks said.

# 9

# A Chopper to Loc Ninh

NICK WALKED into the big, drafty hangar—the op shack at Saigon's Tan Son Nhut Airport—at 10 o'clock on a Wednesday morning, grumbling to himself. He was thinking about what a dumb waste of time this trip to Loc Ninh was, when he spotted Ford Curtis, over in a corner where the folding chairs were, regaling several correspondents who were all laughing and guffawing.

Well, that's a surprise, Nick thought. He had lucked out on this one. This was the first time he'd ever seen Curtis on one of these trips. The old guy seemed more often than not to be using only Embassy sources and pontificating from Saigon. Nick had damn near not come, but if he had skipped this trip and Curtis wrote some fireburner that caught Harry the Arse's eye, Nick never would have heard the end of it. Vietnam might be a very small place, but it's obviously not so small that a lone reporter can be everywhere at once—but try to explain that to your foreign editor when he gets a bug up his ass that you've missed something. And if Braeford Curtis writes about it, it's news—no matter if it's just a thumbsucker, ruminations on the state of his world or his navel, or whatever.

Nick had hesitated about this trip because he'd been suspicious there wasn't going to be much story for the very reason that the flacks in Barry Zorthian's press information office had been rounding up reporters to go view the action. The Viet Cong and North Viet regulars had attacked several friendly bases during the last couple of days in Phuoc Long and

Binh Long provinces, a hundred or so kilometers north of Saigon, near the Cambodian border. It must have been a rout in the U.S.'s favor, or why would the press office be working so hard to show it off? All the same, Nick knew that if the PIO boys were pushing, folks would be going, and gathering news is not a business where you can risk being left behind.

Nick signed in for the flight at the little glassed-in cubicle where a lading sergeant took requests and made assignments for military transport, then made his way through the waiting area of folding chairs to his pal John Simenson, who was in the group with Curtis and the other guys who were obviously going on the flack trip. The place was littered with newspapers and paper coffee cups left behind by reporters or military or Embassy personnel who already had been able to cadge a ride to wherever they were trying to get to. This so-called "shack" was always aswamp with hitchhiking air travelers since there was only one main road running north and south in the long, skinny country of South Vietnam—the infamous Highway One, which the French had long ago dubbed The Street Without Joy. You could take your pick whether you wanted to believe the nickname derived from military debacle or from nightmarish traffic.

Simenson was a great little kid. Nick really liked him. A lot of people even called him Sweet John because he was so nice. Little Johnny was another nickname he had. Amazing the people you meet in a war zone, Nick thought, smiling to himself. Little bitty guys, and beautiful tall women with masses of red hair.

As Nick walked up he heard Curtis say: "Oh, hell yes. When Lyndon decides he wants to talk, he doesn't care where he is and you'd better listen. Sitting on the doniker, as he calls it, wherever."

The reporters and cameramen all laughed, shuffling around and smiling, obviously enjoying Curtis' stories. Nick introduced himself to those around, including Curtis.

"So," he said, turning to Nick, "You work for ole Harry the Arse Bodowsky. I haven't seen Harry since he was working for Life in New York and fell off a barstool drunk in Costello's."

"How'd you know I work for Harry?" Nick was dumbfounded.

Curtis laughed. "You mentioned your paper. I keep up with who gets promoted to foreign editor."

Jeez, Nick thought, this guy is good. Easy, affable. Within the next few minutes, Curtis had gotten around to most of the group, asking the reporters about themselves, putting them at ease, probing a little to see how much combat the young ones had seen. He recalled a network camera technician by name, even though they'd bumped into each other only once, several months ago during Israel's Six-Day war.

Nick's pal Simenson hadn't said a word. The tiny, sandy-haired guy just sat stone-faced and scared-looking in over-sized fatigues, clutching his notebook, a camera and a frayed canteen. Why doesn't the kid speak up? Nick wondered. He has a great story about that war. Kid's too quiet, he's going to have a bad end if he doesn't push himself more.

"Hey, Simenson," Nick yelled over the background noise of air traffic constantly on the move on the field outside. "Tell 'em about the time you met Moshe."

Nick could see John Simenson's choir-boy face turn crimson even under the shadow of his over-sized helmet. Damn, that kid is so young and so shy, it's amazing how he can be such an aggressive reporter, Nick thought.

Curtis gave Simenson a hard look, then his face softened as he said: "You're UPI? You been with 'em long?"

"Belgium," said Simenson. "I walked in off the street in Brussels while I was on a camping trip after college and they gave me a job."

"Good boy," said Curtis. "That's the way to get foreign experience, just be aggressive and go grab the jobs."

Curtis was in top form. As they waited for their chopper ride to Loc Ninh, he shared gossipy tidbits: Jack Kennedy had been having an affair with Ben Bradlee's sister-in-law; Princess Margaret's husband had some VERY strange friends.

He had an anecdote for each of them about someone they knew in common, usually one of their bosses, a vignette, an insider's joke. He's making us feel we're the insiders, thought Nick, part of his charmed circle. All just working-stiff journalists, all on the same team. The tone was conspiratorial, intimate. Any subject that came up, Curtis knew the principals, or he had been there, or it reminded him of a funny story. His knowledge and his contacts were awesome, and the work-a-day journalists were properly impressed.

It was all good fun, as exhilarating shop talk always is, and the reporters were in high spirits when they finally got the call to board their chopper.

As he stood up to leave, Curtis abruptly turned to John Simenson, giving him another hard stare. That's it, thought Nick, it's the stare. He'd caught on to part of the great man's technique. Curtis was staring at the white combat patch that all correspondents wear on their left breast pocket, emblazoned with their last name and their paper or service. Nick chuckled. You got to give the old guy credit, he thought. Everyone of us is sitting here lapping it up, yet he's doing what any of us could, read a guy's name and call him by it.

"Say, Simenson," Curtis said, "I've been sitting here wondering what your story was about Moshe and I think I've figured it out. You're the greenhorn, aren't you, who scooped us all with your Israeli battlefield interview of General Dayan during the Six-Day War? You're one kid I've been wanting to meet, and I want you to tell me how you did it."

Simenson's blush turned him nearly purple. "Well," he said, "I just ran into him." Guffaws erupted from the clustered newsmen, who were picking up their gear and downing the last dregs of cold coffee as they prepared to move out to the field. "Come on, Sweet John, you can do better than that," someone yelled.

"Yeah," Curtis reassured him, "I've been wind-bagging all morning. I want to hear what you've got to say."

Simenson laughed, and seemed to relax a little. "Well, see, when the war just suddenly blew up, UPI was frantic for someone to send. The Brussels news editor got ahold of me in the middle of the night. Then he obviously realized someone as green as me was worse than sending nobody and kept calling back. But I figured he had changed his mind, so I wouldn't answer the phone and just went out and used my credit card and got on a plane and went."

Curtis was already laughing. "I'm getting the picture," he said.

"Well, see, when I got to Tel Aviv," Simenson continued, "most everyone was there ahead of me and Avis only had one car left and it was white."

A gale of laughter erupted from the gathered correspondents.

Simenson turned a lighter shade of pink this time, but went on. "Well, see, they wouldn't let me through at the border crossing, so I just cut off the road and was just driving around out there in the desert behind the Syrian lines and shells were falling and here I am this moving target in that damn white car. I kept zigzagging, thinking that would make me harder to hit. But the worst part, I kept thinking, What the hell kind of story am I going to write? I don't even know what I'm supposed to be looking for. I'll never be able to face the office again."

"So what happened, fer Christ sake?" someone yelled.

"Well, see, first I came on this bunker, and I got out of the car and tried to get in, but the Israeli soldiers there wouldn't let me. They just said to get the hell back to Tel Aviv, I was setting them up as a target with my white car. I finally passed a Jeep with some Israelis and they were yelling at me to get out of there too, but they stopped. And Christ, the passenger in front was Moshe Dayan, who was running the whole show. I asked him a few questions about the war, he gave me straight answers, and I went back and filed. I was the only one to get a battlefield interview."

"You bet your ass you were, kid. What a wonderful story," Curtis said, sticking out his hand to shake with Simenson. "I'm pleased to know you."

It's usual on such trips, whether going into combat or on the campaign trail, for reporters to trade war stories, war stories being the battle of the scoop—how I outfoxed everyone to get that story. But Curtis added a special dimension. He really is a big man in every way, Nick thought, as he watched him, hunkered over, walking under the rotors of the Huey, still puffing on his pipe.

Curtis had always been a hero of Nick's. The big guy was a honcho during the Korean conflict, long before Nick was out of high school. The younger reporter found it hard to believe that here they were, together, in another war and another place. And Ford Curtis *was* a honcho. The average Joe might not know it because Curtis didn't have the television visibility of a Chet Huntley, but every reporter knew that this guy had the stature of a man who is read by and packs a wallop with cabinets and kingmakers. Sure, any good reporter has clout in his own arena, with his own audience—Nick knew there weren't many people around Chicago's city hall who wouldn't make it a point to return his phone calls. But Curtis, well, he reeked of TOP LEVEL access. Gee, Nick suddenly found himself wondering, which came first? His admiration for Curtis or ... No, it was his Uncle Dennis who got him interested in this stupid business. Uncle Dennis, holding Nick's hand, on a Chicago Sunday afternoon at the amusement park or zoo. Dennis on assignment with his Speed Graphic, looking for candid news shots, a pretty girl, her skirt caught by a breeze, kids feeding the polar bear. "Hang on to Dennis' trouser leg,"

Nick's mother would warn as she'd give a last tug to straighten his collar or smooth his hair. "He gets busy with them pictures, he don't remember nuthing." The familiar reproving tone concerning her younger brother's occupation: "Always intrudin' on grief or glorifyin' axe murderers."

Nick climbed aboard the Huey, grinning to himself over Curtis' tale about how he'd gotten the scoop that General Westmoreland would be U.S. commander in Vietnam from Lyndon, while the president was standing, dong in hand, at a urinal. Nick thought about the first time he'd been aware of Ford Curtis' byline. It was a sensitive, bittersweet piece about a 1st Cav unit losing its colors in Korea. "There is no dishonor greater to an honor-bound troop of men than leaving Old Glory behind. That's never before happened to the men of the 1st Cavalry since they first saddled up and rode with Teddy Roosevelt up San Juan Hill." Nick still remembered the lead and he'd probably barely been in high school. Funny, the 1st Cav had to wait for this war to redeem themselves for losing those colors, and instead of horses, the cowboys were riding choppers, airborne mixmasters. But what a redemption!

These chopper jockeys are something else, damned near as fearless as Parks, Nick thought as he strapped himself into his webbed seating and the Huey began its ascent. They can get in anyplace, riding what they call "slicks" for contour flying to swoop in with assault teams, dipping their bigger flying ambulances in to pick up wounded. The killed-in-action rate is a fraction of what it would be without their speed in evacuating the wounded.

Today's jock suddenly broke into Nick's reverie with instructions over the intercom about where to piss or puke. "There's butt cans around the ship. If ya get sick, use the whoopee buckets. In case we're gonna crash, there'll be one long ring. Clasp your hands over your head and lean toward the front. When ya piss in a urinal tube, don't miss. It rusts the deck."

Everyone laughed, everyone seemed in a fine mood. The sky was clear and blue, the air was cooler this far north of Saigon. Too bad we can't just stay up here forever, Nick thought, peering down at the jungle growth below as the Huey began letting down at the fire base just outside of Loc Ninh.

It wasn't something one easily got used to, these landings. The chopper was inevitably taking ground fire, its rotors over which one always had to shout were revved up to deafening, the dirt churned up by the beating blades swirled in a tornado funnel with the chopper and its uneasy cargo hovering and dropping in the vortex, a lumbering, flailing, screaming sitting duck. Nick's stomach on an elevator ride dropped in stages, always a floor ahead of the Huey.

This time the ground fire wasn't that bad, sporadic and light arms. Nick could see the cluster of the living and the dead that awaited the arrival of any chopper, green plastic body bags, the rag-tied, blood-soaked wounded, some standing, some riding a stretcher, medics hovering, holding a plasma bottle high, and a traveling grunt or two, laden with pack and M-16. One guy stood out, no rifle, no pack, just an upturned anxious dirty face staring up with an odd gesture of hand on top his helmet as though he were worried it would blow off in the swirling wind. Perhaps, Nick thought, he's heading home.

The passengers were up and out the open doorway before the skids had even touched down—speed is staying alive. Off, get the wounded on, and away. Nick watched Curtis go out the door ahead of him. Nick gave a nervous last minute tug to the chin strap of his steel helmet, patted his breast pocket checking for notebook and pen, then jumped himself. He had the awful sensation of free falling, wind rushed and he saw rain clouds. My God, I'm in the sky, he thought, I jumped while the chopper was still airborne. Then he saw Curtis ahead of him bounce too hard as he hit the ground, then cushion his fall by bending his knees and rolling. As Curtis stood up, Nick almost banged into him from his own jump. Both nearly leaped another foot when the skinny grunt without a rifle said: "Hi, you guys."

"Jesus Christ," said Nick. It was Angela.

"What the hell are *you* doing here?" Curtis spurted.

"Working," she replied with hardly an inflection, but definitely a grin, hard as it was to see through the grime on her face. "I gotta get back and file and I'm carrying out Parks' film, if there's room for me on the dustoff."

She put her left hand up on her helmet, adjusted her huge duffel bag and headed for and climbed aboard the chopper that Nick, Curtis and the others had just left.

"Well, I'll be damned," Curtis said to no one in particular, as he watched the Huey begin its ascent, drowning them all in a whirl of dust.

On their trip back to Saigon, Curtis' affability wasn't much in evidence.

Several guys commented on the "vagaries" of Curtis' mood, although no one but Nick seemed to tie the change to the encounter with Angela. In fact, no one was in the best of spirits. There wasn't much of a story by the time the rest of the reporters got there. There hadn't been a whopper even from the beginning, just as Nick had suspected. But Parks and Angela had walked off with whatever there was simply by getting there first. MACV had pushed the trip so hard because the body count of dead was extraordinarily lopsided in the U.S.'s favor. But once you led off with the lopsided body count, the rest, from a news standpoint, was downhill.

Nick and the other reporters were used to Parks, knew he stayed out in the field a lot, were used to finding him there when they arrived. Since Parks free-lanced photos, he was aiming at a slightly different market than they were, but if he started hauling Angela around with him, she would add an entirely new dimension. She sold words. If she and Parks got there first and sold to even some rinky-dink paper, the wires could pick their stuff up, and all the so-called well-connected journalists would look a little silly.

But Curtis acted as though it were far worse than just silly. A whacked-out loony Limey and a girl! It made Nick wonder if Corrigan was right about Angela dating Curtis. In fact, the encounter reminded Nick of an old Spencer Tracy-Katharine Hepburn film with the two of them starting out spitting nails at each other. If it had been Nick's movie, he would have called it "The Crucial Encounter of War Zone C."

## 10

## Back to the Continental

NICK HAD little doubt about it, Kevin Leahey was a spook.

He needed a drink to clear his head. Nodding at the Marine guard as he left the American compound and headed for the Continental, Nick mulled over the late evening encounter he'd just had at the Embassy with Leahey. The guy billed himself as a U.S. AID official, an agricultural attaché. That's why Nick had decided to use him as a focal point in the Pacification story. The U.S. claimed that agriculture improved in villages that were "pacified." The term itself was ridiculous. It only meant which areas were on the latest official list as being under government control, and thus Cong-free. Anyone who'd been in the field knew the Cong came and the Cong went and villagers might like it or they might not, but putting a fence around them didn't improve the quality of their lettuce. But pacification programs, by various names and in one form or another, had been part of the U.S. Vietnam strategy from the get-go. Reporters had to periodically take a look at the latest version. Genuine do-gooders were one thing, the CIA and their intrigues quite another. Every instinct told Nick that Leahey's "attaché" status was a CIA cover and that he shouldn't trust the figures on pacified areas the official had finally coughed up, after giving him the runaround for days before handing them over. But careful, Nick warned himself. He knew he was angry because he'd had to go back to the Embassy a second time to get the statistics. Still, that was no reason to decide the guy was a goddammed spy. Made you wonder, though, if the jerk had needed the extra time to cook the books. Maybe the inconvenience was swaying Nick's judgment. On the other hand, Leahey had a good line of patter, and was an easy way to personalize the story. And if his figures were OK, it didn't matter if he was CIA.

It was well past dark, but the Tu Do was teeming as always as Nick made his way down the tree-lined boulevard, breathing in exhaust fumes from the street jammed with ancient mopeds and scooters. He knew he could find Ray Corrigan at the terrace bar if the old Reuters' guy wasn't out in the field. Not a bad idea to run Leahey's numbers past Corrigan for his assessment. Nick had already promised his desk the Pacification story, but he could certainly back out if he doubted the truth of what Leahey told him. The thing was confusing. Corrigan had called Leahey CIA, but the old Irishman liked to tease Nick so much that it was hard to be sure, sometimes, when he was being serious. Parks had made it clear that he thought Leahey was a spook when they'd gone to take his picture and he had called Leahey Mr. CIAster to his face. But Parks said all U.S. officials were spooks, of one form or another. Besides, Parks' brain wasn't wrapped too tight.

Leahey's stated ideas of how to help the South Vietnamese improve their farming methods sounded good—improve the lives of the peasants. But Nick wondered if the so-called attaché might be supplying guns, not butter, in the manner of Pyle, Graham Greene's seemingly well-meaning "Quiet American." Amazing, Nick thought, Greene published that book 12 years ago in 1955, and predicted every bit of this mess. Who learns from history? Obviously, no one. Leahey, the smooth-skinned, baby-faced blond was the grandson of a New York cop turned politician whose ties to Tammany Hall put him on the road to riches while he was still walking his beat. Two generations of Yale veneer for son and grandson didn't hide what Nick saw as the soul of a Connecticut redneck. Nick grinned to himself. Leahey is pretty transparent. Pyle was the soul of sincerity, which made him especially lethal.

I wonder what the redheaded bird thinks about rednecks, Nick let his mind wander as he started up the Continental's terrace steps. She seemed to have the faintest trace of soft Southern in her speech. She had mentioned a North Carolina paper that day at the Follies. What would her woman's intuition tell her about Leahey?

On an impulse, Nick kept his eyes straight ahead as he crossed the terrazzo of the terrace bar, deciding he didn't want to talk to Corrigan or any of the other guys sprawled drinking in the ancient wicker lounge chairs. But he couldn't miss their calls for him to come to their table, so he indicated with hand signals he'd be back in a minute. He headed directly for the lobby. Do not pass go, do not collect $200. It was a gamble, but the redhead lived in this hotel, and sure enough there she was, off in a corner.

Angela had her nose in a book. She was nestled, her left foot tucked under her, into one of the big overstuffed gold-braided red velour chairs that didn't appear to have been reupholstered or changed since the ornate lobby had first been tapestried and gilded to the French colonial tastes.

Colonial mentality, that's what it was about Leahey! Nick was still turning the interview over in his mind as he made his way through the potted palms toward the Beautiful Bird.

Nick grinned as he stopped before her and noticed what she was reading: Bernard Fall's "Hell in a Very Small Place," the newsman's bible on Vietnam.

"Glad to see you're finally doing your homework," Nick said as he walked up. The minute it was out of his mouth, he knew that his opening gambit was hardly as cool as it could have been.

She looked up with a frown and squinted in a way that suggested her better judgment had short-stopped an acidic reply. She visibly took a deep breath, offered a grin that softened her remark and said: "The condescension I could do without."

"Sorry. It sounded that way even to me. I'm Nick O'Brien. Could I interest you in a beer?"

"My God, yes," she said as she snapped Bernard Fall shut without even marking her place. "Just so long as we don't have to talk about what a klutz I was to show up at the Follies on my first day in town." She unwound the long leg curled under her, poked a bare toe around in search of the sandal half protruding from under the overstuffed chair and unfurled herself. Gee, she's tall, thought Nick. She could damned near look him in the eye, well, the chin, maybe, which must make her nearly five-ten.

"Let's get out of here," she said, startling Nick by taking his arm as though they were great, long-lost pals. "Reading Bernard Fall in this spot is unsettling."

"Oh yeah?" said Nick, pulling back slightly and looking at her quizzically.

"This place is a real symbol of crumbling colonialism—faded carpets, thread-bare tapestries. The Vietnamese managed to rout the French from every niche but this one. And here the U.S. press sits on its collective butt."

Nick couldn't contain his laughter. "That's pretty poetic, you shouldn't have any trouble selling that one." They passed over the worn oriental in the lobby, across the few feet of marble terrace and down the steps toward the rag-tag mélange that was traffic in National Assembly Square.

As they reached the bottom step, Nick suddenly threw his left arm in her path, hurled her to the steps, then landed on top of her with a crunch that sounded like he'd broken her arm. "Have you gone craz..." was all he heard before the explosion of a home-made gasoline bomb muffled the rest of her words. Screams and sounds of breaking glass and scraping chairs from the terrace drinkers were nearly lost against the usual cacophony of coughs and backfires from the motor scooters and ancient Peugeots that chugged through the swarms of bicycles and pedicabs that stuffed the tree-lined streets on both sides of the square.

Nick took a quick patting inventory of Angela's left arm, and the bent knees that had gotten him in the solar plexus when he fell on top of her. "Everything seems to work," she said rubbing her elbow, still sprawled and dazed on the stairs. "What happened?"

And he was off, doing a broken-field run dodging through the traffic, a bike running over the backs of his boots, a protruding metal shard from a passing scooter catching and ripping the baggy knee-pocket of his fatigues.

Goddamned little gook, I saw the son-of-a-bitch as he raised his arm to hurl that can, son-of-a-little-fucking-bastard throwing shit at women and children when they're just drinking a goddamned beer. Little bastard, with his black headband, clinging on the rear of a bike, if I can't outrun a goddamned bike in this... but it's not run, it's dodge, no place to run, he's turned around, he's seen me, he's getting off bike, now we'll see who can run, little fucking runt's whole body isn't as long as my legs, I'll have him before he can even get across the grass on the median...

Nick barely had time to tackle the terrorist and bang his head against the ground once or twice before Angela and the chicken-shit cops the GIs dubbed White Mice because of their white uniforms and abusive, ineffective tactics, showed up from different directions.

The Saigon cops moved in, feet and billy clubs swinging, on the two men tussling on the grass. Nick felt a searing pain in his left side from what he guessed was the whack of a boot in his ribs. He tried to roll away. Whoever was kicking was still at it, but the blows were only glancing now with the slight shift away. His real problem was fending off with his raised arms a club coming at him in short strokes from a disembodied white police helmet suspended over easy-rider shades. Shit, Selma revisited, he thought. It was during those heady days of civil rights marches three years before in Alabama and Georgia that Nick as a young reporter had first gotten his head kicked in. Saigon's White Mice cops were operating with the same impunity of Bull Connor's rednecks in Birmingham or Sheriff Clark's in Selma. Nick heard Angela's voice in the high decibels repeatedly screeching the information that he was an American and a journalist and they had no business treating him this way. In fact, those tough little bantams with the storm trooper mentality knew exactly who they were dealing with and they were moving fast to get their licks in before someone bigger than they came along to stop them. Like maybe a couple of MPs.

Angela's indignation was blowing in the wind.

# 11

# Angela Tackles the Mice

ANGELA HAD started out in a level voice trying to tell the White Mice they had made a mistake. But when she saw the grisly working over one of the Saigon cops was handing out to the terrorist with the black headband it was clear they were, indeed, making a distinction between him and Nick. Pretty cagey, she thought. Kicks to the kidneys and groin. Don't want an American beaten to a bloody pulp. She then tried pulling the guy in the wrap-around dark glasses away from Nick, but the bastard just turned on her and started swinging the billy.

"Are you crazy, trying to beat up on a woman?" she hissed.

His laugh was a leer as he reached out, grabbed her shirt at the top button and yanked, tearing the yellow silk where a button ripped off. He then contemptuously dismissed her with a violent shove that sent her sprawling in the grass.

She wasn't hurt and there wasn't time to worry about bruises to her dignity. She had to get help, fast. She was afraid that pipsqueak with the Napoleon complex could end up hurting Nick pretty bad. But what should she do?

She rolled over in the soft grass and crawled on her hands and knees the few feet back to where Nick had been. It was well past dark, but the night sky was lighted by the thousands of neon signs offering drinks and the flashing outlines of gyrating female forms. Enough light to see Nick's form was motionless and several White Mice hovered over him, ready to pounce if he moved.

She had to get to him and scream and keep screaming—some of those hotshot reporters or MPs must be around someplace. She crawled between the legs of one of the cops peering down at him and hurtled her body over Nick's head, the way he had thrown himself on top of her what seemed like days ago. Even if they roughed her up, surely they wouldn't beat on her with billy clubs the way they were doing to Nick.

Her screams pinpointed where Nick was for the reporters who had left the terrace to follow the chase and were milling in the gathering crowd. The screams and the new arrivals worked like magic on the cops. They melted into the crowd like smoke.

Her screams also brought Nick to life. "So much for the power of the press." His words were muffled, arriving somewhere in the vicinity of Angela's rib cage. She felt him try to prop up on an elbow, then fall back.

She sat up in astonishment, expecting him to be half dead. "You're all right?"

"My elbow's shooting fire. But you make a soft pillow," he said gingerly touching a spot on his forearm swelling into an angry red lump. "How'd you land on me? Did one of those bastards hit you?"

"Naw, just ripped my blouse. But I . . . I was afraid they'd kill you."

"It feels like they did. Are you OK?"

"I'm furious, but I guess I'll get over that," she replied with a big grin.

Corrigan, who had just arrived winded and puffing from unaccustomed running, knelt down beside Nick. "You OK, Boyo?" he asked.

"Yeah. Just take a look around for the fucking kid in the black headband."

"Will do," Corrigan said, pushing himself up from the ground with no little effort.

"You're not a bad sidekick in a brawl," Nick said as Angela reached down to help him up. "You're sure a lot tougher than you look."

"You need a good soak in Epsom salts," she said.

"You gotta be kidding. I vote for Scotch."

The gathering reporters began questioning Angela and Nick and the White Mice standing around with an indifferent air. But it was apparent pretty quickly that the Saigon police had no time for reporters or their questions.

"Listen, Jack," said a guy from the AP who had come running from their bureau, a block away. "These two are Americans, and reporters to boot. What the hell are you doing roughing them up? And where's that damned terrorist? I can't believe you let him get away."

"Get rost, asshoe," came the reply in the nasal singsong cadence of the East and the biting, blunt vocabulary of the West. The cop, using his billystick straight-armed to push the AP reporter aside and part the crowd in front of him, strode off.

"I don't believe this," said Angela.

"I hope you'll start believing it," said Ford Curtis, stepping out of the crowd. "That knowledge might keep you alive."

# 12

# Curtis as Dutch Uncle

No one needed to say, let's go back to the Continental. The terrace bar was the logical spot after all this commotion. The correspondents began heading back to the undrunk drinks and turned over chairs left in their haste to follow the action.

"You owe me a beer," Angela said, as she and Nick started to fall in with the crowd heading across the grass and past the tall trees of National Assembly Square.

"Two or three, I'd say," Nick said with a laugh, as they both brushed at their clothes trying to dislodge the dirt and stains and tiny, wet green blades. Angela folded the lapel of the torn silk blouse backwards into the edge of her bra to keep it from flapping open.

Corrigan and his Brit pals joined them, all excitedly spouting their own version of the scene they had just witnessed.

The hubbub didn't subside as 10 or 12 of them began reclaiming the evening's abandoned wicker chairs or a favorite nearby table on the slightly elevated "shelf" overlooking life on-the-go in Saigon. Those few left behind still drinking reported that the bomb thrower had done little damage. The debris of a blown-apart bike was in the street, but traffic was flowing as usual and only one pedestrian had suffered cuts.

Angela found herself finally squeezed in on a straight back chair between Curtis and Corrigan. Nick was across the table.

"I think the lady would prefer Scotch," Curtis said as Nick started to order them both a beer.

"Fine idea," Nick said. "That OK with you?" he asked Angela.

"No," she said. "You said a beer, let's stick with that."

"Let's have both," he said with an exuberant wave of his arm. "We deserve it."

"Sounds good to me," she replied. "Boilermakers should put us back into fighting trim."

Everyone around the table was a bit charged over the excitement of the chase and the idea of physical attack on one of their own. Several correspondents at the next table who had arrived well after the bomb was thrown dragged their chairs over or were slouched around trying to get all the details. Indignation was high.

"Those White Mice aren't worth shit," said one.

"Worse," said another. "The U.S. is propping up this Thieu government, and that's what they're getting for their money."

"They ought to take the hint and get the hell out," said a Brit.

The night wore on, the beer and Scotch flowed.

Angela was taking her shots straight back—there had been three so far—and chasing them with beer.

"You might want to take it easy," Curtis said at one point, "you've had a harrowing evening."

"Yeah," she said noncommittally, not wanting to give him an opening but not wanting to sound too rude. She wasn't sure what he was up to, but she hadn't liked the proprietary sound of his telling Nick her taste in drink. He surely wouldn't be sleazy enough to be suggesting he had established some kind of beachhead here. He was right, though, she had better slow down. She was indeed still pumping adrenaline, but could suddenly end up quite drunk. The guy *was* appealing, she thought as she looked sideways at him—very self-assured, or was it just arrogance? But she found it reassuring, comforting. Whatever, she didn't want to either land up in bed with him *or* try to pick another fight to scare him off. Just one more shot, and she'd excuse herself politely and get out of here. No one was really trying to talk to her except Nick, and it was too difficult to shout to him across the table. After everyone had had a few more drinks, Curtis included, he asked her for about the third time if she realized how dangerous it was here. Each time the question had been couched in slightly different terms, but to Angela they all had the same condescending ring.

"I'm here to work, Curtis, and why should you give enough of a shit to go to the trouble to keep rephrasing the same goddamm question?" she finally demanded. Nick, across the table in mid-swig from his long-necked beer bottle, lowered his drink with a startled look on his face.

"You're an attractive, interesting woman," Curtis replied in a low voice, leaning in close to her. "I'm intrigued by why you'd want to come to such a difficult place."

"You're just miffed because Parks and I got to Loc Ninh ahead of you," Angela responded, following Curtis' lead and speaking softly to cut down on the public display of her pique.

"You sure showed some enterprise, then," he said with a smile. "I just don't think you have any idea how threatening all this is."

"It's just as dangerous for you," she countered.

"That's not the point," he said, with what seemed his first touch of impatience with her.

"What is, then?" she asked, forgetting to lower her voice, as a waiter appeared at the table asking for new drink orders. By this time, most of the folks sitting around had stopped their own chatter and weren't even bothering to hide that they were listening in.

"Well, ah," Curtis replied softly, "with experience, perhaps . . ."

"I'd know how to not get shot? Come on, Curtis, you just don't think a woman should be here."

"Especially one who beats you to a story." Corrigan didn't say it loud, it was mumbled almost into his mustache, his head turned away from Angela and Curtis. But delivered, as it was, with a wink, it roused knowing smiles and nods from those at his end of the table.

"Yeah, Curtis," Nick said. "You were praising John Simenson for his learning how to swim by just jumping in the pool."

"Point taken," Curtis replied with a sheepish grin. "I guess I need to get used to seeing women in combat. But she's a lovely young woman, and I don't want to see her get hurt."

"Neither do I, Mr. Curtis," she said as she got up and said her good nights.

# 13

# The Wild West

ANGELA'S BREATH bounced back on her face inside the gauze mask. She could feel beads of moisture on the puffy delicate skin beneath her eyes. This heightened awareness of her own face, her skin, might be dizziness, a prelude to fainting. But it did make sense for her to be doing this. Betty Lou had insisted.

"You can't understand if you haven't been there," she had said. "A field operating room is indescribable. It's nothing like a civilian doctor or nurse has ever seen."

She's right. How can I capture it? Angela wondered, as she struggled with a rising wave of nausea. So much is happening, so fast. No way to take notes. I don't know what to look at first to try to memorize details so I can get it down on paper.

She'd hated operating rooms from the time she was a teenager. Sitting behind the railing, peering down into the teaching well, gearing up for her own professional future watching her mother. When she looked down now, she found she was wearing combat boots, she knew they would be spattered with blood. The blood was running on the floor. Green plastic body bags. She was in green, too. It startled her. She had forgotten Betty Lou had put her in a surgical gown, holding her arms out to slip it over her fatigues, tie the cotton tabs in back, her hair wound up under the cotton cap, the gauze mask in place. A lower leg with GI boot still on its foot was sticking, sole up, from a white enamel pail off in a corner. Flies swarmed over the green mountain of bodies stacked by the double doors.

Betty Lou Angstrom. A 22-year-old scrub nurse from Kansas. Angela had met her the night before in the officers club bar shortly after bumming a ride from Da Nang on a C-130 bringing in hospital supplies to this MASH unit near Pleiku in the Central Highlands. Bo Parks had kept telling Angela that she needed to go out on her own and get stuff no one else had. So here she was.

"You can bunk in with me, if you want to stick around and write some stories," Betty Lou had said.

Betty Lou! The farthest she'd ever been away from home before coming to Vietnam was the drive to Kansas City when she enlisted. She'd gotten her nurse's training at a hospital about 50 miles from her little home town in southwest Kansas. She'd driven there every day for classes and her intern duty, just like she'd ridden a school bus for four years to the consolidated high school 37 miles in the other direction.

"A grammar school, we had," Betty Lou explained, "but the farm kids were needed at home to work so not enough of 'em went past the eighth grade to make it pay to have a high school in every little town."

Betty Lou was a tiny, wholesome-looking blonde with Shirley Temple curls and a turned up nose and an enthusiastic little girl way of talking that was reminiscent of Debbie Reynolds. But Betty Lou's job was nothing out of the movies.

She put in 16- to 20-hour days assisting doctors doing intricate surgery, many times so tired they would nod off over a patient opened up on the table in front of them. She often scrubbed up standing shoelace deep in blood, the stench of gangrene so strong it would flare up through her sinuses and make her eyes water. She used her farm-girl ingenuity to great advantage when they were cut off from resupply, sometimes for days or a week at a time, by figuring out how to jerry-rig equipment, or how to substitute one thing for another, or how to sweet-talk patients who didn't have enough morphine to get them through.

Angela was staring at the foot sticking from the enamel pail when the double doors burst inward with a whoosh. A team of medics and rolling metal, plasma bottles swaying, charged through the swinging doors like a gang of desperadoes into an Old West saloon with six-guns ablaze.

In one fluid motion, the bundle of what remained of a GI was lifted from the rolling gurney, his life support tubes transferred from litter to operating table, and the surgical team moved in.

"Friendly fire," said one of the medics. "F-4 flying too low when it dropped its load."

Angela edged closer to get a look at the warrior on whom the surgeons were so frantically working. Sandy hair, green eyes, probably about 19. And he had no face. His features were melting away from napalm like a mask of wax, literally running down past his eye sockets, his nose holes, dripping into his mouth.

She stood by for hours in that Quonset hut with its floors running in blood as the doctors and nurses fought to save the young Marine. But his life slithered away just like the skin oozing from his skull.

# 14

# AP Turndown

"Don't you think we've done this already?" The AP bureau guy with the weary eyes and permanent scowl didn't bother to hide his impatience as he handed Angela back her story about Betty Lou.

"Sorry, but visits to hospitals are no big deal," he said from the side of his mouth that wasn't holding the butt that was about to burn his lips. "We periodically send our own reporters to do this. Anyway, you need more names and hometowns of recuperating GIs. This one's too gritty to get much play. A guy's face slithering off? No way."

"Why'd AP in New York give me a camera if they didn't want graphic detail?" Angela persisted, trying to control her voice to avoid any shrill telltale note of anger.

"You know, 'cause staffers can't be every place at once. If you get a shot of a downed chopper, or something like that we don't have, fine. But you gotta know they're not buying pictures—or stories—of slithering faces. We give readers stuff that's too tough, and we're accused of consorting with the enemy."

"Can you suggest someplace else I might try? It would be easier to show it around Saigon than be mailing this story all over to places in the States."

"No, goddamit. You don't seem to be hearing me," the guy snapped. "All of us here are having trouble with our own desks in New York. Everyone wants to sanitize the copy we're filing as it is, make it conform to what the government's saying. No one's gonna go to bat for your stuff. I don't even know you."

The guy turned back to his typewriter and started banging away.

The rude dismissal, Angela thought, these old crusts have it down to perfection. Only God or a shrink would know why I'm so determined to hang in and prove I'm as smart and tough as they are.

She was pulling the door closed on the cubbyhole office with its clattering wire machines and half dozen desks littered with old newspapers, overflowing ashtrays and paper coffee cups afloat with dead butts when the guy hollered out, "Hey, kid."

He had to yell it a second time for her to hear over the clacking of the wires at her back. "Hey, kid." She wasn't prepared to hear it anyway; it was a long time since anyone had called her "kid." At her height, which she had been since she was 17, people did not tend to call her kid no matter what her age or level of experience.

She returned to his cluttered desk with a certain expectation.

"Listen, kid, you're a good writer, vivid. But don't expect that to help much. People are already seeing more blood and gore than they want to see on TV."

"Thanks," she said with a wry grin.

"Sorry," he said. "But that's the way it is."

# 15

# A Retired Spook and the Old China Hands

Robert Komer, the man in charge of the program to subdue the Vietnamese countryside, to win the hearts and minds of the peasants to the U.S. cause, leaned forward across the wide expanse of his blond teakwood Embassy desk, his leather swivel chair bouncing with the sudden movement. The intensity of Komer's message was etched upon his face.

"It's working, Ford, I tell you the Pacification Program is working. You're beginning to sound like some of these Young Turk reporters with their negativism."

Ford Curtis shifted in the champagne colored armchair in front of the big desk in this big office that was forever in the shade because of the anti-terrorist concrete latticework covering its windows. The chair was too soft and deep for him to easily get enough traction to haul himself up and out. But as he struggled to get on his feet, Ford meant for his abrupt departure to send a clear signal that he wasn't listening to any carping about the press, and he sure wasn't taking any crap himself.

"We've known each other too long, Bob," he said, half out of the chair and not bothering to tone down the annoyance in his voice, "for you to take a cheap shot like that."

As he got to his feet, and was towering over the seated bureaucrat, he said with a tight, more controlled voice: "And you haven't answered the question of how your program is any different from the rest of the double-talk. We've had search and destroy, scorched earth, light at the end of the tunnel, war of attrition. What's your word for '*win*'?"

"We *are* winning, Ford," Robert Komer said, extending his arms across his desk, palms open and outstretched in a beseeching gesture. "These young reporters simply refuse to acknowledge that."

Komer, medium-sized, middle-aged, nondescript except for his London-tailored suit and bow-tie, looked the part of the salesman and former CIA agent he was. He was selling the Pacification Program to move Vietnamese from the countryside into protected, so-called secure villages. His enthusiasm was so great for the program he was selling that Lyndon Johnson had bestowed upon him the title of Honorary Ambassador and set him up in a chain of command that allowed Komer to report directly to Westmoreland. Robert Komer had been Harvard '42, a year behind Braeford Curtis.

"Yeah, well, fine," Ford said, ratcheting down his annoyance a couple of notches. "But take a little advice, Bob, and lay off the Young Turks. It seems to me that on the whole they're a pretty good bunch. And it's been my experience that when political types start moaning about their unfair press, they're laying a smokescreen to cover something else. You should be concerning yourself with the buildup of troops in the north, not worrying about things that don't concern you—like how the press does its job."

"OK, OK." Komer waved away any further dispute. "I'm not trying to sell you anything. This Pacification Program speaks for itself."

"Fine. If it does, it does. Get me those figures."

"Well, sit back down, and let me call Kevin Leahey in here. He's our agriculture attaché. He's got it all at his fingertips. Knows exactly which villages are in the program and how well they're doing. Good man."

"Just messenger it," Ford said, having moved across the room, his hand now on the knob of Komer's office door. "I don't want to go over all that now. So, thanks for your time, Bob. I'll be seeing you, I expect, at the ambassador's Christmas reception next month. I understand he's flying in the Mrs."

"How'd you hear that?" Komer asked with a frown. "Bunker really tries to keep tight security on her movements."

Curtis laughed. "You were in the CIA too long. If you're nothing more than a bureaucrat now—like you claim—you ought to quit worrying about the cloak-and-dagger stuff."

As Ford walked out through the high, wide teak doors of the Embassy, the blast of Saigon's heat smacked him with a force that boggled both body and soul.

His broad shoulders sagged under the weight of the humidity, and the flagging spirits he had been trying to hold at bay for weeks flooded his system like a jaundice. He missed his family. There was no order in his life. This war was going sour; its stench—both real and metaphysical—oozed over everything, oozed over them all. The Vietnamese were corrupt as hell and couldn't fight worth a shit. Damned kid journalists with no combat experience, that bright young woman wanting to be a correspondent with few more credentials than a borrowed camera, and you weren't even sure if you could trust the word of a Harvard classmate! The stench indeed.

Christ, I need a drink.

"Well, then, I'll buy you one," came a response from the direction of his right elbow.

Good God! Was he talking out loud and then answering himself? he wondered as he whirled in the direction of the words.

It was John Andre, one of the few career Army boys whom Ford truly trusted as a source. Andre was squinting in the bright sunlight, his hand shading his eyes in the semblance of a salute as he peered up at Curtis.

"So, Ford, Saigon's sent you 'round the bend like the rest of us, eh?"

"You old son-of-a-gun, how are you?" Ford boomed. "If someone had to catch me on the street talking to myself, I'm glad it was you."

"Let me get you to the Rex BOQ for a quick infusion, then we can commiserate about this pisser of a war." Andre took Ford by the elbow and steered him down Thong Nhat.

As they walked into the officers club upstairs over the old Rex Theater, Curtis saw two colleagues at a table near the door. Besides a very large martini in front of each, one had an enormous sirloin on his plate, the other a cheeseburger. Both were sticking French fries into their mouths without benefit of a fork. A bottle of Heinz ketchup was uncapped in the center of the table.

"There's a couple of Old China hands who've been covering wars since almost before you were born, John," Curtis said as he and Colonel Andre paused to adjust their eyes to the dim lighting in the room.

"Yeah, I recognize them from my time in Korea," Andre said. "Not bad sorts, but they're out of their element in this place."

"How so? You mean an officers bar, or Vietnam?" Curtis asked.

"Vietnam, of course," Andre said with a laugh. "What the hell kind of newsman would ever be out of place in any bar?

"I don't know how long you've been here, Ford, but this a different scene than what the old-timers are used to. The place is overrun with rock 'n' roll kids calling themselves journalists. You can see them every day arriving on Pan Am, traveling on tourist visas. They're weighted down with cameras, carrying their clothes in packs on their backs, looking for action, adventure, thrills, cheap drugs. MACV will accredit almost anyone—high school papers, church weeklies."

"Jesus," Curtis said, staring at Andre with genuine amazement on his face. "I didn't know it was that bad. I had an inkling from a young woman who tried to suck me into an argument about the M-16, but I didn't know it was that pervasive."

"No reason for you to. I doubt very many of them are actually working. But the young legitimate reporters are much more in tune with this whole chaotic scene. Those old guys over there," Andre said, nodding his head in their direction, "are anachronisms."

Curtis plotted his move across the room. He was going to have to acknowledge the two at the table, which was so close to the entrance there was no way to take another route, but he wanted to move past fast. He had no intention of sharing the colonel with them. He had known Andre from Korea, where he'd been a mere captain, and had run into him periodically since. He had also been in contact with him in Washington when Andre did a stint at the Pentagon. And the Army man was a sensible and trustworthy source.

As Curtis tried to pass the table with a nod, the guy he knew as Smitty grabbed his arm. "So where do you stand on all this, Curtis? It's clear which side your paper's on, but what about you? You haven't been here long enough for anyone to figure it out."

"I don't know what you're talking about, Smith, I just walked in the damned door," Curtis said, trying to disengage his arm, sensing that the large martini had an ancestor or two.

"It's one hell of a note," Smitty went on, nodding toward the bar, "when the Brits and the peaceniks are conducting our war."

Curtis, his arm still in the grasp of Smitty's old claw, looked in the direction of his nod and saw Ray Corrigan slide off his barstool, pick up his Scotch and milk and move toward them.

"I had 48 hours to get out of Peking when China fell in '49 and I don't intend to be witness to another such Red debacle," Smith said, as Curtis with some difficulty jerked his arm away.

He looked over at John Andre, who rolled his eyes, grinned and said: "We might as well sit down, it looks like you're in for a long afternoon."

"It's already been a long stretch," the Reuters guy said as he walked up and set his milky Scotch down on the table. "I decided the argument was getting out of hand and moved to the bar when Smitty here told me that myself and the youngsters he lumped me in with weren't smart enough to understand what the War Department was trying to do."

"Jesus Christ, fella," Colonel Andre said, "Defense hasn't been called that since even before China fell." He pulled out a chair and circled his hand over the table indicating to the bartender he wanted a round for everyone.

"Yeah, Smitty, you're missing an important distinction there. The U.S. isn't waging war, it's fighting in the defense of freedom," quipped Corrigan, as he gingerly eased his bulk into an empty seat.

"You got that right, pal," Ford said, turning on Corrigan. "You should know that quite well. It seems to me the only time the British and the U.S. have been on the same side during a war was when we had to bail your asses out during World Wars One and Two. If you guys fought half as well as you talk, we could have sat out a couple of big ones. And that brogue spells Irish. Where was Ireland when the Allies could have used help in '42?"

Ford, who up to this point had refused to sit, reluctantly pulled out a chair when the bartender arrived with a tray of drinks.

So in that season of turnings, turning from memories of the comforts of home to the inexorable heat and chaos of Saigon, turning ever so slowly to recognizing themselves as linchpins in a house of cards, and, momentarily, turning away from the specter of the inevitable end of the story, Ford Curtis and some of the seasoned correspondents spent a hot afternoon, in an air-conditioned officers club, cheered on by a member of the United States military, bemoaning the depths to which the gentlemanly art of covering a war had fallen.

# 16

# Dining With Chopsticks

"I'm really glad you kept your promise about dinner," Angela said as she and Nick sat down at a bare wooden table in a noisy, cheap little Japanese joint that Nick heard had stupendous sweet and sour white fish.

"Yeah," said Nick. "Sorry I've been out in the field so much. It's about time we got together after you saved my butt from the White Mice. I'm buying."

"I accept," Angela laughed. "We can call it a celebration of our initiation rites into the hard realities of South Vietnamese justice."

"Oh, boy," Nick said with a grin. "Another one of your poetic riffs."

"And you see yourself as a single-syllable guy?"

"Something like that. So how's it been going?"

"Not terrific, but I'll survive. It's lonely at times. Parks has been great, but some of the rest of these guys are real shits."

Nick laughed. "You're too good looking. Most of 'em are scared they'll get razzed, if they act like they notice you. But they're pretty much an OK bunch."

"I guess," Angela said without much enthusiasm as she picked up the huge hand-lettered paper menu that was entirely in Japanese.

"Gosh, what do we do now?" she asked after glancing over the unintelligible scratchings.

"Two contingency plans," Nick said. He dug a scrap of paper from his pocket. "Yoki Suku, the Japanese correspondent who told me about this place, is supposed to meet us here. But he's drawn me a sort of diagram of the menu in case he's late."

Warm rice wine materialized immediately. Then with Yoki's diagram and the pidgin English of an arthritic, elderly waiter who looked like he was left over from the World War II Japanese occupation, a steady stream of food began appearing. Despite his gnarled hands, the old fellow was deft with the steaming dishes that he put on a lazy Susan in the middle of the table, which he had covered with butcher paper.

"I hear you're having trouble selling," Nick said, stabbing with a chopstick at an elusive shrimp in an aromatic brew of steamy vegetables.

"It's a lot rougher than I expected." Angela leaned over to adjust the wooden sticks between his middle and forefingers. "I've only sold one piece so far, plus good money for the Loch Ninh story that went with Parks' photos. Any ideas?"

"Afraid not," Nick said. "I haven't been here long myself and I've never been a freelance. But let me ask around.

"Hey, on second thought," he said, looking up from his focused glare at the still slippery shrimp. "One guy it might do you good to talk to is John Simenson. I think he had to scramble a lot in the beginning. He probably knows the Europe market. Finally landed his first job as a local hire in Brussels for UPI. Has a wild story about covering the Six-Day War. You know him?"

"Not really," she said, her face lighting up. "But I've seen him on a couple of press trips. Seems like a very sweet little guy. I'll talk to him. Thanks.

"So now, let's change the subject to you," Angela said with a smile. "You're from Chicago, aren't you? I've lost touch with who's doing what there anymore."

"Yeah," said Nick. "You been there? I thought you were from someplace in the South."

"I did an internship, and a brief run, at the Trib."

"No kidding? Damn. The Trib doesn't have anyone here right now. I didn't even know you were a journalist!"

"That's pretty accurate, the way things are going," she said with a self-deprecating laugh.

"Ah, gee," Nick said, squirming in his chair, apparently at a loss for reassuring words. He glanced around the steamy, noisy room, and with an expression of relief watched a scrawny, bespectacled, Japanese in western dress thread his way toward their table through the gray haze of cigarette smoke that lay thick in the air. "Here comes the guy, Yoki Suku. I first met him in Chicago when he was sent from his Tokyo Shimbun bureau in New York to cover one of Mayor Daley's many re-election runs."

"So Nick, you found good food," Yoki said extending his hand in greeting, a big grin on his face. "And this is your fliend," he said with a slight bow as he turned his beam of approval on Angela. "Excerrent. And wercome. I hope you like Japanese lestauant."

"Love it," said Angela. "Quite a find. Most of the joints around here are full of GIs with bar girls on their knees."

"Sit and chow down," said Nick. "I followed your menu directions as best I could. See if you approve." As Yoki dug in with obvious pleasure in their selections, his happy grin turned to one of amusement as he watched Nick manhandle his chopsticks.

The combination of the warm wine and tons of food acted like a sedative on the normally loquacious correspondents. After stuffing themselves, the three sat around smoking and moaning about how full they were. When they finally struggled up from the table, they took a stab at a couple of nearby bars looking for John Simenson, but soon gave in to drowsiness and decided they'd had it for the night.

Yoki turned off toward his digs, and Nick and Angela walked on down the Tu Do toward their respective hotels. Nick was still staying at the Caravelle, which was on the other corner of National Assembly Square from the Continental, towards the Saigon River.

"Well, here we are back at our first crash pad," Angela said with a laugh, referring to the broad hotel steps where Nick had thrown himself on top of her the week before.

Angela shook Nick's hand as they stopped to say goodnight beneath the shadows of the huge flowerboxes that formed the so-called Continental Shelf, the perimeter of the hotel's outdoor terrace.

"Thanks, Nick," she said. "You've fed me, introduced me to a new friend and given me a lead on another. You're a pal."

She kissed his cheek and headed into the hotel, taking the steps two at a time.

Nick is good, Angela thought, making her way across the lobby for the staircase to her second floor room. I really need to make some friends. I'm attached to nothing, stationed nowhere, my moorings of home severed by a divorce from my only anchor. I've got to stop feeling like I've joined the Foreign Legion. I keep thinking of "Beau Geste," that Gary Cooper movie I saw when I was a kid where everyone ended up dead in a lost cause.

She frowned at the faded, cloying rose pattern of the hall carpeting. How could she have been so naive to think she could just waltz over here and feel like a useful human being again simply by working hard? She seemed to be making a mess of everything. I've made a horrible enemy of Ford Curtis with my smart mouth, she thought. Hardly anyone will bother to speak to me except crazy Parks. And Nick, of course. She smiled to herself. I'd be pretty black and blue if the only way to get these so-called gentlemen of the press to trust me is to get beat up by the White Mice with each of them one by one. John Simenson, the little guy, maybe he can provide some practical help. Maybe that could be a bridge for us to become friends: he seems so intense and fierce, great qualities for a potential ally.

Angela turned the big brass key in her door and walked across to the louvered windows overlooking the street, flopping her heavy bag on the bed as she passed. She opened the shutters, filling the room with light from the busy nighttime street. More light than was given off by that puny bedside lamp. She liked prowling around her room in the semi-dark, guided only by the neon from outside. It felt private, moving unseen in shadows, while letting the world in at the same time. Not too isolated or alone, but not exposed either. She looked down into the bustling street and saw Nick, who obviously had been waylaid by the several friends clustered around him, standing in the street talking. She recognized Ray Corrigan, the rest she didn't know. Corrigan was gesturing toward the hotel's terrace and, sure enough, in another moment the group moved in that direction. Angela couldn't see where they sat, since the bar was right beneath her. It crossed her mind to go back down. It would be a good way to become friendlier with some of these people. Nick would pull her in, invite her to join them. Why was she hesitating? What made her pull away?

Instead, she stood at the window, mesmerized by the hyperactivity of the street scene below. She hadn't expected any of this to be easy. A borrowed camera, a start-up roll of film and a promise from her hometown paper to buy an occasional story. Stepping off a cliff with no parachute. She had thought work was the answer. But you tote your loneliness with you. Like a vacuum bubble of space that surrounds you, just like the empty seats on each side of you in the Continental bar. We're observers, not participants, she said to herself as she had said a thousand times before, turning over in her mind the question of why people viewed her as remote, distant. She didn't feel distant to herself, anything but. She always seemed to feel scared, or nervous, or inadequate. She had thought she was having a coronary, arriving here, as she stepped off that plane.

Jackson called her "the metaphor for cool," but he understood. We're observers, not participants. We watch and write it down and move on to the next carnage without skipping a beat. But it's still and lonely when the clatter of the keys stops, and the adrenaline keeps flowing. That's when we head for the nearest bar—slow the pulse and deaden the mind. Stop the world, I want off. Just as her intensity was in work, Jackson's life was in his horn, his nights in sleazy, smoky jazz clubs. Meeting him at that party in San Francisco had forever changed her life. He seemed bizarre, exotic, to a college sophomore sporting the uniform white bucks with red rubber soles, worn, as the code commanded, with white socks rolled tight below the anklebone. She giggled to herself, standing there alone peering out the window in this *truly* bizarre, exotic foreign country. She had thought then that Jackson had looked like a mortician. A lot of people called Jackson "intense." But it went way beyond that: He ignored the "things" of life. He cut through the bullshit, right to the bone. Jackson cared about his horn, his music and Angela, and he didn't waste time on anything else. He'd given her a new view of life, he'd given her moral support. When it hadn't occurred to her to defy her parents and quit pre-med at Stanford, he'd asked the obvious question of "why?" she couldn't quit school and work for a semester to earn money if her parents wouldn't support her rebellion. He moved from San Francisco to Berkeley so she could eventually go to school there. Then he moved to Chicago when she was accepted in the journalism school at Northwestern. "I can play my horn anywhere," he'd said. But she'd left him. Playing a horn in the middle of the night didn't provide them with much togetherness.

And then along came Peter, a man who made bread and grew vegetables in their backyard. A man who "mothered" her, Jackson said. Was that what she saw in Peter, a mother? At the time, she felt madly in love. A home, with good smells in the kitchen. Not a smoke-filled bar every night, if you didn't want to stay home by yourself. A sharing of the same profession, just as her parents had done.

Three years later, Peter left her for a woman who had his supper ready when he got home.

The family circle goes round.

"I do my work, while you do yours," Jackson said. "One of these years you're gonna have to make up your mind, Valentine, do you want yourself, or do you want all this togetherness horseshit."

# 17

# Hey, Johnny, Wait Up

"Hey, Johnny, wait up," Angela yelled as she spotted John Simenson the next morning, hurrying past down the Tu Do just she was starting down the steps of the Continental.

She didn't know the baby-faced UPI reporter any better than any of the rest of the pack she'd seen on press trips, but he seemed sweet and wasn't exactly part of the gang. He put up with a lot of razzing from other guys because of his diminutive size and his air of innocence, although people seemed to like him.

"I'm embarrassed to have to ask," she said as she caught up, "but I thought you might know some European magazines I could try. Nick O'Brien told me you were stationed in Brussels for quite a while."

"Well, ah, I hear you're having some trouble selling," said Johnny.

"They either gripe it's the same as what everyone else has, or it's too different. American editors are wary of anything that might be read as critical of the war," Angela said in a rush, partly from running to catch up to Johnny, partly from nervousness that he was stalling, trying to think of a way to refuse. No one wanted to give someone a reference when they didn't know their work. She gulped and plunged ahead. "I've got this incredible stuff out of a field hospital and they're *all* saying it's too tough for their readers."

"It's rough, I know. But, well. Uh, well, uh, have you got a copy of the story so I can see it?" Johnny asked.

"Sure," Angela rummaged through her ever-present huge duffel and handed him the pages.

Johnny stopped in the middle of the bustling pedestrian traffic for a quick read of Angela's three-page story. "Damn. This is good shit! But nobody'll buy this at home. UPI wouldn't touch it."

"That's what I'm finding out," Angela said. "Got any ideas?"

"Yeah, you're right about Europe," Johnny said as though coming out of a fog and finally getting Angela's drift. Nick had warned her that Johnny had a way of stammering around that caused people who weren't too smart themselves to assume that Johnny wasn't very alert. Angela smiled to herself. Actually, that was probably a help to the little guy, especially in this macho atmosphere. Sources often condescendingly explain or blurt out things to women reporters, because they assume they don't know what they're doing. Nick had said Johnny was "a damned good reporter." Angela suspected his hemming and hawing helped put sources off guard.

"The Europeans don't care, it's not their war," Johnny said. "They're also into writing, scene setting, not just body counts. Yeah, you're right," he said again. "I've got a list of names back at the UPI shack that may help."

"Gosh, Johnny, thanks." Angela was breathless. They'd resumed walking at a good clip the moment Johnny stopped reading. Occupational hazard, especially for a wire service reporter, the feel of forever being on the run, never without a deadline to meet, some paper someplace in the world is always closing pages and could use a paragraph or two to top off a story, make it fresh. Angela suddenly realized that while Johnny may be running for deadline, he also was having to trot to keep up with her long-legged stride. She cut her gait by half as they walked in silence down the Tu Do toward the UPI office and the slow-moving traffic on the river.

# 18

# Halloween with Mrs. Colonel

NICK'S EYES roamed the main room of the tiny villa. The decor was rent-a-furniture circa Holiday Inn. Martini-in-hand Americans were jammed in wall to wall, spilling out onto the scorching patio with its shallow pool, opening and closing the sliding glass doors, letting in blasts of stagnant, hot, Sunday-afternoon air. Low-ranking military brass and junior Embassy staffers were packed too close to see any knees, but the women's were exposed, if unseen, in their abbreviated Jackie Kennedy sleeveless dresses. Even a few little pillbox hats bobbed in the crowd, perched atop stiff bouffants. Five years after she was shot out of the White House, the widow Kennedy was still a fashion presence, especially in an expatriate setting where state-side chic was not precisely up to the minute. Jackie had only recently been caught by paparazzi frolicking in a bikini on some Greek guy's yacht.

Americans sure know how to bring America with them, Nick thought, as the buxom, fat-cheeked colonel's wife who had him cornered droned on. She brought to mind a stout Peter Lorre in drag with the puffy lids of a heavy drinker pressing down on her beady eyes and the three strands of a rhinestone choker pressing in on the thick folds of her neck. The hosts had used Halloween as an excuse to have a party, but this woman in her everyday duds looked like she had taken them seriously and come in costume.

"I just told the colonel this morning," said Mrs. Colonel, "that the lack of patriotism on the part of the press is a true hazard to our boys.

You reporters just don't know what your responsibilities are in a free society such as ours."

There was no way to move on through the crush. Nick thought of spilling his drink down this offensive woman's lumpy cleavage, but she'd probably holler "rape." The party was being given by some junior exec from the U.S. mission. These guys were probably recruited with promises of combat pay and all the PX-priced Jack Daniels they could swill. Nick didn't like hanging out with this kind of official crowd any more than he would do much partying with the pols from city hall whom he'd covered back in Chicago. Socializing with sources not only blurs a reporter's vision, but it can also put him in some ethical tough spots if he isn't careful.

He shouldn't have come, he chided himself, as Mrs. Colonel droned away. On the other hand, how could he work if he didn't cultivate sources? It's a thin line to walk, if you're interested in maintaining any sort of integrity.

He was looking through the haze of cigarette smoke over the fat woman's shoulder when he saw what he thought must be a heat-induced mirage. It was Angela, vivid and unmistakable in a bright blue blouse. She was coming through the door with that creep, Kevin Leahey! The guy Parks called Mr. CIAster. Leahey looked as pompous and smug as ever, wearing what Nick guessed was his Yale tie in spite of the heat.

"I just told the colonel he should speak to the general about it," the colonel's lady babbled on as Nick fidgeted. "After all, reporters simply can *not* be allowed to go around and write down whatever they see. Why, just last week my sister Eloise sent me a clipping from the Indianapolis paper, of all places—she moved there because her husband is in cement—and the story said that soldiers in the Central Highlands had actually refused to go into battle. Now how, I ask you, can we win a war with people writing such things? The colonel said the story wasn't even true. He knew what they were referring to, it's not uncommon, but that's no reason to report it, and it didn't happen like that at all."

The speaker had gotten through this last without ever taking a breath, like a sprinter expanding her chest for the final tape. She's got the lungs for grand opera, Nick thought, as he watched the breathless performance with his own mind gasping for oxygen at the stunning scene of Angela's red head weaving through the crowd with the suspected spook at her elbow. God, he thought, she should have better sense! Dating a source you probably couldn't believe at all. It's bad enough when it pays to wine and dine some guy's secretary. But everyone thinks this jerk is plain dangerous.

Nick's mind was doing somersaults, but he knew he had to bring himself back to Mrs. Colonel. After all this time of listening to her non-stop blather, she finally had said something important, but he was having difficulty focusing on what it was.

"The reporting was inaccurate, or the mutiny didn't happen at all?" he finally asked, sniffing at a possible story about peaceniks among the military.

"What's the difference? That's my point. It's no one's business. We shouldn't be debating that sort of thing in the newspapers," she chirped wagging a fat finger under Nick's nose. "If you want some positive news for a change, you should write a story about how many of the officers' wives are doing Red Cross work in base hospitals."

Ah, Christ. Nick tuned the Old Bag out, realized he had lost Angela from his radar screen, and dialed to his own frequency to debate with himself what he considered one of the major mysteries of life. Why, he continually asked himself, do politicians and assorted other publicity freaks drink with reporters? Were they so dumb they didn't know how dangerous it is, or did they do it on purpose, assuming that whatever they say when they have half a load on will have to be respected as a confidence? If they tell you something that makes them look bad, they figure it's "off the record." But for what they call "good" news, they want to turn you into their personal publicity mill.

Everyone always has an axe to grind with the press, or a story to tout. They're either saying stuff they don't want you to print, or stuff they do want you to print, but they never get it through their heads that they can't dictate to you which is which.

"Don't you agree?" said Mrs. Colonel, almost yelling to break into his reverie.

"Absolutely," said Nick, not giving a damn if he had just agreed that the entire press corps should be shot.

He was getting so desperate he was actually toying with the idea of saying, "Fuck you, you old bat," when he realized Angela was shoving her way through the crowd and once again coming to his rescue. She took Nick's arm with apologies to Mrs. Colonel that she needed to "borrow" him for a minute. She led him straight to the bar, pushing and shoving through the crowd.

"What a break to find you here, pal," she said after ordering them both a Scotch from the Vietnamese houseboy serving as bartender. "I was afraid I was sentenced to an entire evening of spooks and bores."

"You know about that guy you came with?" Nick asked in amazement.

"Kevin? Of course. He's been laying all sorts of what he calls *wonderful* story ideas on me. And I'm the only one in the press corps he's telling." Angela grimaced and held out her hands palms up. "You know the pitch, just because I'm such a *nice* person."

"I was really worried when I saw you come in with him."

She still had her arm linked with his, and she gave it a squeeze. "They've all got their own version of the truth, including your politicians back in Chicago, now haven't they, punkin?"

He laughed. "How'd you get so savvy?"

"Hard work and hard knocks on the police beat in Chicago. My first city editor took me aside and warned me to be careful," she lowered her voice to a conspiratorial whisper, as she reached past a guy seated at the tiny wicker and bamboo bar for her Scotch. "Said he'd seen working the cops turn nice girls into hard women." She lifted her eyebrows in a wry grin. "Same guy also told me that the few women in this business had it tough, but they were good at asking the dumb question that could sucker a source into spilling his guts."

Nick laughed. "If it was Kirkland, I know the old shit. You mentioned the other night that you were an intern at the Trib. But we got sidetracked. The word among the pack is that you were a model."

"When I was younger, I wanted to switch schools and my parents said they wouldn't pay my tuition. Later, it was the only way to make big bucks fast to grub-stake this trip." She stopped, touched her glass to Nick's, downed her drink, then said with a dry laugh, "So the lesson there for women is, if you can't win a Pulitzer, there's always Harper's Bazaar."

"It's hard to figure what any woman's doing here. Is that what you're after—a Pulitzer?"

"I'm here for the same reason you are," she said with an emphasis that told him he was getting a whiff of something important.

"My paper sent me," he responded.

"You didn't have to come. Ask any grunt. The first thing they say when they see a reporter at a firebase is 'You guys are nuts, 'cause you're here and you don't have to be.'"

"That's not the point," Nick stubbornly persisted.

"What is, then?"

"Gee, I dunno. How can I explain what I'm doing here? I'm here, it's my job."

"So? It's the same for me," Angela said as she grabbed a just-vacated stool at the bar, and held up her glass to signal the bartender for a refill. "But don't you ever think about why you do this job, instead of something else?"

"I guess not. But I suppose you do," Nick replied with a grin. "I'm the single-syllable guy, remember? So what's your theory?"

She laughed, and reached for her new drink. "Let's save it for a time when we're totally sloshed. But I do think we serve a much broader social function than just guarding the First Amendment and keeping the politicos honest. We record the lives of Everyman."

"Huh?" Nick said, with a mystified look on his face.

"When we cover stories like fires or missing children, we're validating anguish. We're branding it as a tragedy, instead of random awfulness. Same when we put a grunt's name and hometown in a war story. We're making it personal."

"Oh, God." Nick, put his head in his hands and moaned.

Angela grinned. "You asked for it. You with your pesky, nosey questions."

Nosey, maybe, Nick thought, but there was something that kept stirring in the back of his mind about Chicago. A dim recollection, perhaps, of some female whiz who had graduated a few years ahead of him in j-school at Northwestern, but Martinelli didn't sound familiar.

Before Nick could reply, Kevin Leahey appeared on the other side of Angela, leaned on the bar and began making noises about people who abandon the person who brought them to a party.

"You never heard the expression about dancing with the guy who brung you?" he said, raising an eyebrow at Angela and his empty glass to the guy behind the bar.

"Gee, no, Kevin," Angela said with a smile. "That's a new one. But it's a bit crowded for that, don't you think?"

This guy's amazing, Nick thought. He has an oily way of being flirtatious and disdainful with Angela all at the same time. Everything he says seems to have a double meaning. Angela didn't seem to notice, but it made Nick feel like punching him out.

Nick leaned close to Angela's ear. "Doesn't this guy strike you as smarmy?"

She laughed, turning her head away from Kevin, and spoke in a low conspiratorial voice. "That's one thing models and girl reporters have in common. As long as you're oblivious to suggestive remarks, you're in control. If you ever let your guard down, you're just another piece of meat."

"So, girl reporter, you didn't by chance go to Northwestern, did you?" Nick figured it was a long shot, but it might work as a ploy to keep her attention away from Kevin. "But under another name?"

Angela laughed. "Yeah. Andrews. My ex-husband's name was Martinelli."

It was Nick's turn to laugh. "I'll be damned. Of course. You graduated just before I got there, but I remember running into clips with your byline. You were a star."

Angela rolled her eyes. "Boy, that was another lifetime. Old Higgins had to go to bat for me to get that internship at the Trib over the protest of the city editor who didn't want a female presence in the newsroom."

Before Nick could respond, a guy he recognized from the press office in Da Nang, obviously in town for a little weekend of R&R, squeezed in between Kevin and Angela and started hitting on her.

"It's getting pretty crowded in here," Nick said to no one in particular, and took his drink out to the little walled garden festooned for the occasion with paper lanterns.

Kevin followed, and didn't waste any time bothering to small talk around his interest in Angela.

"I've heard from some of the older press guys that the redheaded broad isn't much of a reporter," he said to Nick. "Is that what you've heard?"

"What the fuck are you asking a question like that for?" Nick exploded, finally releasing some of the hostility that had been itching for a chance to spill out. "You trying to decide if she can be trusted with one of your CIA disinformation exclusives?"

"Jesus, aren't we touchy," Kevin said, his voice bland, his handsome but slightly pudgy face a blur because his blonde eyebrows were almost white. His blue eyes were made even paler under the colorless shadow. "What in hell are you talking about?"

"You know," Nick said, his voice sounding in his own ears like a grade D actor in the kiddies' Saturday-afternoon matinee. Kevin's doughy face was the evil sneer of the villain. These spook guys are probably trained not to lose their tempers, Nick thought, so they don't look guilty of anything.

"The only thing I know is that the broad said she was doing a story on children and malnutrition and how the war has affected the food supply. But this guy Curtis, when I got him some similar figures and mentioned her request, said he wouldn't give it a high priority." Kevin's delivery was sharp and slightly snide. His face then relaxed into a smile as he said his last bit slowly and distinctly as though speaking to someone ever so slightly retarded. "I'm an agrarian economist, remember?"

"Yeah, so I've heard. So why the fuck do you care what kind of reporter she is? Afraid she'll misquote you on the yearly tonnage of Brussels sprouts?"

"I heard she wasn't really a reporter at all, just over here looking for kicks. I don't want to waste my time on someone who's not legit."

"What time you worried about wasting, buddy, the daytime or the nighttime? She's a reporter, and she's a good one, and you're definitely wasting your time for what you've got in mind."

Nick slammed his drink down on a metal Holiday-Inn poolside table complete with striped umbrella and started to stomp off. He whirled around for a parting shot: "And Ford Curtis is a bigger asshole than you are if he's trying to put the screws to her by drying up sources. Especially with jerks like you who only want to plant false stories."

"False stories? You're not making any sense," Kevin said in a dismissive tone.

"You guys have been stirring up trouble here since 1954," Nick said. "You created this mess of a war. And you just keep right on blowing smoke about how one more fuck-up is some new wonderful deal."

Kevin shrugged. "I haven't a clue what you're talking about."

"The CIA," Nick spat out. "I don't know who you think you're kidding."

Kevin just laughed.

# 19

# River Walk

"What's with you and Curtis?" Nick asked with no preamble the next night as he and Angela were taking a walk through the steaming night toward the Saigon River.

She laughed, throwing back her head and shaking out her thick auburn hair as she strode along sniffing for even a hint of a breeze.

"It's this hot and nearly midnight," she said. "My hair's as wet as if I just stepped out of the shower."

"Great. So what about Curtis?"

"What if I said it's none of your damn business?"

"So fine. Say that."

They walked on, down through the bustle of the Tu Do, dodging sidewalk traffic from still-open souvenir shops and noisy bars. Angela stopped several times to study a dress or pair of slacks in display windows of the ubiquitous tailoring shops along the street.

"Satin undies, what a trip," she said, finally breaking their silence, looking at an array of silk lingerie.

"Yeah, fascinating," replied Nick.

"That's what separates the men from the women here," she said.

"No shit," Nick replied, sarcasm dripping from his voice.

"No, stupe," she said laughing. "I only meant that the men are all on an orgy of snatching up stereo equipment at PX prices, while I'm splurging on cute little handmade panties cut wide at the leg like the pinup-girl shorts of World War II. Look at that one, with a rose and a Chinese character embroidered near the hem. They're adorable."

"Jesus Christ," said Nick.

They went on in silence. As they reached the last, suddenly quiet block, the foot traffic left behind, they barely created a shadow beneath the overhanging canopy of towering tamarind trees.

"Curtis is trying to undermine you, and I think you should know that," Nick finally said into the dark as they moved toward the murky black waterway at the bottom of the street. "The man's got a lot of clout. What did you do to him?"

"Not much."

"He's telling sources you can't be trusted, pointing out you have no paper behind you."

"Yeah, Kevin told me."

"OK. Just so you know," Nick expelled a big breath that sounded like a sigh. "It's hard to believe a word Kevin says, but I don't see how he could make this up. He wouldn't even know you and Curtis knew each other, unless one of you told him."

"Well, it sure as hell wasn't me, so it had to have been Curtis," Angela snapped, stopping on the boardwalk along the river and turning toward Nick.

As they stood near the gangway of a floating restaurant, dark and shuttered for the night, the sky suddenly was lighted, followed by the sound that had brought the light. Boom, boom, boom. The B-52s hit or missed their target, no way to tell from this distance, maybe 10 miles. Artillery rockets, chasing after the bombers, streaked the night sky red and yellow. Then just as suddenly, there was quiet again across the river, in that northern section of the area the U.S. military called The Iron Triangle.

"Sorry for the interruption," Nick said with a dry laugh. The two resumed walking along the riverfront.

"So what's with him?" Nick picked up where he had left off. "Did you turn him down?"

"God, we go right on with this mundane, petty stuff, while people are probably dying over there," Angela said, not breaking stride as she flung her left arm out toward the river. "But I guess everybody does. That's how you stay sane."

She laughed. "Yeah, to answer your question. I suppose, one might call it a turndown. But it really didn't get that far. Maybe he could just tell that I think he's a stuffed shirt."

Nick whistled. "Cute. That's what you call not much? You ought to want his help. He's one of the most powerful and respected journalists in the country."

"Respected, my ass!" Angela's voice took on considerable heat. "He's just high on the pecking order because of his paper. It's like the old Boston joke about the Lodges speaking only to the Cabots and the Cabots speaking only to God. Those, quote-unquote, *star* reporters don't dig and report, they speak only to premiers and presidents and highly placed sources."

"Well, shit, you don't mind looking for trouble, do you?"

"He's not worth my trouble, one way or the other. I don't need him or his inflated ego."

"Lady, I think you're going to need all the help you can get." Nick's voice cut through the heavy air like a knife.

"My, aren't we testy." Angela stopped in mid-stride to turn and grin at him.

"Christ." Nick slapped his forehead with the palm of his hand as he turned and narrowed his eyes at her. "It's suddenly hitting me that you're enjoying this. One way or the other, you've got his attention." He paused, but got no response from her except the grin. "Shit! Who can understand women."

She laughed. "Well, he *is* a very attractive man."

That made Nick laugh. "Come on. How do you think you're ever going to learn how to be a war correspondent when you regress into female logic like that?"

Their eyes, dilated in the dark along the quay of the Saigon River, blinked into the thousand lights of hundreds of sampan lanterns as they took a right turn following the interior waterway that flowed into the river. The tightly clustered houseboats bumped gently at both banks of the canal. The span of the Y Bridge was a dark shadow across the water.

Here's another river to cross, Angela thought. Another obstacle? Is that what it means? Jackson played "One More River" on his sax the night she told him she was going to marry Peter.

Jackson had given up the jazz scene in San Francisco so she could go to journalism school at Northwestern. He'd had a regular gig at the

Black Hawk on Powell Street, but, "What difference does it make?" he'd said. "There's another Black Hawk on Rush Street in Chicago. You need to get far away from Stanford, and this doctor bullshit." Her parents had been scandalized—leaving Stanford, living with a man to whom she wasn't married! Jackson said she had crossed another river. The Berkeley marching band always played "One More River, One More River to Cross" at the Cal-Stanford games, the entire tuba section tapping out the repetitive dirge-like rhythm by swaying their big brass horns like so many rows of wheat rippling in a stiff breeze. The song had a significance that Jackson caught; she'd never quite understood what it meant. Another challenge? Another game to be played? Another game to be won? Another war to fight?

Nick watched the shadow-show playing across Angela's face in the flickering sampan light. "So," he said, snapping his fingers, to bring her back. "What's it going to be? Regression? Or you gonna be one of the boys?"

He could barely make out the faint grin as she said: "Just because I've stooped to wearing combat boots and fatigues doesn't mean I've gone to seed."

"Oh, boy, that definitely calls for a 'no comment,'" Nick said.

# 20

# Back in Her Room

BACK IN her room the next day at the Continental, Angela mulled over Nick's fears for her as she brushed her teeth at the pedestal sink in the big old-fashioned, oversized bathroom. She felt fairly certain that Curtis couldn't hurt her all that much, because he moved in a different stratosphere. The ambassador wasn't having *her* over for cocktails or feeding *her* news tips with dinner. She must develop her own stories, stories of hardship and frailty from the rice paddies and villages; second-day stories that skipped over the body counts and zeroed in on the human wreckage.

But she was running into a stumbling block that none of the other reporters had figured on, either for her or for themselves: credibility with their stateside editors. She had worked her butt off on two pieces that she knew were damn good, "exceptionally good," both Nick and John Simenson had pronounced when they'd seen them. But no paper would touch them—war orphans and over-worked, understaffed field hospitals were considered too tough for American readers to take. She finally had scrapped the war orphans altogether and was able to sell the hospital story to an obscure radical journal. Nothing, so far, from John Simenson's contacts.

As she stepped out of her beige silk slacks and her hand-tailored satin panties and into a steaming bath, she could feel herself getting angry again. It made her furious to think about those stories and the goddamned long hours she'd put into them. And even more furious to think about the hellish life of Betty Lou, the 22-year-old scrub nurse from Kansas who had inspired the MASH piece.

Too strong for American readers, editors said. Not too strong for Betty Lou, or Angela, or the kid with the melting, napalmed face, but too strong for readers.

She slipped out of the bath and wrapped herself in one of the enormous near-blanket-sized towels that were a Continental Hotel trademark.

"That's no place for a lady," the foreign editor at the AP in New York had said as he'd handed her the Leica and the credential letter. Everyone had said it, in one way or another. Everyone except her mother, who hadn't minced words: "A low-life profession. But if you must, then get good at it. Go where the important story is."

The steam had dripped off, leaving only a watery glaze as she peered harder in the mirror, running her fingertips lightly over the delicate redhead's complexion that she soaked daily with every imaginable kind of oil fighting the sun. Her poor skin would never recover.

She laughed to herself. Ah, phooey. What difference does it make? I'm not going to get hung up on missing what people back home think of as ordinary, everyday comforts. I've got a new life, a job to learn, mountains to climb.

She padded out of the bathroom, her wet feet leaving their size nine imprints on the faded, once-elegant carpet. She looked around and calmed down. She loved the tropical Sadie Thompson feeling of this huge, old-fashioned French colonial room—her own private cool place, even in the heat of the day. She knew she should be trying to find a cheaper hotel, but a place to call home was very important to her. A quirky trait in someone who had no discernible domestic skills, nor any interest in developing them. That's why she had been so drawn to Peter, he was her nest maker.

The quiet whirring of the fan on the high ceiling made the filmy white curtains suck gently against the louvered shutters. The filtered sun formed a lacy filigree along the creamy walls. As it always did, the circulating air evaporated the moisture from her body, a luxury she indulged in whenever she wasn't in the field and could get back to her room for a quick dip to float away the sticky paste of dirt and sweat that regenerated itself nearly as fast as she could wash it off. Sometimes it required all her grit to dispel the feeling that lice and creepy little animals were running across her spine, or sloshing back and forth under the arcs of her breasts, or perching on her nipples. The stolen baths marked the only time she felt really fresh and comfortable. The icy air-conditioning in most of the U.S. buildings in the city made her skin feel so clammy that she found the refrigerated air almost as uncomfortable as the oppressive heat.

It's a strange life, she thought, and found it instructive that the few women whom she'd met over here—nurses and an occasional reporter—seemed to have gotten their hearts broken before they had been here a month. Living at a fast pace and high intensity, forget it. Guys are lonely, they want some companionship, until they board the plane and go back home to wives or girlfriends. She couldn't risk it. She'd get too involved, be a mess. Someone like Curtis? Catastrophe. She and Peter had left Chicago because Peter got a good job offer. What happened to Angela's career was of no consequence to anyone but her mother.

She lay down on her high antique bed with its brass and ironwork headboard and stared at the whirring fan. The ceilings were wonderfully high, perhaps 15 feet. With the intricate set-in moldings and detailed plaster circles radiating around the fan, it reminded her of her grandfather's house in Cambridge. Curtis was from Cambridge, Harvard. Her father was a Harvard man; Southern, but Harvard. Everyone was: both her grandfathers, her mother's uncle Arthur. That's who Curtis reminded her of—Uncle Arthur. Same hearty, but distant, stuffed front, chewed-on pipe to hide . . . what? A sweet sort of vulnerability, some fear that the secret of their humanity might leak out and leave them flat, with no pomposity on which to fly. Why did he draw her so? Probably because he felt like home. Most of the girls she'd been in school with in North Carolina were now married to men like that—solid, good providers. That's what women are supposed to want, isn't it?

She knew she wasn't alone in her problem of getting stories past editors. All the reporters were running into the same situation in one form or another, with the big difference being that those on staff got paid regardless. If a story of hers didn't run, she got zilch. The hawk/dove split on the war raging back home had editors chary about putting anything in the papers they deemed to be "open to interpretation." Students were rioting, anti-war protesters were marching in the streets, while veterans' organizations and pro-war groups were calling the demonstrators Commies and Pinkos. And both sides accused the press of being on the other side. With the line coming out of Washington often 180 degrees from what correspondents were reporting from the field, editors moving copy didn't know whom to believe. In fact, the Army was putting out information at the Follies on such things as who won what battle and what the casualties were that quite frequently was in direct contrast to what the correspondents were seeing on their own.

But the politics of the situation aside, reporters who had NEVER in their careers had a story spiked because their editor doubted its factual basis, were routinely having stories killed or rewritten or watered down because New York or their hometown city desk felt the story went too far, or wasn't verifiable, or didn't jibe with the official line. The divisions over the war had people nuts back home. Up until this war, it had always been a given in the news business that you go with your own reporter, which means if your reporter has it one way and the wires or another reporter have it another, you double check with your own guy, then you stick with what he says. That's why you have your own—you know his work and you trust him. So when an editor suddenly finds himself in this volatile climate where he's killing his own guy's copy because he doesn't want to be too far out on any limbs, Angela wasn't surprised that they weren't going to get on any limbs with her, a freelancer, whom they didn't know, much less trust.

She padded back to the bathroom where olive drab undershirts and skivvies coupled with pale satin panties and silk bras floated in the bidet with a bar of Ivory her father had sent from home. The steam from her bath had cleared, and as she bent to the task of her hand laundry she had a vision of herself washing white bobby socks one entire summer in the "footbaths" she found in cheap hotels the length and breadth of France. It wasn't until she got back to the States and was recounting her backpacking adventures and hardships that she found out that "the handy little French toilets without seats," as she had described them, were intended for a toiletry other than linens. Here she was again, on the outside looking in, trying to hold her own but losing ground in foreign territory.

She giggled, remembering her comment to Nick about satin underwear. When she first got in-country, she decided that the luxurious feel of satin was the one thing that could make living in those godawful fatigues bearable. But it wasn't long before she had to admit to herself that survival and comfort were the only luxuries she could afford. Silk and satin stuck to the skin like heated cellophane, and the panties crept up the leg at the damndest times! A bra was impossible, just a holding pool for rivers of sweat. Nothing at all was the worst—no place for the sweat to go except pour down your body and cause the coarse fatigues to take some peculiar folds as they got soaked. Cotton was cool and absorbent, and GI T-shirts protected the neck from sunburn. Besides, if she ever was wounded and they had to cut off her fatigues, she wanted plain OD skivvies to stir as little titillation as possible.

Funny what a double-edged word naked is. She always felt exposed without her clothes on, or without proper underwear, except when she was with a man. Or maybe not any man, maybe just Peter. Why had the husband who ultimately didn't want her been the only man she'd ever felt safe with? She had happily thought that she would spend the rest of her life with the nest builder, the homebody, the one her mother referred to as "Angela's ethnic." When she and Peter were first married, he'd taught her how to garden; they'd planted a baby cherry tree in the yard outside their first rented apartment. She hadn't known that you could just go buy a tree, and dig a hole and put it in the ground and it would grow. She was fluent in Latin, a dead language, but not fluent in things living. After she and Peter moved, they'd gone back to see their first offspring, but someone had cut the little tree down. When they had days off together, their outings were to the supermarket and the hardware store. Peter loved the hardware store with all its gadgets to fix up his home. She'd trail along beside him, just watching, her hand stuck in the patch pocket of his lumber jacket feeling connected to someone for the first time in her life. But love, somehow, seemed too hard to hold on to.

"He mothers you, Valentine," Jackson had said to Angela at her wedding party. "You're confused between being loved and smothered. You want a person to be your home. But you're the house you live in."

# 21

# Dak To and Cream Puffs for Thanksgiving

ANGELA MADE contact with a small Swedish magazine in late November that not only bought a version of her field hospital story, but also asked her to go to the Delta to expand on the piece she had been unable to sell about an orphanage there that cared for Eurasian children. She got back depressed about the orphans and hungry for some decent-tasting food. She decided to pamper herself—not even think about starting to write her story until tomorrow—and just eat something indulgent and go to bed with a good book.

The area around National Assembly Square was loaded with sidewalk vendors hawking discarded English-language paperbacks. She decided to wander through the series of shops and table stalls in the tunnel-like passages that ran through the ground floor of the building across the Tu Do from her hotel. She thought the labyrinth's official name was Passage Eden, but lots of folks referred to it as the Alleys of Eden. The Eden Building was at the farthest corner of the block, at Le Loi and Nguyen Hue. That's where NBC and the AP had their bureaus. On the near corner, at Le Loi and Tu Do, was the Givral, a pleasant coffee shop and *patisserie,* where she planned to satisfy her sweet tooth once she had found a book. All the comforts close to home.

The alleys were dark and cool, a bit dank, actually, but wandering through felt like an exotic adventure. Never knew what kind of trinkets you would find. Most of the books she saw were in miserable condition, pages mildewed together, whole sections missing. A few old standbys and a smattering of classics, but most were trash-adventure, or bodice rippers. It was pretty clear why all the Americans around were constantly swapping paperbacks, or pleading with Army pals to pick up books for them at the PX. She was frowning over the cover of a tattered copy of T. E. Lawrence's "Seven Pillars of Wisdom," when Curtis startled her.

"Kind of heavy going, wouldn't you say?" He nodded at the book in her hand.

"Well, if you're into backbiting, this might be just the ticket." She'd said the first thing that popped into her mind, realizing it didn't sound too coherent. She hadn't seen the gossip-mongering jerk in several weeks, but her anger at him was still simmering. Pompous ass. Telling her how concerned he was for her safety, and telling people behind her back she didn't know how to do her job.

"Backbiting? Well, that's a new take on Lawrence." Curtis gave her a big, but rather perplexed, smile.

"Seems to be your strong point, Mr. Curtis."

"What are you talking about? What kind of inference is that?"

"You can take it any way you like." Angela dropped the book, and turned and walked off.

Now she was stuck without a book. The hell with it. She'd go eat a cream puff. And read a magazine, if she had to. She left, smirking to herself. For once, her blurting out without thinking had paid off! Fucking Curtis, he didn't know what the hell she was talking about. Neither did she, but she'd got his goat. Ah, retribution is sweet.

When she turned to her left, heading for the Givral, she ran into Ray Corrigan on his way to the Continental bar. He took one look at her and grinned. "You look like you've just swallowed a canary. You must have scored some scoop."

"Nothing so exciting, I'm afraid," Angela replied with a dry laugh. "Just another encounter with Curtis. I think I won this one."

"Hm," Corrigan smiled and lifted the craggy eyebrows as he chewed his pipe. "You've got the gossip running with that one. Everyone speculatin.' Is it love, or hate, this ting?"

Angela burst out laughing. "You're incorrigible. Good name for you. Incorrigible Corrigan."

"I like that one better than Wrong Way, I'm saying. Been stuck with that for years."

"So tell me something more useful than gossip," Angela said smiling. "I've been out of town for days."

He told her there was heavy fighting in the Central Highlands, and that Nick, Parks and John Simenson had left several days before for Dak To.

"No sense in even thinking about going," Corrigan said, "the fighting is spread out over isolated garrisons up there, the way it has been off and on since September. With no one seeming to notice but me."

"What do you mean, exactly?" Angela asked, her interest perking up. She squinted to focus on Corrigan's face, putting her hand up to shade her eyes from the sun. She wasn't wearing a hat; she'd only expected to run across the street.

"They say there are 12,000 North Viet regulars massed this time. And they're fighting over one bloody, stupid hill. All these flare-ups at remote border areas. First it was on the east near the Cambodia border. Close to here, t'was. You were there with Parks at Loc Ninh last month, weren't you?"

"Yes," Angela said, almost breathless, wondering where this old-time, experienced correspondent was going with this. She didn't want to break the spell by suggesting they have a drink or a coffee together.

"So, and what did you find?" he went on. "A poor thing, t'was. A bunch a bloody dead Cong. Lucky t' find even that. Usually they evaporate, 'n take their dead with 'em."

"But what is it you're noticing, Corrigan, that no one else is?" She saw one of Corrigan's Brit pals dodging through the traffic on Tu Do heading toward them.

He looked at her, startled. "Well, don't ya see now? Sucking the U.S. troops over and over again away from the cities. Into big buildups in these remote areas for cat fights. Now they're up there at Dak To near the DMZ pissing around again. So that's the state of play," Corrigan said, as his pal walked up. "Would ya like t' take a drink with us now?"

"Thanks, but no," she said. "After two days of rice and dried fish in the Delta, I'm going to treat myself to a French pastry at the Givral." She didn't want to have to listen to the Brit whom Nick called Marbles bellyache about the "American" war, when all he ever seemed to do was get drunk at the Continental.

"Sounds a good plan," Corrigan said, as he turned and headed for his favorite table on the terrace.

Angela picked out a booth at the big window of the café with a good view of the square and her hotel. The constant rush of the traffic and the hustle of the Saigon street scene forever fascinated. You never knew what crazy thing you were going to see next. Prostitutes and pimps, street vendors selling trinkets, old women in conical hats with a bamboo pole across their shoulders with pots hanging from each end full of hot *pho,* their fish soup. Beautiful young girls in their long silk *ao dais* wearing elbow-length gloves in this heat, scarves like masks tied across their faces, to keep their skin from darkening in the sun.

She settled in to watch the cavalcade with a pot of hot tea and an indulgent chocolate cream puff.

She looked up, wiping flaky crumbs from her mouth. Unbelievable. How could you pack a family of five on a motor scooter? But there they were, whizzing by. Father and mother fitted onto the seat. A fender bumper with two kids, and a basket on the back with the littlest one.

And there was Nick, standing on the terrace across the street, talking to Corrigan.

And there came Nick. It looked like he was coming her way.

"Surely you're not going to give up a drink for a pot of tea?" she said by way of greeting as he walked in and headed for her table.

He laughed. "I can get a beer here. Happy Thanksgiving." He sounded cheerful, but looked weary. He still had his field gear, camera around his neck, a canteen tied to the duffel he was carrying. He'd been waylaid by Corrigan as Nick headed across the square to his hotel.

"Thanksgiving?" Angela frowned.

"Just got back from pumpkin and cranberries with the troops in Da Nang." He dropped his bag and plopped down hard across from her in the wooden booth.

"Gee, I hadn't realized what day it was. Not exactly fall with leaves turning. So how was Dak To?"

"Corrigan told you?" He asked the hovering waiter for a beer.

"Yeah, he made it sound pretty bad," Angela replied.

"Couldn't prove it by me," Nick said. "So bad we couldn't get in. Well, I got as far as Dak To, but the action was at some Cong bunkers near the Cambodian border. They finally formed a press pool, flew in two wire service guys and a photographer."

"A hill? Where the Cong had dug in deep?" Angela asked.

"Way deep," Nick replied. "Hill 875. So deep the B-52s weren't making a dent, except when they dropped a load on paratroopers already wounded trying to take the hill."

"Jesus! You mean it? U.S.?" Angela put down her teacup with a bang, startling the waiter who had just put a beer in front of Nick.

"Yep, 173rd Airborne. Eight choppers shot down trying to evac the wounded, then they just got bombed to smithereens. They say the bombing killed 20, but I don't know how they can tell. Apparently there are body pieces all over the hill.

"So Corrigan says you've been in the Delta," Nick said.

"Well, that's an abrupt change of subject," Angela said. "You're not inclined to dwell on things, are you?"

"Naw, what's the point?" Nick replied.

"To savor things, understand them, sort them out."

"What's to sort out?" Nick asked, taking a swig of his beer. "Westmoreland is doing what he's doing. And this one's not working out so well. Body parts, bombing your own guys. Speaks for itself. First rule of reporting, if the facts are grim enough, you don't have to elaborate, they speak for themselves."

"You've got to have some feeling about it. Some outrage," Angela persisted.

"Just the facts, ma'am," Nick said, grinning, as he imitated the intonation of Jack Webb on the old "Dragnet" television show. "What am I going to do, write a letter to my congressman? I already have. My congressman reads the Chicago papers."

"Good point," Angela said.

"While you're writing to Everyman, I'm writing my congressman. A hell of a lot of good any of it does anyone."

"I don't know how you can keep working, if you don't feel there is some point to it," Angela retorted.

"I do what's in front of me," Nick said with a shrug. "I'm not heavy into this 'broader social function' shit you were expounding on not long ago. Where did you pick up that malarkey?"

Angela laughed. "An on-the-job lesson I learned as an intern. More than happy to tell you the story. It might do you some good to give a little more thought to what you're doing."

"So, OK, shoot," Nick said.

"It was late," she began, lowering her voice to a dramatic narrative. "I'd tramped all over through snowdrifts, with a copy kid's assignment to pick up obit photographs of twelve children who had died in a community center fire. Reporters had been and gone, ahead of me. But I was the only one who got in to the grieving husband whose wife rescued her own daughter, then died with her arms around two other kids she was trying to save. The guy was just sitting there by himself in that empty apartment. It felt so lonely in there, it was all I could do not to cry. The neighbors were so busy protecting him from the prying press, they'd left him completely alone; his daughter had been sent off to grandma. It was the definitive course in how to interview."

"What the hell does that mean?" Nick asked. He shifted around on the hard bench of the booth, and looked wearier than when he had walked in.

"I just went by instinct. When he'd balk at certain questions—like what kind of person his wife was—I'd back off and take him back to earlier that afternoon when it started dawning on him that his wife might be dead. He wanted to go over and over those details. He told me about driving to the makeshift morgue and walking up and down the rows of bodies looking for her, returning again and again to the center—each time seeing her car still standing, alone, in the parking lot."

Angela's voice suddenly became husky, she stopped her almost whispered narrative, waved at the waiter and asked him to bring her a Scotch, and another beer for Nick.

She kind of shook her head and shrugged her shoulders before resuming her narrative. Beyond the plate glass window it was getting dark. A light went on in the room below hers at the Continental. Corrigan and Marbles were still at their table on the terrace; two people she didn't recognize had joined them.

"I quit being upset by the man's grief and became totally absorbed in the process of how to lead him through the maze of telling his story. We sat for hours, in the half-light of a single lamp, over coffee, oil-cloth on his kitchen table, and I helped him sift through the day. He wanted to talk. Each time he repeated a detail, he came closer to grasping the reality that his wife was gone. I've never been scared again to talk to people about the tragedies in their lives. And I got a story that nobody, *but nobody,* else had."

"You're some tough broad if you can do that," Nick said, a look of something approaching wonder on his face. "Most guys hide under their desks when they see those assignments coming." His eyes left Angela and followed the last customer as he got up from the booth behind them. Nick swiveled to watch the guy walk out the door. A young boy was mopping the floor around them, the waiters were stacking straight-back chairs upside down on the tables in the middle of the room. Nick cleared his throat and squirmed as he turned back to Angela.

But she was on a roll. "Don't be silly. Doctors, lawyers, soldiers, priests all preside over the calamities of people's lives. But only reporters can freeze the event, lift it up for a moment and put it on stage. For an ordinary guy, who's just lost his wife, or his house or his only child, who's struck dumb with incomprehension, we represent society's support and sympathy. Our very presence means, *'This is so horrendous, we're going to record it for all time, put it in the newspaper.'* He's not alone with his grief."

"Well, shit. I've been in this business a long time, and I never heard that one before."

The waiter arrived with their drinks, and Angela looked up to notice it was fully dark outside now. But she could see that Corrigan and his pals were still in the same wicker chairs at the terrace bar where they had been sitting an hour before. She took a stiff slug from her drink.

"Reporters are on their own trip," Angela finally replied. "They're focusing so hard on what's going to appear under *their* byline they don't think about the social function they serve. If they did, it might help them be more sensitive when they talk to a grieving family. Most reporters think their higher purpose is to guard the First Amendment, which, of course it is, but we're also scribes, the recorders of Everyman and what his life is like."

"Ah, shit."

She started laughing. "Now if that isn't the typical thoughtful journalist's response. No wonder we have reputations for being such louts.

"So what about you," she said, with barely a pause. "Tell me about this so-called fiancée, Mary Alice."

"You're not bad yourself at switching subjects," Nick said, flushing. "She's buck-toothed, pimply faced and ordinary. Got turned down from holy orders because of acne, BO and bad breath. So she's on the prowl for some schnook with a briefcase to provide her with babies and pick up the tab."

"You don't make it sound like much of a honeymoon," Angela said, laughing.

"You got the picture. I don't have a lot of interest in being trapped. So let's go to that great Japanese bar Yoki introduced us to, and get sloshed and quit talking about all this heavy shit."

That was the night they learned nine verses of "Koge, Koge, Koge kimi no Booto"—"Row, Row, Row Your Boat" in Japanese.

## 22

# Mr. Ambassador Meets the Press

THE BATTLES were heating up on all fronts. The Viet Cong were getting bolder, and the terrorist attacks on the city were stepping up when the U.S. Ambassador to South Vietnam finally yielded to repeated demands for a press conference.

Everyone in the assembled sea of correspondents was clamoring to know what the hell was going on at Dak To. Reporters were bouncing around in the chairs, raising their hands, shouting their affiliation, each trying to get the attention of the tall, elegantly groomed, gray-haired emissary. But to each repeated query after a reporter was called on and stood up, Ellsworth Bunker, behind the podium, flanked by an American flag on one side and a two-star general on the other, would sidestep and insist that was a question for the military, not the Embassy. The general would then refer the question to MACV.

"Then what *can* you tell us, Mr. Ambassador?" Ford Curtis finally asked, exasperation in his voice. "Can you give us your take on what's behind the announcement that McNamara will resign as secretary of defense in three months? At the end of February."

"Well, now, Ford," Bunker said, clearing his throat, "both the President and Mr. McNamara have spoken about that."

"Let's call it what it is, Mr. Ambassador," Angela said, uncalled on, abruptly standing up. "Now that McNamara has been *dumped,* shouldn't

Westmoreland be next? But the question for those of us here is why the dickens is the general taking the Cong bait and getting sucked in at Dak To?"

There was an all but imperceptible twitch at the corner of his mouth as Ellsworth Bunker rearranged his body weight from one foot to the other, touched a finger to his Brooks Brothers tie and cleared his throat. "The question is what?" Bunker said with a slow frown, leaning forward slightly as though he really were straining to hear. There was only the faintest emphasis on the "what."

He's a master of the stall, thought Nick. And it did seem to have the effect of slowing Angela down. Her surprised look could almost be described as jaw-dropping.

"Mr. Ambassador, sir," she said, taking an audible deep breath, "General Westmoreland said last week in a speech to the National Press Club that we're at the point where, I quote, 'the end comes in view.' Do you have any idea, sir, what he meant by that, in light of the fact that he's sending thousands of troops in to defend isolated American garrisons strung out all across remote areas of the Central Highlands? That what appears to be one of the largest battles of the war is being waged up there near Dak To as we speak?"

Nick, close enough to the ambassador to see that behind his thick, amber-rimmed glasses his pale eyes were watering from the strong TV lights, caught the Bunker tic and chortled to himself. He knew the laconic Vermonter didn't flap easily, but it certainly appeared that Angela's question had scored a hit on his funny bone. Nick looked to his left, caught Ray Corrigan's eye, and raised his own eyebrow in a question mark. The irascible Irishman arched his scraggly John L. Lewis brows with a faint nod, but the clear intent was an answering "yes." Not bad for a greenhorn, his slightly quizzical look seemed to say.

There was no way for Nick to know that Corrigan had planted the seed.

But Curtis wouldn't let it lie. "We've already been told the 173rd took the hill on Thanksgiving Day. Why do we have to go over this same ground again?" He was looking directly at Angela, several seats away, as he spoke. Both of them were still standing.

"We need some answers, not inside-the-beltway gossip of why Johnson finally got smart and scrapped McNamara," Angela shot back at him.

Bunker watched the volley like an amused tennis fan.

There were more than a few scattered laughs from around the Embassy auditorium. Chalk that one up for Angela, Nick thought.

"Well, so, we still don't have an answer, Mr. Ambassador," said Angela.

"Oh, I think you do, Miss," Bunker said with a dry smile, but what looked to Nick like a twinkle in his eye. "We took Hill 875 at noon on Thanksgiving Day. That's progress, I should say. Now if you'll excuse me, I have work to do." He strode from the podium.

A collective groan went up from the assembled reporters.

"Jesus," grumbled Corrigan under his breath, as the reporters began filing out of the hall. "Why doesn't Curtis keep his prick in his pants? Our job is to nail these turkeys, not feed them answers."

"Angela let him have it, don't you think?" Nick asked, as he flipped closed his thin, spiral, reporter's notebook and stuck it in the hip pocket of his jeans.

"There's a bit more at stake here, Boyo, than the skirmishes between those two," Corrigan snapped in his thick brogue. "What the hell's going on between them, I wonder?"

"They gave everybody a good laugh," said John Simenson, joining them as they hung around talking in the lobby of the new six-story Chancery, which had only recently opened for business, after the last one a few blocks away had been taken out by the Cong. They were putting off leaving the air-conditioned building and facing the 100-plus heat of the Saigon streets. "So what's the big deal?" Simenson asked.

"For starters," Corrigan said with a show of exasperation at the young wire-service reporter's gee-whiz enthusiasm, "Curtis is making an ass of himself—personally and professionally. The lady had nailed Bunker about Westmoreland's bullshit, and Bunker and everyone else in the room knew it.

"But the main thing," Corrigan went on, "is that the goddamned Marines are slogging through the mud at Conthien for no apparent strategic reason, U.S. planes accidentally bomb their own positions up there for the second time in three days, Yanks are running into bitter resistance in Quangtri, and Curtis steps on a golden opportunity to get some kind of explanation. Very unprofessional."

"Do you think it all fits into a pattern, a North Viet push of some kind?" Simenson asked.

"Yeah," said Corrigan as he fired up his straight-stemmed, large-bowled pipe filled with Irish tobacco that had the texture and smell of a Donegal bog. Nick always watched this procedure in amazement, wondering why Corrigan's walrus gray-blond lip hairs didn't go up in the conflagration. You could hardly tell the mustache from the little pyre of light colored twigs that Corrigan called tobacco. "I suspect Charlie Cong is making some kind of move around the DMZ that may be only a feint. But it appears the Marines are really digging in up there," the Irishman said through clenched teeth and in between great gasps of drawing breath to set the fire roaring just beyond the end of his nose. "Westmoreland's up to something, but we'll never find out what it is if we have to have 'As the World Turns' acted out every time we get a shot at the ambassador."

"Well, shit," said Nick, "I don't see how you can blame Angela."

"You're a randy big guy, now aren't ya?" said Corrigan in the teasing lilt he used on his younger colleague. "Try to have any kind of serious discussion and it's right away you turn it 'round to the ladies. We all saw you sashaying into the Continental lobby that night looking for her and trying to pretend you didn't see us at the bar. Fucking Greek, always thinking about women."

"You know I'm not a Greek," Nick blurted out, biting his tongue as soon as he said it, knowing he shouldn't allow himself to be baited by Corrigan's razzing.

"I know the lady can do no wrong as far as you're concerned," Corrigan said laughing at Nick's fluster. "But with her making probably $50 to $75 a sale, and not a hell of a lot of those, I don't understand how she can last very long."

"If Angela had a proper outlet for the sensitive stuff she's writing," Nick said with defiance, "she'd be beating Curtis' ass with her resourcefulness."

"Sure, Boyo."

"Well, what should she do?" Nick asked with an earnestness that made it clear he hoped the older, more experienced reporter would have some solid ideas.

"Something to stun 'em, something stunning," Corrigan said pulling thoughtfully at his walrus mustache. "She's got to come up with a blockbuster. Grab those stateside sub-editors by the shorthairs."

"Give me a for-instance," Nick insisted.

"If we all put our heads together," the Irishman said with a wicked grin, "I'm sure we could come up with something."

Unable to stall any longer under the watchful eye of the Marine guard stationed near the reception desk, the three reluctantly moved out through the big teak doors and into the blazing noonday sun.

"God, this is an ugly building," groused Corrigan looking back over his shoulder at the protective concrete grillwork shading the Chancery windows and casting a dappled shadow over the lawns of the walled Embassy complex.

"Yeah, but it's safe," said Simenson. "At least it won't get blown away by Cong sappers like the last one did."

# 23

# Mrs. Ambassador's Christmas Party

Nick doused the lights but left the engine idling as he eased the Jeep up to the curb on Thong Nhat across from the U.S. Embassy. A lithe figure in a loose flowing gown climbed down from the vehicle, glided across the street and disappeared into the shadows under a bougainvillea bush a few feet from the sentry's post at the front gate.

"Here he comes," Nick chortled to his companions as a tall American rounded the corner from Mac Dinh Chi, striding past the eight-foot iron pickets toward the Embassy gate. "The ambush'll work. I was afraid we were late."

As Ford Curtis neared the Marine guard and reached into the left breast pocket of his tuxedo jacket, a hand shot out from the bougainvillea and grasped his other wrist.

"She's really done it! The lady has more spunk than I thought," Ray Corrigan said with a chuckle from the back seat of the Jeep.

"Fucking Curtis deserves it," Simenson said, reaching over from the passenger seat to give Nick a gleeful thumbs-up.

"Is that stunning enough for you?" Nick demanded, laughing, turning to challenge Corrigan.

As Ford spun toward his assailant, he was met by the radiance of thousands of tiny crystal beads shimmering ice-blue and white in the reflected spotlights scanning from the Embassy roof. Angela's flowing dress was a blaze of fireflies in a reflecting pool of sea-green chiffon.

"My God," said Curtis. "I was expecting the Viet Cong!"

"You might wish," Angela replied with a weak grin.

Curtis bowed slightly over his arm and asked with edgy, ever-so-slight sarcasm, "And to what do I owe this pleasure? Is it some kind of dare?"

"Something like that," Angela replied, remembering the two stiff shots of cognac it had taken to get her on her feet. Nick had delivered the handmade dress from the tailor, but was of no use trying to help fasten the dozens of tiny hooks fashioned from loops of silk thread, down the length of her back. Corrigan and Simenson had finally been summoned from their waiting posts at the lobby bar. But of the four conspirators, only little John's fingers were nimble and steady enough to accomplish the task.

"My knees are certainly shaking," she told Ford with as much candor as she could muster.

"Well, stop the knocking and let's proceed," he said with surprising and gallant good humor. "I'm delighted to escort such a breathtaking creature. That dress is stunning."

She grinned, thinking that was not quite what Corrigan had in mind when he had diagnosed her problem as a need to do something that would stun, catch the eye of editors back home.

Curtis, wrapping her hand more firmly around his left arm, took an engraved white card from his breast pocket and handed it to the Marine guard who either hadn't noticed or was too correct to flinch at the lady's unorthodox arrival. "Braeford Curtis and guest at the invitation of The Ambassador and Mrs. Bunker," Curtis said.

"Then she *is* here," said Angela, with an inflection that came close to a squeal.

"So that's it," said Curtis, as he guided her along the path toward the massive teak doors, past the huge tubs of flowers that graced the front of the building, past the vista of the chancery acreage with its sweeping lawns and illuminated shrubs and flowerbeds. "How very clever of you. A scoop that no one else has been able to manage."

"Not a single in-depth interview with her since she married Bunker in January," said Angela. "A two-ambassador household. Amazing. It would really be a coup if I could get her to talk to me."

"Quite. And she's your kind of woman: Commutes back and forth from her own embassy in Nepal. But you didn't have an invitation. How'd you guess she'd be here? Security was supposed to be tight."

"Jesus, Curtis, you're not the only one in the news business."

"Those cowboys outside in the white NBC Jeep put you up to this?" Ford asked in the droll manner he had perfected to an art, looking very solemn, puffing on his pipe as they waited for the elevator in the Chancery lobby. But there were laugh lines playing around his eyes.

Watching him closely, trying to read his mood, Angela saw a slight quiver on his lower lip as he bit hard on his pipe stem. My God, she thought, the man's sense of humor is so dry he even tries to hide a grin.

"White's not the best color for camouflage, you know," he said, his teeth still on his pipe, and without so much as a smile.

At that, her pent-up tension came rolling out in a fit of uncontrollable laughter. The more she tried to stop herself, the more she howled, unable to get out a coherent word. Several other dignified-looking couples shifted in embarrassment as they waited for the elevator to the ambassador's reception. Angela was so doubled over with laughter she had to lean against the wall—and Ford—for support. The more a general and his tight-lipped wife stared, the more Angela laughed. "You really are a good sport," she managed to sputter out to Curtis.

"You're OK yourself," he said, as he caught the laughter infection, a release from his own terrified moment of thinking that he was being kidnapped.

"You're not angry? I was afraid you'd kill me," Angela managed to get out, still struggling to get mirth under control.

"No," he said with a grin. "How could I help but admire your enterprise?"

As the elevator dumped them in a spare, business-like reception hall, with its eagle and great seal of the United States looming over the festivities, Mrs. Bunker was there to greet them.

"Madame Ambassador," Curtis said with the laughter still in his voice, "here is a young lady who has gone to some little trouble to meet you." Watching the tell-tale twitch at the corner of his mouth, Angela took several deep breaths trying to keep from breaking up again.

"Why, how nice, and thank you," said Mrs. Bunker, extending her hand to Angela. The ambassador's wife was a stout, pleasant, fiftyish matron with short, streaked gray-blonde hair worn in a loose page-boy. A gardenia corsage was pinned to her gold, brocaded floor-length sack-style dress with mandarin frogs at the collar.

"I'd like to spend some time chatting with you," said Angela, taking the older woman's hand. "I'm a reporter, and I'm dying to know what marriage is like for two ambassadors commuting back and forth between two embassies."

"Well, my dear," Mrs. Bunker said with a warm smile, but no acknowledgment of the request for an interview, "I think we're very lucky. At least we're serving on the same continent."

"Could we speak later, perhaps, about an appointment? Should I contact your secretary?" Angela persisted, speaking fast, hoping to gain some ground before Mrs. Bunker turned to greet the next guests in the receiving line.

Carol Laise Bunker was as swift as she was diplomatic. "By all means, write my secretary," she said with the soft trace of a Virginia drawl. "I'd be glad to see you in Nepal. Saigon is not my bailiwick, and it wouldn't be proper for me to be holding interviews here. Besides," she said with an almost wicked little grin, "I'm a newlywed. And I'm sure you'll understand that during the all-too-brief periods that I'm here, I like to spend as much time as I can with my husband."

Startled by the older woman's candor, Angela was charmed and, at the same time, blushing. "Oh, I understand. And thank you so much," she stammered in her nervousness and relief that she had accomplished something of her mission. Corrigan would never let her live it down if she totally failed.

As she turned away, she heard Ellsworth Bunker greeting Curtis: "I'm delighted you could make it. And Berenice? Is she with you?"

"No," replied Curtis, "she and Ford Four are in Cambridge. He's in his second year there, you know."

"How time gets away from us," said the 73-year-old parchment-faced Bunker with what passed in him for a grin. "It's certainly taking its licks out of me. But I still say, Braeford, if you had any sense you'd send your only son to New Haven for a proper education."

"And, of course, have him take up rowing while he's there," Curtis responded, holding up his end of the banter that was the ambassador's way of acknowledging their long acquaintance. "Dean Acheson always said you were the coolest freshman the Yale crew ever had."

"So he did. So he did. Acheson was a fine secretary of state, but his judgments weren't perfect on all subjects," said Bunker in his quiet way of poking fun at himself.

As Angela started to move away, Curtis caught her by the elbow and steered her between himself and Bunker. "I'd like you to meet a colleague, Mr. Ambassador."

"My pleasure. I do think I've seen this young lady at a press conference or two, the red hair looks familiar. But I must say, crystal beads and chiffon reveal wonders that baggy fatigues hide."

Bunker's formal, abstracted exterior hid any surprise he might have felt at seeing Curtis with Angela. The sharp-eyed ambassador rarely missed much and the sniping between the two of them at his recent press conference had certainly gotten his amused attention. But Bunker smiled benignly at the handsome couple using his usual diplomatic trick of focusing on a middle distance between himself and whomever he was negotiating with. He then turned the same smile on the next person in the receiving line.

"This is not the most elegant setting in the world for a diplomatic supper," Curtis grumbled as he and Angela moved on to pick up drinks and tiny limp canapés from long linen-covered folding tables set up along the walls. "Linoleum tiles on the floor and Marine guards in short white jackets trying to look like waiters. Their goddamned combat boots are showing beneath the cuffs of their tuxedo pants."

"Maybe Bunker's taking special precautions because his wife's here," Angela suggested. "The traveling back and forth is not going unnoticed. I read in The Times that some Iowa Republican was complaining about the cost of a jet being provided to fly Bunker to Nepal to, quote, 'further his romance.' The honorable representative called it 'disgraceful.'"

"They certainly fly in everything else to provide the comforts of home. I wonder how much it cost them to get that giant Christmas tree here," Ford said indicating the towering Douglas fir loaded with lights and ornaments in one corner of the large hall. "It must have come by refrigeration all the way. You'd never know it was Christmas in this heat."

"So," Angela said, giving Curtis a quizzical look. "Ford Four! You call your son, Ford Four?"

"What?" Curtis said, looking startled by the abrupt change of subject.

"Is that model priced above or below the Mustang and the LTD?"

Curtis' face reddened, but his look was one of disbelief more than anger.

"You're incredible," he snapped. "You can manage to look and dress like a lady when you have to, but you certainly have trouble acting like one."

"Ha," Angela said with a brittle little intake of breath, "that from the *gentleman* who has been going all over town bad-mouthing me?"

"What in heaven's name are you talking about?" Curtis asked with an annoyed frown.

"I have it on good authority, Kevin Leahey, for one," Angela replied, as she turned to exchange her empty for a fresh glass of champagne from the tray of a passing waiter. "You know. The guy who works in the Embassy—out of Komer's office."

"The pasty-faced fellow with no eyebrows?" Ford frowned again, this time with the strain of recall. "I didn't even remember his name. Only that he had on a Yale tie. Seemed rather excessive in this heat. He brought some figures Komer had promised."

"You obviously had time to discuss me." Angela's tone was indignant.

"That's nonsense," Curtis replied.

"Oh, really?" Angela said with arched eyebrows and a look of disbelief on her face. "No discussion of *so-called* reporters without papers behind them?"

"I, ah," Curtis said looking uncomfortable. "I don't know. There may have been some general discussion. But, good lord."

"Yeah, right."

"Now see here," Curtis said, his voice heating up. "That is utter nonsense. I had just heard how many people were over here for a lark, shocked by it. I may have mentioned the subject in general, in passing, but to think I discussed you specifically would be a bold-faced lie."

"A lie? That sounds like the CIA," Angela said with a laugh.

"CIA," Curtis said, looking startled before a slow grin of recognition broke out on his face. "Well, sure. If he's working with ex-CIA meister Bob Komer, that would be logical, wouldn't it?"

"Hm," said Angela. "I really hated to think you would actually be trying to do me in."

"Farthest thing from my mind," Ford said. "Quite the contrary. I find you very appealing."

He paused, gave Angela a long look, then said quietly, "But I seem to have been on the wrong foot from the beginning."

"Let's not get off track here," Angela replied, nervous with this new direction. "Ah, do you have any idea why they didn't have this party at their little house on the grounds? Seems like it would have been much nicer than this institutional feeling."

"That's not the ambassador's residence," Ford answered. "The mission chief, George Jacobson, lives there. Bunker's house is about five blocks away. They're here because they're nervous about security. Something's brewing, but I can't figure out what. There's talk of a buildup in the north, kamikaze attacks. They're worried."

"Oh?" Angela perked up. "What do you think it means?"

"No shop talk," said Ford.

"Come on," Angela said, "if it's just a rumor, it's not anything I could use. What makes you feel something is brewing?"

"Why don't you just enjoy the party?" he said as he motioned to a passing waiter for a refill of their glasses. "Champagne for the lady, a martini for me."

"Well, if you don't want to discuss the war, how about your personal life?" Angela said in a casual tone that belied the bite behind her words. "I didn't know you were married."

"Isn't everyone?" His response sounded as off-handed as her statement.

"Not necessarily."

Angela heard the too-hard edge to her crisp reply and took a gulp of champagne. Well, she had managed to bring the friendliness to a thundering halt, she thought, but it serves the fucker right for his flipness. She stared at the rim of her goblet. Her eyes lowered, she still knew he was staring at the crystal bead she could see heaving gently on its perch at the tip of a chiffon-covered nipple. Oh God, it took her breath away—the nipple was totally erect.

"I'm sorry, I've been rude," she finally blurted, still staring down at her glass, held stiffly, two-handed, in front of her.

"I'm sorry I was so cross," came his awkward reply.

"OK, let's shake on it." In her nervousness, she shot her right hand out, still holding the goblet, champagne arching in seeming slow motion across the great divide, splashing Ford's face, then trickling down the starched white front of his dress shirt. "Oh, Jesus!" she said, instinctively moving to brush off what she had spilled, but stopping, her hand in mid-motion as she saw the peculiar look on his face.

"I'd rather kiss and make up," he said.

"Oh, hell," she said with a forced grin. "Don't start that." Her response was flip to cover her blush, to try to show she considered the remark a joke. But Ford didn't act as though he thought anything was very funny. She grabbed his upper arm in a bluff, palsy way. As she did so—leaning against his arm—she felt a return push that told her he was double-checking what was abundantly clear, that she was wearing no bra.

"Come on," she said, feeling the blush move down her neck as she pulled at him, "let's join the frivolity. Thanks to you, I've got my work done and it's time to play." She leaned back, still tugging at his arm, and turned on her most radiant, flirtatious smile. "Please," she said.

"I've still got work to do," he replied with a smile as tight as hers was broad, using a handkerchief to brush at the dampness of his shirtfront. "I may show up at these bashes wearing a tuxedo, but I always consider myself on the job."

Angela looked startled. "I'm really glad to hear that, Curtis. I guess I've thought of you as kind of a dilettante."

He stared at her in stunned disbelief, and then roared with laughter. "My dear child, you can't be serious. Without any ego implied, I am one of the most respected newsmen in America. And you, an unconnected freelance, are calling *me* a dilettante! Amazing. You're so brash, I think I'm falling in love with you. You're incredible." He gripped her upper arm and pulled her to him. "Don't you have enough sense to realize you're supposed to be awed by me?"

His face was so close she could have stuck out her tongue and tasted the martini she could smell on his lips. He was peering at her in an almost threatening way, and he was hurting her arm. But the funny quiver line was around his mouth. Her legs felt rubbery, her head felt light, and it kept flashing through her head that maybe her shoes were too tight.

"I, I'm sorry," she faltered. "If you'd acted this much like a real person before, I probably would have been awed. It never occurred to me you had a sense of humor, especially about yourself."

She could feel his breath in little puffs on her face. "Let's get out of here," he said as he tightened his grip on her arm. "That goddamned dress is driving me nuts."

"Jesus, Ford, not so loud," she hissed, coming a little bit back to her senses. "We're jammed into this roomful of people."

"Who gives a damn? If there is a man in here who doesn't want you, there's something wrong with his plumbing. Let's go."

"We . . . we haven't had dinner," she said.

"What the hell does that mean?"

"I don't know, I . . ."

"Angela, I'm not going to have you do this to me again. Are you interested in seeing me or not? I will not be a schoolboy standing on your doorstep with my hat in my hand."

"You're married."

"For Christ sake, so what? You're not a child, and these games are not becoming."

"You're right. And this has gone quite far enough," she snapped, trying to jerk her arm away as his grip tightened, her anger and her good sense coming back in a rush. "You wouldn't speak to me or anyone else like this in your *set* in Cambridge. I'm not up for grabs here any more than I would be there. Put your manners back on, mister!"

Ford's head snapped back as though he'd been slapped. His face was crimson.

"You've been going around telling the world I'm a rotten reporter, or no reporter at all. You've treated me like what you call a camp follower," she went on, her choler rising. "And now your wife's not in town and all the sudden I look pretty good."

"That's not quite it," Curtis said, his voice flat and cold as a stone.

"What IS IT, then?" she asked, her voice as cold as his.

"If you're not smart enough to figure that one out, it's not in my vocabulary to tell you."

"Curtis," she said softly, "I didn't come to Saigon looking for a fling. I've got a job to do and I don't intend to let romance mess up my head." She could feel strength coming back to her voice as the force of her own words hardened her resolve.

"Pull yourself together," she said too loudly, then lowered her tone, struggling to get back her equilibrium, "and start working the room. You have a job, too. You said you think something's brewing; we should be trying to find out what it is. When supper's over, I'm leaving. At midnight, my coach turns into a pumpkin."

He let go of her arm without a word, and she walked over to a nearby group to join them in conversation.

After supper, Curtis watched through a front window of the Embassy as Angela ran down the walk, past the flower tubs, to the white NBC Jeep, snagging and ripping the sea-green chiffon as she climbed into the backseat.

# 24

# Miss Kim's Paradise Bar & Grill

As Nick elbowed his way into the crowd in Kim's Paradise Bar & Grill in early January, the noise level was so intense that The Rolling Stones' "Honky Tonk Woman" was no more than a percussive thump. Several of the ladies that Miss Kim's ads in GI publications referred to as "charming hostesses" smiled or made not-so-subtle gestures as he passed—talk was neither necessary nor hearable. Nick had made his way to the end of the long bar and was trying to order a BaBa beer when he was stopped in mid-motion by what he saw at a table across the room.

In a booth behind a curtain of bamboo beads was Angela and their Japanese friend Yoki Suku with a B-girl Nick knew as Princess.

"What the hell are you doing in a joint like this?" he demanded, pushing through the curtain that parted with a hollow tinkle.

"Hi, guy," Angela said, brightening as she saw him. "Sit, and have a beer. This is Tuyet. Tuyet, Nick O'Brien. We're doing an interview."

"Hi, Nicky," said Princess, a tiny Vietnamese whose delicate beauty was all but obscured by slathers of pancake makeup and black lines so thick around her almond eyes she looked like an escapee from kabuki theater.

Angela's eyes for an instant took on the same dilation of wonder as she looked quickly from one to the other then visibly thought better of saying anything beyond, "Oh."

"Well, for Christ sake, I'm not a monk." Nick's face flushed to the very roots of his dark curls.

"No one ever said you were," Angela replied.

"Ford Curtis is married, you know," Nick said.

"What the hell has that got to do with anything?" Angela snapped.

"Ah, Angela insist I bling her here," Yoki injected nervously. "It's, ah, place she choose for intelvu."

"Tuyet's telling me about her life. So get off it, both of you," Angela said briskly, breaking the tension. "I may not be able to sell it to *Family Weekly*, but someone'll buy it. Slice of life."

"Maybe," Nick said with a shrug.

"You guys are so busy covering battles you're ignoring what's happening to this country," Angela said. "There are 56,000 registered prostitutes in Saigon, a huge percent with VD. The garbage and sanitation systems are at a standstill because the workers all have jobs with the Army or catering to GIs. We can't just keep ignoring all this."

"Ah, jeez," said Nick, squirming uncomfortably on the wooden bench of their booth. "I'd never sell that to Harry the Arse. I'm here to cover a war."

"Editors say same in Toyko," Yoki said, nodding in agreement with Nick.

"So, OK," Angela said. "If we only want to talk about war, what about that Cong pamphlet I hear they distributed at the Embassy? About an upcoming attack? The guys I overheard discussing it just shrugged it off. When I asked for a copy at the Embassy press office, they said there weren't any left but that it was just Cong propaganda anyway."

"Yeah," Nick replied. "Some so-called captured documents saying that troops would flood this whole area, including Saigon. But everyone brushed it off as just a morale booster for the VC. Is that what you heard, Yoki?" Nick asked, turning to his friend who had been nodding his head "yes" as Nick talked.

"I never saw, but I hear," the Japanese replied.

"So they translated them, and gave copies out?" Angela shook her head in disbelief. "What the hell is the point of all that? Aren't our troops concentrating more in the North? What does Corrigan think?"

"I don't know the answers to any of those questions," Nick replied. "I haven't seen Corrigan since your big deal Embassy Christmas party, and Westmoreland says the end is in sight. Beats me."

Angela laughed. "Okey-dokey. I guess that takes us back to GIs and sex."

"Ah, shit," Nick said, just as the curtain parted with a tinkle of bamboo. Miss Kim, in a silk embroidered mandarin jacket, her hair piled high with an anchor of ebony sticks, motioned with a quick jerk of her head for her employee to get back on the job.

As Yoki scooted out to let Tuyet leave, he ambled over to talk to some friends he'd spotted at another table.

Nick and Angela sat in silence for a few moments as Nick studied the label on his beer bottle and Angela scribbled more notes from the interview with Tuyet.

"What was this guy Martinelli like?" Nick suddenly blurted.

"Peter?"

"Your husband."

"He was terrific. Sweet. A good newsman."

"So?" Nick asked, but Angela didn't respond.

"So, what happened?" Nick asked again.

"I fouled it up," Angela said, matter of factly. "He wanted . . . I don't know. Something missing in me, I guess. He just picked up and left one day without discussing it. Throughout the divorce, I never could get him to tell me exactly why. I wasn't enough of a homebody, I guess."

Nick cleared his throat. For once he was out of questions.

"So what about you?" Angela asked. "Do you come to Miss Kim's often?"

"Naw," Nick said, flushing, noticing with obvious relief that Yoki was heading back to their table.

"Gee, Nick," Angela said in a teasing tone, "I don't know why you don't want to talk about it. I told you I'm doing a story on Saigon's bar girls, and you obviously could be a good source of information."

She was startled to see ever brighter shades of red begin creeping up from his neck. Even in this smoky, yellow light, his face looked as though it would be feverish to the touch. He seemed like a school boy, but she would tease him out of that. She wouldn't want to hurt him. He was a friend—solid, funny. And so damned good-looking, those gorgeous violet, Elizabeth-Taylor eyes and long black lashes. An awful lot of women would kill to get at him.

"Yoki," Angela said, as the Japanese correspondent sat down, "what do you think of a buddy like this who holds out information on a story you're working on?"

As Angela gestured toward Nick and saw the stricken look on his face, and then noticed that poor, solemn Yoki looked almost as stricken, obviously trying to dope out if this was anger or another form of strange occidental humor. Angela burst out laughing. "Come on, you guys, you both look like you're at a wake. Men never have an ounce of humor when it comes to sex. You're both still upset over my coming to this sleazy bar."

"Ah shit," said Nick, "you just talk too much."

"Well, sweetie," said Angela still grinning, "I'm only trying to find out if Princess is an old friend or just a passing acquaintance. Even though you're engaged to the girl back home in Chicago named Mary Alice, I get the distinct feeling that you and Mary Alice are not on the same wave length."

"Mary Alice Moriarty and her mother cooked that one up," Nick said hotly.

"Oh, really?" Angela delivered it as a question, raising her eyebrows.

"With a little help from my stepmother," Nick replied sharply. "She figured the Moriarty family has a social standing that is something to aspire to." He said it with a bitterness that made both Yoki and Angela wince.

"I'm sorry I've been teasing, kid," Angela said softly, leaning over to pat Nick's hand. Yoki slid away, without a word, to resume his table-hopping.

"Nick, what happened to your mother?" Angela asked, her hand still on his.

"She died, that's all."

"Why are you so angry about it, still?" Angela asked.

"I was out riding my bike when it happened, having a good time."

"But you were just a kid."

"Yeah, they sent me out, she'd been sick for a while. But I should have known."

"Known what?"

"I don't know. She just was gone when I got back."

"What was she like?"

"Nice," Nick said, his eyes focused on a far place. "She was nuts about William Powell in 'The Thin Man,' he said with a smile, as his eyes came back to Angela. "That's where my name came from, Nick Charles. Everybody kids me about being a Greek. But she named me Nick and my sister Nora."

Nick thought of another movie that ran a lot in his head, one that had haunted him since he was a child, a flashing neon light playing in sepia tones over a messy room and a slovenly woman in a dirty wrapper.

"Nora, that's a good Irish name," Angela said with a laugh. "I suppose you even had a dog named Asta."

# 25

# The Lunar New Year

When Nick had first arrived in-country he stayed at the Caravelle. Not as classy as the French-colonial Continental across the square, but it had one enormous advantage as far as he was concerned: More often than not, things worked. Antique buildings may have quaint charm, but he saw nothing quaint about antique plumbing or rotary ceiling fans. The Caravelle was '50s modern and had air conditioning. Exterior decoration was a few glass bricks and neon letters announcing the hotel's name and proclaiming the location of Air France's office. Most of the press guys assigned to established bureaus had more permanent digs, but Nick's paper was rotating someone in and out of Saigon for 60-day stints, and even those were periodic. So his editors weren't about to take a lease on an apartment. "What the hell do ya want, permanent residence?" his editor, Harry, had asked when Nick had broached the subject. "Ya wanna feel settled, buy a farm. We ain't providing a place for you to put up a geisha. Forget it, kid."

Decent rooms and apartments were hard to come by because of the explosion of the American "presence" in Saigon, but Nick had kept on the lookout for cheaper quarters, or a villa to share, figuring if he could cut the hotel bills and thus the cost of keeping him there, the paper might let him stay longer. Through John Simenson, he finally landed a cot in one of the apartments UPI maintained as living quarters above its bureau down by the river. Once he got his foot in the door, so to speak, it was pretty easy to hang in. There was always one of the guys taking R&R to Hong Kong, or someone in the process of being rotated in or out from the States, or a reporter whose wife was coming over for a couple of months, so he would move out to an apartment that some other guy being rotated back was giving up.

Nick had been crashing in the UPI apartment for a little over two months, since just after Thanksgiving. He finally had his own little cubby-hole room after having had a bed of his own for a while, then moving to a couch, and on more than one occasion tossing a sleeping bag on the floor. It was nomadic and a little disorienting, but Harry was happy—Nick was keeping expenses down so Harry wasn't getting flak from *his* bosses about letting Nick stay beyond his intended short tour.

Nick was jolted awake there on a night in late January. He had returned in the early morning hours exhausted from a quick trip to I Corps, the area around the Marine base at Da Nang, where the Viet Cong were raising some new hell, causing speculation that they were planning fresh assaults all over the country. For an instant, Nick couldn't figure out what woke him. A dream, maybe, that he was back at the press camp in Da Nang listening to the mortars. He sat up, disoriented. He could hear sporadic fire in the distance, small arms. Then he felt the low scream of a 40 millimeter and the shudder of the ground as it hit. Shit, he thought, this isn't Da Nang, I'm in downtown Saigon in the United Press apartment across from the Majestic Hotel. What the hell is going on?

The room was full of smoke. Bits of rock-like hail were raining down on him. Nick grabbed the pants he'd tossed at the foot of his bed hours before and pulled them on over his skivvies. Moonlight poured through a hole in the wall that hadn't been there before he went to bed. Shaking debris out of his hair, he gingerly groped through the rubble on the floor for his boots, found them, crawled to a chair where he'd thrown his shirt and jacket before falling into bed, grabbed his notebook from a table and got the hell out.

There already were several people in the bureau office downstairs, and just as Nick arrived two MPs burst in.

"Douse the fucking lights," ordered an immense black man whose face loomed in the glow from the streets as nothing more than two rows of giant gleaming teeth beneath a white steel helmet.

"What the hell happened?" asked John Simenson, barefoot, wearing nothing but jeans.

"Shelling. Viet Navy HQO just in back a here."

The big MP barely had the words out of his mouth, and another explosion rocked the building. Everyone dropped, flattened on the floor.

"Shit," Simenson yelled at the MPs from under a desk, "this is Tet, Viet New Year. What the hell happened to the truce?"

"Some fucking truce," grumbled Nick.

"Don't blame us, man, we just work here," said the big MP, then he laughed as though he considered himself a real card.

"You and your damned sense a humor, Peterson," snapped his partner, a scrawny sour-faced blond whose sharp, pinched features were nearly lost in the shadow cast by his oversized white helmet. "These turkeys don't think that's funny."

"The Embassy and Tan Son Nhut is both under attack," said the big black guy. "We was on our way there, but got ambushed. That's why we come in here."

"You *was* on your way to which, the Embassy or the airport?" asked the UPI deskman in knee-jerk, reportorial fashion—a little snide, yet forever seeking clarification, make sure you got the facts straight, even if you won't need them.

The MPs ordered the reporters to secure the bureau, got them moving to pull down the iron grating across the front of the building and haul a couple of heavy office desks over to barricade the front door.

"Christ," said Nick, "maybe the shellings I went to check out yesterday around Da Nang weren't just isolated incidents. I also heard reports that the truce had been broken in II Corps in the Central Highlands. Maybe the whole damned south is under attack!"

"See, I told ya, Peterson," said his partner, the dour MP, "Clark Kent and the boys here is scared. You shouldn't be funning with 'em."

"Fuck you," said Peterson, as the same words echoed in Nick's mind. But he had more important things to worry about than this slack-jawed, slow-witted asshole from Lower Slobovia. Nick just hoped he never ran into the creep in a dark alley some night, or some day in the outer office of a general he was trying to interview. Hard to tell sometimes who was on whose side in this goddamned war, he thought, as he watched the bureau guys set up a single, shaded lamp and test their telex to see if they could get through to New York. He knew there was no way they were going to tie up that single line to let him send to his paper in Chicago. Besides, what the hell would he file? He hadn't a clue what was going on. But he had to start finding out. It was about one or two o'clock in the afternoon back in the States and he had only a few hours to meet his early deadline. The UPI guys were already moving a bulletin that Saigon was under attack. Presumably, AP had as well, which meant alarm bells would soon be ringing on every wire machine in every news office in America. It went from here to the UPI office on 42nd Street in New York, or to AP in Rockefeller Center, then NY would start sending, and those bells would start to ring.

Nick started up the Tu Do for the Embassy at a dead run, but soon slowed to a trot and then a fast walk. Jeez, he thought, the United States Embassy under attack? Those MPs were pretty excited, they probably had it wrong. The streets seemed like any other night at—he looked at his watch, again—3:30 in the morning. Actually, maybe it wasn't as noisy and active as usual. Some of those GI bars normally went all night. But a lot of things were shut down because of Tet; Vietnamese gone to their families in the countryside, GIs on R&R because of the truce. Shit, another Pearl Harbor? Catch everyone asleep at the switch? He passed the Caravelle and the Continental. He noticed several room lights flick on in both of the hotels, but the streets were deserted and the quiet was starting to feel eerie. The occasional short bursts of small arms fire felt almost reassuring. At least he wasn't in some "On The Beach" nuclear dead zone, or the only human survivor of an alien space invasion. He had been on the street about five minutes and had passed only one Vietnamese on a bicycle and a Jeepload of MPs when he heard heavy shelling from the direction of the presidential palace. At almost the same time he saw tracers in the sky over in the direction of the airport. What the hell was going on? The tracers could almost be Tet fireworks.

He took a right just beyond Cathedral Square. He saw a strange dark mass up to his left a block ahead at the corner of Hai Ba Trung and Thong Nhat, the street the four-acre U.S. Embassy compound faced. He stopped in his tracks to reconnoiter and figure what his next move should be—it was to get behind the nearest tamarind tree and then try to adjust his focus in the dark to make some judgment about what the mass was. The blob seemed to move as separate pieces and then reform as a mass, sort of like an amoeba or sea jelly. As Nick inched closer from tamarind to tamarind, he realized the pieces were people, but Viet Cong? ARVN? What? Just then the sound of a grenade exploding came from the direction of the Embassy compound, followed by about 30 seconds of rifle fire. He hugged a tree and waited.

He inched closer. By the time he could discern that the sounds were

English, the argot was also clear: journalese! He moved over to join them.

Several of his colleagues, along with some MPs, were not exactly what you'd call pinned by fire; but in effect they were held down because they couldn't get any closer than this street corner, about a hundred yards from the Embassy entrance, without some sniper taking a pot shot. Nobody seemed to know what was going on. He was told a small hole had been blasted in the Embassy compound's eight-foot-high concrete wall. He could barely make out what the MPs said was a bullet-riddled black Citroen wrecked in the street just beyond the Embassy gate with a dead Vietnamese at the wheel. An abandoned Jeep was in the street nearby.

"Why the hell is everybody standing around a half a block away?" Nick asked.

"In the interest of your health, Mac," said one of the MPs, hanging back at the corner with the reporters. "The Cong's inside the Embassy, but we can't tell in the dark where their snipers are to take them out."

The thumping sound of an approaching chopper turned all heads skyward. The reporters watched as a Huey made several passes at the Embassy's roof-top helipad but each time was driven back by automatic weapons fire of snipers guarding the approach.

A few derring-do types talked half-heartedly about trying to scale the compound's walls to take a look at what was going on inside, but the general feeling was that if the MPs were holding off until dawn before they made an assault on the Embassy gates, maybe it would be just as well for the reporters to sit back on their pencils and let the pros do the assault number.

Nick was impatient with the commando posturing. What they really needed to worry about was getting their own jobs done. They had few hard facts beyond knowing for sure that the Embassy was under siege, and the filing situation was a nightmare. Most of the print guys generally filed through Reuters, which fortunately was close by, just back across Cathedral Square. Nick didn't need to be told by those who already had been over there that the place was awash with screaming maniacs. Not only was the Reuters wire clogged and the lineup to file long, but many of the guys around had the same near-impossible task as Nick did, of having to be both legman and rewrite.

Some outfits had several guys on the job plus a stringer or two, which meant two or three reporters could be out picking up information and feed it back through a runner to the guy back at Reuters who could both write the new stuff up and stand in line to file. But man, Nick thought, it was him against the world. No way to phone stuff in, no way to do anything but try to cover all the bases himself, figure out what was going on here, then back to Reuters, then cool his heels standing in line there.

Nick was pondering this as he made his way across Cathedral Square. He hated like hell to leave the Embassy corner. He was sure as soon as he left, the MPs would make their assault on the compound and he would miss the whole thing. But he simply had to get a few graphs off to his office to let them know they could count on his getting some kind of eyewitness account to them, at least for the later editions.

He finally got something filed through the Reuters mess while keeping a sharp eye out for any Vietnamese hanging around who might be able to at least do some running for him—he'd never dare hope to find one competent to string. On the whole, the Vietnamese stringers weren't much good, anyway. You really couldn't rely on their information being accurate; a lot of them were inclined to sit around talking to each other at the Pagode café, swapping rumors. A number of American press guys had gotten stung more than once by two or three Vietnamese sources all corroborating the same so-called fact, when, in fact, the information had been generated on the Pagode grapevine.

Nick felt relieved as he made his trip back across Cathedral Square to see from a block away that his competitors were still all hanging at the Hai Ba Trung corner—at least the Marines haven't stormed the Bastille without me as witness, he thought. Marines, Christ, he wondered, where are they? Speculation back in the Reuters line was that the Marine guards inside the compound must have been killed. It was hard to tell just how big a war he was in, but in the predawn dark, the city still seemed pretty quiet despite the periodic explosions of grenades and rifle fire. Back with the little group in front of the Embassy, the consensus was that only a few VC sappers had stormed the U.S. compound through the hole blown by a bazooka and that this almost surely had to be a limited action.

As daybreak Wednesday, January 31, 1968, approached, relief and Angela arrived about the same time. The minute Nick spotted that long-legged graceful stride, he knew who it was long before he could distinguish her from any other shadowy figure in combat polyester.

Jesus, he thought, she's the answer to my prayers!

"I figured you could use a legman," she said as she walked up. "Sorry I took so long. With all the Tet firecrackers we've been hearing for days, it took a while to wake up and realize this was different. Besides, I had a late night."

"Am I ever *glad* to see you," Nick said with a wide grin. "You're hired."

"What a mess," Angela said. "Everyone is on holiday leave, or partying. I was myself until after midnight. With some high-level military intelligence officers. I'm pretty wrecked."

"Oh great," Nick said with sarcasm. "No wonder we're caught with our pants down. The spooks were at a party."

"Yep," said Angela. "So tell me what you want me to do. But first, I picked up some info when I ran into a PIO near Lom Son Square after I came out of my hotel. He said the VC sappers didn't get into the Embassy itself, just the grounds, and most of 'em are dead by now. That's when I decided to come up here. Figured you'd need someone to go file for you."

"Do I ever. But there's nothing new here since I last filed. It's been like this for hours. How'd the press officer know so much?" Nick asked. The night sky suddenly turned white over the Independence Palace a few blocks to the west as U.S. planes dropped flares to light up enemy positions.

Angela and Nick both momentarily ducked, then looked skyward before she answered. "Came from the Embassy coordinator. You know, the guy lives in the little villa on the grounds."

"Yeah, George Jacobson, *mission* coordinator," Nick corrected.

"Whatever. Anyway, Zorthian, the press office boss, phoned Jacobson, who described the whole thing. Said they never got in the Embassy. Jacobson has himself locked in his bedroom, or something."

"Jesus. Good angle. OK, did the guy you talked to say what else is under attack? I mentioned the airport, the Viet Navy HQO and the palace when I first filed."

"Several billets, he said, both enlisted and officers' quarters. A bunch of . . ." Angela was interrupted by the distinctive whine of a rocket, at enough distance to be barely discernible, then the thud of its explosion several miles to the west, in the vicinity of Cholon, the Chinese section of the city. She began again, "A bunch of fires around the city. He said that Westmoreland said the Embassy is highest priority."

"Shit, yeah," Nick said. Then he laughed. "Obvious reasons. Not just the symbolic value, but it's smack dab in the middle of where all the reporters are based. And here we are. No one's going to hop a bus and go see what's happening at the airport. And American readers won't give a rat's ass about South Vietnam's Independence Palace."

"Jesus, you're such a cynic," said Angela.

"A realist," Nick replied. "Besides, a couple of the wire guys took a buzz around to see what was happening and got pinned down by VC fire for their trouble. So they came back here."

They both looked over as a Jeep pulled up across the street from the Embassy gates. Before the two MPs could get out of the vehicle, they were blown out by a stream of bullets from an automatic rifle. A sharpshooting Marine, standing in front of the gates, bent down on one knee and provided cover while several other MPs ran across and pulled their wounded buddies out of the street. The sniper was silenced.

Overhead, another Huey came into view and appeared headed for the compound. The gathered newsmen stopped talking among themselves, looked skyward as a collective face and seemed to hold their collective breath. The chopper dipped, hovered above the Chancery roof, and disgorged its load of paratroopers, their M-16s held aloft as though they were leaping into rice paddies. Most of their boots were on the roof and on the run before the chopper's blade runners touched down.

"I'd better take the Reuters shift this time," Nick said to Angela as he prepared to take off. "You cover this end, and I'll alert Harry that you might be filing in the future." Before he could move, the gathered MPs broke through the Embassy front gate shooting and throwing grenades. The gathered newsmen rushed behind them into the compound, flashbulbs popping and cameras rolling. The grounds were littered with dead Cong wearing red armbands, wounded Marine guards, dropped rifles and the debris of exploded ordinance.

"Oh my God," said Angela, "what a sickening sight."

"Yeah," Nick replied, as several of their colleagues brushed past him headed for the Chancery, exclaiming over the large shield of the United States lying in the rubble, riddled with bullets.

Angela grabbed Nick's arm. "George Jacobson," she mouthed, rolling her eyes and nodding her head to indicate a right turn toward the back of the building where several MPs were being trailed by an NBC cameraman. Nick looked at the retreating backs of the reporters going into the chancery.

"Good idea," he said. "You go. I'll follow these guys, before I head for Reuters."

Angela trotted after the small group moving through the grounds. The heads of shot-off flowers carpeted the lawn, fallen palm fronds created a zigzag course, bullet-scarred trees stood sentinel as she cautiously picked her way past an AK-47 that she didn't want to accidentally trigger. She passed the prone form of an Asian man wearing a black headband whom she did not fear because his body already had become home to swarms of buzzing flies and insects.

As she rounded the corner of the big building, she spotted the small white stucco villa set back among the trees that she had been so curious about.

A middle-aged white man in striped pajama tops was gesturing wildly from a second-floor balcony. As she stopped to watch, one of the MPs ran over and tossed a pistol up to the man, who then disappeared back into the house. Angela moved over to the cameraman, "Is that Jacobson?" she asked.

A blast of automatic fire rang out, and the MPs rushed the villa. A moment later there were two shots.

"The last were small caliber, maybe that's good," Angela said to the cameraman, who was much too engrossed in his work for her to expect any replies.

Jacobson walked out his front door a short time later. "I was lucky," he said. "The guy who came at me was already wounded, and his shots went wild."

Angela knew that with the sound of the shots, several of the other reporters were likely to come running. So she beat it back across the lawn to find Nick as quickly as possible. They met halfway.

"You might want to get over and file this," she told him breathlessly, as she stepped over a dead VC lying by a flower tub of geraniums. "A network was there, but they won't be able to get their film out today."

"Shit, yeah," he said. "You muck around here, and pick up whatever else you can. Westmoreland is likely to show. Get whatever spin he puts on this, then meet me at Reuters as soon as you can. Don't wait for him if it's much more than an hour. Harry can patch him in from the wires. We need to map our strategy." He started running for the Embassy gate, and Angela ran alongside filling him in on the story he would file.

"Jacobson said the Cong guy was creeping up the stairs. He figured he probably had hidden in a room downstairs while Jacobson was locked in his bedroom for hours giving the lowdown to Zorithan over the phone. The pistol was a .45. Oh, the MPs also threw Jacobson a gasmask 'cause they were going to lob in teargas canisters, not knowing if, or how many, Cong might be in the house."

"Get names on any MPs?" Nick asked, still on the run.

"No, sorry," Angela said. "They were all still in the villa, and I didn't want to wait to get to you once I got the confirmation and quote out of Jacobson."

"That's OK," Nick said. "This is fucking fantastic to have this *this* early. Harry the Arse should be mighty pleased."

"It was the 101st Airborne, by the way, that landed on the roof. And, oh, did you know Jacobson was a retired Army colonel?" Angela asked, panting as she trotted past another dead Cong and out the big gate of the Embassy.

"Yeah," Nick said.

"Well, damn," Angela said. "I wish I'd known. Embarrassing. I asked him where he learned to handle a gun so well. He was nice about it, but I felt like a jerk."

"You'll live," Nick said with a grin as he took off at a run. "Good luck with Westmoreland. Don't let me down."

THE GENERAL showed up in a starched, immaculately pressed uniform, toured the disorderly scene and then talked to reporters on the Embassy grounds. The bodies of dead sappers scattered around the huge tubs of flowers ringing the main building served as a backdrop for Westmoreland's remarks. The blood from dead and wounded Marines had by now dried, but had not been scrubbed away.

The North Viets and Cong had been deceitful in breaking the truce, he told the assembled reporters, but their "well-laid plans went afoul... American troops went on the offensive and pursued the enemy aggressively."

Angela and the other assembled reporters exchanged skeptical, if not astonished, glances at Westmoreland's upbeat assessment. But all dutifully reported his remarks, along with the factual information that Saigon, Hoi An, Da Nang, Pleiku and Hue, among scores of other cities, had all been hit in surprise attacks within the last 24 hours, and that all were still burning.

Westmoreland also said 19 "enemy" bodies had been found on the premises, although that information was "clarified" within a matter of hours. Actually, four of them were Vietnamese employees of the Embassy. One died frantically waving his U.S. Embassy employee card. But as every reporter knows, there is always more than one and usually several sides to every story. One of the four "faithful" employees may well have been a ringer, a person who helped set up the assault. He was nicknamed "Satchmo" and had worked at the Embassy for years, even at one time as the ambassador's chauffeur. Marine eyewitnesses said he had fired on them during the battle, and a 9-mm pistol was said to have been tucked in his belt when his body was found. The body count for the U.S. was reported as much lower: Five MPs dead and only two Marines. The contingent of Marine guards had stayed holed up in the Chancery, effectively keeping the attackers out and confined to the Embassy grounds.

The American flag was raised anew over the Embassy at 11:45 a.m. Saigon time, but Angela had already left to make her way back to Reuters to meet Nick as she had promised.

They worked like that for days. They wrote stories about the failed attempt to take over the Saigon government radio station to broadcast propaganda tapes, the house-to-house fighting in Cholon, the burned-out buildings and desolation in the garbage-filled, rat-plagued city. Nick felt they were golden. "The gold-dust twins," he called them. Angela not only walked like an oiled machine, she worked like one. She was fast, she was resourceful, and she didn't hand out any crap. She picked up her share of the workload and expected Nick to do the same.

It never occurred to either of them that Harry the Arse, his foreign editor, might not see it exactly the same way.

# 26

# The Pagode

Nick was fidgeting with the spoon in his empty coffee cup, wondering whether to order a second but hesitant, not wanting to move, afraid to tamper with whatever mood was behind the frown creasing Angela's forehead.

She hadn't said a word in the fifteen minutes since they'd walked into the open-sided Vietnamese joint called the Pagode. He'd ordered them both coffee from the elderly Chinese waiter while Angela walked over to the American-style jukebox and dropped in several coins. The locals paid no attention to them, going right on with their smoking and chattering, or silently shoveling rice or slurping *pho* soup from bowls held almost up to their mouths.

The streets here, around National Assembly Square, were eerily quiet, with traffic and commerce reduced to a trickle compared to the usual frenetic pace. The Pagode, a few doors up from the Givral on the Tu Do, was across the street from a side entrance to the Continental Hotel. Things were calming down on this end of town. The battle for the Embassy, the presidential palace, the radio station, were long since over. The Viet Cong had been routed from most of Saigon and from Tan Son Nhut airport, but they still held Cholon, the Chinese section of the city. Hundreds if not thousands of civilians had crowded into schools, hospitals, churches and pagodas to escape the fighting. Many had been rousted from their homes by Cong who said they had come to liberate them, and entire blocks were still afire or had been destroyed by rockets. A good part of the rest of the population still seemed to be hiding behind their drawn shutters. Jeep-loads of armed soldiers roamed the streets enforcing the strict (shoot on sight) curfew. The national police chief had shot a prisoner, his hands tied behind his back, at point blank range in a public place in front of two photographers. But a few shopkeepers were beginning to make tentative stabs at getting back to business. Sanitation trucks had begun to roll, trying to clean streets strewn with garbage, spent munitions and the unidentified dead, who were being hauled to a mass grave at the edge of town. Gangs of street kids had been well ahead of the trucks, looting the pockets and purses of the fly-and-blood-encrusted, bloated bodies long before they were removed.

"I guess you're a Gerry Mulligan fan," Nick finally said, clearing his throat a second time, his voice still raspy. "That's the third time we've heard the same song."

"I guess," said Angela, listlessly stirring her cold coffee.

Nick had finally had a chance to talk to Harry an hour before. It was the first time in the several days since Tet began that he'd been able to have a thorough conversation with his foreign editor. With the chaotic conditions, their communications up to then had been limited to snatches of conversation. Or more frequently, just filing stories and hoping that Harry had gotten them and liked them. Nick assumed Harry was patching from wire copy as best he could when he ran into holes or questions.

Harry, it turned out, was happy as a pig in shit with the stuff Angela and Nick had been sending him. He'd given Angela a double byline with Nick on several of their joint pieces, and had used all the stuff she had written on her own.

And Harry hadn't given Nick any flak about what he had promised to pay Angela. Nick knew that meant the old skinflint must be hauling in compliments from the brass for having been "clever" enough to come up with a first-rate stringer right in the middle of the biggest news event of the war.

The Viet Cong had attacked over 100 cities and towns during their surprise Tet offensive. But with Saigon and most of the others relatively secure, the news focus had shifted to Hue, the imperial capital. It was still under heavy assault, and enemy combatants—Cong or North Viet regulars—held a good chunk of the city, including the Citadel, the ancient, walled imperial grounds.

But Harry had overruled Nick's suggestion this morning that one of them head north to Hue, so Nick and Angela had come to the Pagode to plan what stories they would go after in the next few days and how to divvy up the work. Vietnamese journalists hung here a lot, but Nick figured it was unlikely they'd run into any Americans and have to forestall their planning session.

Instead, Angela was sitting here brooding, elbows propped on the green Formica-topped table, listening to "My Funny Valentine" over and over.

Good as Angela clearly was, Harry couldn't bring himself to completely cut Nick loose and trust all of Saigon to a stringer. "And I'm sure as hell not sending any broad into combat, you stupid fucker," he had screamed at Nick over the crackling Vietnamese phone system. His voice had been fading in and out, but for that outburst every syllable from Chicago came through loud and clear. Angela was standing right next to Nick in PTT, the phone and post office on Cathedral Square.

Nick had hoped she hadn't been able to hear what Harry said. But watching her now, it seemed pretty clear that she had.

God, she looks wiped out, he realized with a start.

Sitting across from her at the small table, he took the first good, up-close look he'd had in days. It suddenly hit him that he'd been too busy to pay any attention to anything except the way she worked. She had black circles under her eyes and her skin was drawn and pasty, with no trace of makeup, and it seemed like she had on the same clothes she'd been wearing when he'd spotted her several days ago striding up Hai Ba Trung.

"Jeez, you look exhausted," he said, as he watched her light a new cigarette from the stub of the old.

"Aren't you?" she asked, without a trace of expression.

"Yeah, but you look ghostly. You're not going to faint or cry or anything, are you?"

She managed an almost imperceptible tinge of smile around the eyes, but her voice was still flat and lifeless. "No, I won't faint or cry. But I do think I'm running on the last dram of adrenaline I can dredge up. I definitely need to crash for a day."

"OK, fine," Nick said. "We can figure out tomorrow what our next move will be."

"I think Harry made that perfectly clear," she said, with a curdling sarcasm that required a great deal more energy than one would expect considering her zombie-like state.

"Oh, come on, Angela. Don't pay any attention to what that Neanderthal said. Besides, he's been giving you bylines and using your stuff. He's getting used to you. Give him time."

"Why does he need to get *used* to me?" she said through clenched teeth, grinding out her cigarette with a fury that clearly had Harry's name on it. "What am I, some kind of freak? What the fuck difference does it make if I'm a man or a woman. They don't run my picture in the paper, only my stories. I did the work, I busted my butt. He liked my stuff. It was certainly more than just adequate."

"You were fast, you were accurate, I've told you that. You came up with a couple of great features. You nailed the story about the total disappearance of the White Mice, leaving no cops to patrol the streets. We had Jacobson, thanks to you." He just looked at her, he didn't know what more to say.

"Nick, I want to go to Hue. Or at the least be trusted to cover the mopping up operation here without your having to oversee me as though I were retarded or crippled or something."

"Jesus, Angela, don't talk like that. There's nothing wrong with you, people just have to get used to you, that's all."

"Sure, kid, you're right. I'm never grateful enough. That's always been my problem," she said as she got up and dropped a 50-piastre tip on the table. "I'll go home and get some beauty rest. When I'm not so tired and vulnerable, I'm more careful to know my place and not step out of line."

"That's bunk, and you know it," Nick snapped.

She tousled Nick's hair as she stood over him. "Sure, kid. I'll see you tomorrow."

She slung her campaign bag over her shoulder and strode away, an aura of class weaving among the Formica-topped tables, the Pagode once again becoming the tacky chrome and glass joint it was before she entered.

# 27

# Marshall Fields and a Green Kitchen

NICK WAS starting up the steps of the Continental when he spotted her. He'd held off until after 5 the next evening, figuring he'd give her plenty of time to rest. Everybody knows women get depressed when they're tired. He had planned to knock on her door and tell her to put on her best duds and he'd splurge for a fancy dinner, either here or at the Caravelle across the street. Couldn't go far with this curfew.

But there she was, at a table just at the top of the steps, and she looked radiant. Her face had a glowing pink tinge to it almost as though her translucent skin were reflecting the watermelon silk shirt she was wearing. Then Nick realized with a jolt that the animation in her face was the raptness with which she was listening to something Ford Curtis was saying, as she leaned across the small table, seemingly hanging on his every word.

Nick wanted to duck aside, but there was no way.

"Nick, hi." Angela had spotted him. "Why don't you join us?"

Curtis didn't look any happier about the invitation than Nick felt, and of course Nick said he was meeting some friends.

"We'll talk tomorrow," Angela said, as Nick started to head for the standup bar off the lobby. "I looked for you at Reuters this afternoon," she caught his arm before he could move on, "but someone there said you'd filed earlier. I sent Harry a story I ran across this morning about a shoe merchant whose business was destroyed in the fallout from the attack on the presidential palace. The guy had worked his way through Northwestern selling shoes at Marshall Fields in Chicago."

"Wow, great home-town angle," Nick said as he moved away, "I'm sure Harry'll love it."

As Nick hurried across the square early the next morning on his way to call his foreign editor, he spotted Angela drinking coffee on the Continental terrace. He could tell by her body language that she intended to join him, so he moved quickly to shortstop her at her table. He didn't want her overhearing another turndown.

When he started to make small talk, she cut in. "Are you on the way to call Harry?" she asked. "Yeah," Nick replied, blushing. "But I wouldn't hold out a lot of hope for Hue."

"I'm not," she said.

Nick tried tackling his foreign editor a short time later from the cavernous, ornate hall of the PTT, but Harry was still adamant. He said the stuff Angela was filing was good, he had no complaints about her work, but she was to continue working under Nick's wing and as an adjunct to him.

Harry's stubbornness aside, Nick had a fine day. Angela developed a really good tip about an eyewitness who gave much more detail than had previously been reported about the sappers who attacked the runway at Tan Son Nhut. That led them to not one, but two good stories. They both were pleased with themselves and in a happy mood when they got to the terrace for the evening cocktail hour. Several guys stopped off at their table to chat and two or three sat down with them.

Nick leaned back in his wicker chair, stretched out one of his long legs to rest on the seat of a chair on his right and drank his BaBa beer. He felt good, he decided, in spite of the letter he'd gotten from Mary Alice Moriarty hinting that if she didn't hear from him soon, she was going to give him up for dead. "I know you're alive," she'd written, "despite having had only two letters in four months, because I see your byline in the Trib nearly every day. But somehow, that's not quite enough." The girl always had had a decent sense of humor, he thought. In fact, she was a decent enough sort. "I'm beginning to think mother may have been right," Mary Alice had continued, "she said all along, you know, that your going off to Vietnam when you didn't have to sounded like a ploy to break our engagement."

"Now then, Tiger, tell us how t'was you dug up the Marshall Fields shoe salesman." Ray Corrigan, seated at the terrace table, was razzing Angela. "If it hadn't been for the picture of himself and the address of his store, I would have sworn on me mother you had worked a bit of invention in creating him. Wonderful quote about the building collapse sounding just like the rumble of the Chicago El."

The easy banter and teasing made it clear to Nick that Angela had acquitted herself well in the last few days not only with himself and Harry, but with whomever she had run into whether it was at a press conference, on the street or banging away at the old upright in the Reuters office while she waited her turn to file. It seemed as though she had indeed finally become one of the boys. With these thoughts running through his head, he asked how she'd patched up things enough with Curtis to have been having drinks with him the night before.

"I ran into him in Reuters. He needed to verify a minor detail before he could file." The Chinese waiter handed their drinks order around the table. Angela paused for a beat, a wide smile spreading across her face. "I gave him the phone number of a Vietnamese bureaucrat who was able to give him his verification."

"You look like the cat with the canary," Nick said.

Angela picked up her Scotch glass and continued as though she hadn't heard. "Ford seemed to be dumfounded that I had sources of my own," she said. "As if I wouldn't, as long as I've been here." An ever so slight condescension crept into her tone. "He's amazingly naive."

"What's so funny?" she demanded when Nick had started to laugh.

"Nothing," he insisted.

"You think it's funny because people probably say I'm naive."

"Well, you did help him. And he's a competitor."

"Leave the lass alone," Corrigan laughed, poking a sharp elbow at Nick, who was seated to his left. "Let her have her fun. She deserves it."

"I gave him a phone number. That's all," Angela was defending herself to the table at large, despite Corrigan's blessing. "I'm not going to give someone a real tip that would lead him into a competitive story, but I'd never hold back a phone number on someone planning to do the digging himself." She turned back to Nick. "Ford wasn't startled that I *gave* him the number, he was startled that I was resourceful enough to *have* it."

The terrace was jam-packed and noisy. Corrigan suggested that they all go over to the Caravelle roof or the Rex BOQ for steaks. It was never any problem to find an Army guy around to sign them in for dinner at the officers club, and it was always a treat to dine on Kansas-fed beef flown in from the States.

They ended up settling on the Caravelle, picking up a few more people along the way and taking a big table in the Champs Elysees, the hotel's roof-top cafe. It was a good evening. Everyone was having a fine time, Angela included, when Nick suddenly realized she had gotten really pissed. He never did find out if someone had made a remark that angered her, or if she was just drunk and brooding and talked herself into a snit. Her moodiness over Harry's turndown, the strange fear that Curtis seemed to trigger, who knows? Nick couldn't put his finger on it.

At one point in the evening when someone mentioned Curtis' name in passing, she piped up and said, "He's a green kitchen." All the drunken heads swiveled to stare at her, all the foreheads frowned from the strain of focusing on the great wisdom of the remark, then some guy slurred, "Shure, baby, whatever you shay," and everyone went right on talking and tippling.

"Yeah, he presses in on you just like an avocado stove," she said to no one in particular.

The nonsensical remarks made Nick realize how drunk she was, and he decided to try to get her home. Half the men in the place were hitting on her, but she seemed to be in her usual top form of keeping her distance without seeming the least bit unfriendly. She didn't argue when Nick said it was time for her to leave. He was guiding her through the lobby of her hotel, when she suddenly jerked her elbow out of his grasp.

"I don't think I'm, ah, going to be available to work with you for the next few days," she said, squinting her eyes in a frown that was an apparent attempt to focus on Nick's face. "I've got a couple stories I want to develop on my own. Another river to cross."

He knew of no sane way to field that, especially with a drunk, except by saying, "Suit yourself."

"That's what I plan to do, suit myself," she said, with a slur and a wobble as she drew herself up to her full height.

She did a regal curtsey, holding on to the sides of her beige silk slacks as though they were billowing out to the width of a ball gown.

As she pulled herself up, she said, "See ya, Nick, after I check out the perfume," and strode toward the stairs leading to her room.

## 28

# Missing

NICK WAS ambling down the Tu Do about three days later, lost in thought over the story he had just filed at Reuters, when Ford Curtis stopped him on the street. "I thought that stringer was working with you permanently," Curtis said, with a tight smile and little more preamble than a hello. "But I haven't noticed her around with you lately."

"Naw," Nick said, knowing that didn't answer anything and that it would force Curtis to either ask what he wanted to ask or shut his face.

Curtis, of course, shut. Nick had guessed that Curtis wasn't about to go public with his interest in Angela, but got satisfaction out of skewering him, at least to that extent. Let him put his married ass on the line, if he really has anything to say, Nick thought.

A couple of days after that, Nick ran into Bo Parks, who, of course, didn't fool around and came right out with it. "Where's the Bird? Is she OK?"

"Sure. She's working on something."

"For you, mate?" asked Parks.

That set Nick to wondering and finally to worrying. After two or three more days he and Parks approached the manager of the Continental and found out that Angela was paid up to the end of the month and that her bed hadn't been slept in for over a week.

They leaned on the manager to let them in her room for a look-see, but it didn't tell them anything except that her clothes and her typewriter were there, which meant she hadn't packed her bags and flown back to the States in some fit of pique. In other words, she was fucking missing!

Nick felt like kicking himself around the block and back again. Sure, they'd all been working like crazy. But Curtis and Parks hadn't been too busy to notice! Nick had just made the stupid assumption that Angela was pissed at Harry, so she was off doing a magazine piece for someone else. But she couldn't be off any place for eight or nine days with no typewriter and no clothes. What a jerk he was!

He and Parks hit the mini-bar off the lobby for a couple of quick belts trying to calm down and figure out what to do next. There was nothing to do. What could they do? Report a missing person to the police? That would be a joke. Those bastards didn't care. Look at how they'd beat up on Nick when he was trying to tackle a goddamned bomb thrower. This whole country was upside down, the city in chaos, in the middle of a war with no front lines. Where do you start to look for someone? Tell the army to send out an APB for a long-legged white woman with a camera over her shoulder? The camera! Parks and Nick hotfooted it back to the manager and got in a shouting match with him over opening up the room again. He finally relented, then watched their every move as they searched the room, but the camera wasn't there.

There was no way to tell if she had taken extra clothes, who the hell knows how many changes of clothes a woman has, thought Nick. But she had taken her camera, so she was going on an assignment, right? Where could she be?

The two ran down the massive winding staircase to the lobby and started spreading the word among the other correspondents in both the standup bar and the terrace, but no one had seen her. Parks and Nick got so drunk talking about what to do, Nick finally just lost track of everything.

The next thing he knew Ford Curtis was trying to shake him awake, and he finally realized it was the middle of the night and he was back in a lounge chair he sometimes used for a bunk in the UPI apartment. He couldn't focus on anything the way his head was pounding. Curtis finally just stuck Nick's head under a cold water faucet. Nick couldn't remember later what he told Curtis. Nothing much, probably. He didn't know anything to tell. He just remembered Curtis being angry as hell.

Curtis and Nick both seemed to have the same kind of head the next morning, but in the light of day and after orange juice and coffee on the Continental terrace, the two of them, along with Corrigan, Parks and several other guys, decided they had to map some kind of strategy. The first step, obviously, was to check Army flight manifests out of Tan Son Nhut for the morning after Angela got drunk and told Nick she was going to suit herself. After Nick told them Harry wouldn't let her go to Hue, everyone was in agreement that she probably had decided to try to get there on her own.

"Oh, sweet Jesus," Nick suddenly slapped his own forehead and closed his eyes as a light went off in his head.

"What?" the others at the table asked in unison.

"Out with it," bellowed Ford.

"Perfume. She said something about perfume. I just thought it was more of that junk like how she loves to buy hand-tailored satin underwear."

"You IDIOT," screamed Ford, as he knocked over his chair leaping up to go start making phone calls.

"Oh, Boyo," Corrigan said with disgust, bending over to pick up Ford's upturned chair. "You know you have to cross the Perfume River to get into central Hue. Why didn't you tell us that sooner?"

"I didn't make the connection," Nick said miserably. "She didn't say river, or maybe she did. But not at the same time."

Curtis returned to the table not long afterward with the information that she had, indeed, gotten a hop on a C-130 into Da Nang, then the trail went cold.

"They say she was manifested on a flight there, spent the night in the bunks at the press center, but they have no more record," Curtis said in a forlorn tone.

The only response from those at the table was a deathly silence.

"It doesn't make sense," Curtis persisted, as he looked from face to silent face. "Someone's got to have seen her."

His words hung over the terrace table, playing against the background static of Saigon traffic that was almost back to normal.

"I made 'em go right to the top with this." Curtis was almost apologetic, as though trying to reassure the muted, somber group.

Then his voice rose an octave and took on more heat as he began to fume. "Damned sergeant was about as helpful as a politician trying to explain what we're doing in this God-forsaken country in the first place."

So there sat a table full of normally loquacious reporters—

speculative, cynical, inquisitive men. No one said a word. Blank faces, eyes focused on some inner place, the place where one greets tragedy with the thought: "It could have been me."

Curtis really is an OK guy, Nick thought, going off on his own private travels. He's impressive with his hotshot sources, knows how to play them. Got more information in a few minutes than I could get in a few hours. Yeah, so? He didn't find Angela, did he!

But he's top-notch smart. I wonder if he's going to catch on about this war? Catch on that high-level sources may be able to get you info fast on a flight manifest, but they aren't where it's at. You spend time in the field, you get the grunt's view of what's *really* happening. Stick with official military and Vietnamese sources and you end up filing stories closer to what Washington is saying and wants to hear. It didn't take Angela long to figure that out. That's why she was so pissed when Harry wouldn't let us go to Hue. Jesus, it's my fault that she's lost. What's wrong with me that I didn't notice sooner? We're never going to find her. Vietnam really is a different kind of war. A civilian population using guerrilla tactics against a conventional army. Curtis' sources think that with its firepower and superior forces, the U.S. can reach its "geo-political" goals, whatever the hell that is. But the reporters talking to foot soldiers know it's a fight against a hit-and-run, ever-changing enemy. The peasant girl who cleans your hootch, the mama-san selling vegetables in a village, the kid riding by on his bike, could like as not be carrying the wherewithal to blow one of your legs away. All the firepower under the sun doesn't work against an enemy you can neither identify nor find.

"So," said Nick, pulling himself back to the painful present, "what do we do now?"

The reporters at the terrace table knew Angela had flown north, which they'd already guessed. Curtis' contact had said she'd been turned down for space on a helicopter to Phu Bai air base just south of Hue, they knew the sergeant had told her she could sit in the Da Nang airport and wait for space available back to Saigon, and they knew that the sergeant had been ticked off by her crisp, blue response to that suggestion. Curtis had threatened the guy with something dire if he didn't make damned sure she wasn't on any manifests in any direction, but they all knew ahead of time the answer: she wasn't. No one had seen her for eight days. Where was she? Christ, probably dead! Da Nang was still under heavy fire, Hue and Khe Sanh still under siege.

Curtis was still fuming: "Imagine that little prick telling me Angela had probably gotten a flight back to Saigon without being manifested by 'wiggling her ass.' The little bastard."

Some of the other guys were startled by Curtis' outburst, not all being close Angela-watchers like Nick. They were slowly picking up that Curtis sounded like a man on fire, but were still remembering back with some mystification to the not-so-long-ago days when Ford Curtis was grousing over her Loc Ninh scoop and was a leading exponent of the war-is-no-place-for-a-lady school.

# 29

# The Bus from Phu Bai

THE RICKETY local bus was lurching—if you could call its snail's crawl a lurch—along two deep ruts in what passed in these parts for a major road. The Street Without Joy, Highway One, the only main route between north and south. It was supposed to be about eight miles or so from Phu Bai to Hue, but it could take a day to get there at this speed. The driver already had gotten out twice to lift the hood and peer at steam boiling up from the engine. Christ, what a foul odor, Angela thought, then burst out laughing, the sentence barely formed in her head, as she made the connection between that expression "foul," and the caged chickens and other order of "fowl" surrounding her on the bus. That was actually a rooster in the rack right over her head. God, these people were staring at her enough as it was, she mustn't sit here laughing out loud like a slaphappy lunatic. They'd really think she was crazy if they knew she was smiling and cackling to herself over the derivation of a word.

Well, hell, she doubted the words were related, anyway. But she decided to look it up in her Oxford Dictionary just as soon as she got back. Probably never, at this rate. Probably going to get herself killed, smart-ass that she was, trying to show Harry the Arse that she could strike out on her own. A stubborn, dead idiot, that's what she'd end up.

This old bus was a lot like the one she'd ridden in Mexico City once as a kid, on spring break, the only vacation she'd ever taken with her parents. It was on the wide tree-lined *Paseo de La Reforma*. They'd gone to the Reforma Hotel to see the Diego Rivera mural that had shocked the world when it was unveiled in 1939, showing Roosevelt and Churchill's heads on the bodies of donkeys. Her mother wanted Angela to see it, living history, part of her education. Maybe that's why they never took her again. They wanted to relax on vacations, bask in tropical winter sun, tired quickly of the burden of history lessons for a child. Let the nuns do it. The nuns she was sent to on a whim of her mother's, not because any of her family was Catholic.

She and her parents had walked across the broad *paseo* and seen the beat up little bus belching black diesel fumes, with people and live chickens hanging out the windows. They'd gotten on the bus, just for a lark.

"I did it for a lark." That was the punch line of one of Peter's silly jokes. When the lady robin's newly hatched egg wasn't robin's-egg blue, the mother bird told her accusing mate, "I did it for a lark." Curtis. Good grief, why did that make her think of Curtis? Because she wanted to sleep with him, that's why. Was she on this bus and now in an awful jam because she was running from what obviously would be another painful entanglement? That was silly! She damned well wanted to prove to Harry—and everyone else—that she could do the job as well as any of them. Hopping on a bus picking up local workers from the Phu Bai air base was probably not the wisest—or safest—thing to do. But she hadn't wanted to risk being refused a ride on one of the military convoy trucks that were hauling fresh troops and reporters into Hue from the base. Why couldn't she find the serenity her mother had with her father? He would let her do and be whatever she wanted and always loved her. Never any competition, even though they both were doctors. Forget it with Curtis. The big man. Don't even mention the fact he's married! Sure people have flings in wartime—everyone's lonely, scared, wants some normalcy. I can't risk it, too raw, too vulnerable. But Curtis feels so safe, protective. Yep, same thing she fell for in Peter. But we know how that ended. He left me for a pleasant, dumpling of a woman who mended and weeded and baked pies that didn't come from the frozen food section of the A&P.

It had been the end of the workday for them both when she ran into Curtis at Reuters. It was a natural to walk on down the Tu Do, and stop at the Continental for a drink. Curtis initially had suggested the Caravelle rooftop for old time's sake, since that was where they had first met. For all his outward no-nonsense, he really was a romantic, Angela thought.

"I'm so happy we cleared up that misunderstanding about that fellow in Komer's office. I want to celebrate," Curtis had said.

Angela had laughed. "The guy's name is Kevin Leahey, and you should remember it. He's a real prick."

They walked across Cathedral Square past the red brick Notre Dame with its strange, skinny, dunce-cap gray spires and its rose window, pale in comparison to its namesake in Paris. The main post office was straight ahead, sprawling the equivalent of two blocks, a mad mixture of red-tiled roof and bits of rococo plaster detailing the façade and the big archway over its entrance. Its clock said 5 p.m., she had made all but the earliest editions in Chicago. Her next deadline was Saigon's curfew at seven. "I wonder what happened to the Five O'Clock Follies?" she said aloud. She'd been too busy to ask or worry about it.

"They're claiming things are rosy, according to what I hear. Haven't been there," Curtis said. "And giving enemy body counts that are absurd. They get higher and higher each day. No one believes them."

They took a right, and headed the couple of blocks down the Tu Do, which felt like a pathetic carnival grounds after the crowds are gone. Garbage lined the streets, rats scurried away at the sound of their footsteps. It was much cooler than usual, helping a bit to keep the stench down. An occasional wisp of wind would pick up a discarded food wrapper and carry it a few feet. Only the beautiful old trees that canopied the street were lovely reminders of what life was like only the week before.

"Kevin Leahey," Curtis mused. "It seems a lifetime ago, that Christmas party at the Embassy before all this Tet mess. You were so beautiful in that stunning green dress."

Angela laughed again, nervously. She was attracted to this man. He was powerful, smart, had a good sense of humor, but he spelled danger. She was coming off a bad fall with Peter, never quite understanding what she did wrong there. Wrong? She was a person who easily blamed herself whenever something went awry. She had a tough act to follow in her mother—a woman who never seemed to falter, or be unsure about anything. This guy is really nice, she thought, but a no-no. "Why don't we just stop at the Continental," she said, "and make this a quick drink? I'm bushed, as I'm sure you are. We've all been going at full tilt for days."

"Well, you clearly have," Curtis replied with an intimate, engaging, smile, lifting his eyebrows at her ever so slightly. "I've been on the lookout for Chicago papers to keep track of how you're doing. Harry must be mighty pleased."

"Gosh, thanks." Angela could feel her face warm at such a nice compliment from such an impressive source. Amazing, he was actually going out of his way to read her stuff!

Just up from the hotel, they passed a Volkswagen dealership with a fly-specked paper sign stuck to its window offering to replace a VW fender for $21.09 plus labor. The auto shop was shuttered but the Princess Bar next door appeared to be limping along with some day business despite the strict curfew.

At the Continental, Curtis maneuvered them to a table close to the entrance steps away from several other correspondents who were already seated on the terrace.

"You know Harry? I'm surprised," Angela leaned forward in her chair with interest, just as the waiter brought their drinks.

"I know most people who have been in the business very long," Curtis replied.

The Phu Bai bus bounced along, and Angela tried to remember how Curtis had talked her into going to dinner. Curfew the excuse? The big dining room, or the hotel's interior courtyard only a few steps away? She couldn't remember. Give her a couple of drinks, and she's always game for anything. Did she think he might put in a good word for her with Harry? That's ridiculous. Nick couldn't budge the Arse, and she would never expect Curtis or anyone else to go to bat for her. She hadn't even mentioned her flap with Harry to him. But Curtis' wonderful confidence in himself and his world was so reassuring. Reminded her of her mother's assurance, but Angela never felt a part of that. Her sweet father, on the other hand, was reassuring in the warm way that she had mistakenly thought she had found in Peter.

The little bus came to another one of its abrupt stops. The locals riding along with her had been unusually quiet for the last few minutes. They had seemed intent on peering out the windows, and pointing. She could only guess they were hoping the landscape would offer a clue to what the latest fighting had done or what they were going to find when they got home. Many of the houses they passed were in rubble, their stone walls collapsed, their roofs caved in. There was a steady stream of refugees slogging along heading south, pots and pans, food stuff, attached to bamboo poles on their shoulders, barefoot children tagging along lugging whatever they were big enough to haul. A skeletal-looking water buffalo on bended knee was stubbornly refusing to budge as an old man with a wispy Ho beard tugged at its lead. The road that had seemed a decent rut when she first got on the bus now looked like a muddy riverbed. The cool weather they felt in the south had obviously been a cold rain up here. The driver did a grinding, shifting thing, and the bus lurched into life again. The chattering from the passengers that burst out felt like a collective sigh.

Curtis. She had been warning herself for a couple of months to be careful. She had been drawn to him from the very beginning. That first night in the rooftop bar, all the rest of them looked like children. He had been the man who stood out in the crowd. And he had a way of taking charge without seeming to that was nice. He'd smoothly had a Chivas in her hand on the rooftop bar before she had had a chance to say "no." But then again, there are little warning signs: telling Nick what *she* wanted to drink after that fight with the White Mice, without consulting either Angela or Nick.

"The *loup de mer* is usually quite fresh. Will that suit you?" he had asked as the waiter hovered, white towel over his arm, tiny lights strung in the trees of the Continental garden, as though there were no war going on, no curfew outside.

"You know you were right about that M-16 jamming debacle," Curtis said, raising his glass of wine to her. "I did some checking after you brought it up that first night we had dinner. Clever on your part. You pay attention. We mustn't let our professional egos get in the way of what I hope will be a very good friendship."

"Gee," Angela said blushing. "That's very flattering coming from you. Here's to *friendship*," she said clinking her glass to his. "But to be honest, Mr. Curtis..."

"My God, please. It's Ford," he said with a startled frown.

"Yes, the fish will be fine. But please, no head," she said to the waiter.

"I don't understand you," said Curtis, failing to keep a tone of exasperation from his voice. "It feels like you go out of your way to be distant."

She gave him a wry smile, and shook her head slightly. "Yes, it feels safer that way."

"Safe from what?" he asked.

She played with the long stem of her wine glass, the slight smile still there, but her eyes unfocused, as though she were searching through the card catalogue of her mind for the right words, or perhaps trying to identify the feelings.

"I don't know exactly," she finally said, seeming to study the cutlery, then picking up a butter knife and drawing imaginary patterns in the white linen table cloth. "I guess I'm on shaky ground about everything. I'm sorting. I'm trying to learn—the hard way—a new job, a new way of life, a new culture. I'm just coming off a shattering divorce."

She looked up and gave him a dazzling smile. "This all sounds like so much curbstone psychology. I guess the bottom line is that there are an awful lot of horny men around here, and I need to be careful."

Curtis who had been watching her intently, as he sipped his wine, looked like he had trouble swallowing before he burst out laughing at her last remark.

"You never cease to amaze," he finally said.

She had glowed at the remark. The man treated her as though she were a fascinating creature. Listened to her theories, laughed at her jokes, all the while maintaining the benevolent smile of a doting parent whose offspring can do no wrong. As Angela had warmed to his attentions, the electricity between them had fairly crackled in the humid air of the palm shaded garden.

He had held her chair, filleted her fish, and she had the fleeting thought early on that she wished she had had a chance to at least freshen her makeup. And when it came time to say goodnight, she almost didn't.

As she stood at the door of her room, he took her face in his hands and kissed her lightly on the lips. She had a memory flash of her hardened nipples under the sea-foam chiffon at the Embassy party. That night she had had the absurd thought that her high-heeled sandals were too tight. Tonight she was wearing jungle boots. She was about to suggest he come in for a "nightcap." Besides, she reminded herself, it was dangerous to be out on the streets after curfew. They would Shoot to Kill, the MPs said. Good excuse as any. Better than most, actually.

She giggled now, causing several bus passengers to again stare at the tall redheaded foreigner, thinking back on her meeting with Curtis at the Passage Eden at Thanksgiving. It was strange happenstance that she had had that Lawrence book in her hand. She had insulted Curtis' manhood. What a hoot. "Backbiting." Ole T.E. was into some kinky things with little Arab boys, but all she had meant was Curtis' gossiping with Kevin.

As the kiss at her hotel door had turned more serious, she had felt herself going under. I'm going to lose myself, she thought. Just totally disappear. How nice. How lovely.

"I'm nearly twice your age," he said, "but you are the most incredible thing that has ever happened. I would love to devour you."

That brought her to. That was scary. The thing she feared. He meant it in a sensuous way, and it was, indeed, a very sensuous kiss. But she could fall down the rabbit hole. Disappear inside of him. He was reading her copy, watching over her, letting her know he knew her editor. "Good night," she said, "and thank you for a lovely dinner. It's been swell."

Chickens and their droppings couldn't possibly account for that horrible smell. Looking across the aisle of the rickety bus lurching its way to Hue, Angela decided the odor was coming from the body of that little samurai-warrior-looking fellow wearing sandals made out of old Jeep tires. The damned bus was stopping again.

"All aboard, we're on a mighty mission." Mac Wheeler had swooped her away to Phu Bai. That crummy lading sergeant in the dispersal shack in Da Nang told her to get back to Saigon. Hue was OK for the guys, but not her.

"Hey, whoa. Calm down, little lady." The lanky cowboy had stepped between Angela and the sergeant, the object of her wrath. Mac's eyes were as light as the sky, edged by deep leathery lines from a lifetime of squinting into the sun. His grip on her arm said he wasn't going to let go.

"Sergeants can be mean as horseradish," Mac had said. "I seen fellas strung up for saying less than you just laid on that dude."

"I have been standing here for two solid hours watching him manifest one correspondent after another," Angela fumed. "It's enraging."

"Well, now, cain't say as I blame ya. But I'd bet we could figure out something if the two of us was to put our minds to it. Where ya trying to git to?"

He bought her a hamburger, regaled her with stories of his barnstorming days in West Texas and flew her away to Phu Bai in his slick. He didn't try to tell her what she could and could not do. A free spirit, like she wished she were.

The chopper jocks are all hotdogs, but the guys who fly the slicks are the aces with their low-level contour flying. Skimming low over the terrain, following its bumps and hollows to stay beneath the reach of heavy artillery, they ferry small groups of grunts in and out on search-and-destroy missions. Often as not, turned into ambulance drivers on the return trip.

Funny, when several of Mac's pals had stopped by their table at the officers club, there was an undercurrent to the usual razzing about which of the jocks faced the most danger. The big cargo gunships had obvious advantages, but . . .

The brakes of the creaky little bus squeaked as though they were rubbing right against the brake drum. Cute, she thought. Get killed covering a war because the brakes failed. If the bus kept stopping like this, she was never going to get there. And if she did and it was after dark, then she'd *really* be in trouble. In fact, she was finally beginning to let seep into her consciousness what she had been tamping down for quite a while now: that she was already *really* in trouble. What the hell would she do even if it was broad daylight and the bus dropped her off at the farmer's market in central Hue, if there was such a thing? She couldn't just go to American Express and ask for the listing of a cheap but clean room with hot water for the night. She obviously wasn't thinking very straight when she got the bright idea for this trip.

The bus stopped and didn't start again. Angela heard some jabbering and looked up. She saw soldiers boarding who clearly weren't GIs. They wore palm-leaf helmets and were carrying Russian-made AK-47s, which she recognized by their metal stocks. Her heart racing, she tried to scrunch down, but she was at least two heads taller than anyone else around. They couldn't miss her, sitting there squeezed in among the chickens. And that mean looking little dude with the square backpack was heading straight for her.

# 30

# Falling Short of Hue

THE HAND came at her, and it flashed through her mind that his insignia was on his collar, not his epaulet. Red. Was he going to slap her? No, he grabbed her upper arm, and yanked her to her feet. That hurt like hell, she thought. I guess an adventure writer would call it a vice-like grip. She almost smiled at the thought, then immediately wondered why she felt the need to keep making jokes to herself when, in fact, she felt like her heart would stop? But the situation *was* laughable. When she stood, her captor had to reach up to hold her arm, she was so much taller than he. His eye level was just about at the top of her breast. He sort of shook her as he dragged and pulled her off the bus, all the peasants with their chickens staring, and cowering, and silent.

Off the bus, feet on the ground, she was surrounded by soldiers who looked like regular North Vietnam Army. Their packs, their helmets—no peasants in rubber sandals, these. They were pushing and shoving and milling about her—five, it looked like, although she thought another guy had walked over to a stand of trees with what appeared to be a hand-held radio of some sort. The ground was nothing but mud, she was sinking down over her bootlaces. Her camera, which was around her neck, was the first thing they grabbed for. Behind her, she heard the little bus crank up, then chug away. Jesus, now what? But her immediate problem was in front of her.

"I'm a journalist, *bao chi*," she kept saying, trying to sidle over to more solid ground. The insignias came clear now. A guy with a black star on his red and yellow stripe pointed a rifle barrel in her gut. She held her hands out in a soothing gesture, pointing to the higher ground. OK, he nodded, pointing to the same spot with his rifle. She moved over slowly, so as not to excite anyone. At least she had found a bit of solid, dry dirt. They babbled at her. "*Bao chi,*" she said again. She held out her plastic-encased MACV card, which hung from a dangling cord around her neck, and pointed to the white, identifying patch on her shirt pocket. Pointed to her own face, then the picture on the ID.

It didn't seem to register. Their facial expressions, angry looks, exaggerated gestures looked to her Western eye like people who were getting a mute, stone-walling response. Her response was anything but that. She'd never been more earnest in her life. She was turning her pockets inside out to show she didn't have any weapons. Offered them the several packs of cigarettes and a package of peanut butter-cheese crackers she had on her. They took them, stuffed them into pockets of their loose, green cotton uniforms. But they just kept chattering in Vietnamese, to her and each other, as though this were a traffic jam, or a fire.

The soldier with the hand-held communication device strode back into the group, and began barking, not chattering. He had three stars on his collar. If she remembered rightly, stars were for enlisted men, not officers. They all had one star, except this guy. One little shrimp of a fellow with sad eyes beneath an oversized helmet pulled some rope or twine from his pocket and grabbed one of her hands. She instinctively jerked away, and three of them were on her in a flash. She fought them off, throwing elbows and kicking—again, it was instinctive, not rational, not thought out. She landed in the dirt with a thud, hitting her chin. The barker was really barking now, and someone straddled her, grabbed her arms and wrenched them back. Another held down her flailing legs. Her wrists were bound together. It felt like hemp. Someone tied it tight, then gave a couple of good yanks, and it burned into her skin. The barker let out a string of stern-sounding yips, and the bonds on her hands were not only loosened, but she could feel slack in the rope that meant her arms weren't bound so closely together. Someone helped her to her feet, and she faced them.

Six, there were. She was chattered at again, and again drew blank stares when she repeatedly said: "I don't understand Vietnamese. I don't know what you're saying. *Je ne comprend pas,*" she tried her high school

French. This standoff proceeded for what felt like a lifetime. Then finally, a kid who looked all of 15, sporting two canteens and what appeared to be a loose canvas bag full of rice, stepped forward. He nudged her in the back with the butt of a rifle, and jerked his head forward in a gesture that seemed to mean "walk." So she did. She followed the leader as they crossed the muddy road, past a forlorn family of five who appeared to have all their belongings with them, and began plowing through the underbrush that led into a jungle of trees.

# 31

# The Search

"Hue is a bloodbath. No word for it but carnage, butchery." Ford Curtis stirred another spoonful of sugar into his coffee without seeming to notice he'd already put in two, his buttered croissant untouched on his plate. "When the bastard North Viets found the people didn't rise up to greet them as liberators, they just began mowing them down."

Curtis had been to Hue twice already since the Tet offensive began. Everyone at the table knew he was scheduled to head for the Marine outpost at Khe Sanh that afternoon.

Nick shifted uneasily in his wicker chair. Curtis seemed really wound tight over Angela's absence. Nick had decided to just not think about it. Push it out of his head. But it was hard to do with Curtis ranting. Saigon felt like it was getting a bit back to normal after the Tet debacle. The usual street traffic buzzed around the Continental terrace square, the tamarind trees provided the same filtered shade, their feathery leaves unmoving in the humid, early morning air. They all had jobs to do, but Curtis raved on.

"They arrived with death lists of the most minor functionaries. Dragged them from their homes, clubbed to death, buried alive. The streets are littered with bloated bodies."

Nick didn't want to think about it. He was in Saigon, not Hue. Angela was a big girl, she'd do OK. He couldn't afford any more hangovers like the one he'd had after he first realized she was missing. He had to get to work. Had to find some angle no one else had today, so he could file something different than what the wires would have. The other correspondents at the terrace table for morning coffee had already made it clear they didn't see what anyone could do about finding Angela.

"Besides," said one, "the broad shoulda known better. Going off like that by herself."

Curtis persisted. "Thousands were shot—children and old people, priests and nuns, herded together, then left to rot where they fell. The Marines are coming in from the north and the south, and God help those in the middle. There's hand-to-hand combat in the streets. Refugees pouring out, trying to get across the Perfume. Hue's a main juncture, both rail and shipping."

"Yeah, fellow, most of us have been there," said a photographer from an Oslo paper. "We're in a war. What's your point?"

"If Angela was able to make it there," Curtis replied in a scathing tone that sounded as though he didn't consider the questioner quite bright, "she's probably already dead, or worse. She wasn't in the U.S. compound with the rest of the press, or I obviously would have seen her. I just got back day before yesterday."

Yet here he was suddenly talking about making still another trip into Hue instead of going to Khe Sanh.

Jesus, Nick thought, he's really going public about Angela.

"You're crazy," said a correspondent from one of the news magazines.

The Viet Cong and the AVN still held the Citadel in Hue, but U.S. Marines had pretty much secured the south side of the city, leading to the general speculation that it was only a matter of days until the last of the snipers would be blown out of the walls of what was left of the Imperial Palace.

Khe Sanh was another matter. It was a mountain-ringed plateau camp held by five battalions of beleaguered Marines who would starve or run out of ammo if U.S. forces didn't knock out enemy artillery blasting away at the base's tiny aluminum-matting airstrip. Cargo planes dropping off fresh troops, supplies or correspondents were coming back riddled with holes, or not coming back at all. In other words, Khe Sanh, near the DMZ, had the potential for becoming America's Dien Bien Phu, which nearly 14 years before had been France's Vietnamese Waterloo. French generals had picked the small, isolated valley in northeastern Vietnam as an ideal spot to lure in the Cong's predecessor, the Viet Minh, and destroy their army in a "set-piece" battle. Instead, the

French garrison was kept under siege by a hit-and-run guerrilla force for 56 days. The French couldn't get supplies in to their beleaguered troops, while the guerrillas were said to have been resupplying with coolies and bicyclists running, riding and trotting through the dense mountain underbrush. Dien Bien Phu was surrendered on May 7, 1954. The French had suffered some 9,000 causalities at a remote fort that had no strategic value, and France had lost its will to fight the Indochina War to hold on to its colonies.

Ford Curtis not only had told his office he was going to take a look for himself at the siege of Khe Sanh, he was one of the leading proponents of the theory that Khe Sanh would fall in the same way, and probably on the same day next month—March 13—as the 14th anniversary of the attack on the French at Dien Bien Phu. True, at that point the Khe Sanh siege, which began Jan. 20, would only be 52 days old instead of 56, but the symmetry was too deliciously apparent to ignore. The icing on the speculative cake: General Vo Nguyen Giap, the mastermind of the French rout, was thought to be calling the shots in Khe Sanh.

But today, Ford Curtis didn't seem at all obsessed with Khe Sanh.

"Hey, Curtis, I thought your paper wanted you in Khe Sanh, not Hue," an Agence France-Presse reporter said, a knowing smirk on his face. The turkey's picking up the drift of Curtis' new obsession, Nick thought. But I don't see what's so damned amusing. The guy barely knows Angela, so what does he care.

Strangely, on that 1968 morning in early February, Curtis seemed the only one oblivious to his own drift. He sat there expounding on what apparently were to him perfectly legitimate professional reasons for his going to Hue.

Nick absentmindedly dunked a French roll in the inch of cold coffee left in his cup, thinking how he'd never dare try handing a line like that to his foreign editor, Harry. But then, he didn't have Curtis' clout—or gall. It probably would never occur to any of Curtis' brass back in New York that he'd simply gone off the deep end over a dame.

Jesus, come to think of it, the smitten bastard had given Nick an idea! He'd try to somehow sell Harry on a story about "Our Reporter Found!" That would sure as hell be a story no one else had.

"Listen, Ford, I think I'll go to Hue, too," Nick blurted out. "With the two of us looking, we'd have a better chance of finding her." By the time the sentence was out of his mouth, he'd slapped some *piasters* on the table to cover his share of the bill and was off, yelling over his shoulder: "I'll see you at the airport."

The startled looks at the table flashed an instant replay in Nick's head as he moved down the steps of the hotel's terrace at a trot, the initial images missed in the whirr of clicking slides of Angela in various stages of distress snapping before his eyes. Bo Parks' voice followed him down the street, narrating the replay: "Don't be a bloody fool. I just got back from Hue and so did half the snappers in this town. She's not there."

Nick got to the UPI apartment in double-time, but Harry hadn't answered him on the Telex by the time he had his gear together. Since Chicago was fourteen hours behind Saigon time, Nick figured he might still catch Harry in the office if he phoned from Tan Son Nhut Airport.

When Nick found Curtis in the op shack at the airport, he had already signed them both on for the next flight to Da Nang, their first leg. It was clear to Nick that Ford had had to throw his weight around to get one seat. The fact that he had gotten two at the last minute was awesome.

But his hyperactivity was setting Nick's teeth on edge. Curtis was pacing, chewing his pipe, running his fingers through his salt-and-pepper hair.

"That damned sergeant said it'd only be a few minutes, twenty already," Curtis said, looking at his watch for the umpteenth time.

"I guess we're lucky to get on the list." Nick wished Curtis would just sit down and shut up. He picked up a three-day-old paper lying among the litter on the folding chairs of the hangar.

"Lucky? Christ, we have to get there." Curtis jammed his pipe into a side pocket of his fatigues, not bothering to mind the ashes that tumbled out.

But Curtis was also acting like the two of them were asshole buddies, confidants. Nick found that part confusing. He barely knew the man. It put Nick on his guard, but Curtis seemed sincere. He certainly has a way of making a person feel like a big leaguer, Nick thought. No wonder he dines with presidents while the rest of us peons eat beans.

"Jesus, I'm behaving like some lunatic kid," Curtis said, yanking the tobacco-less pipe out of his pocket and sticking it in his mouth. "I've got to get hold of myself. But I've got to find her and get her out of this damned country."

The dope doesn't seem to know she doesn't want out, Nick thought, but figured it was wise to keep his mouth shut. He made a stab at keeping his face neutral.

Curtis looked directly at him through the silence. Finally with a frown of concern, he said, "You surely can understand the wisdom of that, Nick."

"All I know is we have to find her."

"You're right. Sensible. That's why Angela trusts you."

"But she doesn't trust you, does she?"

He looked like Nick had hit him. He stared for a minute, glared maybe. Took a draw on his empty pipe. "You don't mince words, do you?"

"Not when it's important."

Curtis screwed his mouth into a thoughtful gesture, he appeared to be rubbing his tongue against his teeth with his mouth closed. "I like people," he finally said, "who know how to get to the point. And you're right. She has no reason to trust me, and I don't think she does. Rather the opposite, I'm afraid. She strikes me as unusually wary, not just of me, but of everything. Is that the way she strikes you?"

"Yeah."

"Do you have a clue why?"

"She's a woman in a man's world."

"Of course. But that's a bit simplistic, don't you think?"

"Maybe. But if you're looking for clues, that's a good place to start."

Curtis grinned for the first time all morning, and put his arm around Nick's shoulder. "For the rest of it, I'm on my own, huh? Fair enough. You're a good man, Nick. And smart. Angela's lucky to have you in her corner. Now let's go find her!"

Twice while they waited for their Da Nang flight, Nick had persuaded the tech sergeant in the flight prep shack to patch him through to a civilian phone line to try to reach Harry. The longer it took, the more nervous he was getting. He pretty well knew Harry wasn't going to buy this trip.

When he finally got through, he found he was right: "We'll keep using the wires on Hue. We need you where we can get in touch with you."

Harry wavered a minute when Nick told him Angela was missing and it would make a great story to play up "our reporter" lost and then found in the midst of the most dramatic battle of the war.

As Nick stood there at the gray metal, standard-issue military desk with the sergeant and several other GIs shaking their heads and rolling their eyes at his proposal yelled over the scratchy line, he could picture Harry, writing the headlines in his head and already laying out a full page of combat photos. But he picked up on the folly of it almost as fast as the dudes back at the terrace table at the Continental had. "How the fuck you gonna find anybody in that mess up there? The goddamned Marines are reclaiming that city house by house and block by block. You can't go walking around looking for some dame. Jesus, fella, it sounds like it's time you were rotated back!" Click.

The flight had been called by the time Nick got back. He was embarrassed to tell Curtis he couldn't go, but Ford was gathering up his gear to board and had already retreated into a distracted, aloof shell. Poor bastard, Nick thought, maybe the full realization of what he was doing was finally beginning to hit him. A big part of Curtis' reputation was built on his ability to cut through complex issues, bureaucratic bullshit and obfuscating personalities to render the muddy clear. But incisive thinking does not always signal insight into self. Anyway, he didn't register much more than slight eyebrows and a puff on the pipe, which he had finally refilled, over his brush with the reality that there are people who go where their desks tell them instead of informing their desks where they're going to go. He probably wasn't even embarrassed to have to tell the Army that the publisher of The New York Times had a hitherto unknown previous commitment and couldn't take a ride in their airplane.

Nick hung around watching the final loading of the C-130. Those Hercules were amazing, and well named. They could carry almost anything. This one had just run a two-ton truck up its rear belly ramp, before closing up getting ready to take off. Reports had come back that trucks like that were being used to convoy troops and supplies from Phu Bai into Hue. Funny, those Herks always looked to Nick like they had just crash-landed, they were so squat to the ground. Nick just kept standing there, ruminating, wondering why he didn't move. No reason to hang around. It was as though he didn't want to let go of Curtis. Fancy that! He felt at loose ends, or something. Curtis gave off an aura of order, a feeling he could put everything right. The old correspondent sure had some kind of luck or charm working for him, Nick thought. Maybe he really *could* find Angela.

When the cargo plane finally did lift off, Nick just stood there on the busy field and felt a horrible emptiness, an awful depression, the worst since he'd gotten in-country. Everyone is depressed here all the time, he thought. It's not only the senselessness and brutality of the war, or perhaps that was the given, but on top of that was the oppressive heat, the jungle rot and mildew of everything you touched, all overlaid by a smog of cordite that mingled smells of food and fish and fresh fecal matter that lay like a pall in the stagnant air.

He knew he'd better shape up his head and get back to work or he was going to end up on a funny farm. Without quite realizing it, he'd followed Curtis halfway out to the plane like some kid scared to leave his father. Almost like with Uncle Dennis, holding his hand, on a Chicago Sunday afternoon at the amusement park or zoo. Dennis on assignment with his Speed Graphic.

Nick roamed around Tan Son Nhut's commercial terminal deep in thought for some 10 or 15 minutes before he suddenly realized that he had been wandering, looking for he knew not what. When he came to, he stopped for a Turkish coffee and a ham sandwich on a French baguette at a food stand that also served up *pho*. He stopped at a newsstand and wondered at the array of languages on newspapers that all looked suspiciously stale, even if he couldn't translate them. He watched the businessmen and tourists come and go. It could have been Paris, or Indianapolis!

God, this country is weird, he thought, the way things just go on no matter what, kids still flying Tet kites when the city was under rocket attack, peasants working the rice paddies in the middle of a firefight. He wandered over to watch the commercial flights coming in. A Braniff plane with its brightly painted fuselage was parked over to his left. He watched civilian passengers deplaning from a blue and white Air Vietnam DC-4, businessmen with briefcases, fragile wispy women in their silk *ao dai* high-necked gowns and pantaloons. A strange sensation of *deja vu* came over him as a tall, willowy Vietnamese in a conical hat and black peasant pajamas that were too short stepped through the plane doorway and started down the metal stairs. Jesus, that glide, it was as though . . . his mind was playing tricks on him, this was the very gate where he'd first seen Angela. But it was no Vietnamese, nobody could walk like that. He'd never seen a Vietnamese man that tall, much less a woman. What the fuck was going on? Harry might be right, he thought, maybe he needed to be rotated back.

A mean breeze whipped those black pajamas and the woman put her left hand up to hold on to her big peasant's hat. She reached the bottom of the steps and started across the tarmac. It was her, it had to be! Nick couldn't move, he was rooted to the spot. Christ, he'd gone completely round the bend! He finally just stood there and started yelling her name, and he could feel all the little guys with white coats and butterfly nets start to make their moves. Instead, the pajama-clad figure stopped, looked in his direction, then arms flung wide started running toward him. It was her! It really was her!

She came running, or more kind of bouncing, as though she were moving over earth clods of a newly furrowed field on some sort of weird shoes of thick, black cloth. Her left arm was up, palm down on that crazy hat, holding it from sailing off in the wind. She was out of breath when she landed in Nick's arms.

"I've been worried crazy. Where the hell have you been?"

"With the Cong."

"Well, you're certainly dressed for it."

She started to laugh, and gave him the biggest hug he'd ever had, she nearly squeezed his breath away. And then he couldn't tell if she was laughing or crying. Some of both, maybe.

"Are you all right? Stop crying, let me look at you. What the hell have you got on your feet? They didn't hurt you?" He held her at arm's length, and she looked great, that goddamned hat had finally fallen on the ground. Her hair was kind of funny, sort of matted and kind of opaque, or something, sort of like seaweed. But otherwise she looked great, even the seaweed hair was OK.

"I'm fine, just sort of exhausted and hysterical."

"The Cong? What hap . . . ? Where's your camera?"

"Wait 'til you see 'em. They're right here," she held up some kind of bamboo satchel. "They let me keep my camera, and I've got rolls and rolls of shots in here."

"They let you take photographs? My God, Angela, where were you? Were you a prisoner? What were they up to? Why'd they let you take pictures?"

"I don't know. I just don't know what they were up to. Clearly, they figured they'd get some sort of propaganda coup by holding me and then letting me go. But I'm here and they didn't hurt me and I've got my film. I'll tell you all I know AFTER I've had the hottest bath in the whole world. Let's get out of here."

"The story of a lifetime and all you can think about is a bath!"

"You better believe it, kid."

"We'd better call Harry."

"There's no hurry. This one can hold. No one's got it but me."

## 32

## Selling the Story

FORD CURTIS didn't cross Nick's mind until they were well settled down and half drunk in the little front sitting room of Angela's hotel digs.

First things first, Nick ordered ice and a bottle while he waited for Angela to take her much-advertised bath.

As he stood, drink in hand, at the open Parisian-style window/door overlooking Assembly Square, mulling over the sparse details he'd so far dragged out of Angela about her capture, he marveled at the hominess of this room. With its desk and easy chairs in front, separated from the bedroom and bath by a teakwood bookcase divider, it was like a tiny little house. The divider shelves were filled with her amazingly eclectic assortment of musty, battered books, old pictures and odd colorful trinkets and bits of fabric. Most of the stuff looked like it had been collected from the nearby markets, or the stalls and tiny storefront shops that lined the streets around.

Black and white photographs of war were tacked to the creamy walls.

Gosh, Nick thought, I don't have much more than a portable typewriter.

So how was he going to pitch this thing to Harry? It all seemed strangely political. A good-looking woman spends 10 days with the Cong. Well, mostly with them, and short spurts with the fellows who captured her. They clearly were regular North Viet Army. They'd moved her around. They don't torture her, they don't rape her, they encourage her to talk to captured Americans, and they let her come out with pictures! Doesn't make much sense. No one's going to even believe this story, unless the pictures really hold up.

Unbelievably, they had made it to her room without anyone seeing them. The taxi took them to a delivery door of the hotel and they scooted up a back stairs. At that point they didn't want anyone quizzing her until they'd had a chance to sort out her stories, and figure how to break them and to whom she should sell. Her peasant garb made a great disguise. She'd insisted on that conical hat right up to the very end, she'd even worn it into the bathroom. It seems she knew her hair looked like seaweed and could hardly wait to wash it. Nick said he sure was glad to know that all those shampoo commercials advertising shiny, manageable hair for ladies weren't just a bunch of bull.

"They're true," Angela explained to him with a grin. "Plain old soap really does make your hair dull and straw-like. Especially the dinky pieces of lye-type shit I occasionally got from the Cong."

When he asked if she was going to make a big point of that in the piece she was planning to sell to either Look or Life, she glared at him. Nick burst out laughing. "You've been a prisoner of the Viet Cong for 10 days, and your main goddamn concern is your hair."

She finally emerged from the bathroom with the hair still wet and wrapped in a Carmen Miranda-type turban. She was wearing a thick, hotel-issue white terry cloth robe and white athletic socks.

"How are the feet?" Nick asked.

"Not bad. The blisters are starting to heal and turn to calluses. The soak in hot, hot water felt sooo good, you can't believe."

"OK, let's roll."

He handed her a glass with a little ice and a lot of Scotch, and a notebook and pen. "I got to get ahold of Harry soon. You got to give me a lead or a digest line, a few details so I'm prepped to tell him what to expect."

"Shit, Nick," Angela said with a frown, ignoring the offered notebook. "I don't quite know how to break this down. I have POW interviews to offer. As to what happened to me, there's no drama. No real story. I walked, then walked some more, then got up and walked again. My feet were like mushy cantaloupes. My biggest fear some days was that I might have to have my feet amputated. What's heroic or dramatic about being too embarrassed to take a pee and end up wetting your pants?

Or having a deathly fear of sunstroke? Yeah, sure, your heart's in your mouth. Who wouldn't be scared? But pretty soon it's your life. These guys who are marching you around are just guys. Some occasionally offer you a cigarette, some are pretty hard-nosed, a few menacing. But they're disciplined. They're well-indoctrinated with the party line. They're fighting for their cause, so they're not going to foul up and harm me when I'm high profile. Word had obviously moved up the line pretty fast that they had a two-headed prize: a journalist *and* a woman."

"The drama is in your getting out alive. You know that as well as I do," Nick replied. "An eyewitness to the Cong. That's the story. That and the grilling they kept giving you every time they could move you on to another English speaker."

"Yeah, you betcha. I'm their propaganda tool," Angela said, this time her frown turning to a grimace. She picked up her empty glass and stared at it for a moment, then put it back down on the little teak table between them. She reached behind her to retrieve the Scotch from the bookshelf, unscrewed its cap, and took a long swig from the bottle. She then picked up the empty glass with her other hand, placed it on the bookshelf, and firmly set the bottle down on the teak table.

Nick laughed. "Now we're getting down to business. Hey, whoa, what about Curtis? Maybe I should try to get a message to him while I'm out. The poor son-of-a-bitch is on his way to Hue to look for you."

She took the news with a lot less emotion than she'd shown for her seaweed hair.

"Jesus, Angela, what's wrong with you? The poor bastard is out there risking his job and his life looking for you and you're as cool as though I told you he went out for a pack of chewing gum."

"Ford's not risking his job. There's plenty to file on from Hue."

"What does he file if he gets dead?"

"Quit being melodramatic. You said he was supposed to go to Khe Sanh, so what's the difference?"

"The difference is, I guess, the guy's willing to make a fool out of himself over you."

"Nick, leave me alone about Ford." She reached for the Scotch bottle and took another swing.

"The poor sap's in love with you."

"I'm afraid there's no room in Ford's life for more than one war correspondent."

At that point, Nick gave up on Ford and tackled the subject of another winner on Angela's Hit Parade of Men—Harry the Arse.

"Him, you need," Nick said, standing up to go, hoping to leave no room for argument. "I'll buzz up to the post office and see if I can get a phone line through."

He got Harry—at home. After the foreign editor had cleared the sleep out of his ears, he was overjoyed. Really. This was one hell of a story. And it belonged to them alone. Angela had some fantastic pictures, or at least she thought she would, once she had a chance to develop them.

Harry suggested the best way for Angela to get maximum exposure was to let Life or Look magazine take their choice of the shots along with first rights to her eyewitness account. "Daily life," he said, "you know, the stuff about how to wash and take a shit is fine. Obviously done delicate, can't get too graphic. You sure gotta hint, a course, 'bout fear of rape. Delicate again, you know the drill." Harry was perfectly willing to take second choice of the photographs, since there would be plenty to choose from. Newspaper photos are so grainy anyway, it didn't make that much difference. But Harry planned to break the spot story of Angela's capture and safe return under Nick's byline. Harry even offered to call an acquaintance at Life to negotiate the sale.

The big problem was figuring out how to get the pictures through. Harry was worried that if they transmitted the shots through AP, which was the usual route, AP photo guys at transfer points along the line would see them.

"Embargoed exclusively for us," said Harry, "we aren't running any great risk that some other paper would actually use one, but we sure would be announcing the story to the world."

Harry and Nick had finally decided the safest route was for Nick to put the undeveloped film in a net bag tagged for delivery to a friend of Harry's in New York and put it on a commercial flight or one of the government-contract runs that Braniff and a couple of other airlines made regularly transporting GIs back and forth from the States and Okinawa. It would cost them a day that way, but since Angela was the only source of information for the story, they figured there was no way to lose it.

"The broad's golden," Harry said. "She's on her way now." He said he'd set up the deal with Life just as soon as dawn came up in New York.

"All you kids gotta do is get your butts to a couple a typewriters," Harry yelled, then hung up.

When Nick reported back, Angela was dressed and the red hair was restored to its buxom life. Her portable with a blank sheet of paper rolled in was open on the teak table beside the Scotch bottle.

"Looks like the Scotch has been getting a better workout than the typewriter," Nick quipped, as Angela leaned on the sill of her open balcony door staring out at National Assembly Square.

"Yeah, well tell me what Harry said," Angela said, barely turning toward Nick.

"I'm going to write the news story," he replied.

"What's that all about?" Angela demanded, turning to stare at him.

"Simple. Someone else breaking it spot means the wires and everyone else will pick up the story of your capture. That'll be great advance publicity for the magazine's weekly spread with your first-person account."

"Well, maybe..."

"No *maybe* about it. Harry knows what he's doing. Just sit down and get to work. Besides, you've got tons of stories—the American POW interviews, you name it. The magazine can take its pick there, too. You'll have plenty left over for later Sunday features for Harry, and still some to sell to a monthly mag."

Angela, in a defiant gesture, silently crossed her arms over her chest and leaned back against the sill.

"OK, babe, sit down," Nick ordered.

Startled, she picked up her portable, carried it over to her desk and sat. She turned the typewriter so that it faced Nick, who'd moved over to stand near her. She then looked up at him with the most forlorn look he had ever seen.

"God," she said. "My life depends on this. What if I can't do it?"

"Just put your fingers on the keys and tell us what happened," he said quietly.

She lit a cigarette, inhaled deeply, laid it down and began to type, not looking at the keyboard, never taking her eyes off of Nick's face.

"I was petrified when they first stopped the bus and came aboard. It seemed like they headed straight for me," she wrote. "I suppose I wasn't all that easy to miss, squeezed in the way I was among the farmers and their wares and chickens."

"Way to go," Nick said, as he sat down to finish his Scotch.

But when he finally pulled the last page of Angela's story out of her typewriter, he frowned.

"Looks good, but I dunno about this," he said, jabbing his finger at the page. "This line might give you trouble."

"Well, hell," she responded. "It's the truth. Whether it was a setup or not, I can't help it if the few American POWs I saw were getting humane treatment."

Nick didn't give Curtis a thought for days. He and Angela were buried in work. Everyone they knew and plenty they didn't were all interviewing her. The weekly newsmagazines, all the networks, the BBC, Der Spiegel, Le Monde, even Japanese TV. Angela was queen of the mountain for days.

Then one afternoon as they were bouncing along in a pedicab, returning from an interview at the Embassy, she said: "You know, I think maybe I'm ready to take on Curtis."

"Take on Ford Curtis! Lady, are you crazy?" Nick screeched. "If he's got a brain, he'd shoot you on sight. You leave him lurching around like a fool, don't even bother to make a call to let him know you're alive, haven't inquired once of anyone whether he's dead or alive in Khe Sanh or Hue. What are you going to take on, his ashes?"

"I heard yesterday he's in Khe Sanh, and was inquiring after me from someone who had just arrived. He was said to be extremely impressed when he heard about my POW interviews."

"Angela, no man's going to love you for your POW interviews. Whatever happened to apple pie?"

"I haven't a clue, love. The guy who told me also said he was coming back in the next few days."

## 33

# On the Hot Seat

IN THE midst of all the commotion over her release, Angela walked into her hotel lobby late one afternoon, and the desk clerk, with a nod of his head, indicated a U.S. staff sergeant in sharply pressed khakis seated among the potted palms. "He wait two hours," the clerk said.

When Angela introduced herself, the sergeant, Manly was his name, said: "I have a message for you, ma'am," and handed her a brief note. It requested that she come to the office of a Colonel Adams to make an appointment. That was it. No explanation, just an address in downtown Saigon. Sgt. Manly, a freckle-faced red head with a slight nasal wheeze, said he had no knowledge of what was in the note, so he couldn't explain what it meant.

The next day, in the nondescript office of a downtown building that seemed to house mostly import-export companies, a military clerk gave her an appointment a week hence. He was breezy about the procedure.

"No problem, ma'am," he said. "We always just like to talk to folks who've had a run-in with the Cong."

On the appointed day, Nick sounded equally nonchalant as he and Angela walked from her hotel, across Le Loi, over to what everyone still called the Old Rex Hotel, even though the U.S. had commandeered it years before. "Don't worry, it's routine," he said.

"How can you be sure?" she demanded.

"It just figures that they'll want to debrief anyone who got behind enemy lines. That Life magazine with your shot of the two Cong grinning on the cover sold out of the PX like lightning. I had a hell of a time getting ahold of a copy myself." He tapped the duffel he was carrying, indicating he had his stashed safely away.

"Have you got it? Let me see that." She stopped dead and held out her hand as they were weaving their way through the ever-clogged traffic. A pedicab and two motorcycles swerved to avoid hitting her, as passengers and drivers yelled abuse. A big black Mercedes came to a screeching halt.

Nick grabbed her by the elbow and pulled her across to the curb. "Jesus, what's wrong with you?" He unzipped his bag, fished around and handed her the magazine.

A budding smile of ownership spread slowly across her face as she held the magazine in her hands and stared at the familiar red and white logo across the top of a black and white photo. The shot was of two of Angela's Cong captors wearing wide grins, black headbands, and flip flops made from old rubber tires. One cradled an AK-47, the other held his with the stock resting on his bended knee, leg propped on a rock, the picture of a conquering hero. Angela's story began on the cover, and jumped to a three-page photo spread inside.

"Jeez, you've seen it before, haven't you?" Nick said, sounding perplexed.

"Yeah," she said with a laugh, but with the same beatific smile on her face, "but it's nice to see it again."

"Come on," Nick said, grabbing her arm, "you're going to be late for your appointment with the spooks."

"What do you think they want? Really," Angela asked, stopping again, and holding up sidewalk traffic this time.

"I don't know, Angela," Nick's tone was slightly exasperated. "But they're probably a little pissed that an American was with the Cong and they had to find out from a magazine."

A sentry at the Rex directed her to the appointed room, and she climbed the steps to the second floor. She cleared her name with a guard at the door, and knocked.

An Army officer wearing horn-rimmed glasses immediately opened the door, and waved her in. Clean cut, a bit nerdy, he was as tall as the top of her shoulder. The room was spare. A number of straight back metal chairs lined the walls, shades were drawn against the glaring noonday sun.

"Miss Martinellli. Thank you for coming in," said the officer whose hand was still on the doorknob. It looked like he'd had a manicure. "Won't you have a seat," he said, waving her to a metal chair placed in the middle of the room. "I'm Captain Jacobs."

He gestured behind him, nails flashing in the light. "This is Major Lewis and Colonel Matthews." Her eyes were adjusting to the dizzying first impact of sun glare coming through the shades, compounded by the flicker of fluorescence. She stared in the direction of his pointed arm. Two vague shapes materialized in a circle of chairs. Must be Marines, she decided, squinting, as she tried to make out their uniforms.

"And this is Sergeant Brandon." An enlisted man sat against the wall, out of the circle. Air Force. So, it's going to be an ecumenical occasion, she thought.

"He will take notes on our conversation," Jacobs continued, as Angela took her seat, "which we will also be recording. Do you have any statement before we begin?"

"No, sir," Angela said, placing her large shoulder bag on the floor at her feet. "I understand this is routine for anyone who was a POW."

"Well, right." Jacobs smile was tight. "But since you aren't military, Miss Martinelli, it's a bit difficult to think of you as," he paused and looked over at the major he had identified as Lewis, "a prisoner of war." The major closed his eyes briefly, and nodded his head slightly. A "yes" of approval, the nod seemed to be. Jacobs appeared to be relatively young, under 40, Angela guessed. His bearing was stiff, rigid, not the stance of command, but rather that of rectitude. The two other officers looked older and more relaxed.

"We appreciate your coming in on such short notice," said Jacobs. "But we only *recently* became aware that you spent some days with the Viet Cong. Or was it the NVA?"

"I believe it was both, sir," Angela replied, but wondered if that was a question she was expected to answer. The stenographer hadn't begun taking notes. Obviously these guys became *aware* that she had been with the enemy by reading her story, which made it clear the NVA had handed her over to the Cong. So, are they just pissed, or is this going to be like a court, where they'll try to trip me up?

"For the record, please," Jacobs nodded to the sergeant stenographer to begin, "state your full name."

"Angela Andrews Martinelli."

"Andrews is your middle name?"

"My family name."

"Then you should properly be addressed as *Mrs.* Martinelli?"

"I'm divorced, sir."

"Martinelli is still your legal name?"

"Yes, sir."

"You have described yourself as a journalist. Are you affiliated with any known news organization?"

"I freelance."

"You write for a number of publications?"

"Yes, sir. I have sold quite a lot to the Tribune newspaper based in Chicago."

"How did you come to spend time with the Viet Cong?"

"I was taken off a local bus somewhere between Phu Bai and Hue."

"Had you made arrangements ahead of time to be taken off?"

"Of course not." Her voice rose in anger, she sat up straighter in her chair. What the hell does that mean? she wondered.

Jacobs paused to read some notes in his hand, and Angela took the moment to look around the room now that her eyes were more adjusted to the light. One of the vague Marine forms in the center, seated in a leather swivel chair, was clearly the man Jacobs had ID'd as Colonel Matthews. His face and posture were more relaxed than the other two, his snow-white hair indicated he was probably a good 10 to 15 years older. Jacobs continued. "Well, now, the area around Hue was pretty dangerous territory at that time. How were you in a position to even find a local bus, if someone hadn't given you directions?"

"I knew Hue was only about 10 miles away. So I went out and stood at a bus stop with locals leaving the air base after their shift was over."

A low chuckle rose up from Colonel Matthews. "I would say you're mighty enterprising, Miss Martinelli. Did you ever think of joining the Marines?"

Angela smiled. "No, sir, can't say that I have." Was this the one who would be her ally? Even the North Viets seemed to know about the Good Cop, Bad Cop routine.

"We know you were questioned, Miss Martinelli," Matthews continued, "tell us about that."

"They would periodically show up, two NVA officers, and set up—out in the open—what felt like a military tribunal. They'd put me in front. The two would sit at a table, a beat-up old wooden table with wobbly legs. One was young and stern, wore round, John Lennon glasses. Even wore a pistol on his belt. I understand that was a sure sign of an officer. A pistol—similar to an American .45 caliber."

"It was the same two men all the time?" Jacobs asked.

"Yes," Angela replied. A picture popped up in her head of the Good Cop Viet interrogator. He could have been Uncle Ho, himself: benign, sweet smile, soft voice. But I better not say that *anybody* was nice. I've already raised enough hackles among the old farts in the press corps by saying I didn't see any POWs who had been mistreated. But nice or not, none of my captors ever seemed to believe that I was just out wandering around, looking to write down what I saw. They're going to kill me. That same nightmare over and over. If I don't sign this paper they're waving in my face, they're going to kill me. But strangely they never did threaten me with anything. They just kept acting like any reasonable person could see it was illogical that I just wanted to write what I saw.

"Did you see any other weapons that you could identify?" Jacobs asked.

"The men who took me off the bus had AK-47s. At one point I saw some men carrying B-40 rocket launchers."

"You seem to know a lot about weapons."

"It's part of my job, sir."

"My notes indicate you were on a manifest into Da Nang air base, but we don't seem to have any record of your movements from there." Jacobs paused, clearly waiting for an answer. Angela tried to keep the expectant look on her face, as though she were waiting for the question, even though its implication was clear. There was a long silence, no sound in the room other than the air conditioner, which emitted a slight whirr.

"Miss Martinelli?" Jacobs finally said, making it a question.

"Yes, sir?" Angela replied with a question mark of her own.

"It's well over a hundred miles from Da Nang to Phu Bai," Jacobs said, in a controlled voice that barely skirted impatience. "How did you get to Phu Bai? Another local bus?"

"Oh, no sir," Angela said. "I got a ride on a chopper."

"What kind of chopper?"

"I'm not sure, sir. It was Army, I think."

"Was it big or little, Miss Martinelli? You recognize the caliber of weapons. Surely you can tell one chopper from another."

"Absolutely, sir. But this was so quick, the weather was bad, I just hopped aboard, I was so happy to get a ride." This pimply faced prick would love to bust Mac Wheeler for giving her an unauthorized ride. No way, she thought.

"You can't tell us . . ."

Colonel Matthews interrupted, his voice friendly. It could have been a question from a history buff at a cocktail party. "I'm eager to hear more about your experiences with the Cong. Now just how did the NVA hand you over to them, and how could you be sure which was which?"

"The men who took me off the bus had stars on their collars, palm leaf helmets, and they wore shoes. Regular North Vietnam Army. After a day or so, they handed me over to Cong. They were in Ho Chi Minh sandals, had much more rag-tag uniforms. And they identified themselves as NLF, were very proud of it. People of the National Liberation Front, they would say." Yeah, a few said it, she thought, but not a lot. No one said much of anything to her that she could understand. That was part of the awfulness: the isolation, not understanding, not knowing. She was glad when the NVA came around. They had a translator with them. It meant endless questioning, but at least it was someone she could understand.

Colonel Matthews spoke again. "Please go on, Miss Martinelli. It's clear from your face that you are reliving painful memories, but this information is invaluable to us."

Angela was startled to be brought back to the present. "I'm sorry. I . . . the translator spoke impeccable English. I never did find out where he learned it. For those grilling sessions, they would gather round the table in the open, guys with rifles, squatting on the ground. Amazing how they could squat, could sit for hours in that position, with their feet flat, their rears just a few inches off the ground."

Major Lewis suddenly piped up with a question. Another country heard from. "Mrs. Martinelli, were you harmed in any way? *Any way* at all?"

"Not physically, no."

"By that can I assume you mean you suffered psychological damage?"

How should she respond to that? Yeah, it made me a nut case? I have constant nightmares? No, it was a walk in the park?

"I . . . ah, what can I say? It was stressful, frightening. I assumed they would kill me. Kept wondering each day, if that was the day. How would they do it? I hoped it would be a shot, not a knife."

"Do you have any idea just why you were released, unharmed?" Captain Jacobs, stepped back in. Were these guys competing with each other? An inter-service rivalry? Were they trying to throw her off balance, coming at her from different directions?

"No, sir. I don't."

"Can you make a guess?" Jacobs' tone was sarcastic.

"I've already speculated in print, sir. I suppose they had some propaganda purpose in mind."

"But you don't know what that was?" his voice was practically a sneer now. "Didn't you write that you saw no American POWs who had been mistreated?"

"That's right," her voice came out defiant; she tried to get it under control. Stay bland, but it wasn't easy. "I actually interviewed several," she said in a more modulated tone. "But they had all only recently been captured. Perhaps something bad would happen to them later. But I didn't *see* any who had been abused, sir."

"And you felt it necessary to write that?" Jacobs asked. His voice, at this point, was as level and bland as hers.

"Yes, sir. The question of *why* they released me was an obvious one. I had to address that question to the best of my ability."

"There's one question you didn't bother to address in your story here." Major Lewis, his voice sharp, brandished a rolled up copy of a magazine with a red logo. "That's where you got the money for your plane fare back from—Hanoi, was it? Or who dressed you in the black pajamas?"

"I was given what my captors referred to as *clean clothes,* sir, and taken by military truck and dropped off at the airport in Hanoi. There was a commercial airline ticket waiting in my name. It routed me through Phnom Penh, then back to Saigon."

The major put the magazine back down in his lap and turned and gave a hard stare to his colleague, the colonel. A slight shrug was Matthews' only response. A silence ensued, with no sound other than the air conditioner and the faint din of traffic that seeped though the sealed windows.

Angela shifted in her chair.

Captain Jacobs finally picked up the slack, and droned on with endless questions about weaponry, locations, food supply and how the Viet Cong traveled through the countryside. After four hours of questioning, Angela was finally dismissed. They all smiled and shook her hand.

"You're a mighty lucky lady," one said.

When she later replayed the grilling in her head, it was clear the main thrust was, "Why had the Cong let her go?" That question was on her mind, and everyone else's.

# 34

# Choices

BLACK OR white? The choice seemed to boil down to that. A black silk, or a white linen? She hadn't worn a dress in so long it was nice to have the luxury of such a minor dilemma.

She slipped the silk from the weird bamboo curlicue that passed for a hanger in these parts and opened the second door of her armoire/closet. She hadn't opened this door wide enough to view herself in its full-length mirror for a month or more. Right arm across her chest, she held the dress against her body to study the effect. The black looks hot, she thought, the white cooler, more demure. Cool is what I need, I think, to slow down what may be turning into a headlong rush.

Showered, legs shaved, makeup in place, and with an extra squirt of perfume, she started down the wide, carpeted stairs in her high heels and the crisp white dress.

There he was, Curtis, waiting in the lobby. He looks like he took as much care to dress as I did, she thought. Clean-shaven, no safari jacket, an expensive looking summer suit. As he watched her coming down the last few stairs, his smile lit up both their faces. She could feel her widening grin matching his.

The party hosts were friends, or more likely sources, of his. The first thing Angela noticed was that the house had air conditioning! The elegant woman who greeted them at the door appeared middle-aged, and her slightly lock-jaw speech bespoke New England. She quickly introduced Angela and Ford to the nearest couple (a bird colonel and his wife), her mauve taffeta skirt whispering against the intricate Persian carpet as she moved on. A waiter appeared to offer champagne.

"Nice to meet you," the colonel's wife stuck out her hand. It was square and firm and brown. No nail polish, a no-nonsense hand, surprising in this setting.

"Ah yes," said the colonel, looking at Angela with the light of recognition. "An interesting case."

"Case?" Angela replied, a questioning look on her face.

"Well, yes, of course, you were the woman who was captured. But perhaps I shouldn't be mentioning it. Is it classified?"

"Classified?" Ford looked from one to the other. "What are you talking about?"

"Well, now, there's John and Barbara," the colonel said to his wife, nodding his head toward a couple who had just entered. "We haven't seen them in ages. We must say hello. Nice to have met you," he said, as he took his wife by the elbow and steered her toward the new arrivals.

"What was that all about?" Ford turned a bewildered face to Angela.

She laughed. "I had a debriefing yesterday. Just a bunch of boys playing cloak and dagger."

"I love the moxie of your brave front," he said, smiling, brushing a stray wisp of hair from her cheek, "but are you sure it's not something we need to worry about?"

"They wanted to know what I'd seen, and I told them. Don't worry," Angela assured him, smiling inwardly at his concern, "I think it was fine."

"You certainly will let me know if there is anything I can do to help. I know most of these fellows, or at least their bosses."

"The debriefing experience should make a good follow-up story to my capture stuff," Angela said.

"Good idea," Ford replied. "I also think it would be smart to do a piece looking at the possibility of Giap's involvement in the siege at Khe Sanh. We're coming up, you know, on the anniversary of the French rout at Dien Bien Phu."

"That's your bag, Ford, not mine," Angela said with a laugh. "I'm not as hepped up as you are about that theory."

"I still think your capture put you in a position to write about it," Ford replied. "But let me hustle over to the bar and get us a real drink, then we can explore this more."

Angela smiled.

I don't want to explore it, she thought. It's a cockamamie theory.

She took the opportunity to look around the room. It was tastefully decorated with Asian art and furnishings. Its most striking feature was tomato-red walls. Silent waiters, dressed in black and white, glided about offering silver trays of canapés or fizzing glasses of champagne. A full bar was set up at one end of the room. The guests were standing, holding drinks, a few perched on small chairs of bright silk. A smattering of military, several older correspondents whom she had seen around, but didn't know. The rest of the 30 or so guests were unidentifiable, as far as she was concerned. Embassy employees? Expats? She had no idea. But they were all well turned out. Definitely a cut above those she'd encountered at that Halloween house party. God, that seemed a million years ago. Four months. A lifetime. The last time she'd worn a dress was the Embassy Christmas party. She'd been with Curtis that time, too. Wonderful to feel like a real person once in a while amid this chaos. He was going to be her anchor of normalcy, but she must be careful to see it only as that. He's got a wife back home, joyless marriage, to be sure, but that's not the biggest threat. The real danger was the undertow she felt in his presence, the way his smile lit up hers. But it could be a trap, she warned herself. Take your eye off the ball. Start trying to please someone else too much, and you will disappear. Again.

"Why the frown?" Ford asked, as he handed her a Scotch.

"Just pondering independence," she said with a smile.

"Independence? For the South Vietnamese?"

"No, me," she replied.

"Good Lord, you seem to have plenty of that."

Ford took her arm to steer her to another couple, and she instinctively squeezed that arm tight against her body, and rested her head for a second on his shoulder. The silk of his dark suit touched her cheek, and she turned with a smile to brush at any makeup that might have been left behind. In a fluid movement, he moved his eyes from her face to the couple he was introducing. She nodded, but didn't catch their names. She really should be writing the story about the debriefing. She had scribbled some notes when she first got back, but hadn't begun to write. She felt she needed some kind of interesting lead-in. She couldn't assume new readers had seen her old capture stories. She really should do it tonight. But she had a feeling she wouldn't. Was she falling down the rabbit hole?

"You're frowning again," Ford said. He turned to face her directly, backing her up slightly as he passed his arm over her shoulder to lean his palm flat against the bright red wall. "What are you pondering this time? I hope it's us. We make a very handsome couple, you know."

The gesture made the Christmas party flash in her head: His heavy breathing, as though he'd been running, the tingle in her toes. She leaned her head back, resting it against the wall, and watched his face, so close to hers. His features almost seemed to melt, they took on such softness as he looked at her. He's going to kiss me right here, in front of all these people, she thought. He almost did, they were nose to nose when he stopped himself.

"My God, let's not make a spectacle," he said, and gave a hearty, happy laugh.

A waiter came by offering more champagne, a couple Ford had known in Moscow stopped to chat, and the hostess dropped by to say in her clipped tones that she hadn't meant to neglect them and wasn't Saigon absolutely sweltering.

Shortly thereafter, Angela and Ford took a taxi to his place.

# 35

# Love Birds

NICK WAS heading up to the Givral to get some breakfast the following Sunday, when he spotted Angela and Curtis arm in arm, loaded down with packages and a pair of lovebirds in a bamboo birdcage. They both were eating ice cream cones as they poked along through the bazaar of a million antique, ordinary and bizarre items. It was the first time Nick had seen Angela in several days. She had landed some good assignments, so hadn't done anything for Harry in a while. It was a clear morning with a rare breeze off the river, and for once Saigon seemed bright and shiny, not overhung by the pall of incessant heat and cordite. But the glow may have emanated from those two. Angela was exuberant, bubbly. Curtis wasn't much less. They really seemed happy together, Nick thought, and tried not to think much more about it than that. He didn't understand this kind of stuff, so why bother? They spotted him, and despite his objections, had insisted they all go for a late brunch together.

By the time the three of them were nearing the top of Nguyen Hue street, Angela had acquired a jade bracelet, a sea green silk *ao dai*, a black lacquered fan, and three story ideas. Curtis said the jade colors were "smashing" with her green eyes and auburn-red hair. Nick realized with a start he'd never even noticed before that her eyes were green, and her hair always seemed pinned up under her combat cap or a helmet, except for that time when he'd noticed it looked like seaweed.

He wouldn't have given it much thought even now, except that he saw the way her face lit up when Curtis made the remark. She seemed to glow as though a bulb had been turned on underneath her skin. Curtis seemed to have a way with everybody, Nick thought, not just generals and presidents. It flitted across his mind that he should think of clever things like that to say, but he wasn't big on noticing hair colors and stuff. He just noticed when he liked it—or maybe when he didn't. Mary Alice Moriarty, she was definitely a blonde, he was almost sure of that. Maybe blondes somehow stuck out more. But, here, walking up Nguyen Hue, he had trouble conjuring up Mary Alice's face. And her eye color, forget it.

He certainly had no trouble conjuring Angela, her face, her walk, her vibrance, so what the hell difference did the color of her eyes make? Details are important to a reporter, you have to notice them. But that's different. When you're working, you make a point to look because you're going to have to write it down to convey an impression to a reader. He consoled himself with the thought that at least he remembered to say nice things to Angela about her work, and that he knew more about it than Curtis did.

When the trio got to the end of the street stalls of clothes and food and trinkets and gems and black-market U.S. cameras and weapons and electronic equipment spilling into the boulevard from under the brightly colored sidewalk awnings and umbrellas, they did a quick turn through the stores inside the Passage Eden.

It was there Curtis bought Angela the black satin nightgown. Jesus, Nick felt embarrassed. It seemed as though Curtis was going out of his way to look for things to buy her, as though she didn't have her own money or something. They had barely settled into a booth at the Givral for brunch when Curtis started telling Nick with obvious pride about the story ideas Angela had come up with before they ran into him.

"She sees stories in all these people. A million wire pieces have been done on the open black-marketing of U.S. equipment and weapons, but she talked one of the Vietnamese merchants into letting her spend a day with him and tracing the route the stuff takes, from PX, or wherever, to his sidewalk stall."

"How the hell did you talk him into that?" Nick asked, startled, putting his orange juice glass down with a bang. "The guy could be setting himself up for arrest."

"Of course I promised no names, including no names of GI suppliers. Beyond that, I guess I just . . ."

Curtis laughed, and broke in. "Beyond that, she appealed to his ego, implying he had the genius of Thomas Edison and the ingenuity of Henry Ford to be such a brilliant businessman. She wants the world to read about his savvy entrepreneurship. She's a clever lady. It's hard to pinpoint quite how she does it. And it's good to see her finding stories in town, don't you think?"

So much for Nick's having a lock on compliments about her work! He chomped down on his tough-crusted French bread with a vengeance, biting the inside of his mouth for his trouble. If anyone had asked Nick at that moment, he would have said that Curtis was every bit as clever as she. Although he wondered how long this "in town" shit was going to last.

Curtis had another special route to Angela's heart. It had to do with General Giap and Curtis' Dien Bien Phu theory that the 1954 French rout was going to be duplicated in Khe Sanh. Curtis had decided that Angela possessed some special insights on Giap. She not only had been with the Cong, but had been interrogated by some soldiers who were clearly North Vietnamese regulars and even more clearly had purposely released her to get some message back to the West that none of the correspondents had yet discerned. Curtis was hoping she could resolve the question of whether Giap was directing the assault at Khe Sanh.

Since Giap was North Vietnam's defense minister, it seemed pretty silly to Nick to be worrying whether or not Giap was personally directing the I Corps assaults—his hand was certainly in there one way or another. But lots of the columnists were continually debating among themselves and writing thumbsuckers on the fine points of the fall of Dien Bien Phu, drawing elaborate analogies between that and Khe Sanh.

Anyway, Angela seemed to Nick to be happy with Curtis taking her seriously and treating her like an expert on The North Vietnamese Mentality.

# 36

# Bosom Buddies

LATER THAT week, Nick ran into Curtis at Saigon's Tan Son Nhut Airport.

They had spotted each other and nodded hello before taking seats among the folding chairs in the corner of the big hangar where they waited for their assignments for military transport. As usual, the place was a mess with the debris of eat-drink-and-read-on-the-run reporters, but Nick salvaged the sports section from a two-day-old paper he hadn't read.

He was engrossed in it, when Curtis moved over into the seat next to him, which had just been vacated by someone whose flight was called.

"Where you headed?" Curtis asked.

"Americal Division HQ," Nick replied. "Planning to go out with a few patrols."

"Sounds good," said Curtis. "I'm headed the same place. Got an interview scheduled with the commanding general. See if he can give me some heads up on why Westmoreland doesn't see that Khe Sanh is a setup by General Giap. You know, don't you, that we're heading right into the anniversary of Dien Bien Phu?"

"Yeah, I've heard your theory on all that," said Nick. "That Giap is sucking in the Marines for the same April disaster he fed the French."

"Not just *my* theory," said Curtis. "Lots of people see it coming."

"So I've heard," said Nick, trying to return to his paper.

But Curtis wasn't to be deterred. He expounded at some length on what he saw as the tell-tale signs that Khe Sanh was disaster waiting to happen. Nick got the distinct feeling that New York newspaper readers also were going to get a strong dose of the Dien Bien Phu thesis the next day with their morning coffee.

It's funny, Nick thought, how a reporter almost always can guess what another has just finished a piece on. A guy who hasn't started to write a particular story will say just that and be hesitant and exploratory in discussing it. But if he's just finished writing, he'll deliver a monologue on the subject as though all these thoughts had just come to him. When you pick up the paper the next day, there's the speech you heard the night before. Nick's antenna told him he was getting a Curtis pre-publication monologue.

"Angela has handled herself amazingly well with this whole capture business, don't you think?" Curtis suddenly said in mid-sentence of a long rendition on Giap.

"Yeah."

"She worries me, though, she doesn't seem to be afraid of anything."

"I dunno. Doesn't do much good to worry about things like that."

"Who? Me or Angela?" He laughed nervously, as though he were embarrassed by trying to pin Nick down.

"Both. She couldn't go into combat situations if she thought too much about the danger. You worry too much about the risks of loving someone like her, and you're gonna be in trouble."

Curtis cleared his throat and fumbled with his tobacco pouch.

"Well, actually, Nick, you were an enormous help to her. And very generous, I think."

"Generous?"

"A lot of reporters wouldn't go out of their way to make a competitor look good."

"Angela's not exactly a competitor, Ford. She works as a stringer for my own paper."

"Yes," said Curtis, "but thanks to you."

"She saved my butt during Tet," Nick retorted, frowning and shaking his head at Curtis as though the older man were stupid.

"You can turn it aside as much as you want, Nick, but you've been good to her, and I know it. And I want you to know that."

"I like her." Nick shrugged. "She's a good reporter."

"Are you in love with her?"

"Jesus, Ford!" Nick was so startled he dropped his newspaper he'd been trying to get back to.

"Sorry, I didn't mean to embarrass you, but, ah . . ."

"Yeah?" Nick demanded. "But what?"

"I really like you, Nick. You're a fine young man."

"So what are you trying to tell me, Curtis?"

He didn't respond.

"Are you trying to say that Angela prefers you to me? Jeez, you really are old-fashioned. You're trying to do the honorable thing!"

"Maybe something like that," Curtis said slowly, frowning as though he were pondering Nick's comment. "I'm also not inclined to fly by the seat of my pants. I have a penchant for clarity."

"Or maybe you're just trying to fuck me over," Nick snapped. "To get me to stay away from her. Angela and I are friends, and you better not try to mess with that.

"You want to know something else, Curtis?" Nick went on, building up a head of Irish steam. "You and I can't sit here, looking for a hop to Chu Lai, and divvy Angela up, or decide her future. You ought a just let things be, take them as they come."

Curtis didn't say anything for a long time, he just puffed his pipe. Finally, with a rather shaky grin, he said: "Well, what do you think of my theory about Westmoreland?"

Nick laughed, relieved. But he was even happier, shortly thereafter, when their flight was called, breaking into the new silence between them.

In the milling and shoving of boarding, Nick got the feeling again that Curtis made a point of taking the web seat next to him. But with the noise of the chopper, there was little opportunity to talk. When Nick pulled out his newspaper again and tried to focus on it, he found his mind wandering to Curtis and just what he was up to. Ah shit, he thought, all this emotional stuff isn't my bag. The hell with it. Things are just what they are. He didn't like thinking about feelings and crap like that. As they skimmed over the treetops of the countryside below, he stared out the chopper window, looking for distraction. He found it, at least momentarily, and chuckled as he watched a grunt with a pack and an M-16 peeing in an already gummy-looking rice paddy. So much for our helping the Viets improve their food supply, he thought.

As they began their descent, Curtis leaned over and shouted: "While we're here, maybe we can have a beer and talk some more. I'm interested in your take on how to cover what you call 'this different kind of war.'"

"Sure," Nick yelled back.

They deplaned into the noisy, chaotic atmosphere of the Da Nang field, where every manner of bomber, chopper and supply ship was taking off and landing.

Curtis grinned and shook Nick's hand in the dusty rotor wake of a little Huey taking off. "I appreciate the advice," he said. "But don't be overly solemn about your advisory role. I can't stay humble for too long, or I'd never be able to write another line."

Nick laughed. "I'm not too hot at the Ann Landers stuff. The 'different kind of war,' I can handle."

Curtis put a conspiratorial arm around Nick's shoulder. "We all feed off our own arrogance, don't we? If we didn't have that, we'd never have the gall to write down the first word."

"Yeah, I guess so," Nick said. "I never thought about it."

"And speaking from that arrogance," Curtis continued, "I don't mind telling you, Nick, the reason I'm able to hang on to the position I've attained is that *I am* able to listen." He grinned, again. "At least, like the proverbial mule, once someone has succeeded in getting my attention by hitting me between the eyes with a two-by-four."

# 37

# Chopper Down

For the purposes of war, the long skinny country of South Vietnam was divided into four military regions. I Corps was at the top, the five northern provinces. Da Nang was I Corps' approximate halfway mark down the coast. A vast U.S. military sprawl had grown up around that city; the headquarters of the giant Americal Division was in nearby Chu Lai. The cities of Phu Bai and Hue and the coastal resort of Hoi An were also in I Corps, as were the inland fierce battle sites of Khe Sanh, Quang Tri and the A Shau Valley.

Curtis and Nick spent several days with separate field units operating on the perimeters of the combat center sprawled along the South China Sea at Chu Lai.

They were a fine few days for Nick. He had the incredible good luck of going out on a search-and-destroy mission with a squad of 13 men that contained not one, but two guys from Chicago. That gave him what editors always want, what they call "the local angle." On the fourth day, when Nick got back to his digs at the BOQ that was set aside for visiting press, Curtis had left him a note saying Angela had shown up that morning. She was trying to make her way to a "pacified" village in the vicinity, so Curtis had talked the post commander into giving her a hop on a resupply chopper heading in that direction. It would make a special touch-down to let her off. Curtis had decided to tag along, the note said, and apologized for missing the bar date he and Nick had set for that evening.

Nick decided to tag along, too. He knew it was an impetuous thing to do, but what the hell.

He flagged a Jeep driver who was dropping off a visiting officer, and cajoled him into giving him a ride back to the transport section he had just left. Nick figured he might be able to get some kind of hop, even though it was getting late in the day.

But when he made inquiries about getting his own special touch-down arrangements, he was told a pitched battle was raging in the village where Angela and Curtis had been headed.

"That chopper your pals were on crashed right after it dumped them off," the lading sergeant told Nick.

"What the hell happened?" Nick demanded. "Curtis' note said it was a pacified village."

"Shit, you know how much you can depend on that kind of info. Pacified one day, Cong in there the next," the sergeant replied.

"Yeah, probably stupid Curtis relying on CIA handouts," Nick said. "Holy crap," he muttered to no one in particular. "I bet he's been talking to that goddammed Kevin."

That sleaze-ball CIA spook, Nick thought. Bills himself as an "agriculture attaché." Kevin was notorious among reporters for issuing mimeographed lists of so-called pacified villages that either didn't exist at all or were sure as hell not pacified. Nick had tried to warn Curtis that hanging out with Embassy types was nothing but trouble. And if there was one area for sure where official sources rarely jibed with what you could see with you own eyes, it was the pacification program.

"So what the hell happened?" Nick demanded again of the sergeant, nearly shouting this time.

"Calm down, fellow, how the fuck should I know? Damned reporters. Made a special touch-down to drop 'em off, and all hell broke loose. Small arms maybe took the Chinook down."

"Jesus, they're down there? In the middle of a firefight?" Nick demanded.

"All I know is pilot radioed before the crash. Two gunships and a rescue dustoff all trying to get in under heavy fire to pick up whoever's left."

"Anyone alive? Can they see?" Nick asked, his voice suddenly low and constricted.

"Reported seeing three, carries a crew of five," the sergeant said.

# 38

# The Cong in a Palm Tree

FORD AND Angela had been poised to move as the Chinook's runners touched down in the red soil. She scooted down the lowered ramp of the open tail section a second ahead of him, but in that instant Ford noticed her jungle boots were caked red like a foot soldier's. Nick was right, there are two ways to cover this war: from the smoke-filled rooms or from the rice paddies, but it is almost impossible to keep a foot in both worlds.

The politicians can't stop you from writing what you see, thank God for that, but your own goddamned editors can, Ford thought. If you are going to battle New York, you need to be in the field with the grunts, REALLY know what you're talking about and forget the damn dinner parties at the ambassador's house.

As Ford stepped off the ramp under the blast of the chopper's rotors, his boots squished in the soggy ground, the oppressive, moist air weighing down, the sweatband in his helmet already sticking to his hair.

Christ, Ford thought, I've spent years developing my ability to synthesize, to hone in on the larger issues. There are a million Young Turks clawing their way through their city rooms to get assigned here, to cover one battle after another. One battle that is the same as the next; only the names of the dead change to protect the generals from running out of cannon fodder. Assigned, hell! That wonderful, vital, gutsy woman running in a crouch in front of me, her boots caked with the red clay of a veteran who instinctively moves in a defensive zigzag even in a safe zone, a pacified village.

The rotor-driven wind tunnel suddenly and violently changed directions. It was like running into a wall of dust and rock particles at 60 miles per hour, and it kept wildly reversing itself at high speed. Ford couldn't move. He was being beaten back and forth in place by a swirling, changing funnel of dust. He could barely see what he thought was Angela ahead, like a shimmering mirage in the red clouds.

Behind him, the door gunner's weapon began an incessant rat-a-tat-tat as it methodically swirled in a wide spraying arc of fire that encircled him. He could feel the thuds under his feet as the rounds riddled the ground just behind him, he could hear their whistle as they tattooed the swirling dust around him. He was being shot at by the chopper he had just left! Was there enemy fire ahead of him? He didn't sense any.

Even after he heard the Chinook crash, stilling the twisting and vibrating of its disabled rotors, the rat-a-tat went on as though the machine gun were jammed, the gunner's fingers frozen to his trigger.

"My God, Kevin," Ford said as he looked over his shoulder at the wreckage, and the rat-a-tat-tat finally stopped. When he turned back, Angela was zigzagging ahead of him toward a clump of trees, her left hand up, holding on to her helmet as she scrambled through the underbrush and muck.

A grenade exploded to Ford's left as he ran, and to his right he saw a figure in black headband fall from a palm tree, still clutching a rifle.

Angela was breathing in deep gulps as Ford reached her, huddled, doubled over behind the clump of bamboo stalks.

"Jesus, Angie, are you all right? You haven't been hit, have you?"

"Stomach cramps. What the hell happened?"

"Small arms took it down, I guess," Ford said. "I haven't heard anything big. Are you sure you're all right?"

"I can see a couple of the crew over there," Angela said, pointing, still gasping for breath. "One of them picked off the dude from the tree. Hard to believe he could take down that gunship with a rifle."

"It's quiet now," Ford said. "Looks like there were only a couple of them around."

"Yeah," Angela said in a snide tone. "So this fits your idea of pacified?"

"That sonofabitch Kevin," Ford snarled.

"What the fuck has Kevin got to do with this?" she snapped.

# 39

# Colonel Andre Demurs

FORD CURTIS shoved and beat his way through the mass of kid-faced GIs, drunk and spilling drinks, hanging over the Hendrix-blaring jukebox or drooling down the nearly nude bosom of one of the Princess Club girls. Towering over the crowd, Curtis could see that Colonel John Andre had gotten there ahead of him, but not by much. He was still three deep from the bar, although he'd somehow managed to get a beer.

The correspondent's rage was such that it was all he could do to keep from punching out some of the innocents blocking his path. He had called and insisted on this appointment with Andre the minute he and Angela had landed at Tan Son Nhut. They had spent the previous night at the BOQ in Chu Lai after hours of waiting for a rescue chopper to get them and the surviving crew members out of their "pacified" village. Two crew dead, the other three wounded. If he and Angela hadn't been there to apply a tourniquet and the most basic of first aid, the injured pilot probably would have died before help came. How in the devil could a rifle take down a Chinook?

"What the hell is going on?" Curtis stormed, as he finally reached Andre. "This Kevin kid, an aide at the Embassy, gives me the names of pacified villages and I'm damned near killed trying to land in one. Obviously, my hide is no more expendable than any other grunt's, but what kind of intelligence is this? On the part of the Embassy? The Army? Do any of these assholes have ANY idea at all what they're doing?"

"Ford, I'm not in any position to comment," Andre replied stiffly. "I agreed to meet you because you're a friend."

"I understand. I'm not trying to put you on the spot. But I can't believe what I'm seeing."

"No comment."

"My God, John, you're a pretty straight shooter. If that's all you can say, I suspect it means things are even worse than I thought."

"No comment."

"Christ! I never thought I'd see this day. I'm going to end up lumped in and bundled up with the peaceniks and the Young Turks. What a hell of a note."

"What a hell of a note, indeed," Andre said as he finished his beer in a gulp.

"Let's get out of this dive," Curtis yelled, bending way down to reach the ear of the diminutive Andre. "I need a drink and I'll never get near the bartender. I only suggested this joint because I figured there was no chance of our being seen or overheard."

"I didn't *say* anything to you, Braeford."

"I know you didn't, Colonel. Your silence tells me more than I ever wanted to know. I've got some heavy restructuring to do in my thinking."

Andre gave Ford a quizzical look, them seemed to smile, almost to himself.

They left behind The Animals and "We Got to Get Out of This Place," only to trade the bar and its din for the unending clatter of the streets. As they made their way down the Tu Do headed for the quieter Juliette bar downstairs at the Caravelle, Ford had the sudden premonition that in years to come, when he would think back on this chaotic time, his strongest memory would be his yearning for quiet. Peace goes with quiet and this country would never find it. Ford would find some future serenity, he felt sure of that, even if he was temporarily confounded by this strange war and an uncertainty he had never before experienced in his personal life. The strength of his writing was his ability to cut through disorder and find coherence, and that was his personal strength as well. But he also knew with an eerie, icy certainty that for this impoverished, pathetic country, there would be no calm, no peace. And probably not for many of these young correspondents, either, who were frantic, intense, getting torn up. He *must* find a way to protect Angela from that.

"We've given this country a legacy of chaos, haven't we, John?" he said to Colonel Andre.

"Don't be so dramatic, Ford," the Army man replied with a laugh. "Keep in mind that the French were here before us, and before that, the Chinese. And even the Japanese squeezed themselves in for a while."

Ford laughed. "You're right, as usual. The American myopia."

And as they walked along, Ford saw her—intense, frowning, leaning across a table at the Pagode café, engrossed in a conversation with Nick. Those two are amazing, he thought, the way they can share their work, trading notes, story ideas, sometimes even sharing the writing. He realized they must have been on to something, or they wouldn't be in that sleazy little place where only the occasional Vietnamese journalist showed up. Ford had instinctively been operating on the premise that it would be wise to stay on the good side of Nick, but this scene reinforced that notion in spades. But, what about my marriage, he thought? What about Berenice? We have a good marriage. At least I had assumed so until recently. Angela is causing me to lose all sense of perspective. *Angela is causing,* that's a ridiculous way to think. What am *I* doing to myself? Running off like a crazy person to Hue, thinking I could find her. Am I totally, hopelessly falling in love with her? Or is this just some kind of overreaction to the fact that Berenice refused to come to Saigon?

A zigzagging motor scooter broke into his reverie.

"Watch it, fellow." Andre grabbed his elbow as they were dodging traffic, trying to cross the square between the Continental and the Caravelle.

Ford looked to his left at the broad steps up to the National Assembly, an exquisite white Rocco. Berenice would have loved that building, he thought. After 27 years he certainly knew her likes and dislikes. But was his marriage no more than that, predictability? Apparently not! The memory came back with a jolt. He'd certainly been blindsided when she suddenly announced she wasn't coming to Saigon.

He'd taken a cab from their home in Boston to Ford Four's dorm. Funny, he'd gone to his son, not his daughter. Why? It hadn't been a conscious choice. He supposed he'd simply expected more understanding. But it was clear over dinner with his son that while he was trying to go easy on his old dad, he really was on Berenice's side. But what the hell could you expect from a kid who claimed to be a flower child while driving a $10,000 Corvette at Harvard, his tuition paid by his parents?

"Let Mom do her own thing," was precisely the way Four had put it. Her own thing. Good heavens, hadn't she always! He'd fought his own stuffy Brahmin parents like crazy when he'd announced before he'd even graduated from Harvard himself that he was marrying his French tutor who was Jewish and whose father was a Talmud scholar to boot!

She was a foreigner, she had dark hair and eyes. Although she was less than a year older than he, she was two years ahead of him in school—already had her master's degree. And now his wife and his son and Angela were all accusing him of having misogynist tendencies. How absurd! He clearly gravitated toward brilliant, independent women.

In the early days of their marriage, when they couldn't afford both a nurse and a housekeeper, he had not only spelled Berenice with the children if she had an important class to attend, but he had actually changed diapers! By God, he was the only man in their set who babysat, and he certainly was the only one with a wife who had a PhD in anything, much less Byzantine history. And when he started getting foreign assignments, he took his family with him. His kids had been to Moscow, London, Paris, Cairo. And they'd had a fine home each place, none of this living on booze and cigarettes and canned beans like a lot of correspondents. Berenice had gone out of her way to make a comfortable life for him.

"Earth to Ford," Andre said waving and snapping his fingers in Ford's face. "You seem off in another world."

"Sorry, I guess I was. The noise around here is so intense it rather causes one to withdraw, doesn't it? Let's find a seat in here and have a drink," he said as they entered the Caravelle lobby.

They settled in at a small round table in the posh, quiet bar with its mirrors and thick carpets, its expensive drinks.

"I'm glad you're here, Ford," Andre said after they had ordered. "Most of the journalists of your stature bop in for four days, talk to two or three generals, then go back to the States and pontificate."

"This place doesn't lack for reporters, John," Ford said with a wry laugh.

"Yeah. But we've talked about this before. A lot of them appear to be nothing more than tourists looking for cheap thrills. Or Neanderthals."

"Neanderthals?" Ford didn't quite laugh, it was almost a grunt, a harrumph, that seemed to emanate from his belly. "That's about the way I feel. There seem to be no rules or code of conduct for anything anymore. People marching in the streets back home, the government here is corrupt, not sure if we can believe our own . . . or our military. And yet the press is facing the accusation that it's unpatriotic to attempt to describe the chaos."

"You seem to have a pretty good handle on what's happening. I was thinking more of a guy like Smitty," Andre said with a grin, referring to the Old China Hand he and Ford had run into at the Rex officers' club a few weeks ago.

"He's out of it. He doesn't at all get what's going on. He's still in the Cold War mentality of seeing a Commie under every bed."

"Yeah," Ford said with a frown, chewing his pipe. "I've picked up some vibes that he and several of his cronies have been asking questions about Angela's politics since her capture."

"I'm ashamed to say, some of the Army brass are asking as well." Andre leaned over to the next table, picking up an ashtray and matches, since Ford was knocking his pipe into the one on theirs. "But you gotta know there's always going to be insinuations about a woman under those circumstances."

"Insinuations?" Ford bellowed, as several startled customers looked over and stared.

"Take it easy, fella," Andre said with a laugh, putting his hand on Ford's arm and patting as though he were trying to steady a wayward horse. "Sorry. That was a crude way for me to put it. You've got to realize Angela is suddenly pretty high profile." He shook a cigarette from the pack he had placed on the table and lit up.

"My understanding was she'd had a thorough debriefing. Surely that cleared up any questions?" Ford's tone was almost plaintive, his frown that of a protective father.

"So far as I know, it did." Andre said. "People just like to gossip. It relieves the tension."

"Of course," Ford said, calming down. "But her hanging out with all these sort of Beatnik types doesn't help."

"You can say what you want about the kids," Andre shot back, "but they've got the rhythm, the feel of what's happening here. Guys in your league generally don't stay. If they do, their disillusionment with what they see is recorded with the thunder of a whale rolling over."

"Are you trying to tell me we can't win this war?" Ford said, so startled he stopped and took his ever-present pipe from his mouth so he wouldn't choke on the smoke.

"I'm not telling you any such thing. That's not up to me to even *know,* much less *tell.* I'm telling you the old rules don't apply here—for soldiers or for journalists. I don't know what the answers are, but the *questions* have got to be different."

# 40

# Chopper Theory

"That chopper wasn't shot down," Angela said to Nick, her shortness of breath betraying her excitement before they'd even had a chance to settle themselves into the worn black plastic chairs at the Pagode. "There was no heavy artillery coming at it."

"What the hell are you talking about?" Nick asked, impatience in his voice, as he turned and signaled the waiter with two fingers for two cups of coffee.

"It crashed. It wasn't shot down. It was just little pings of small arms," she said, struggling to keep her voice low and to control the hyperventilating that dogged her, marked her in her own eyes as too emotional for her job. "Those things are as big as a house, and armor-plated. You can't bring them down with a rifle."

"Did you mention this to Ford?"

"No."

"Why not?" Nick demanded. She could hear his impatience again. He was still upset and angry because she'd almost gotten killed. Or more likely, because she'd been with Ford when it happened. "Shit," he'd said, when she'd gone looking for him this afternoon as soon as they were back from Chu Lai, "nice to know you're still alive. I hung around there for hours till I knew you'd gotten out. Your hotshot boyfriend sure knows how to pick 'em."

"Quit being angry with me for almost dying. I . . ."

The elderly Chinese waiter interrupted, setting down two cups of coffee, two spoons, cream, he made quite a ritual. "Thing more?" he asked.

"Yeah," said Nick. "Give me a shot of that whiskey you keep stashed behind the bar." The waiter shuffled off.

"I don't know why I didn't tell him," Angela said. "I just didn't. We're already starting to squabble a bit about my work. And he was the one who got us there in the first place with that stupid Kevin telling him I should see pacification at first-hand instead of running around writing 'peacenik' stories. Peacenik, shit. Like how understaffed our field hospitals are?"

"OK, OK. Get off Kevin and get on with it." He put the urgency of his words to Angela into a hurry-up motion directed at the waiter, "Where's that drink?"

Then turning back to Angela, he picked up his thread. "You said Ford got an up-close dose of what disinformation is all about."

"Did he ever. He was in a rage with Bob Komer and Kevin. He acted like they personally were trying to get me dismembered. He couldn't seem to decide which was worse, the thought of some disfigurement to my gorgeous body or to the First Amendment."

"Which won the race?"

"Probably my gorgeous bod. We know which of their heads ultimately rule men, don't we, sweetie?"

"Jesus, you can be crude," Nick said, shaking his head, and pouring a shot into his coffee cup from the bottle the waiter had placed on the table.

"Just realistic, to quote you," she replied with a grin. "Angela with a black eye-patch or a stump below the knee would definitely lose some of her adornment value."

"Adornment value? You're sick!"

He held out the whiskey bottle. "Want a taste?"

When she shook her head, he said, "Then just get on with the chopper story."

"There's another part. Remember Mac Wheeler, the pilot who took me from Da Nang to Phu Bai?"

"No," Nick replied, with more sarcasm in his voice. "I don't remember Mac Wheeler. You never bothered to tell me much more about your capture than what you wrote for Life magazine."

"Well, Mac bought me a hamburger in the officers club before he took me out to my infamous bus ride that landed me in the soup instead of in Hue. There were several other pilots sitting with us and one of them was bitching about those Chinooks. Something wrong with them. The other pilots shushed him, but I think it was only because I was there. It clearly wasn't a new topic for any of them, but they didn't want him talking about it in front of me."

"Maybe their small heads just wanted to talk to you—they didn't want to bother talking shop," Nick said, not letting go of his sarcastic tone.

"Now who's crude? Will you please calm down and listen? I may really be on to something big here. I'm talking about a major mechanical fault with the Chinooks."

"Every time you turn around, there's another man hanging over you."

"You knew it wasn't a woman who helped me out after that damned lading sergeant wouldn't let me on a flight, even though he was finding space for male correspondents as fast as they showed up. The chopper jock was from Texas, he was good looking, six-foot six and his name was Mac Wheeler. Anything else you want to know?"

"Speaking of boyfriends," Nick said, nodding with a slight move of his head toward the sidewalk, "here comes Ford down the street with that scrawny chicken colonel."

"Who is he?" Angela asked.

"Name's Andre. Most of the guys say he's pretty dependable as a source."

"Could he help with this?"

"Get real," growled Nick. "The military's not going to admit they're crashing their own choppers."

"I think that's what they're doing. I think the blades of the fore and aft rotors banged into each other!"

Nick just blinked at her, stunned, as though he hadn't heard.

"Are you sure?" he finally asked.

"No, of course not, you idiot. How could I be sure? I just think it. But I've been going over and over that crash in my mind. The chopper was lifting off fine behind us as we were running away from it. Then there was an enormous thud and it suddenly went crazy."

"Yeah, but anything could have hit it," Nick said skeptically, even though he slowly took a pen and notebook out of his breast pocket.

"You're right. But I don't think anything did. It didn't act that way. I've kept trying to remember what it sounded like. Those two overhead rotors whirl at some gigantic speed. It'd probably be worse than two cars crashing head on at a hundred miles an hour, or something."

"That's one hell of a story, if it's true," Nick said. "But you could never prove it."

"Not with Mac Wheeler, that's for sure. He was singing that old World War II song, 'Praise the Lord, we're on a mighty mission' when we were flying into Phu Bai. He believes in his mission, Nick, but his friend didn't. The guy wanted to tell me something was wrong, but the others wouldn't let him. He was a gentle guy with a milky white complexion and a perpetual sunburn, a sweet smile. He just wasn't a cowboy like his pals. It was hard to think of him as a chopper jock."

"What did he say?"

"Something like, 'Just because they said they fixed the '47's pylons doesn't mean they did. The rotor gear boxes are still fucked up.'"

"Goddamned cowboys," Nick said softly. "They'd rather get killed than admit anything's wrong with this war."

# 41

# Late for Dinner

IT WAS at about this time that the gossip revved up a notch about Angela and Curtis. He had one of those colonial pastel villas out on Cong Ly, and word started sifting down to some of the correspondents that he had begun having little dinner parties for high-level Embassy and military personnel. Angela always seemed to be at these little *soirees* and acted as hostess. Reports were also sifting back that the villa's décor was taking on a decidedly "feminine" touch.

This phase ended rather abruptly one night when Angela got tied up in Da Nang, trying to find Mac Wheeler's pilot friend who had blabbed about rotor problems on the Chinooks. She didn't make it back in time for what Ford seemed to view as her "own" dinner party.

Even though there had been only four people at Ford's, most of the guys in the press corps heard a number of conflicting versions the next day about how the infamous dinner degenerated into domestic slapstick. And Nick and several others had grandstand seats for a fight after the party that took place in a pedicab in front of the Continental.

The next day, Nick tried to piece together the sequence of events as best he could.

There were a few things from all the versions that everyone seemed to agree on. As dessert was being served, Angela had shown up dirty and tired, dragging her pack and steel helmet and tracked red clay from her jungle boots across a white oriental rug she and Ford had bought only the week before. Ford was light and controlled. "The back door's not a bad idea, my dear, if you're going to be tromping around in working boots."

"Damn," said Angela, when she saw what she had done. "My beautiful carpet. How will I ever get that clay out?"

"Sorry to be such a mess," she said to the guests, whom she didn't know. "Just give me a minute and I'll clean up."

"What kept you?" Ford asked.

"It was . . . uh, a chopper crash," Angela stammered. "I . . . it was important."

"What could possibly be so fascinating about a chopper crash in this place?" Ford delivered the line with a wink in his voice, as though he were attempting the role of straight man to a comic's routine.

But one thing led to another. The guests, persons of some position at the Embassy, were subjected to an unremarkable domestic squabble: no redeeming characteristics, no clever repartee, no zinging one-liners. The gentleman guest recalled it as mildly amusing, or so he said in recounting the tale to a friend of his from Time magazine. But his wife was said to have been scandalized, and didn't mind saying so to the Embassy wives who heard her indignant version over bridge.

A friend of Nick's who worked in the Embassy told him she heard the reason the wife became so indignant was that as Angela and Ford got deeper into their fight, Angela hadn't even bothered to hide that she was bored by these little intimate dinner parties with people who weren't even her friends.

Nick's contact also described the Embassy wife as "an aging blonde cheerleader-type without a hair out of place." Nick chuckled to himself on hearing this. He could imagine Angela's reaction to the woman.

So, the tale went on, Angela's stance had been that the houseboy could cook, they'd all been fed, so "what the hell difference does it make whether I'm late or not?"

"My God, you can't fly in the face of every civilized convention like some hippie," Ford sputtered his cheeks spotting crimson.

"There is nothing *uncivilized* about having a job and doing it. That is a higher priority than killing time with pointless socializing."

"You certainly bore easily. You're the only living human who found it dull being a prisoner of war," he snapped back.

"I didn't say I was bored, for Christ sake, Ford, don't twist everything around."

"What did you say, then?"

"That the days were uneventful and that I eventually got over being scared."

"And you wonder why I worry about you!" Ford's anger suddenly seemed to dissipate, this last expelled in a puff, no more than a whisper.

"First I'm uncivilized, then a fool. You certainly can turn on the charm when you set your mind to it."

Angela grabbed up the duffel bag she had tossed on a low Japanese stool only moments before, turned to the Embassy couple who were both ashen with embarrassment, and said, "I'm truly sorry, but there's no way we could sit here smiling and chatting as though nothing has happened," and she stomped toward the door.

"Where the hell do you think you're going?" Ford yelled.

"To find Nick and get drunk," she said as she slammed the door behind her.

"The hell you are," Ford said, following her out.

The next thing the Embassy couple heard was the engine of their own car starting up in the courtyard outside. As they ran to look out, they saw Ford roaring away in hot pursuit of Angela who was at the wheel of Ford's car, speeding down Cong Ly toward town. The couple's Vietnamese driver stood bewildered in the spot where their Mercedes had been the moment before.

# 42

# Pedicab Fight

FORD, CHASING after Angela down Cong Ly, shifted the unfamiliar little Mercedes into low feeling like some teenaged drag racer. What the hell am I doing, he asked himself? Had he completely lost his mind? He had walked off and left guests in his home; the gossip, he knew, would be all over Saigon. He saw with relief that traffic was light this far out from downtown, but still heavy enough that Angela probably wouldn't notice him following her. He felt that he would be able to keep his little white Peugot in sight, at least for the moment.

Angela was rude, he thought, absolutely rude to Jim's wife, whatever her name was. She's always like that. Says she has nothing in common with the wives, would rather talk politics or battle strategies with their husbands. How can you have a life with a woman like that? No sense of propriety. No order. You'd certainly never see Berenice standing up her own guests, then arrive wearing men's clothes and wreck a rug of such fine quality that it should be handed down to the children.

That's the problem, he decided, swerving to avoid a bicycle loaded so high with what looked like kindling that from the back he couldn't see the rider. Order and form mean nothing to Angela. For Berenice, with her European background, they are everything. Angela is all color and texture and rhythm, and Berenice is form.

He slammed on the brakes as a couple on a motor scooter shot out from their parking place on the sidewalk. "Damn kids," he spat out to his empty car. But he could see that Angela was stopped, too, at a red light.

My God, he thought, I'm turning into a nut over this woman. I'll probably be arrested for driving a stolen car. What a stupid end to a distinguished career—rotting for the rest of my life in a Vietnamese jail. That's a little melodramatic, he laughed at himself, but I'll certainly lose my job if word gets back that I've gone berserk. Why don't I just drive back to my house now, maybe I can catch Jim before they've called a cab, or worse, the police.

Ford could see Angela pulling some kind of maneuver up ahead. Now what the hell was she up to, he wondered. She was cutting through the park, which was fine, made it easy to keep tabs on her. He was not going to let her escape. No matter what happened, he was not going to lose this woman from his life. But, hell, he thought, that would probably mean he would spend the rest of his life hanging out in smoke-filled bars talking about newspapering. Funny, that's close to what Berenice had said to him: "I'm sick of dragging around and constantly having to recreate the order of my life while you preen and pamper your ego and your 'career.' You're the 'star,' you're in the spotlight, and I'm just a stagehand. Well, from now on it is my *own* life I'm living, not yours!"

As he sped through the dark park, his headlights played shadow finger games on the car's hood with the sentinel trees lining both sides of the road. He was having no trouble keeping Angela in sight as she sped toward the central city, but he knew he could easily lose her once they got to the monument circle in front of the Independence Palace. If she's determined to lose me, he thought, that would be the place to do it. I'd better make my move now.

He got close behind his own little white Peugot and tried to force Angela over to the curb several times, but only succeeded in what looked like a childish game of bumper tag. After he had banged into her from behind for the third time, she managed to get a car ahead of him in the increasing traffic as they approached the palace, and she took a left down Thong Nhat through the park that ended at Cathedral Square.

At the end of the park, she made a quick right at the cathedral. As Ford made the turn, he saw that she had abandoned the Peugot, parking it half up on the sidewalk of JFK square just behind the church. He saw her running, dodging through the clogged traffic, then she grabbed a pedicab heading in the direction of downtown. Ford wasn't far behind. He abandoned Jim's Mercedes right in the street behind his own car, yelling, "Follow that cab!" at a startled coolie as he leaped into the gnarled fellow's pedal-driven rickshaw and sent him pumping down the Tu Do, breathlessly trying to catch up to Angela.

As his fast-pedaling driver brought him abreast of Angela's carriage, Ford leaped out running, grabbed the hood of her pedicab and climbed in, only to see her pull the same maneuver, going out the right hand side and catch another cab on the run.

RAY CORRIGAN was slouched down in one of the wicker chairs facing Nick across several empty Tiger beer bottles on the Continental terrace while Nick expounded his theory about secret incursions into Cambodia. "I tell you we can't just sit by and . . ."

Corrigan was looking out at the street and suddenly burst out laughing.

"What's so goddamned funny? Nick asked.

"Take a look over your shoulder," Corrigan said.

Nick turned around in his chair in time to see what appeared to be two cyclo drivers in a dispute, both waving their arms, an open rickshaw pulled in front of a covered pedicab apparently blocking the second one's path. "What the hell?" he said, turning back to Corrigan with the question.

"Look again," said the burly Irishman, sputtering with laughter.

Nick swiveled back to see more than the usual snarl of traffic pulsating around the battling coolies with another pedicab added to the core of the gridlock. Ford was tugging on Angela's arm as she tried to climb into the third cab.

"JESUS, ANGELA," Ford screamed over the sounds of the traffic and the jabbering drivers, "let me pay these guys off or we're both going to land in jail. Be sensible. You told me yourself how brutal those White Mice can be."

"Oh, for Christ sake, all right," she snapped back. "We look like fools tying up traffic and fighting in the middle of the street. But hurry up, this is embarrassing." Ford had thrown a wad of bills at the two disgruntled hackies and was back in the cab with Angela before she got the last words out of her mouth.

"What are you so afraid of?" Ford asked as he climbed in and said, "*vite*" to their new driver. "Couples have arguments, and we've had our first. And I'm sorry. I apologize. But you can't run away every time we have a little quarrel." He tried to put his arm around her, but she pulled away, and sat sideways in the cramped cab seat, as the hunched little coolie cycled down toward the river.

"It wasn't a *little* quarrel, Ford," Angela said, her voice softening a bit. "I just can't take all that domestic shit. It's a trap for me."

"All I ask is a little common courtesy to a guest," Ford said in a level, reasonable tone.

"Oh sure," Angela said, clearly starting to get riled again, "night after night of my making small talk with some Embassy wife. I don't see you wasting your time talking about how tough it is to find a good hairdresser in Saigon, but I'm supposed to while you talk war and politics with her husband. I am not a helpmate, Ford, and I'm not a decoration. If you can't pull off your little dinner parties without me to pass the fucking peas and engage some nitwit in knit one purl two, then you better quit having them."

"Well, you not only look like a grunt, you talk like a grunt."

"Damn right. Because I'm covering the war from where it's happening, not from rumors picked up over soup."

"That's a bit of a low blow, don't you think? I still manage to hold onto my job, even if I'm not out playing cowboys and Indians like you and Nick." As those last words came out of his mouth, Ford put his hands to his face in a grimace. "Oh God," he spread his hands wide and looked at Angela. "Why do I keep letting you bait me into these arguments? You do it on purpose to keep distance between us."

Angela gave a dry laugh. "Yeah, you're probably right about that." The pedicab driver bumped along and made a right turn at the end of the Tu Do, and peddled past the river. The rhythmic pat-pat of the cycle's tires against the pavement syncopated with the soft slapping of the river against its moorings.

Ford suddenly spoke into the quiet. "I want you to come back to the States with me, have a life together. I've already written to Berenice asking if she wants a divorce. "

"What?" Angela's voice was strangled.

"I'm hoping that way not to hurt her. Let the divorce be her idea. She didn't want to come here with me."

"Ford, oh my God, please. Don't be getting a divorce on my account.

I can't deal with this." She put her right hand out in an imploring way, and squeezed his.

He put his arms around her. "Don't worry. It's going to be all right. You don't have to decide anything now. We'll go along for a while just as we are. I promise."


NICK AND Corrigan had watched the pedicab with Angela and Ford visibly arguing until the vehicle moved out of sight heading for the river. They were startled a few minutes later to see it heading back up the Tu Do with the two of them fused as a single shadow in the back of the cab.

"How long do you think that will last?" asked Nick.

"Nothing's forever," Corrigan replied.

# 43

# Le Cercle Sportif

ANGELA AND Nick sat eating *pho* and drinking coffee late one morning at a scarred, beat-up table in Bunny's, a joint a few doors off the Tu Do down toward the river. The room was heavy with smoke and the smell of stale beer, all trapped in moisture from a clanking air conditioner.

The place usually came to life only at night, but there were already several drunks at the bar, including two Westerners in civilian clothes who, Nick speculated, "are most likely GIs who lost their way home last night.

"They're probably already on report, or listed as AWOL," he said knowingly to Angela. He was slightly grumpy and trying to reassert his credibility, having just been beaten by her in a game of pool in Bunny's back room. That room with its peeling paint and worn green felt had a view through fly-specked windows onto the enclosed courtyard-alley of typical daily life in Saigon. Rickety, outside stairs wound up to cold-water, one-room apartments. In the alleys, children were raucous in their games, music blared, laundry hung out to dry on wooden stair rails, garbage went uncollected.

The fact that Bunny's jukebox wasn't blaring the usual—either Hendrix or Janis Joplin—seemed further evidence to Nick that the suspect GIs were hung over. An elderly Asian with a straggly Ho beard leaned on the bar as he slurped some indefinable liquid from a porcelain bowl.

The slow-moving, youngish Caucasian waiter, who finally came over to Angela and Nick's table to refresh their coffee, also appeared a bit green around the edges.

"Looks like it was rough around here last night," Nick said with a laugh as the waiter refilled their cups. Nick knew from the grapevine that the guy was an ex-GI who had mustered out here when his tour was up, but was too strung out to bother returning home.

"Same as always," the waiter mumbled, putting little enthusiasm into his response.

"It's so damned sticky, I don't know why we're in this dump at this hour," Angela said after the waiter walked away. It was a rare day when both had filed early and had decided to bag work for the afternoon and head for Bunny's to play pool.

"Never been in at this hour before," Nick replied. "Feels weird with no one around, especially no cuties offering Saigon tea." He was referring to the colored-water drink that bar girls sipped while they encouraged GIs to keep drinking alcohol. The girls were paid by the house according to how much "tea" they drank.

"That's always been a question for me," Angela said. "I've heard stories that a good deal of these so-called 'B' girls get guys drunk, pick up their cut from the bartender, and excuse themselves and meet their boyfriends or husbands waiting for them outside."

"Absolutely," Nick said. "That's the way a lot of young women earn their living. Some of 'em aren't prostitutes at all. Often that's the only income the family has."

"Gee," said Angela. "These GIs pay for several rounds of $2 Kool-Aid served in tiny shot glasses, then they go home alone. They must be bummed."

"Mostly too drunk to do much, one way or the other," Nick said with a laugh. "So, I hear you and Ford had quite a nice little dinner party the other night."

"Ah, hell, not you too," Angela said, a disgusted look on her face. "Let's get out of here and do something civilized."

"Like what?"

"Have a *citron presse* poolside at the Cercle Sportif, take a swim, and then have a proper lunch."

"Ha. That's rich. I hear they serve champagne."

"Yep," she said with a grin. "Let's do it."

"How'll we get in?" he asked. "You're not a member, are you?"

"Ford is. We can go on his."

"So what's with you guys, still lovey-dovey? No more spectacular public fights?"

"I'll answer all your impertinent questions at the Sportif," Angela said, getting up from her chair and throwing a few piastres on the table, her bowl of soup half-finished. "Come on." She tugged at Nick's arm. "We can make quick stops at our hotels for suits, then walk over. We're turning into such bar rats, it's disgusting."

THEY SET out—Angela in a fresh pink silk blouse with bathing suit and city map in hand. Nick sugguested a slightly different route from their usual one up the Tu Do and past the Cathedral to Reuters. Instead, they cut through the Passage Eden across from her hotel so they could walk past the old French Colonial city hall. They gawked like tourists at the twin, red-tiled, mansard roofs, framed by the frilly white filigree that trimmed the ornate, block long, two-story building. Angela pulled out her camera and started taking pictures, while Nick struck comic poses.

"It's a day off, what the hell," he said.

They didn't really need their map; they were only a couple of blocks to the left of the Tu Do. But the area was a bit more residential, without quite the honky-tonk feel of what they considered their own neighborhood.

"So, did you see the latest reference to my *so-called* capture?" Angela asked Nick as they strode along.

"Which one?" Nick replied with a grin. "There've been several conservative nuts implying it was some vast left-wing conspiracy that got you released."

"Yeah, I know," Angela said. "Ford hasn't been taking it too well."

"How about you?" Nick asked, giving her a sideways glance as they neared a once-grand, French-style townhouse.

"Who cares," she said with a toss of her head.

She then stopped dead in her tracks and grinned at Nick. "That was stupid. Of course I care. Especially when I know that it's not just conservative commentators back home, but even some of the guys around here who are making snide remarks, suggesting I slept my way out of captivity."

"Ah, jeez," Nick said, so startled he dropped his duffel on the sidewalk as he turned to face her. "Who would be crass enough to let you hear that?"

"You've heard it, right?" she asked. She leaned against the metal poles of the fence surrounding the small, overgrown yard of the faded, once majestic old house. She opened her duffel, searching for a cigarette.

"They're jealous, petty pricks," Nick said heatedly. "What matters is you landed a story no one else had."

Angela laughed as she lit up a cigarette. "I couldn't have said it better myself."

"Those guys are assholes," Nick's indignation picked up steam and rolled on. "You don't have to be some giant brain to figure out the Viets had *some* propaganda motive in mind. Otherwise, they simply would have knocked you off, or raped you, or made some other ghastly example for the rest of us. Look at the brutality in Hue. Thousands slaughtered in the streets, a big part of them women and children."

Angela zipped up her bag and had started to move on when she suddenly threw back her head and laughed. "With all the dues I've paid—getting constantly passed up for jobs because I'm a woman—tough shit if some weird advantage finally fell my way."

They reached familiar territory, Thong Nhat, the street the American Embassy was on. They had come out to the side of the forested park surrounding the presidential palace, instead of at its front. Circling around to the back of the park, they found the Sportif, nestled in among tall, scrawny pines. This had been the country club for Saigon's elite since the 1920s. It boasted badminton, 15 tennis courts and an Olympic-size swimming pool.

Approaching the serene, cream-colored building with its duplex verandas set off by white wood-carved balustrades, they passed clay courts equipped with night lights.

"How about some tennis?" Nick said with a grin. "I'm sure one of those is the infamous Court Number Five."

"What about it?" Angela asked.

Nick chuckled. "Westmoreland used to show up every day in his whites and take a lesson there, until some broad from the AP wrote about it."

"I didn't know they had any women in their bureau."

"They don't. They just sent this one over from New York to do some features, but she burned Westy's butt. He gave up his Sportif membership.

The story coupled his tennis lesson with what was happening in the field at the same hour, and it didn't go down very well with the folks at home."

"God, what a business," Angela said with a dry laugh. "Meanwhile, I'm a Commie because I got captured."

They picked out a couple of shaded, poolside chairs, before Angela went off to change into her suit. Nick had put his on under his slacks, so he just slipped out of them and pulled off his T-shirt to start getting some sun on his back while he waited.

When Angela returned, she still had on the pink blouse, open over a shocking pink one-piece bathing suit. Nick's heart skipped a beat, when he realized she had on that same incredible, floppy big hat he'd first seen her wearing coming off the plane when she arrived in Saigon.

A waiter in a white jacket came by and, at Angela's insistence, they ordered the club's signature *citron presse* instead of beer.

"It's nothing but fucking lemonade," Nick yelped when he tasted it. "Sour, at that."

"I told you this was going to be a civilized day," Angela replied. "You can have champagne with your lunch. But first, we have to take a swim, get our exercise."

"Jeez, when push comes to shove, you certainly know how to be a pain in the butt," Nick said, sucking on his lemonade straw. "Before we do our calisthenics, want to fill me in on what you've been saying you learned from your capture?"

"It's something I'm serious about, Nick," Angela replied. "You always make fun of what you call *my theories,* but I don't understand how you can be serious about your work, yet not give much thought to why or what you do."

"OK, fine. Just go on," he said.

"Remember when we talked several months ago about the story I got in Chicago that snowy night after the fire? This was a repeat of that same lesson. No matter what the tragedy or circumstance, people always want to talk. It's an emotional sorting process. Those Cong guys wanted to talk, they wanted to tell their side of the story. I knew that, sensed it, and it helped me from being scared. I just kept telling myself I was on a story, that these guys were feeling important because I was taking their pictures and writing down what they were saying. I talked to some South Side street-gang members once who were the same way.

They bragged about killing anyone who got in their way and all their other exploits. But they loved showing off and trying to shock me. One of the guys, named 'Ice Pick Slim' or something, kept pointing at my notebook and saying, 'Now put this down,' before he'd lay another shocker on me. He ended up being indicted for the robbery-murder of a cabbie using an ice pick, but I wasn't scared of him. He was having a great time spouting off while I wrote it down. I know you make fun when I say this, but there is a real social value in being a scribe, writing down what's going on. It gives people a legitimacy, makes them feel that the routine of their everyday lives has some significance. I've seen the same thing with the grunts. They're awed by us, somehow, because we have the power to bring some meaning—a moment of spotlight—to their lives."

Nick just bowed his head in weariness and drained his lemonade glass with a loud sucking sound. The social-shit pet theory again, he told himself. He should have known better. She never even stops to take a breath. He thought she was probably right, she was a smart lady, but he'd heard her sing that song too much already. And she never cut loose about anything but journalism. He decided to try to change the subject by asking about Ford.

"Yeah, well, speaking of spotlights, is Curtis still convinced your subconscious knows more about General Giap than you realize?"

"Jesus, Nick."

"I can't wait till he hears you're going to Khe Sanh with Parks."

"How'd you hear about that?" she snapped.

"Angela, we're not all blind. Parks picked up that you dread telling Curtis you're going, especially with a known crazy like Parks. We're all on your side in this, Angie, and we're scared Ford's going to ruin you."

"Ruin me?" Her laugh seemed to have a genuine element of surprise. "Ruin me? Come on, sweetie, whatever are you talking about?"

"You're a hell of a good reporter, Angie."

"Thanks for noticing."

"Let me finish . . . And Ford is trying to hold you back, and you know it."

"Ford thinks you guys are trying to get me killed."

"See what I mean!"

As always for Nick, she was full of surprises. She leaned over and took his hand and squeezed hard, then said in a husky whisper: "Nick, baby, I keep promising you I've lived through this before and I'm going to be all right." She stood up, and walked to the edge of the pool.

"It's you and Ford I'm worried about," she said, then dove in.

# 44

# Finding George

ANGELA WAS on a quest for a chopper jock, but she didn't even know his name. She thought she remembered that his first name was George. It wasn't easy. It didn't make much sense with so little to go on. But whenever she was out in the field, she would describe him, ask other pilots, mechanics, if they knew the guy with the carrot red hair. What she didn't tell them was that he was the one who had first triggered her theory about the Chinooks' rotors causing them to crash.

Then in a screwy twist of fate, *he* spotted *her*. She was just stepping on the elevator, leaving the rooftop bar at the Rex BOQ with some friends, as he was getting off. He stopped her, put a hand on her arm, and she told her friends to go on.

"George?" She was tentative, not at all sure that was the right name. But she knew she had her man; same soft grin, flaming hair. Perhaps even the very same dreadful, short-sleeved Hawaiian shirt, but the tan shoes had a spit shine.

"Yeah, George Rodgers," he said, sticking out his hand. "Glad to see you're OK. I heard Mac Wheeler flew you into a mess. Let me buy you a drink." He waved his hand toward the bar she had just left.

She was afraid to turn George down, scared of losing him again. But she didn't dare dawdle and be late for dinner with Ford, not after the row the week before. Which, ironically, had been triggered because she was out searching unsuccessfully for a sweet, red-haired chopper pilot called George who was too outspoken and soft-hearted for his job.

"Perhaps another time," George said, and she was ready.

"Let's make a day of it, a working day," Angela countered, slightly out of breath in her excitement at finding him. "I'll ride around with you, and see if I can't sell a piece about life on the run as a chopper pilot. I hear you guys are not supposed to fly more than four hours a day and that most of you routinely fly eight or ten."

He laughed, rubbed his right thumb across his chin, its pink stubble barely visible on his sunburned face. "I dunno that I want to be in the centerfold of an exposé. But you're welcome to come along." His grin resembled a spreading blush, the blue eyes twinkled. "My crew would love it. Most of 'em will probably even shave if they know you're coming. But I think you're crazy, my girl. Mac said you were captured. That wasn't enough for you?"

"I have to earn a living. What I can pick up sitting on my butt in Saigon isn't terribly salable."

"OK, kid," George replied, "you're on. I just don't want to see you get hurt. And you know, don't you, I fly Medevac? I'll go out of my way to hang on to you, but you could sure get left behind at a firebase, bumped by wounded."

"Understood."

# 45

# Tracking George

WHEN THE rescue call came, Angela was lounging in a ready room of the 101st evac squadron near Pleiku, sipping at tepid black coffee in a Styrofoam cup and working a week-old New York Times crossword puzzle.

It was early, and had already been a long day. She was waiting for her second hop, hoping it would be more newsworthy than her first. Actually, it would be her third hop, if you counted the before-daylight flight up here from Saigon to hook up with George Rodgers.

She put down the crossword puzzle and looked at her watch, nearly 10 a.m. She'd been sitting here for two hours waiting for George to return. The wretched coffee was working a hole through her stomach lining, and she had absolutely nothing in the way of a story—spot *or* exposé. George had been right, on their first ride out shortly after 0600 he'd filled up with wounded and had had to dump her coming back. Poor George, she knew he'd been distraught over leaving her at the LZ. He'd given her a forlorn shrug and thumbs-up signal as he leaned out his right-hand window before takeoff. As he rose, she could see him through his Plexiglas chin bubble, straining to keep sight of her. But she had been just as glad to be left on the ground at the firebase. The action was over, nothing particularly newsworthy in what had been a limited skirmish, so it had given her a chance to just chat with some of the grunts. And a couple of the wounded guys George had flown off with were so badly mutilated that she couldn't bear to look at them. One had his belly blown open with his guts all hanging out and another had been hit in the face and the skin was gone from the right side of his jaw. You could see how the teeth fit in their sockets just like on a skull model in a dentist's office, except this one was swimming in blood.

She had been relieved not to be crammed into the little Huey with them even for the 10- or 15-minute ride to a MASH unit. One of these days, she was afraid she would throw up right into some poor GI's wounds and cause him to die. Fine doctor she would have made, she thought.

The pilot who had brought her back here shortly after George took off was less than pleased. It seemed he would rather have had more wounded than transport her.

"This ain't no ferry boat for fucking reporters," he'd yelled when he finally spotted her white correspondent's patch after they were in the air. When she'd clambered aboard, she had grabbed a webbed strap, sat, and kept her head down and her helmet on. They'd been airborne for at least five minutes before the pilot jerked around and looked at her hard, after the co-pilot said something into his speaker tube, then gestured his head in her direction. She couldn't really hear him over the roar of the rotors, but she could read his mind, if not his lips: "Bad enough a reporter, but a fucking broad, besides."

So here she sat in the ready room, ready and waiting. George was already out again when she'd gotten back, and the jerk-face who ferried her in wasn't about to take her back out. "No more fucking broads," he'd roared as he'd stomped off to await the next rescue call.

When it came, it was about a downed Huey. There was sure to be something in that. Wounded and dead Marines were routine, nothing to peg a story to, just blown apart by a nameless mine or brought down by a faceless enemy, you needed more than that. But a downed chopper—shot down, maybe. That could be a story!

The little Hueys generally had only one rotor. If they did have a second one, it was way out on the tail. No way for their blades to collide with each other like her theory about the Chinooks.

She needed to get to the crash, but freak-face, who'd been waiting for a call, probably wouldn't let her back on his chopper. Maybe she should just tough it out, maybe he was just a grandstander who wouldn't really have the guts to keep her off the flight. If she kept her head down, maybe he wouldn't recognize her.

She stood up, crushed out her cigarette and took a last swig of coffee.

She was still stuffing the unfinished crossword in her duffel as she picked up the crew's trot falling in alongside the door gunner. He did a double take, then gave her a quizzical look as he snapped the chin strap on his helmet. She wasn't sure if he was trying to tell her something, then he rolled his eyes skyward. Her helmet, of course. She had picked it up automatically, but had forgotten to put it on. She snapped it on—fast—stuffing the long ends of her hair up underneath and looping it around the inside leather strap. It wasn't easy to do, running and hanging on to her gear with her left hand. But she got it up, then reached in her back pocket for a bandana she'd made out of some ripped-up jungle utilities. She stuffed that partway into her left breast pocket, so that it dangled out and covered the white patch that said, "Martinelli, *bao chi*," Vietnamese for correspondent.

The pilot seemed not to notice, or at least paid no attention to her during the ride. But when they were on the ground near the crash site, all hell broke loose. It's possible he could have mistaken her for a medic while they were airborne, but it was more likely that he was relishing the idea of throwing a fit on the ground and then leaving her behind. As she jumped off, he started yelling and calling her names.

A tall, good-looking captain came out of nowhere. "No press allowed," he ordered. "And no cameras."

"Are you in charge here?" Angela tried to keep her voice neutral. Who was this guy and how did he suddenly materialize? He was in starched khakis, not jungle gear, a yellow kerchief bloused at his throat.

"You're going to have to get out as best you can," he said, as though he were unaware she had spoken. "Crew and supplies from the downed bird have priority."

"I don't want to leave now. I want to take a look," Angela said. "What happened? Were you on the downed chopper?"

"None of your damn business."

"Come on," Angela replied with the sweetest smile she could muster. "What difference can it make? I'm not going to touch anything."

"That's right, 'cause you aren't getting close enough."

"Hey, I've got a right to take a look and take pictures." She could see past the captain that several men in uniform were moving back and forth from the Huey to the downed helicopter, which was not quite visible behind a stand of trees.

"Who says?"

"I do. What the hell are you trying to hide? You got an A-bomb aboard there or something?" Shit, she thought, I shouldn't have lost my temper. Guys in flight suits or fatigues, obviously from the downed chopper, were boarding the Huey. One was limping, and needed help, but the rest were moving under their own steam. The uniformed guys, all with yellow scarves, appeared to be some sort of crash site team. They were offloading equipment, and climbing aboard the Huey with it.

The big captain moved toward her with his right arm extended menacingly at the elbow as though he meant to *accidentally* jostle her with a shift of his crooked arm that would have given her a good crack along the side of her head if she hadn't ducked out of the way.

As she moved past him he whirled, whipped a long-barreled Smith & Wesson .38 from a holster on his right thigh, leveled it at her and said, "Don't take another step, that's an order."

"My God, are you crazy? You'd shoot me for walking a hundred yards just to look at an American aircraft?" She was trying to keep her voice calm, but over the pounding in her own ears it sounded like a screech.

"I'd as soon shoot you as look at you, cunt."

It was all she could do to keep her voice steady, but she didn't dare totally back down.

"If you're that crazed, I'd be nuts to challenge you but I've certainly made a mental note of your name and patch, Captain Kellaher. It'll be interesting to find out if you go off the deep end like this often."

God, she thought, he's wonderfully handsome, except his face is too square. Why are blue-eyed blonds supposed to look like angels? Those blue eyes were vacant, just like Bobby Kennedy's eyes the one time she'd seen them at a press event in Chicago, unfocused, vacant, looked right through you. Kellaher laughed, and the laugh was vacant, too, unattached.

"Gonna put me on report, are you, cunt? Well, I'm shaking in my boots. See ya on the evening news, sweetheart."

He kept those spacey eyes on her, a faint smirk on his face, while he deliberately replaced the special sidearm in its hand-tooled holster that had the look of human skin. Nick had shown her a shop in Cholon that specialized in such souvenirs for ghoulish GIs. The proprietor would also string you a necklace of ears. The captain shifted the yellow kerchief at his neck and strode off to the downed bird a few hundred yards away behind the trees.

Angela suddenly realized several enlisted men had clustered around to watch the show. She sensed they were more embarrassed for her than hostile, but no one said a word. She felt like a fool, more than a fool, sick with the humiliation for the way that captain had treated her. No one had *ever* spoken to her like that. Her mother had always warned if she was going to use the kind of blue language she did people would treat her "accordingly," but this was the first time anyone had *ever* spoken to her that way. Slime is the only word she could think of, it was the only thing she could feel. She knew she must say something to these men, she couldn't just stand here like a fool, but she couldn't think of anything. She was so mortified.

"Don't let him get you down, miss. The man's not worth dirt."

She looked, but wasn't sure who had spoken. Judging from the resonance and cadence, it was probably the hulking black man, with the grenade launcher slung over his right shoulder and sergeant stripes on his sleeve. He looked older and more at ease than the other three who were all just babes.

"Yeah, Kellaher's weird," said a snaggle-toothed little black kid who looked all of about 15 with such over-sized boots it seemed he might walk right out of them. Those horrible teeth, thought Angela. That's supposed to be one of the few advantages of getting your ass shot at—Uncle Sam will spring for fixing up rickety teeth.

"What a dreadful experience," she said. "What on earth could be in that plane that he doesn't want me to see?"

"Nuthing. He just mean—and crazy."

Angela turned to look at the speaker and smiled when she saw him. He was a string-bean with a bad case of teenage acne whose jive knees were ever on the move, even to the point of keeping time with his own chewing gum. Good grief, every one of them is black, Angela realized with a start as she made a point of taking a close look at the face under the fourth helmet and saw what looked like yet another poor street kid. The liberals are damned right. Where have all the white boys gone? Off to college, that's where, and left the poor and the black to fight their war. Except for that damned demented captain. That bastard was not only white, but she would have bet money he was a rich kid, to boot. Again, tell-tale teeth. Those perfect, straight translucent teeth were always a dead giveaway: a good, expensive orthodontist from the age of seven. Wonder how he got to Nam? Probably the same way she had—volunteered.

"Well, what's going on here? Were you guys aboard the Huey?" she asked, as the little group circled around her.

"It weren't no Huey. A Chinook. Coming in to evac us. We was on a search-and-destroy," said Jive Knees.

"A Ch-47's a bit big, isn't it, to be doing taxi service for a single squad?" Angela asked, trying to keep her voice calm. A Chinook!

"It was some kind of coordinated gig," the sergeant replied. "Not sure ourselves what it was, but they was to pick up a number of us strung out along this ridge. We was told we was out here on a search-and-destroy, but there wasn't no one around, no Charlie slant-eyes for miles. And some big shot was aboard that Chinook, kept radioing down asking us questions. They was up to something, but I can't dope out what it was. Running patrols out from a command ship? Silly, don't make no sense. And Kellaher there was sure on the scene awful fast. That Huey you come in didn't lose no time, but the captain was already poking around by time you all touched down."

"The whole thing sounds bizarre," Angela said. "Is anyone dead? What are they hiding?" She looked from one to the other, hoping their faces would tell her something. But the little she could see under the big helmets told her that for them, it was just another day in Nam. God, she thought, I'm wired, too upset and curious to be scared, and they're taking it all in stride.

"Beats me, miss. We don't know nothing and they ain't about to tell us nothing, neither." The leader of the little group gave her a big grin and a shrug as he dropped his pack on the ground, canteen clanking against his grenade belt, as he shifted the launcher to his other shoulder.

"What's your name, sergeant?"

"Brown, ma'am. Oscar Brown. From Detroit."

"Hey, I've been there a time or two," Angela said, cooling down from the captain and warming to the sweet, friendly sergeant. "Almost took a job at the Free Press."

"Did ya, miss? Well, now, you almost a home girl! I delivered them papers when I was a kid. Won my first airplane trip in a carrier-boy contest. Threw papers in Paradise Valley. Tore down now for urban renewal."

She needed to get back to the subject at hand, she thought. She couldn't let these guys just walk off. The sergeant was clearly rearranging his gear in preparation for a hike. Where the hell would they go, she wondered? And how the devil would she get out of here?

"Oscar, did you see that ship go down?" she asked.

"Ah-huh," Oscar replied. "We was watching for it to pick us up."

"Did something go haywire with the rotors, as though they'd been hit?"

"Yeah, looked almost like they hit one t'other, they reversed themselves or sumthin'. Caused an awful ruckus down here on the ground."

Oh good lord, she thought, that's it. It's happened again. I've got to get pictures. But that damned lieutenant is liable to shoot me.

"Yeah," said young snaggle-tooth. "It was blowing up rocks and shit, almost like a volcano."

"Volcano? Whadda you know about volcano?" Jive Knees asked derisively.

"You know, rocks and shit. I'm from Toledo, ma'am. You ever been there?"

"Afraid not, other than driving through from Chicago to New York."

"That's where it's at, all right. Right on the way."

"What's your name?" Angela asked.

"Lester, Lester Flanagan. And the string bean here, he be Dwight Pepper, and that other guy is Spike Jones."

Angela laughed when she heard the name of the old-time goofy bandleader. "That surely is your nickname, Spike."

"No'm. My momma called me that 'cause she said that was a guy made her laugh. Guess she was right, you laughed."

"You got me laughing again, Spike, I guess that is a happy name to have. But I've got to quit laughing and get to work. I've got to get some shots of that plane."

"You better not, miss, that crazy Kellaher might really shoot you. Wouldn't be the first friendly he's *accidentally* put away in the field."

"Lester," Angela said with a shudder, "I hope you're kidding."

"No, ma'am," the kid said solemnly.

"Oscar," Angela said, in a near pleading tone, "I hope you'll help me get out of here."

"A course, ma'am," he replied with a big grin, and a little snort of laughter. "We wouldn't leave nobody here with that nut."

The little troop pulled themselves together and moved away from the line of trees that obstructed the view of the crashed chopper. The terrain was mountainous and rocky, covered with brush and tall pines. Oscar got on the radio asking what they were to do now that the big bird was out of commission and couldn't pick them up.

While Oscar was on the radio, Angela stared over at the crippled behemoth that had shirred a path through the forest as it crashed a few hundred yards away. No signs of any crew, other than the two or three she'd seen being helped onto the Huey, but the others could have been spirited away before she arrived. Captain Kellaher was poking around the copter and appeared to be directing several men who were all wearing berets, probably green, but she couldn't be sure at this distance. She had a long-range lens, and she had trees and hilly terrain for cover. She knew she should get off some shots. But she still didn't know what she was looking for. She'd felt with a certainty after the Chu Lai crash that small arms hadn't picked off the big gunship. Nick had reluctantly agreed that if the gear mechanism or transmission wasn't working properly, the meshing of the two huge overhead rotors could have been thrown off enough for them to hit each other. A Chinook's fore and aft blades had to synchronize as they rotated because they literally were within touching distance of each other. A rotor hitting a rotor would do a lot more damage, fast, than a bullet or two.

She couldn't tell for sure from this distance, but she thought the rotors of the downed chopper looked mangled. And the ship was upright—it hadn't fallen over or nosed in. She realized she had to get some photos, and quickly. Kellaher and his guys seemed to be nosing around, picking up things or taking pictures or measuring, but they probably wouldn't notice her with this many trees for cover. She moved over to the protection of the group and positioned her body as much as she could behind a tree before she started taking her pictures. The men all rolled their eyes at each other at her daring, but none of them tried to stop her. Spike Jones seemed fascinated by the process of her angling for shots and looked like he was dying to get his hands on her equipment, but he didn't say a word. Intent as she was, she still made a mental note to show him something about how the camera worked once they got aboard an evac chopper.

Oscar had gotten orders for them to make their way some distance down the slope they were on and they would be picked up there.

Overhearing Oscar on the radio, Angela was stunned to find out they were in Cambodia.

"How could that be?" she demanded of Oscar.

"No *be* to it miss, we just here, that's all."

"Cambodia is supposed to be neutral."

"You got that much of it right," said Oscar with a wide grin. "Now let's get ourselves situated down the hill so that chopper can set down nice and easy and transport our asses out a here."

# 46

# Sweet George

ANOTHER DAMNED hike, Angela thought, as she heaved up her gear and fell in single file behind Oscar, with Dwight Jive Knees behind her, then Lester the snaggle tooth and little Spike bringing up the rear. It didn't matter which side you were with, just like her hike with the Cong, the poor dogface bastards always had to end up walking. Ford was obsessed on the subject of her fearlessness—or what he took to be her lack of fear—over her capture. She'd never been able to explain that walking is not a fearful occupation, just extraordinarily painful and tiring and boring.

"I worried sick about getting blisters," she'd say and it would absolutely enrage him. But trying to walk with blisters, trying to walk with menstrual cramps, trying to walk with what passes for clean rags chaffing between your legs, trying to find a discreet place to relieve yourself when you're in thick jungle undergrowth and don't dare stray from the path being hacked ahead of you, is hardly the stuff for do-and-daring stories of heroism. It may make you famous if you live to tell the tale, but it hardly makes you heroic to say you survived because you learned how to walk with blisters.

Heroic, that's a joke, she almost laughed out loud. Mustn't do that, she thought. I had to restrain myself on that bus to Hue from laughing, talking to myself. I guess my timing's weird about laughing. I laugh when others think I should be crying, or quaking in my boots. Funny expression, quaking in your boots. Perhaps from American frontier days? Cowboy boots? Ford thinks I'm too dumb to know when to be scared. Not stupid, just *inexperienced in warfare*. Oscar said it would only be a klick, a kilometer or two. Seems like it's been twice that already, but this terrain isn't difficult. Just hate the thought of endless walking.

She could hear a distant whir, and Oscar was setting off a smoke grenade to mark an LZ clearing. That must be their deliverance. Wouldn't it be nice, she thought, if Mac Wheeler were at the controls. Silly. Last she heard he was still stationed at Phu Bai. She'd meant to ask George, but she hadn't had a chance to talk with him. They'd gotten their first call so early, and it was impossible to talk with him at the controls, nearly impossible under any circumstances in those damn noisy choppers, especially the little ones.

Oscar yelled at her to get her camera put away: "That whirly bird is getting close and we don't wants to hold 'em up." As the chopper neared, she could see it was a Huey with its little turned-up dragonfly tail, which always reminded her of the whale symbol used on Nantucket Island, where she'd spent summers as a kid with her grandfather. Maybe it was George coming back for her. She hoped so. She liked George. Besides, he might tell her more about Mac Wheeler.

George and Mac were buddies from flight school at Fort Wolters, they were both in the 1st Cav, but there the commonality ended. George flew Medevacs—he called himself the flying ambulance driver. Mac flew the little Hueys called slicks. Mac didn't call himself "ace" or "hot dog," but that's what he was. The lanky, smooth-talking cowboy was part of an elite airborne assault team that thrived on low-level, contour flying. They dipped in and out of hot spots, flying often in formation, to deliver and then pick up small patrols of jungle-fighting grunts, or else the belly crawlers out on what they called lurps. Long-range reconnaissance patrols, ha. Fancy name for guys with painted faces and twigs growing out of their helmets who endured leeches and every other manner of degradation as they skittered through the vegetation, trying to dope out what the enemy was up to.

George, on the other hand, was a diminutive, low-key guy who seemed terribly mismated to a helicopter. In the real world, he'd worked for a tiny New England commuter line flying six- and- eight-seaters between Boston and Providence and the islands off Cape Cod. Most chopper pilots seemed to have a swagger, a presence, at least most of the ones Angela knew. To her, they all seemed tall, rangy and swaggering.

George was the exception—slight, with his gentle face and clear, milky-white complexion that was always protected by the bill of a baseball cap when he was in the sun. If need be, he even wore the cap under his flight helmet. The only flamboyant thing about George was his carrot-red hair.

The wind blast from the rotors was beating up the dust around Angela's feet and whipping the rolled cuffs of her too-big fatigues. As the ship lowered she could see its big red cross painted on its blunt nose, then finally its tail number. It was definitely George's chopper. Angela had asked him that day over hamburgers in Da Nang what in the world he was doing in a place like this. George had smiled at the bluntness of the question.

"My ex-wife remarried and moved to a ranch in Montana and took our five-year-old with her. I tried to get a job somewhere in the area, but couldn't. I figured if I was never going to see my daughter again, I might as well go someplace where it didn't make any difference. I guess it wasn't such a wise choice, but I was in such despair at the thought of rarely seeing Lucy anymore that I wasn't thinking too straight. I'm a short-timer now, closing in on release day soon."

Dwight "Jive Knees" Pepper gathered up Angela's gear so she could focus on rolling up her cuffs and getting out of the path of the descending chopper. If she didn't move fast it was going to land right on her head. As it touched down, Pepper shoved her in the open doorway, threw in her gear, and climbed in after her. Oscar and the rest of his patrol followed. George was indeed at the controls. His face lit up as he turned in his seat and recognized Angela, picking herself up from her sprawl on the Huey's deck. The door gunner and the crew chief both gave her thumbs up when they saw her. She wondered where the medic was—he'd been aboard earlier this morning. She moved on forward, while her patrol pals settled down behind. Before she sat in the webbing strung behind George's armor-plated seat, she gave him a peck that half landed on cheek and half on the cold steel of his olive-drab flight helmet. "Man, am I glad to see a friendly face," she yelled at him over the whumping rotors. "I got my ego badly bruised by a vile-tempered and crazed captain who doesn't take kindly to the press."

George grinned his sweet smile: "Squat and we'll get out of here. Looks like all your buddies are aboard."

As he turned away from her in his seat, Angela strained forward to get a first-hand view of the complicated process of getting the chopper in the air. She'd done some homework, so she'd have some idea of questions to ask George about his job.

In what seemed to be one fluid motion, he adjusted the speaker tube on his helmet, put his left hand on the pitch-control or lift-off lever and reached for the control stick between his legs. Once he did that, she knew from her reading, he would then have to start manipulating his left and right foot pedals. It's a wonder, she thought, that they can ever get off the ground, much less pull off their hot dog stunts.

As she leaned left to look at the console between George and his co-pilot, a deafening explosion shattered the cockpit's Plexiglas bubble and in the instant before Angela threw her arms up to shield her face an image flashed of George's helmet rising off his body and hanging momentarily suspended in space. She knew she should fall to the floor, but she couldn't, or wouldn't, she wasn't sure. She just sat there tangled in the webbing, her knees wedged against the armor-plated back of George's seat. The huge hole in the windshield was a whistling wind tunnel the rotors still whump, whump, whumping overhead, debris and dirt slapping her face. Lester's volcano, she thought. But she just sat, stunned, unmoving, watching the spider web patterns form as the shattering glass cobwebbed outward in slow motion in ever-widening circles, first the webs spreading and then breaking up and finally falling into the cockpit. Blood from under George's helmet came slowly, too, at first, then rivulets, then in great unleashed gushes.

Seconds before, they had been inside a bubble, a plastic cocoon, and now she was in the eye of a storm in the middle of a pick-up-sticks toy prism with all the khaki-colored glass pieces shattering into a million parts. And she just sat, unmoving, and stared. What to do? It seemed to take an eternity for the thought to form.

Finally, there were sounds, the scream of what was apparently a second mortar, yes mortars definitely do scream, at least when they're that close, but it went past, didn't hit. Other screams inside the chopper, unfamiliar voices, and a low moan from Spike Jones: "Momma, Momma, oh Momma." And the machine-gun, the rat-a-tat-tat, so familiar, so incessant you barely heard it. Thank God, the door gunner hadn't been hit.

And Oscar's voice: "Miss, you gotta move, miss, we gotta get the pilot outta the seat. The co-pilot dead, too, his seat's a mass a twisted steel, him crushed in it. We gotta get at the pilot."

For the first time, Angela looked down at her own body. Her fatigues were splashed with blood and brains and pieces of carrot-red hair. She managed to extract herself from her squatting place, bits of flesh falling from her clothes as she rose and moved aside. Oscar and Lester Flanagan struggled to extract George from his seat, Oscar at the head, snaggle-tooth wielding the feet. They lifted him over the back of the seat, the helmet and the bloody mass it contained lolling, barely connected to the body. They placed what was left of George in the tail of the chopper. Then Oscar moved back toward the pilot's seat.

"Oscar," screamed Angela, at last finding her voice when she saw where the sergeant was headed, "what the hell are you planning to do?"

"Ain't nobody else, miss. The pilot dead, the co-pilot done bought the farm, and the crew chief breathing, but that's about all."

"Oscar, you don't know how to fly."

"Who says? I used to do cleaning up work around City Airport in Detroit when I was a kid, to earn me flying lessons."

"When you were a kid!" Angela screeched as the sergeant gently, but firmly, pulled her out of the way, and shoved her back into the hands of Lester Flanagan. "Oscar, you're a middle-aged man."

"I was a chopper gunner on my last tour, you know." He sat in George's seat and began rotating the disk control stick between his legs, trying to adjust the earphones and speaker tube he'd ripped from George's helmet.

"Jive Knees, can't you do something?" Angela pleaded, turning and speaking over Lester's head, to the tall kid behind him. She flashed on how strange it was that she used her private nickname for him, but he responded with no more notice than if he had answered to the name forever.

"No'm. Spike, he in a pretty bad way, and so's the other dude from the crew over there. We gotta get 'em some plasma fast. They done told us when we called for this here chopper that things was pretty bad, with strikes up and down the ridge—'at's why it took so long for these dudes to get here. Those mortars is trained right on this spot—slant-eyes must need glasses, only hit us with one so far. We gotta move, or we all in the dirt."

The machine shuddered and bucked and started to lift, then dropped, then lifted, then back down. Angela was almost knocked off her feet, and she sat back down, fast, on the nearest webbing along the side of the chopper. It was like a yo-yo. The thing finally got several feet off the ground without diving back down, then suddenly whirled in place, doing a complete about-face.

At first, everyone living and conscious on board was frozen in petrified silence, but after a while they all started giggling and laughing and showing other signs of shock or hysteria. It must have taken Oscar several minutes of those up-and-down, whirling-around, back-and-forth maneuvers before he managed to get the ship airborne. The only thing that could be said in favor of what he was doing was that he made them a moving target instead of a stationary one. The little ship took a number of small arms hits, but nothing that did any more damage than what Oscar was doing to it. Angela wondered if maybe some kind of gyroscope had been hit and that's why they were spinning so.

She couldn't take her eyes off Oscar. As though watching would will them aloft. But after a while, when she looked to her right out the open door, she could see tree tops beyond the arc of blue sparks spurting rounds from the Huey's machine gun. Funny, they looked red during night-flying but almost blue in the daylight.

Looking that way, she also saw the gunner as he got hit. He slumped forward over the M-60 he was straddling, with his legs hanging out the door, then fell sideways. The way the ship was pitching and tossing, she thought for a second he was going to slide out the door, but Jive Knees noticed, too, and reached out a long arm to halt the crewman's slide toward the open sky. No more tree tops, my God, Oscar had actually gotten them aloft.

I wonder if this is fear? Ford keeps saying there is something wrong with me not to be afraid. It feels like nothing, and I don't know where I'm going and will most likely die. I'll pretend my mind's a pudding, it feels like a pudding. Chocolate? No, blood red. Blood pudding? What's that? Where have I heard that expression? Must make my mind go blank, and then if we crash or die, I won't be afraid. Wasn't very afraid after capture, only at first. Don't know what I'm supposed to think or feel. Keep my mind blank, don't think. Don't know how else to do it. I wonder how the men do it? They don't talk about their fear, but Ford loves to talk about the lack of mine. Make me face up to my fear, he says. But don't want to. What if I see it and don't like its looks, and just go to pieces and start screaming and break the looking glass? What then? Don't want to think, can't think about anything except swimming in a pool of warm water.

# 47

# Oscar Flies

SHE THOUGHT of Spike Jones and the camera. She'd promised to let him explore it once they got airborne, promised herself anyway. And now here they were, she and Spike, hurtling to their fate together. Hurtle was a bit strong, lurching was more like it. She'd been lurching along that day she was trying to get to Hue, but she wasn't in the air then.

Being on the ground hadn't helped Spike. His feet had still been on the ground just starting to lift himself into the Huey when the mortar hit. George lost his head and Spike lost a foot, it was left behind still in his boot when Oscar finally got the chopper airborne. Dwight had found some kind of first-aid kit and wrapped gauze around the bloody stump, but she was afraid Spike was going to bleed to death. The medic was missing, where was he? He must have been wounded earlier, or he wouldn't have left. The wind was roaring through like a gale. It took all of her strength to just sit up against its force. Hueys are already open on both sides, the blown-out cockpit was creating still another wind tunnel. She was clinging to the web seating, her back pushed for balance against a small space of side wall.

She couldn't bear to look over at Spike, but what difference did it make? Looking wouldn't help keep him alive. All the blood, it was like watching her mother doing surgery. She was better with words, or at least she consoled herself with that. But words hadn't helped her much with the Cong, or maybe they had, no one was sure. Something helped her there, but what the hell was going to help her here? Sweet Oscar Brown? Sweet Georgia Brown, just as likely!

The lurching wasn't so bad now, Oscar was catching on. Dwight was doing something with the radios and Lester was trying to minister to Spike and the wounded gunner. Dwight had fiddled with the gunner's headset, then finally moved his rubbery jive knees up to the console between the two pilots' positions to try to plug in the earphones there. He was all angles, bent like an India rubber man, trying to situate himself. He tried but failed to squeeze into the co-pilot's seat, which was a mass of twisted steel and bone oozing blood. She couldn't hear what was being said, but Dwight and Oscar were clearly talking to someone. A someone, she hoped, who could help guide them in. Angela finally could stand the suspense no longer and made her way back to the spot just behind the pilot's seat, where Oscar now sat.

"What's happening?" she screamed at Dwight to be heard over the rotors and the roaring wind whipping through the open cockpit. "Have you made contact with someone who can tell us how to land?"

"Yes'm, Oscar talking to 'em now. We tol' 'em we needed to land fast on account a Spike, but they making us go on further where they got a real landing field, not just a LZ at a MASH."

"Are they going to greet us with a fire truck and foam just like in the movies?" She'd made Dwight grin, she was glad for that. "Yeah," said the gangly kid, "all that shit. Just like the movies."

Dwight's grin had thawed Angela's brain a little—she had to break the log jam up there somehow. She'd sat here with her mind wandering, trying to float, trying not to focus on where she was, but she suddenly realized she had a lot of thinking to do. As hopeless as their situation had seemed, she felt blood returning to her cheeks and breath returning to her body and the thought came that she just might live to tell this tale. If so, she had to start planning fast about how she was going to get this story written and filed. She'd be damned if she was going to be scooped on her own near demise!

She pulled a pencil and pad from her left breast pocket and started making some notes. As numb as her brain had been, she had to make sure she had all the points at her fingertips so she could dictate, if need be. How was she going to find a phone? How was she going to be able to file? Well, wherever they landed it was obviously going to be with a bang, which would bring the brass running and she'd just have to tell whoever was in charge she had to make a stateside call, *pronto*. If they did end up landing in a rice paddy or the like, she'd just have to insist on quick transport to some kind of command center. God, she really felt she was coming to. How wonderful. That rigor mortis state was awful. Now she was feeling the opposite, hyper and tingly with her heart beating fast high up in her chest almost like it was moving up to her throat. She wondered if it were possible to get so scared you could vomit up your heart? Oh Jesus, Angela, how gross.

Tree tops again, oh whoa! That's what was the matter with her heart, Oscar was trying to lose altitude and he didn't do it very well—that was her stomach, not her heart, getting crammed up her throat.

Landing is the difficult part, she knew, even for experienced pilots. Tree tops were whizzing by. Good grief, she thought, we're going much too fast. He's got to slow down. Slow down, Oscar, slow down, and suddenly she heard that she was really screaming it: "Slow down, Oscar, slow down. Jesus Christ Almighty, SLOW DOWN!"

They were whizzing over tents and huts, a huge base stretched out below, but Oscar apparently heard someone's admonition because he slammed what would have been the brake pedal in a car, but isn't in a Huey, and the ship spun around in the air 180 degrees, then started to spin the other way, but its forward speed was definitely slowed. There's always something to be grateful for, Angela thought. Thank God she'd strapped herself in. Even so, the turbulence was bruising her ribcage. They were back to the yo-yoing and wobbling and spinning of their take-off, but things were a lot safer now, no mortars for one thing. For another, someone down there was telling Oscar exactly what to do. They'd gotten over a big airfield, they weren't high at all. Angela could see everything, all the grunts and mechanics scurrying around like crazy on the ground. They really did have a truck with a big foam hose. She looked over at Jive Knees and grinned, pointing out the activity below. Such a movie! It all looked familiar; all the good guys always survived these rescue scenes. She saw GIs scurrying over to a couple of parked helicopters. Are they going to come up and wave us in, she wondered, or are they just wanting to get the choppers out of the way, afraid we will land on top of them?

My God, of course, what a wonderful adventure. They're going to send them up, hover next to us and send someone across to set this baby down. Just like in the air circus.

That was too bizarre. How could they ever do that? She watched the activity on the ground, as Oscar maintained a slippery hover. It looks like they're going to send up one of those huge flying cranes. Guys were climbing in the chopper, those things are Chinooks, too, how ironic, she thought. Don't know the zillions of model numbers, but whatever version it is, they've got it hovering so a ground crew can attach the chopper's sling hook. Must remember to ask the model number. Some of the grunts call 'em Shithooks, instead of Chinooks. She smiled to herself. Don't need *that* detail. They can lift tanks and trucks and even other choppers with those things.

But it didn't make any sense that they could hover next to us, Oscar wasn't competent to hover without banging into everything nearby. The big air crane came into view off to her right. She could see the co-pilot as no more than a blur through his Plexiglas bubble. He looked like he was giving Oscar a thumbs up. The Chinook made a couple of stabs at trying to get closer to the Huey, but each time it did, the Huey would start drifting toward it. And as it did, Oscar would let out a string of curses, then some violent gyrations would erupt. No way for the Chinook to safely hover in close with Oscar at the helm. Angela had studied a bit about the chopper's maneuvering capabilities before she'd gone out with George, and she knew the pilot had to obtain a perfect balance between the two sticks and the foot pedals. Each tiny movement in any one of those things could throw off the chopper's equilibrium. Two hot dog pilots could hover fairly close to each other, even overlap their rotors a bit if they were really showing off, but no way here. The Chinook pilot finally dipped his main rotor slightly to the left, in the manner of a fixed-wing pilot waving goodbye, then it shot straight up and seemed to move above them. Shortly, there were periodic loud bangs on the roof of the Huey. Their sling hook? But what in heaven's name could they hope to accomplish? They could certainly haul the Huey, Angela knew that, but how could they get hooked up with the Huey's rotors still whirring?

The banging continued for a short while, Jive Knees was shouting into his radio headset, then he and Oscar just looked at each other and shook their heads.

"Shit, you guys, what's going on?" Angela yelled at them.

"Oscar gonna land," Dwight yelled back. "They tol' him how."

With that, the Huey suddenly dropped.

Angela looked out, and saw the ground rushing at them.

"I think I'm going to need the whoopee bucket," Angela yelled at Dwight Pepper, as what little breakfast she'd had rose in her throat.

He grinned. "'At's what the floor for, miss."

Oscar finally slowed the ship and managed to get it into a hover, 10 feet or so off the ground. And Angela managed to get her stomach under control. We're safe, she thought. Couldn't be much of a crash from this short distance.

She saw Oscar push down hard on his left stick and the Huey dropped like a shot. When the skids hit the ground, the chopper shot straight back up in the air.

Angela started laughing, she could feel hysteria on the rise. "Oscar," she yelled, "More subtlety with that stick!"

Dwight wasn't laughing—he'd been thrown across the ship from his standing spot next to Oscar and had banged against a side wall.

"You OK?" Angela shouted over to him.

"Yes'm," he replied, and then grinned. "But I 'spect you right on that *sutatee* word."

Oscar tried getting the Huey down a couple of more times, each with a bit less bounce than the try before. Finally, the skids hit down, and stayed there.

# 48

# Oscar Lands

SOMEONE TOOK her arm and guided her off the chopper. When her feet touched the ground, she would have fallen if it hadn't been for whoever that someone was, holding her arm. Her legs just went to jelly, wouldn't support her for a brief second.

She looked around the big field in a daze. The sun was beating down, as always, and the heat made the shimmering aircraft look like they were rolling at her through a mirage. The Army did, indeed, have everything out but a brass band for their arrival. Fire trucks, foam had been sprayed on the runway. It looked like the entire staff of the base was on hand cheering from the sidelines. A short, potbellied little chicken colonel was running around, just like a chicken with his head cut off, blathering about putting Oscar up for the Medal of Honor. "What a great way to get a freebie trip home," beamed the big black man. "The President have to pin it on you, don't he?"

In the excitement of landing and the commotion of getting the wounded and dead off first, it took a few minutes to sort out just how bad the casualties were. But by time they'd ducked under the still whirring rotors and walked off the field—away from the noise of planes and choppers taking off and landing—they heard the worst. The gunner was still alive, but the crew chief and Spike were dead. The door gunner was the only living member of the five-man crew Angela had started out with at 6 that morning. The medic had been killed on a previous run, after Angela had been bumped by wounded. Some story about a day in the life of a Medevac crew.

Oscar broke down and sobbed when he saw the stretcher with Spike's bloody stump protruding from under a blanket that had been pulled over his face. Lester and Jive Knees just stood there, staring, their young faces old in acceptance. Angela could barely stretch her arms around Oscar's big frame, but she tried to comfort him, as the two of them stood there in the middle of a hangar and cried and rocked in each other's arms.

The colonel was circling and hovering. It felt to Angela as though he thought he were on stage in front of a big audience. "A man that brave, yet sensitive enough to cry over one of his men. This sergeant epitomizes the American fighting spirit."

She felt like screaming at the jerk. But she needed the colonel's help. I've got to calm down, she thought, focus. And his schmaltzy quote would be perfect for her story. She gave Oscar another big hug and took so many deep breaths that they made her feel dizzy. She then turned to the colonel, high-volt smile in place, and told him she needed a direct line to the States. "Absolutely," he said. When she asked him how to spell his name and then wrote it down in her notebook, he nearly fell over himself, barking out orders to transport her double time to his own office.

"Oscar," she yelled out, as the big guy was being lead off for a debriefing. "This'll take about an hour. I'll find you and we'll get shit-faced drunk. OK?"

"'At sound good." He was led off by two young Air Force officers in starched, short-sleeved uniforms, Jive Knees and Lester listlessly following behind.

After she'd called her story in to an ecstatic Harry in Chicago, she ran into another war at the base's club bar.

"Only officers," the officer in charge said, putting out a hand to block Oscar from entering.

"Well, *I'm* not an officer, you asshole, and I'm allowed in here, so so is he," she screamed in a voice that even she could hear was flirting with hysteria. And in she marched. Oscar didn't want to come with her, but Angela pulled him in, insisting. Because of Oscar's momentary celebrity, and no doubt the prospect of fisticuffs with a female potential nut case, the officer backed down.

The light was dim, the place was smoky. It took them both a moment to adjust their eyes. It was well into the cocktail hour, and the place was jammed. No empty stools at the big mahogany bar on the left. Angela finally spotted a lone, vacant table in a corner, and pointed Oscar in that direction. "What're you drinking? I'll pick 'em up, and be right over."

Before they could move, a voice came at them over the din. "Why don't you folks sit right down here, and let me buy you a drink?" It was the enlisted man behind the bar, who was pulling a draught as he spoke. He put the glass down and waved his arm to encompass the eight or nine seated officers, who to a man had swiveled their heads in the direction of the newcomers. "Everyone here wants to hear your story. That's all we've been talking about."

Angela hesitated, looked over at Oscar, who merely shrugged. As they moved toward the bar, a young tow-headed lieutenant with a crew cut jumped up to offer Angela his stool. They were stood to several rounds and peppered with questions, Oscar especially. A chopper pilot among the group kept repeating, "You're some hell of a fellow, I just can't believe you could do it." Angela was grateful for the diversion of the how-dija-do-it questions. It delayed the time of talking about Spike and George until she and Oscar were more anesthetized. But finally she said, "Hey, guys, thanks for the drinks and the good cheer. But Oscar and I need some time alone."

She picked up her Scotch, he his bourbon, and they found another spot against the back wall.

"Talk about Spike." Angela delivered it almost as an order, as they settled into their seats. "I think it will help."

"He was such a kid, you saw yoself," Oscar said, his big brown eyes pooling up. "I's in this as a career. These chillen just pulled off a the streets."

They talked about George, "He a good man," Oscar said. "Some a these jocks gets too big fer their britches. But Captain Rodgers, he a good man. Always talkin' 'bout his little girl. Jist wanted to git outta here and go home."

They drank some more, and Angela got tearful. "I'm scared, Oscar. I don't know what's happening to me. Am I crying for George, or myself? What am I doing here?"

"I suspects you ought to go back home, ma'am. Get outta this place. No reason a'tall for you to be here." Oscar put his big hand on her shoulder, and awkwardly patted up and down.

"I can't seem to think about George," she said, tears running down her face, as she signaled the waiter to bring another round of drinks. "All I can see are his brains and carrot hair splashed on my fatigues."

She spent a big part of the hours before dawn retching in the toilet of the BOQ where she was staying.

I just can't face Ford, she thought the next morning, as she cupped cold water in her hands from the faucet and splashed it on her face. The mirror over the sink shot back a grim sight. Her face looked almost green, eyes red and puffy. Her tongue felt and looked like cotton, hands sore and raw from her death grip on the Huey's webbing. She decided she would just stay here a day, get some food in her and try to pull herself together. If she went back to Saigon, Ford would worm everything out of her. "Now tell me," she could hear him say, "just what exactly happened? How *can* you keep putting yourself in these situations?" She couldn't deal with that now. She needed all of her strength. Besides, Parks was counting on her, and she couldn't let him down.

# 49

# The Big Question

KHE SANH, that's all anyone seemed to talk about. What was its strategic importance, or did it even have one?

Nick hadn't been there, but Curtis had. And so had the rest of the correspondents drinking and arguing about it, sitting on the Continental terrace.

Even though it was early evening, Curtis was clearly already drunk, and becoming more obstreperous by the moment. "It's a setup. It's a trap. They're trying to entice in the enemy. Whatever correspondents happen to be around will end up as sacrificial lambs."

Nick grimaced. Angela and Parks were in Khe Sanh. They had been gone about a week.

"I doubt Westmoreland has ever viewed us as lambs, Curtis." The snide remark was from the Brit whom Nick referred to as Marbles. The asshole's got a milk mustache, Nick thought. It was the first time he'd noticed that Marbles had taken to the Scotch drink, probably hoping that would make people take him seriously.

Nick thought back on the cryptic early-morning message he had gotten from Angela through the UPI office that he was to tell Parks to meet her in Da Nang rather than at Tan Son Nhut airport in Saigon. Nick had obliged, and Parks went off to join up with her for their trip to Khe Sanh. Parks had gotten the photo assignment from some British mag and the editors were delighted when he suggested Angela do a story to go along with his pix.

Angela also had asked that Nick tell Ford she was going directly to Khe Sanh, instead of coming back to Saigon. Shit, Nick had thought at the time, he didn't want to get into the middle of that crossfire, so he had just called Ford's office and left the message with the first person who came on the line.

But for the rest of that day, Nick had been in an uneasy, cloudy mood. He knew Angela must have been through something bad; the part of the message for him was brief: "I'll fill you in later." All he knew was that she'd left the day before to spend an easy few hours riding around with some chopper jock. She also seemed to think the pilot might have some insights that could help her reporting on the Chinook's rotor problems. Funny, Nick had had a bad dream about Angela the night she left. It was mixed up somehow with an anecdote he'd heard about Dickey Chapelle, the raucous fast-talking dame who was forever offering the gratuitous advice to always stay in the footprints of the guy walking point. A booby trap finally got her while she was out with a patrol. Dickey's obit contained the ultimate compliment from a grizzled Marine that "you couldn't tell her from a grunt," and the Corps had named the central press shack in Da Nang in her honor.

Corrigan and Curtis arguing brought Nick's mind back to the table.

"The place is a nightmare, a hell hole, name your own adjective," Curtis was all but yelling. "Shallow bunkers, reinforced with rags and bunting and dirt, half falling off the overheads like peeling paint in some South Chicago tenement."

"Fine. Fine," Corrigan retorted with impatience. "No one is disputin' that. But what no one is bothering to explain is why the Marines have never really dug in. You're one of the ones, Curtis, who keep insisting that there's going to be a fierce attack, just like Dien Bien Phu. But they're not fightin', they're under siege. Just pinned down in that tiny base camp inside a two-mile perimeter."

"Right," said Marbles. "I say, it's been that way for some time now. Besieged, going on perhaps two months."

Dumb Brit, Nick thought, can't even say "been." Makes it sound like *bean*, some kind of lima bean. He signaled the waiter for another beer, and frowned the guy away from asking Curtis if he wanted another. Several empty martini glasses were already lined up.

Curtis didn't notice. He was drumming on about Khe Sanh. A

reporter from the Des Moines Register had joined the fray, as well as a photographer from the San Francisco Examiner.

"Everyone here has had his ticket punched, Curtis," the photographer said. "And we've all asked repeatedly what's up with Khe Sanh. Doesn't make any sense. Saigon came under attack, and all those troops were sitting around up *there*. Nothing up there, for Christ sake."

"You can't say that, man," the Des Moines guy said heatedly. "There's some big guns trained on that camp, shelling away."

Curtis rolled on. "There is nothing approaching proper sanitation. The trenches alongside the bunkers are running with mosquitoes swimming in slop and garbage and empty C-rations and piss."

The vehemence in Curtis' voice brought back to Nick the day Angela had mimicked Ford's reaction when he found out she was going to Khe Sanh with Parks.

"It's not bad enough you're going to that hell hole, but with that lunatic besides! You're sure to get killed." Angela's rendition had amused Nick at the time, although he somehow couldn't blame a guy worrying how he'd make love to a woman after she'd stepped on a Claymore mine.

Curtis had seemed like a jerk, interfering with her work, when Nick first heard the story. But as the days had worn on with Angela and Parks gone, Nick began to change his estimate. He really began to pity Curtis, watching him move around like a shadow, like a hollow shell. Even his voice had the resonance of an echo. The ambassador called a press conference during that period, and when Curtis got up to ask a question, everyone had to strain forward to hear him, those patrician oval tones wavering and breaking up as though they had been delivered through water. His question, "How much longer is Westmoreland going to stand still for the siege of Khe Sanh?" was the question on everyone's mind. But when Curtis asked, it was clear he was thinking about Angela and not the besieged Marines.

The military brass kept implying that they hoped the enemy would launch an all-out attack on the camp, but none of the reporters who had been there could figure out how the pinned-down Marines could defend against it, if it came.

The tiny metal airstrip that was the camp's only lifeline was truly a sitting duck. The North Viets' big guns a few miles across the border in Laos were trained on that spot. Before you could hear the engines of an incoming transport, you would hear the big guns start up. The airstrip was littered with the scraps of aircraft that hadn't outrun the guns. Smaller artillery and snipers were dug into the surrounding hills. The officers club that the Seabees had come in to build had been shelled down to a few scattered planks and sticks; the beer hall sat roofless for a time before its walls finally returned to the dust.

The incessant shelling and the fog and bad weather were extracting an exorbitant toll. After mid-February, when the huge Hercules C-130s stopped flying into Khe Sanh because of the heavy losses they were taking, some of the hot-dog pilots of the lighter, more maneuverable C-123s got the touchdown-to-takeoff time as low as one minute flat. Mechanics at Da Nang airbase told Detroit News reporter Bob Pisor that a day or so before the C-130s were banned, they had counted 242 holes in the wings and fuselage of one of the behemoths that had limped in from Khe Sanh.

If you weren't waiting for the next plane out, you were waiting for the camp to be overrun. Waiting to be killed during the half-wakeful state that passed for sleep as you lay atop your cot dressed for combat. Waiting to be trapped in your bunker, by flamethrowers or napalm, your flak jacket and boots on fire, the already suffocating, putrid air actually igniting like the greasy debris at the mouth of a gas well.

"We've all been there, we know what it's like," Corrigan said, still trying to calm down Curtis, knowing, like all those at the table, just who in Curtis' mind was the sacrificial, hapless correspondent. "Angela will be all right. She's got to do her stint like everyone else."

"She's not everyone else," Ford snarled back. "No one is everyone else when it comes to that sink hole. Why does she have to go through it like everyone else? My mother hasn't been through it. I'd kill myself before I'd let my daughter suffer an experience like that." And Ford Curtis began to cry.

"Ford, for Christ's sake, Ford," Nick pleaded. He couldn't remember ever having seen a man bawl like that, and he felt absolutely panicky.

"Angela's like us, Ford. Jesus, she's not like other women," Nick blurted out.

"You little twit, can't you get it through your head that she thinks she's invincible?" Ford shouted at Nick. "She's led a charmed and privileged life. She doesn't understand that there are people out there with mortars who really don't give a shit that her mother went to Radcliffe. That lack of fear is going to get her killed."

Braeford Curtis' fist crashed down on the bar table, then in a wild swipe sent drinks and long-necked Lone Star beer bottles skidding across the floor. Before anyone could get up or stop him, he kicked his chair back from the table and was gone.

# 50

# Khe Sanh

BO PARKS took a last long drag on the roach he'd stuffed away in his fatigue jacket for just this special occasion—landing in Khe Sanh. Not more than a two-dragger, what was left seemed to turn to smoke in his lungs and between his left thumb and forefinger. He'd purposely left himself just a drag.

Coming or going from Khe Sanh was a terrifying business. The airport's waiting room was a trench alongside the strip. Grunts going home or on R&R to China Beach, lay curled in the fetal position alongside correspondents straining to hear the engines of their deliverance over the pounding of their tap-dancing hearts.

Dragweed, ha, ha. Parks grinned, his thin lower lip slightly parted over the rotting teeth. That's rich. No point going into battle totally flying, miss the fun. No good, either, burning weed long in these closed-up babies, Hueys more privacy with their open doorways, never know when some uptight brass ass going to take a whiff and start giving ya shit. But a little toke just the thing to steady the nerves.

There was a set pattern to the choreography of arrival or escape, and if you missed a beat or an entrance cue, you could be dead. The deplanees all knew they had to get out fast, with touchdown to takeoff time as low as a minute. Speed wasn't the only risk. You could be nearly trampled to death by the guys trying to get on. At a certain point, just after the plane's wheels touched down, a lucky stiff leaving Khe Sanh had to climb out of the trench and make a run for the spot where he estimated the cargo ship would roll to its momentary rest. He had to hurdle or end run the ever-present body bags with their attendant swarms of flies as he tried to gauge his moves so he wouldn't have to wait, exposed, while the plane's door rolled back and the incoming personnel and correspondents jumped out. And, of course, one always had to be mindful of the stampede of deplanees heading to take your spot in the trenches. If you got caught in a wave of runners moving toward the trenches, you could be swept back and miss your ride as the plane taxied for takeoff.

Maybe a little song, Parks thought, a couple of deep breaths and spin on in, my man. Everybody look what's going down, Parks and Angela round and round, everybody look what's going down, round and round, there's something happening here, what it is ain't exactly clear, everybody look what's going down, round and round, down. Almost in, gotta run, ready set, two for the money, three for the show, 69 at the ready, check the gear: spectacles, testicles, oh blimey that feels good on the pood, pud, wire-rimmed spectacles are eyeglasses, spectacular spectacles are firefights you see with your eyeglass spectacles or your long-range viewfinder, camera, smile for the birdy, the bird's a bit of all right, OK, checking her gear, Foxy Lady, the bird, cool, smooth like velvet, if the landing were only smooth as the lady. There goes Angel, out the down, Angel hits the ground, Angel heads for the trench, there goes Carpenter, out the door, Carpenter, hits the floor, see Carpenter run, Carpenter makes the ditch, there go more, four on the floor, here goes Parks, walk, don't run, if there's a man with a gun, he may be a man with a banjo . . .

"Parks, get over here, run, for Christ sake!" Angela was screaming at him over the screaming sounds of Khe Sanh. So this was Khe Sanh, glad to meet ya, Khe Sanh, enchantez, voulez-vous, and how are you. Angela's eyes were two slits, underneath the helmet bobbing up over the rim of the trench. "Get over here, you idiot, you're asking to get shot loping along like that."

Should have had me lens out instead of in me duffel, great shot of the bird lying on her stomach upright along the trench wall, sell it to Vogue, what the well-dressed lovely wears to work at the DMZ, one two three, what are we fighting for? Don't ask me, Uncle Sam needs a helpin' han, got hisself in a terrible jam, don't ask me I don't give a damn, next stop be Vietnam.

THEY HOOKED a ride in a Jeep with a young Marine from West Virginia. "Culpepper. Lance Corporal Jim Culpepper, ma'am."

"Where can we find the commanding officer?" Angela asked the stocky, dark-haired kid with the big hands and massive forearms, as she climbed in the front seat and Parks in the back. Culpepper wore a helmet and heavy flak jacket, but his fatigue sleeves had been cut off and rolled. The fold held a pack of Camel cigarettes. His right, upper bicep was tattooed with the red outline of a heart. Inside it, gleaming white against his tanned, leathery skin, were the words "*Hot Damn.*" That's a first, Angela thought, a white tattoo. She could hear Parks singing to himself in the back seat.

The sky suddenly darkened as the gray, transparent mist that had hung over the hills when they landed morphed from charcoal to several shades of black.

"Better drag out your ponchos," Culpepper warned. As he shifted into gear, Angela felt the first sprinkles. "Haven't been a day in a month didn't rain. I'll take you to TOC."

She pulled her poncho from her duffel, but before she could get it over her head or ask what TOC was, the skies opened. The rain fell hard and fast in straight sheets.

"Pretty awful here, I guess?" She said it as a question, hoping to draw out Culpepper. Water was running down her face, as she turned to him, her hair in red streaks plastered to her head and neck. Her clothes underneath the poncho were wet and sticking to her skin.

"Awful ain't the word," Culpepper's reply was almost a snort. "Left West Virginia so as not to spend ma life underground, like ma dad in the mines. And what've I got? We live underground. Day and night. Like rats. Just burrowed in. No fighting. Just burrowed in, waiting fer the enemy."

The thunder of an artillery round all but drowned his last words. "And here *he is.*" Culpepper jammed on the brakes, and yelled at Angela and Parks to "hit the dirt."

She threw herself sideways out of the Jeep. Dirt, hell, she thought as she hit the ground. It's nothing but mud. She lay there as several more shells exploded, trying to burrow in, just what Culpepper had been griping about. She couldn't judge how close the strikes were. They were random, hitting all around. She could hear the screams of the wounded. Those shouts of "corpsman," "corpsman," seemed to be coming from every direction. A round, which sounded like a howitzer, connected with something flammable, she could hear the explosion turn into a roaring flame that whooshed as it burned. She could feel people running. The thuds of shells hitting. The ground she lay on was vibrating. How long will this last? Not long, probably. She had heard before she got here that the incoming was in spurts. Random and relentless. Up to several hundred rounds a day was common. A thousand was high, but as many as fifteen hundred had been reported. She had been told that Khe Sanh was about waiting. And here she was, waiting for the shelling to stop.

"That was a bit of a bitch," Parks said to her, with his snaggletooth grin, as they climbed back in the Jeep after Culpepper finally shouted to them it was OK.

At least Parks has sobered up, she thought. Thank God. Would hate to present ourselves to the commanding officer with him as high as he was when we flew in.

When Culpepper dropped them off at the Tactical Operations Center, the captain in charge laughed at the sight of them, muddy, soaking wet. "Welcome to Khe Sanh," he said.

"Sorry." He quickly amended himself with a smile, shook their hands. "I didn't mean to sound inhospitable. But, as one of your colleagues wrote a few weeks ago, we're in the center of the bull's eye."

"The V-ring," said Parks. "The dude was right on."

Angela looked around. The bunker was huge, well-reinforced, well-lighted. They were deep underground.

"This place looks swell," she said to the captain, trying to keep her teeth from chattering, the underground damp no help for her wet, clammy clothes. "I'd heard you guys weren't well dug in."

"This one's it," the captain said, waving his arm to encompass the place. "An old French bunker that was reinforced by the Seabees. We Marines don't like avoiding a fight. The rest of our digs here aren't very permanent."

That night she lay in an eight-by-ten foot cave they speciously called a bunker. She was rigid, waiting, lying there listening for the scratching sounds, her nostrils filled with creosote. They had told her a kid from Cleveland was Medevaced out this morning, his face a mass of rat bites. Surely they couldn't get at her face through the poncho. Of course they could, just chomp! She felt like she couldn't breathe—she had to have some air. Like those warnings on plastic bags from the cleaners: Don't let your kid play with this. She'll suffocate with a bag over her head.

This isn't war. What is it? Trying to sleep in a coffin-sized cave. Still in her clothes and boots that had never dried out. Rigid, afraid to stir the poncho covering her face and hands. She'd tried her helmet, but she *really* couldn't breathe then. Listening, waiting for the onslaught of the rats. A Marine bunker, hell. More like a Marine latrine. The stench. The body odors of those who had lain here before her. Crumbling dirt from the unreinforced walls falling in her face or pinging on the poncho.

# 51

# Battle Fatigue

When Angela got back, she didn't seem the same. Nick couldn't put his finger on it exactly, but the best way he knew to say it was "pinched," kind of puckered up. "You know, like what guys mean when they say someone has a puckered asshole," he told Corrigan.

The big Irishman laughed when he heard that. They were at the standup bar in the Continental, each looking for a quick belt before bed, after a long night of the usual journalistic machismo on the terrace. Nick would never have mentioned his Angela observations to the full crowd. But even Corrigan didn't give him an easy opening. "Jesus, boyo, no wonder Harry's always on your ass. If you tried that with any rewrite man I ever knew, they'd hang up on you."

"Well, hell, this psychological mood stuff is hard to explain," Nick said, turning one of his milder shades of pink. "A shrink probably would use some dandified expression like withdrawn, but she isn't that. You've seen her. She talks and walks and laughs and smiles, but it's a pinched kind of smile and the laugh seems a little loud and forced. Don't you think?"

"Yeah, kid, you're right," Corrigan conceded. "She looks like her pucker factor is getting high. Battle fatigue."

Nick had had the feeling ever since she'd been back that Angela and Curtis were just sticking off to themselves. Whenever he did see them, they were openly lovey-dovey. Nick finally asked Parks what he thought was wrong with Angela, but he said he hadn't noticed any change. Crazy fucker, Nick thought, how would he know? He loves war, calls it sexy. He had told Nick that life in the V-Ring, as AP's John Wheeler called Khe Sanh, was the ultimate high. And all the grunts had "grooved" on Angela. "The bird was first rate, really first rate," Parks said, "except she vomited a lot."

The odors of Khe Sanh, as with all of Vietnam, were what stayed with you even more than sights and sounds. More than one correspondent dwelled on the sensation of gagging or retching as his most vivid souvenir of the beleaguered Marine camp with its barrels of smoldering oil and shit mixture, stacks of blood-soaked fatigues and socks cut from the wounded and piled outside the triage tent of Charlie Medevac, its open running sewers, and things burning everywhere from the constant enemy strikes. Even the trees seemed on fire, gouged and scarred as they were with shrapnel. But Nick figured Angela must have been a lot more uptight than Parks said if she really was going around throwing up all the time. She was a cool lady and probably just didn't talk about how nervous she was.

Parks told Nick that when he and Angela were ready to leave Khe Sanh, the weather had gotten even worse, if that was possible—the ceilings had been described as zero-zero all month. So they had to hang around an extra day and a half waiting for a lift out. Parks said tensions were running especially high, but Angela was calm. "When we finally made our run for that sucker, Luke the Gook was blasting away at us and chaps were screaming and yelling and cussing, and some of 'em were near crying, lying on the floor of the plane praying and cussing Thanksgiving, or whatever. But the lady was cool."

Nick finally spotted Angela at a press conference and told her he'd spring if she'd go to dinner with him at L'Amiral. She looked startled at his offer to pay. They usually went Dutch. But she seemed pleased, and Nick was happy at the chance to get her off to himself. He figured if he plied her with good food and plenty of booze, he'd get her to talk and find out what was bugging her.

He got something quite different from what he was expecting.

It turned out she was a nervous mess. He got his first clue soon after they arrived at the restaurant when she twice insisted on changing stools at the bar before they were even seated for dinner. She said she'd never noticed the anti-terrorist iron grating covering the windows— although it had been there for a long time—and wanted to move "in case someone throws a grenade in." Telling her that's what the grating was for—to deflect a grenade—didn't seem to help.

They were barely seated at their table with the oversized French menus in front of them, after two quick Scotches at the bar, when she confided her big secret. "Nick, I was terrified." Nick just started laughing, which seemed to infuriate her.

"I don't see what's so damned funny," she snapped as she tore apart a French roll and distractedly stuck it in a pad of butter without the usual civility of first picking up her bread knife. "I've just confessed to what an unregenerate coward I am, and you find it amusing. Is it beyond you to be serious about *anything*?" She was really fuming.

"You're not a coward, Angie. Far, far from it."

"Nick, I was terrified."

"Thank God. It's evidence you're not stupid. You know what cowards are. They cut and run and don't do their jobs. You've been through one piece of bad shit after another. You disappeared into Khe Sanh before anyone could question you about that chopper ride after the pilot got blown away. Jesus, you need to talk. The only thing I know about that is what I read in Time or Newsweek. Sensible people are terrified, cowards cut and run."

"Well, yes . . . I . . ."

Her face lit up at what he was saying, but she seemed confused. "You don't understand."

"I understand. You were traveling with Parks. And Parks is nuts. The guy has been practically blown away twice, and he doesn't give a shit. Angie, there's a screw loose in the guy, everyone knows that. You've heard people talk about it. You've talked about it yourself. You can't judge your own behavior, or anyone else's, against that kind of litmus."

"Who do I judge myself against? I've gotten as jumpy as a menopausal old lady. And I just kept thinking, 'The men are right, I can't take it.' It was horrible."

"Parks said you were wonderful."

"He did? You're kidding!" She was absolutely screeching, she was so excited. "Well, what did he say? When did he tell you that? Why didn't you tell me?"

"He said you were wonderful. I didn't tell you because I haven't seen you. I had to invite you to this fancy dinner to get you alone for a few minutes."

"Why would he think I was wonderful? Did he tell you I was throwing up all the time? I've been throwing up for months, but Parks was the first one to know. I was mortified."

"He told me. He also told me guys were crying and pissing and praying lying on the floor of the plane getting out of there, with the plane taking small arms hits, and that you were smooth as velvet."

"I can't believe it," she said, throwing her hand to her mouth in that age-old feminine gesture that mimics the startled beauty-pageant winner. She reached across the table and gave Nick's hand a big squeeze. And the dam broke.

"Oh, God, am I glad I have you to talk to. Oh, Nick, it was so awful. But the worst fear was that I just didn't have the guts to stand up to it. Those poor, sweet, baby-faced Marines with their haunted eyes and hollow laughs. They tore my heart out. I was so afraid I was going to start crying and not be able to stop, and just cry and cry and keep crying until I was hiccupping and hysterical, and then I didn't know what they would do with me, they would say, 'Get that hysterical woman out of here, she is hiccupping and crying, and we have a war to fight and she's hysterical and crying and get her out of here she's impeding the war effort because women always cry and that's why we don't want them around.' But I didn't cry, not once, not even about George."

And Angela starting crying and hiccupping in L'Amiral Restaurant in downtown Saigon and Nick didn't know what to do. But this time he didn't panic, like he had when Ford had started crying. Nick just gave her his handkerchief and patted her shoulder and decided not to tell her that he was beginning to think she and Curtis might have more in common than he had first thought.

She didn't kick over her chair, as Curtis had done. She cried only for a little while. Then she laughed, with a little edge of hysteria to it as she dabbed at her eyes with the huge white linen napkin and blew her nose with Nick's handkerchief.

Nick patted her hand and gave her a glass of water.

"Drink," he instructed. "And I'm going to order for you. The most expensive thing on the menu. Maybe they have pheasant under glass. How 'bout that?"

"Oh, Lord, no. It's liable to remind me of a dead rat."

He ignored that, trying to proceed to a subject that would calm her down. "Who's George?" he asked.

"The chopper pilot whose head blew apart into my lap. He was . . ." She hesitated.

"He was what?" Nick prodded.

"A friend," she said.

"Jesus, lady, you obviously need someone to let you blow a little steam. What's the matter with that stupid fucker, Curtis?"

"Oh, he was so glad to see me, and I was so glad to see him, and I couldn't bear to talk about most of it. So we've just sort of clung together, soaking up warmth, playing Monopoly and Scrabble and two-handed bridge. It's been wonderful, just being together. He's a safe harbor. I wish it could always be that way. Besides . . ."

She faltered, unsure, frowning.

"Yes?"

"I don't quite know how to say this. I hadn't really dragged it into my consciousness until just now, but I felt, somehow, that he thought I had failed, been a sissy. That seemed to give us both a certain kind of relief."

"Oh?"

"It's confusing. I guess he assumed I was scared, but that's not exactly it. As you so nicely reminded me, everyone is scared. It's another thing."

"Like what?"

"I don't know. He assumed something that he and I aren't talking about, and I don't like the gap it's causing between us. But I don't really know what it is."

"That you didn't want to be there?"

"Yeah." She jabbed her index finger at Nick, excited with the discovery, nearly toppling her fluted crystal water glass in the process. "That's it. Because my real fear was that I was a closet coward, there was no way to talk to him about how terrified I was in Khe Sanh or how mindlessly numb I was on that chopper ride out of Cambodia. But in his mind, it's settled: I was afraid, I've learned my lesson, I shouldn't have been there, and variations of my coloration of yellow don't matter."

"Angela! It's no shade of yellow we're talking about. It's red-blooded, healthy terror."

"Yeah, you're right. I was nauseated with fear. But I did not, repeat did not, ever, once, think that I shouldn't have gone to either place. It was my job!"

Nick just looked at her and grinned. She was getting back her animation—alive and glowing.

"Don't laugh. Oh, I do feel like such a fool. But it is exciting to discover I'm not such an awful failure and coward as I thought."

"You were a prisoner of the VC for 10 days, and you seemed OK"

"Being a prisoner, even seeing George blown up in front of me, was nothing like the oppression of waiting at Khe Sanh. Almost holding your breath, not knowing what was coming next, having too much time to think, lying awake all night, living like rats underground.

"Did you ever think," she blurted out after a pause for breath, "about a rat biting your face?"

"Ah, not actually," Nick replied, deadpan.

"That place is crawling with 'em! The first night, Parks and I stayed in regular Marine bunkers. How can people live like that? A claustrophobic cave? I'd heard about the rats; I knew. I slept in my clothes and boots and spread my poncho over my face and hands. Listening for the scratching sounds. Promise you won't ever tell anybody, Nick, but I couldn't bear it if something like that happened to my face."

"Female vanity rears its beautiful head."

"Don't tease me!"

"I tried to keep as low a profile as possible." She rattled on, breathless, running her sentences together, ignoring periods, as though she would never stop talking. "I wore my helmet, always, I damned near slept in it. In fatigues, who can tell me from a grunt. I'm tall and not especially 'endowed,' as they say. But word got around fast there was a broad in the land, and the Seabees insisted I stay at their bunker. I tried not to ask or expect any special privileges, but boy did I leap at that one. Although later I found out most all the correspondents stay there. It was a dream place, they don't call it the Alamo Hilton for nothing—spacious and reinforced and lighted—compared to what I'd been in the night before. No dirt fell on your face during shelling. I could quit breathing in the creosote smell from my poncho over my face. But I still kept being sick to my stomach. I really didn't make a terrible spectacle. But I felt so ashamed of myself."

"I was worried you might be pregnant."

"WHAT? Are you crazy? You silly, silly, silly!'

"What's silly? Parks said you were calm and cool and in control and throwing up. And you got back to Saigon and withdrew from your friends. Who's silly?"

"Me, I guess."

At home in a Khe Sanh bunker, February 1, 1968. AP photographer Eddie Adams, right, and Robert Ellison, of Empire News, who was killed at Khe Sanh on March 6.

That wonderful grin. Suddenly she seemed calm, to have wound down. The chatter stopped. She even took a few bird-like bites of her veal marsala.

"Now that's better," Nick said after a while. "So when do you get back to work, woman? All this falderal is costing you money. Harry wants you to do a piece on Khe Sanh. Newsweek's coming out with a cover on it, it's leading all the nightly newses. They're going bananas in the States over what Khe Sanh means. You can give him the full shot: Do your fear number with the rats, the chaos of the place. I'm sure he'd take some analysis on whether we can hold Khe Sanh, and if so, why the hell we want to, stuck off where it is not even in a natural pathway of invading North Vietnamese."

"Ah, you did most of that for Harry already, didn't you?"

"Yeah, but that was a month ago, and everyone feels this thing is coming down to the wire. The tonnage our B-52s have been dropping in those hills has got to mean something. Why aren't the Marines properly dug in? Westmoreland is going to have to explain himself soon, shit or get off the pot, if you don't mind my being vulgar."

"I don't know," she said, her voice trailing off.

"What don't you know?" Nick snapped.

"Ford . . . There is something reassuring about . . ."

"Oh, for Christ sake."

"I'm too tough to be a proper woman, Nick."

"Jesus, Angela, I can't deal with all this. You're not tough, you just have more sense than most broads. You're the one who said you weren't going to let Curtis fuck up your head. Does all this have anything to do with what happened to you in Pleiku? What did happen to you in Pleiku? Did you figure out anything more about your theory of the rotor blades banging together and causing crashes? More to the point, do you really believe you were in Cambodia?"

"You read the newsmagazines."

"Cut the crap. You can't fall apart on me. Harry's expecting you to file on Khe Sanh, NOW. Pleiku was yesterday. Cambodia is tomorrow's story, if we really secretly have troops in there."

"Nick, please let me fall apart."

"No way."

"I need someone to love me."

"There's always me."

"Oh, Jesus. We're too good friends for that."

"Why can't we be both?"

"I don't have the answer to that. I've never been able to pull it off. You get in the middle and somehow all the rules change. You don't belong to you anymore."

# 52

# The Second Battle of Dien Bien Phu

AFTER SHE filed her Khe Sanh piece to Harry the next afternoon, Angela headed back to the Continental terrace to meet Nick. She was in a fine mood as she strode down the Tu Do from Reuters, feeling as though she could breathe again, wondering if the air really were fresher and lighter than usual. She was back on track. Nick had browbeat her into getting back to work. She had hung around Reuters until Harry had cabled back, saying her piece was OK. Now *she* was OK. Fine, good, wonderful.

She spotted Nick at a table with several correspondents including Corrigan and Marbles and, of all people, an old guy they called Smitty. She didn't know him, except by reputation, which wasn't good with the younger correspondents. Most viewed his approach and opinions as withered and ancient as his gnarled bones and stooped, skinny frame. As Angela remembered it, he was one of the so-called "old China hands" who had gotten Ford riled with their insinuations that she must have slept with the enemy to have gotten away alive from her capture by the Cong.

"So, Lass," Corrigan greeted her, "Boyo's been filling us in, he has. Says you've joined the parade of pundits who are pontificating on Khe Sanh."

"Afraid so," she said with a laugh, as she raised her hand to catch the attention of the old Chinese waiter gliding by with a big wooden tray loaded with empties.

"Graduated, so you have, from reporting, to telling us what to think, and how you feel." Corrigan swiped at the ubiquitous milk in his huge mustache, and signaled the waiter he'd have another Scotch chaser. "We can use a fresh eye on the Khe Sanh debacle."

"What are you talking about? We've ragged it to death," Nick quipped. "Everyone's got his pet theory."

"True, that is." Corrigan laughed. "Most of the views are represented right around this table." He swept his arm to encompass all of them, eight men in various stages of slouch and inebriation. "We're only missing the fall of the French, from your *pal*, Curtis." The old Irishman put an ever-so-slight sarcastic emphasis on the word "pal," as he lifted his bushy eyebrows knowingly at Angela.

Arguments about the enemy's intentions at Khe Sanh, or Westmoreland's—depending on the angle from which you approached it—filled most waking off-duty hours during those early days of March. There were the diehards, like Curtis, who clung to the idea that there was a connection between the siege of Khe Sanh and the rout of the French at Dien Bien Phu. No matter that that was 14 years ago, they argued that the same Cong general was in charge of the troops in both places. And the anniversary of the start of General Giap's siege of the French was March 13. Still others believed that the masses of enemy troops said to be surrounding Khe Sanh were figments of Westy's imagination, that he had been duped into diverting large numbers of U.S. troops to northern I Corps thereby allowing the enemy to go his merry way during Tet, pounding hell out of the cities. Developments in the anti-war movement back home had compounded the speculation that the Khe Sanh mess smelled of politics. Eugene McCarthy, a second-term senator from Minnesota and former college professor, was challenging the war, and it looked very likely that he was going to win more Democratic delegate votes than the President of the United States in New Hampshire's upcoming primary, the first of the season.

"So what's your position?" Corrigan's friend Marbles asked, shifting in his wicker chair and resting his elbow on the table to peer directly down at Angela, seated at the end.

She, like every other reporter who ever lived, was only too happy to expound on the piece she had just written.

"Well," Angela said, taking the last swig of her first beer, and putting the bottle down with a smile.

"So? What's your position?" Marbles asked again. "Nick said you got into some analysis, after you got over talking about the rats."

She took a deep breath, and signaled for another beer to a passing waiter, who was weaving in and out among the packed tables of the terrace. Tet had been nearly six weeks ago, tension in the city was easing up, and the feel of people relaxing just a bit was almost palpable. "First off, despite the appalling appearance of the camp, the Marine casualties aren't that severe compared to other battle zones. It's possible Westmoreland has a point in claiming that the incessant close-in B-52 raids are clobbering the VC."

"I'll be damned," said Smitty, seeming to rise from a slumber, "maybe she's a kid with some sense, after all. Actually give the military credit for knowing what they're doing."

Angela laughed. "Sorry to disappoint you, Mr. Smith, but there are several other possibilities."

"Like what?" he grumped.

"We've all heard the theories," she said. "That the fight there is a diversionary tactic by the Cong, or the reverse, that Westmoreland wants to suck in the Cong for reasons known only to him. The most sadistic speculation is that the Marine base is some sort of public relations pawn."

More than a few commentators had speculated that Johnson and Westmoreland needed a win they could point to. This war with no front lines, an elusive enemy, and nothing other than nebulous search-and-destroy missions gave the media, the U.S. public and its politicians little to sink their teeth into. Everyone needed a specific battle and a tangible victory. And a number of reporters had begun to wonder out loud if Khe Sanh might not be the place chosen to dig in for a symbolic do-or-die stand. Precisely what the French had done so many years ago at Dien Bien Phu, losing their foothold in Southeast Asia.

"Stuff and nonsense," said Smitty.

His comment triggered a chorus of comment. Everyone was either talking or shouting at once. Marbles took his usual Brit position that the war was wrong, therefore the U.S. couldn't possibly do anything right. Corrigan, being Irish, even though he worked for an English newspaper, never took a knee-jerk British position on anything. "But," he said, "there clearly is something fishy about Westy's desire for this so-called make-or-break battle at Khe Sanh." A fellow from Milwaukee couldn't be heard over the din, but his remarks didn't make much sense anyway. The several other Europeans, including a Norwegian photographer, stayed out of the fray, listening to the Americans and Brits hash out what the Vietnamese and everyone else but the Americans called "the American war." In general, most of the European correspondents, with the exception of the French, viewed the war with such righteous indignation that they didn't even bother arguing about it. And the Asians were mostly too circumspect to say much one way or the other. Nick, meanwhile, with his anti-analytical bias, was loudly chiding everyone for "chewing the thing to death, instead of just covering the war." And Smith, of course, was red in the face, from repeatedly shouting, "All you young idiots are systematically losing the war for America!" Finally remembering to include his contemporary, he turned and sputtered, "As for you, Ray Corrigan, you were always an iconoclast about everything."

Corrigan burst out laughing and took control of the situation by spreading his hands over the table, "Gentlemen, stop your engines," he said, loud enough to be heard over the din. "Calm down, calm down. We all seem to be missing the point that the lady here, with the usual feminine touch, is giving everyone his due."

"Yeah, good show," Marbles replied sarcastically, "she's covered all the bases, so she can't possibly be wrong about anything."

"I found that there seems to be good evidence that the Cong have stopped tunneling to repair their forward trenches," Angela said defensively. Sitting, as she was, at the opposite end of the long table from Marbles, she looked past him over National Assembly Square and saw Curtis heading in their direction. She remembered with a start that Ford's houseboy was supposed to be cooking dinner for them tonight.

"I say, what's the tunneling all about?" Marbles asked, just as Curtis walked up, swiped a chair from another table, and squeezed in, now making them 10. Before he had even ordered his Scotch, Curtis brought up the rife speculation that McCarthy might upset Johnson in New Hampshire, asking others at the table how they viewed it.

The non-Americans, to a man, all expressed interest and curiosity about the significance of the vote.

"How does this thing work, exactly?" asked the Norwegian photographer. "How does a fellow from Wisconsin..."

"Minnesota," injected Nick.

"Wherever. How is he allowed to stand for election in New Hampshire?"

Smitty interrupted. "Curtis," he said, "you're old enough to have some sense. What's your take on the siege of Khe Sanh?"

Curtis frowned. "Jesus, Smith. I haven't been shy about expressing my opinion on that. But it's a subject we probably ought to just leave alone."

"Yeah?" Smitty was slurring his words a lot more than he was even 15 minutes ago.

"The Marines are not dug in properly, that's clear to anyone," Curtis said with a finality that suggested that was the end of the subject.

"So?" said Marbles.

"So," Curtis said, clearly irritated, "the camp will be overrun. There seems no question of that. The rest of it is my opinion. I know a lot of people don't agree with me, but I think it will be on the 13th of this month. Great psychological victory for General Giap. Dien Bien Phu, and all that."

"That's nonsense," said Smith. "Westmoreland knows what he's doing."

"Look what they were able to do at Lang Vei, a short *seven* miles from the Khe Sanh base camp," Curtis countered. "With only a few tanks, the Viets overran those Green Berets and trapped them underground, dropping satchel charges and grenades down their bunker vents."

"Green Berets! For Christ sake, Curtis," Nick said, clearly steamed. "There were only 12 of them there. That was an outpost guarded by South Viet Rangers. Besides, that was a month ago. Everyone thought the NVA was going to keep right on rolling into the base camp that night, but the situation has changed since then. South Viet regulars repelled an attack on their sector of the main perimeter night before last. You heard General Sidle say two weeks ago that it was 'illogical' that the NVA hadn't attacked before now. And Angela says there's hard evidence that the Cong has stopped repairing their forward trenches."

"She's already explained her theory to me," Curtis replied. "*Sources tell her that,*" he said in an almost breathless, mock radio-announcer voice, "that our troops are using stethoscopes to detect the lack of underground tunneling. Come on, thus the Cong are pulling back?"

A strained silence enveloped the table. Even Smitty, the man who forever seemed tone-deaf to nuance, turned, without a word, to stare at Angela.

"The tunneling has stopped, Ford." Her lips barely moved, her jaw line was rigid. "We all know, *don't we,* that the Viet Cong is fighting this war mainly through tunnels. They live underground, they have hospitals and kitchens and weapons manufacturing *underground*. If they've quit burrowing around Khe Sanh, it most likely means something. Probably that they're not really interested in *taking* Khe Sanh. Just interested in keeping us hung up there."

"Angela, goddamit," a flush was moving up his neck. "You're going to make yourself look foolish going into print with off-the-cuff opinions. Stick to reporting what you see."

"Reporting facts is excellent advice, Braeford," her voice was stone cold. "The problem here seems to be we're all seeing different things at the same scene."

"That's absurd. You're just not used to combat," he snapped.

"And that's a load of crap, Curtis," piped up Smitty, the old China hand, startling everyone at the table. "I can match you war for war, buddy boy, and I think you're all wet with your Dien Bien Phu theory. And that's all in hell it is—theory."

Curtis flushed slightly, and seemed to grind his teeth a bit on his pipe stem, but by time he had cupped the bowl in his hand and drawn the pipe from his mouth he was able to drawl in his richest Brahmin tones: "Perhaps you're right, Smith. I guess we're all inclined to get carried away by this impossible war."

"Amen," said Smitty.

Curtis stayed maybe five minutes more, until the tension had defused a little, then excused himself and left. He didn't once look at Angela, and she spent the time until he left looking at her hands in her lap. She switched to Scotch, the next time the waiter came around.

She could hear herself chattering too much, a bit too loud, but it somehow felt necessary. Everyone else at the table seemed unusually subdued. Neither Khe Sanh nor Curtis was mentioned the rest of the evening

After they'd closed the bar, Angela went home with Nick to the UPI apartment. He said he'd give her the cot and he would sleep in the big chair.

# 53

# Cheap Weeds

Something was dragging Nick back to wakefulness. The smell of smoke? The feel of someone's presence? Smelled like Gauloise. Cheap French weeds. Didn't make sense, must be a dream. Was he the one smoking, but too drunk to know it? Smoking in bed? Had to rouse himself. Head too heavy to lift. He stuck his hand out exploring for the familiar—the floor, he had pulled the cotton pad off his cot and lain on the floor. Why? As he probed farther, his fingers touched something slimy. He jerked his hand back, but it clicked through his brain that the feel was satiny, not slimy. The synapses suddenly made a connection. Angela's satin panties! He sat bolt upright.

"I was out of cigarettes, these things taste like burning rope," her voice came from somewhere out of the darkness.

A pinpoint of cigarette glowed a few inches off the floor near the boarded-over window at the end of his room. As Nick's eyes adjusted to the shadings of dark, the outlines of Angela's form began to take shape: sitting, legs up, hands on her knees, the cigarette's tiny beacon drawing a pathway of light as she'd take a puff, then return her hand to the top of the pyramid that was the geometric shape of her long legs at rest.

"I'm sorry about what happened," she said to Nick's silence. "It was dumb."

"What was dumb about it?" He was bewildered and couldn't hide it. Or, too groggy to want to. It had been like a dream, but the best one he'd ever had. Angela had been drunk and obstreperous over Ford, then she was in Nick's arms and then they were on the floor, laughing and giggling, ripping off their clothes, touching and kissing tender spots in the tenderest ways.

And now she was trying to back off, saying it didn't mean anything. He strained for some sign from the other end of the room, a sound, for her breathing to see if it was quick and nervous, or if she really was as casual as her last remark. But he couldn't tell over the labored pounding of the ancient air-conditioner. He could hear the growling of the WC down the hall with the wooden tank that needed its chain rattled, but Angela's presence was marked by nothing more than the firelight and strong smell of her burning cigarette.

"What was dumb about it?" he demanded again, this time nearly shouting. He waited a moment, watching the cigarette's path in the dark, then lay back down. "Who gives a shit," he said into whatever article of clothing he was using for a pillow. He was too tired, anyway, to keep awake for some long-winded explanation.

"Nick, I'm sorry," he heard her say as he drifted back to sleep.

STILL UP to my usual stunts of backing off and fucking up lives, Angela thought with disgust as she took another of the foul-smelling fags from the pack she'd found in a pocket of Nick's jeans before she put them on.

If she could just get out of here, go home and take a hot bath. Bidet was more like it. Jesus, yes! Nick with all his prostitutes and nurses. But she was trapped, bedraggled, in Nick's Levis. Couldn't find her slacks. Nick was probably sleeping on them, wrinkled beyond redemption. She had meant to stay at Ford's last night, they had planned to have dinner "at home," as he called it. She'd practically been living there lately. Thank God, she hadn't given up her room at the Continental, as he'd been urging her to do. What a mistake that would have been. Imagine having his place be her home and having to go there and face him now, in this state?

Should never give up your nest. It's your well being, sense of self. A room of one's own. Track what you want on your own carpet. Peter's maiden aunt Maria used to call it "spitting on your own stove." Funny, Angela thought, when she was young and newly married, she hadn't quite understood that. That first little house seemed so much to belong to both of them, to her and Peter, her wonderful nest maker. Teaching her how to make his grandmother's spaghetti sauce, how to plant a cherry tree. There were always good kitchen smells, and flowers, and hominess in that little house. She'd grown up such a wild thing, such a flawed domestic, never baking brownies or sewing doll's clothes, just books and baseball, or racing her bike to beat all comers. Peter was grounded. Sensible. He even taught her to make friends with the morgue attendant on her police shift. That way you could get a beat on any new stiffs long before the other reporters did.

Nick was restless, mumbling in his sleep. Once he shouted out what sounded like "Maggie, don't leave me."

It seemed an endless night, Angela alone with her melancholia, her battle fatigue and the banging, dripping air-conditioner. She kept trying to shake off ghosts of George with no head, and Khe Sanh Marines with no legs, and herself with no face, eaten away by rats. She ducked out once to the john down the hall, worried she'd run into one of the UPI guys and be mortified. She'd thought about going and sitting on a wharf down by the river, but she first had to at least clean up a little, fresh makeup. But she couldn't even find the light switch in this silly-ass little room.

Besides, she had to stay and face the music with Nick. She couldn't just sneak out. She had to make him understand. What?

How the hell was she going to explain it to him, if she didn't understand it herself? And so the night went, cigarette after burning-cardboard cigarette. Except on some primitive level Nick *did* understand. He just didn't think about this kind of maudlin crap as much as she did, but he was every bit as evasive of domestic entrapments as she. He was so dismissive of Mary Alice and any commitment to her. Yet he longed for love and warmth, Angela was certain, just as she herself did. He also understood that the price was always too high. What, she wondered, had made him that way? Who had preceded Mary Alice?

She watched the light come, ever so slowly, the city shapes begin to appear as out of a lifting fog through the grubby sheet of plastic that covered the partially boarded-up mortar-hole in Nick's bedroom wall.

She'd had a sense for a long time that he was awake, but it was only with the increasing light that she could see that he was unnaturally still, the tossing and mumbling had stopped. She hauled herself up from the floor and padded in her bare feet over to peer down at him. His eyes were open, they hadn't blinked open at her approach. He'd obviously been awake for some time, lying there on his back, his hands behind his head, staring at the peeling ceiling, no doubt with no better idea of what to say to her than she had of what to say to him.

"Nick, listen to me," she pleaded. "You can be mad at me, you can scream at me. But I won't let you hold it in and hate me."

He turned his head enough to at least look at her, without changing his stony, impassive expression.

"What the fuck does that mean?" he asked in a tone that complemented the harsh sentiment.

"Who's Maggie?"

"Nobody."

"You yelled her name in your sleep."

"I doubt that."

"You did. I heard you."

"So what are you doing wearing my pants?"

The ice was broken. Angela laughed, dropped down beside him on the floor, as he instinctively covered himself with whatever manner of bedding he could grab. She rubbed her hand through the soft hair of his chest, stroked his cheek. "You're using my slacks for a pillow, so I couldn't leave. Besides, I knew I'd have to unthaw you a little, or that Irish stubbornness might not allow you to ever speak to me again."

"You don't deserve it."

"Yes, I do. We may care a great deal about each other, but we'd make a rotten pair. You know that."

"No, I don't."

"You do, goddamn it! Don't try to tighten the screws on me. I already feel bad enough. And don't get your fucking nose out of joint and screw up the best friendship either of us ever had!"

She emphasized this last with a playful, but sharp slap to his bare chest, a friendly love tap with a sting. He grabbed her wrist and pulled her toward him. She rested her head on his chest, he with his arms around her, as he rocked her gently to and fro.

"What'd we do now?" he asked.

"I don't know," she said. "I'll never be able to face Ford."

"Christ," Nick bellowed, "You always worry what Ford thinks. Never me."

"So what do *you* think?"

"Well, shit, I dunno."

"You're a big help," Angela said with a laugh.

"You ought to dump him."

"I'm in love with him."

"What in hell for?" Nick demanded, pushing her away to arm's length, holding her there, gripping her by her upper arms. "It doesn't make any sense."

"He's charming, witty, at the top of his profession . . ."

"That could be H.L. Mencken who, I might point out, is dead."

"Mencken was hardly charming," Angela countered.

"So, they have even more in common than I thought," Nick said with a laugh.

"At least Ford's a grownup, which is more than anyone can say for the two of us."

"I knew there must be some logic in there somewhere," Nick said.

"Oh, hell, I don't know, smart-ass. I guess I don't create my own serenity or security, somehow. I climb out on limbs . . ."

She stopped at Nick's far-away expression. "What?"

"Sounds like what you need is a mother," he said.

Nick didn't realize how close to the mark he had come. She recoiled from the insight as though it were a slap. Instead, she turned her mind to Nick and what she saw as his lack of self-awareness, his lack of connectedness. So she mistakenly assumed she understood that look on his face, the look that usually accompanied some smart remark. In truth, he was remembering the day at Tan Son Nhut when he and Ford were trying to get a plane to Hue to look for Angela. Nick was recalling his own strong feeling that if anybody could find her, it was Ford. Angela, of course, had found herself.

"Maybe so, or a wife," she snapped back. "But then, so do you. Look at this room, it's a mess."

"I don't feel the need for a conventional life," he said, with the emphasis clearly on the "I."

"Go ahead, finish your sentence, but I do. Right? And then I have trouble living it."

"Well," Nick said with a superior shrug, "you're the one who can't seem to figure out what the hell you want."

"I know exactly what I want," Angela said. "To be left in peace so I can get my work done."

"I don't interfere with your work," Nick said quietly.

After a while, Angela brushed her teeth with salt and her finger, Nick took her slacks to get pressed, and she finally left his room in the late morning, figuring that with Nick in and out of the building, anyone seeing her come out then wouldn't think anything of it.

"I *cannot* believe you're such a prude," Nick had said. But he clearly understood. He didn't even make a smart retort when she said all three of them would be compromised, not just her, if people thought she were sleeping all over town.

She went across the square to her room at the Continental, took a hot bath, changed clothes and prepared to head out to Ford's villa. She planned to use her key to get in, and bring home the clothes, makeup and other personal things she had gotten in the habit of leaving there.

Ford, she knew, had an afternoon appointment with Ambassador Bunker and Bob Komer, the pacification chief, so she wouldn't have to run into him when she got to his house.

# 54

# The Pink Villa

THE LITTLE villa was pink stucco with a walled front garden off the street. A towering date palm dominated, just as the huge elm had reigned over the yard of her childhood home in North Carolina. But this was Oriental formality, a rock garden, tiny pool spanned by a miniature red-lacquered bridge, and a blaze of tropical flowers, hibiscus, wisteria, ferns, wild orchids. Even a cocoa-bean tree! A heady floral sweetness hung in the haze of the late afternoon sun, reminding Angela of the gardenia smell that had enveloped the perfume counter of the five 'n dime in Chapel Hill when she was a kid.

As she put her key in the door, Angela thought of how important a home was to her, yet how little energy she had for creating one. The great thing about overseas assignment was servants, houseboy, even a gardener. Ford, for all his moving around, was rooted, solid. That was nice. Like Peter, except Peter never wanted to leave Illinois. It was Kim Chi's day off, she'd have the house to herself. She hadn't yet decided if she should just gather up her things and leave, or stay and face Ford's wrath. It was probably better for them to stay apart for a while. But she must have the decency to face him. She couldn't just take her things and run. Perhaps she would wash her hair, put on her new Thai silk kimono, laze in the garden and let her hair dry in the sun. Burn away some of the booze and the dissipation from her mind and her soul. She'd be able to think more clearly, gather her strength to try to resolve things with

Ford. If they could only be at peace! Their passion for each other was pushing them apart instead of bringing them together.

But as she opened the door, stale, hot air hit her with an ominous blast. Something was strange. A dank smell lay under the heavy air as she moved cautiously through the short hall into the main room. The first thing she noticed was disarray, things out of place, topsy-turvy, like the disorder of a crime scene following a robbery. Then she saw him, in the overstuffed leather chair he'd insisted on buying at the PX, even though it was much too heavy and didn't go with anything else in the room. He was sitting, somehow hardly resembling himself, a strange idiot-grin on his face, eyes staring, uncomprehending.

"Ford, my God, what's wrong?"

He didn't answer. His wide-open eyes barely flickered. "Ford, what the hell is wrong?"

She looked frantically around the room, taking in the sordid scene. Empty whiskey bottles, overflowing ashtrays, a discarded sock, books and newspapers, a dirty fork, a scattered deck of playing cards, a cup of cold coffee with a dead butt floating in it, an apple core resting on the plastic grooves of a long-playing record, the turntable making its endless rounds, automatic changing arm stuck, moving up then down then across, eerily trying to discharge a phantom record.

Beyond, the dining table was set for two, tall tapers long since had sputtered out and melted down into free-form wax designs on the high gloss of the polished blond wood. Fruit flies buzzed over a once-elegant salad, resting on its wilted lettuce leaves.

Ford was dead drunk.

Angela passed her hand back and forth in front of him. She snapped her fingers, she slapped his face. His eyes registered almost nothing. He was awake and breathing, that was about it. Angela could tell he recognized her, but he couldn't form any intelligible words and had almost no reflexes at all.

She remembered the fat-cheeked southern boy from VMI whom she and other passengers had walked the deck with all night. They had poured coffee into him, trying to keep him alert and alive after he had nearly OD'd, trying to drink a fifth of vodka in a chug-a-lug contest with some of the crew on the Yugoslav freighter carrying them all to Tangiers. Joe, whatever his name was, had won the bet, but nearly lost his life. Ford was close to that state.

She ran to the kitchen and turned on the fire under the kettle for hot coffee, filled a pitcher with water and ran back and threw it in his face. He hardly blinked. She tried to get him on his feet, but he was dead weight. Back in the kitchen she dumped some instant coffee and some of the hot water in a cup, and filled the pitcher again with cold water.

After three dousings with the icy water, and sips of the steaming coffee from a cup held to his stiff lips and spooned in, his eyes began to move a bit. She finally got him to his feet and with the help of a dining room chair used like a walker—she pulling and tugging and pushing—they finally inched their way across the living room, through the bedroom and into the bath. She scooted him, fully clothed, into the shower and turned on a blast of cold water. His voice, come back at last, arrived in full force as he huddled shivering against the white tiles, protesting the icy stream. But he still was too uncoordinated to do much more than yell.

As she reached in to hand him his third cup of steaming coffee, he deliberately set the cup on the floor, then grabbed her wrist and pulled her into the shower with him.

"I'm getting my clothes soaked. Are you crazy?" she yelled at him over the pounding of the water as she struggled to keep from getting wet.

"I've still got mine on, join the party," he said, laughing as he maneuvered her against the tile wall of the stall, pinning her there with his own body, taking her head in his hands, kissing her hard on the mouth.

Coming up for air from the deep kiss, the cold tiles at her back, she could feel her boots filling up with water. Ford rearranged the angles of his lower body more precisely against the curves of hers, then leaned back from the waist to look at her. She knew he liked to watch her face when he touched her breasts. It was guaranteed success. He knew just how to roll the nipple between his thumb and forefinger to call them erect, causing her to focus on a distant place. He was watching now. She felt her tension drain away as he traced the outline of her nipples, beginning to harden and show themselves as her silk shirt took on more water and began to cling to her skin.

"You're still drunk," she said, running her fingers lightly across his lips, then over his cheek, across the top of his ear, and brushed her lips across his.

"Guess so," he said with a grin as he tugged at the zipper of her water-logged slacks.

This time she kissed him, feeling herself go under, float away, drifting in that distant pool, the rose-colored space of weightlessness that signaled her intense desire—always—for this man. It took almost nothing to trigger, a glance, a touch. He was like a magnet. When she was a little girl, the hairdresser in Chapel Hill had a black metal square at the end of a long stick that she used to pick up hairpins. The pins would stand on end, literally leap up off the floor to cling, to flatten themselves against that powerful attracting force. That was how he made her feel.

Angela rubbed against Ford like a cat, she wanted these wet clothes off, hers and his, to be skin to skin. The feel of his body was a heating blanket, a warmth, for aching muscles and sore psyche. The water was still pounding down on them but she had no awareness of the cold, only the sense that there was warmth, radiating, waiting for her if she could only get through the layers of clothes. He had just about gotten the slacks off, she alternately tugged at the buttons of her shirt, then his.

As he pulled at her slacks she looked down, shaking the slacks off, pushing with her feet to step out of the soaking encumbrance, she laughed when she saw the extent of his throbbing impatience for her. "Even so drunk," she said.

She struggled free of her panties around her ankles, and he found his mark, banging her hard against the wall. She was jolted, again and again, as he drove himself home, his hands on her swollen nipples, his head thrown back, moaning her name, the cold water, unnoticed, unfelt, still raining down on them.

As she anticipated the last thrust, waited for the final familiar "oh, yes," he said instead, "Nick," and deflated heavily against her, his body spent, his head sagging to her shoulder.

Panting, struggling for air, she gently moved his head up and brushed her lips against his, trying hard to get her breath.

"It's you I need," she said barely above a whisper. "You I love." She felt the involuntary shriveling as he slowly exited her body, felt the water for the first time as it pounded down on them. They were suddenly shivering, both of them. She swaddled them each in a giant, terry towel she had swiped from the Continental. They moved to the bed, their arms wrapped around each other, and slept that way. "I'm so out of control over you," he said as he drifted off. "I love you so desperately."

"I know. I know," she said to his already snoring form. "That's the heartbreaker," she said softly. "How we adore each other."

After their nap, the rest of the afternoon and evening became a collage in her memory, snapshots of her and Ford making love, a family album of lovers.

Sitting on the bed eating leftovers from the fridge, Ford giving Angela instructions on the proper use of chopsticks.

Replaying the album from *Guys and Dolls*, the record that had been spinning aimlessly when Angela first entered the living room.

At one point, they made love on the living room floor, and, at another, standing by the kitchen sink, and then in the back garden by the pond while she was trying to read and dry her hair. It started all over again when he accidentally touched her breast as they dipped water out of the pond to rinse the sweat from their bodies. This time they ended in the pond, frolicking among the algae of the lily pads.

And finally, they agreed once and for all, for the umpteenth time since they had known each other, that he would return to New York when his career dictated, and that she would follow when hers did the same. In the meantime, he would begin the legalities to disentangle himself from Berenice and find an apartment that could be home base for him and Angela in New York.

The only discordant note was while they were sitting on the bed eating with chopsticks. Ford stated rather than asked, "You were with Nick, weren't you."

"I was drunk. I told him I was sorry," Angela replied.

"Told *him*? What about me?"

"Nick's the one who'll get hurt. You and I have each other. Besides..."

"I know," he interjected, "I set it up. I was awful to you at the bar. But Jesus, you can't go off and sleep with someone every time I raise my voice!"

"You surely must know I'm sorry! But that's not the point. We have to stop hurting each other. You have to quit tugging and I have to quit pulling."

"Amen," he said.

In the morning, Ford went off to face the ambassador and try to explain why he had missed his appointment the day before and hadn't even bothered to call.

# 55

## Dinner at Eight

CANDLE FLAMES skipped along the cut edges of long-stemmed goblets. Nick's wine glass actually hummed when he rubbed his finger fast around the rim to see if fine crystal really could make music. Angela was in an evening skirt, a ribbon in her hair. Easy to forget where you were, that there was a war going on—expensive china, sterling fingerbowls. Class, with the faint scent of mimosa.

Curtis sat at the head of his table and made good sense about the war. "We're destroying this country, its culture, its economy, and its natural environment. We've been misinformed, or even downright deceived, about what we came to save, and the folks at home—the public, the minor politicians, the editors—are finally beginning to catch on."

Nick had been ousted from the UPI apartment that morning. Two of the agency's New York editors and the Tokyo bureau chief were flying in for a firsthand look-see at what was going on in Saigon. So there went Nick's room, the borrowed cot, even the big chair. He had run into Angela at the Pagode shortly after he got the bad news, and she not only invited him over for dinner, but said she was sure Ford wouldn't mind if he bunked on his couch while the visiting firemen were in town.

"I think I might mind, if I were him," Nick said, wondering if Ford had guessed where Angela had spent the night after their flaming argument last week.

"Don't be silly," she replied, and had changed the subject, leaving no opening for further comment.

Actually, the offer was a big help. Nick was relieved. He could have tried to scrounge something, but it might not have been all that easy because the entire press corps was in a state of flux. Things had been changing fast, militarily and politically. March 13th, the 14th anniversary of the start of the Dien Bien Phu siege, had come and gone. Shortly thereafter, the 1st Cav swept in on their flying horses of Operation Pegasus to "rescue" the Marines from an enemy who seemed to have evaporated like smoke into the Khe Sanh hills. Westmoreland then went to Washington to announce on the White House lawn that the battle for Khe Sanh had been won.

Angela had told Nick at the time that Ford had been stunned, not only by the fact that he had been off base with his Dien Bien Phu thesis, but by what he was beginning to see as the "folly" of the war. At that point, there were still a few diehards arguing about whether Westmoreland had been suckered into diverting troops to Khe Sanh, away from the surprise Tet attack on Saigon, but within weeks Lyndon Johnson had announced the general's reassignment to Washington and the president's own intention not to seek reelection.

In this charged climate, editors at home were beginning to decide the war was over and were calling guys back like crazy. Harry was getting antsy, too, so Nick was trying to keep a low profile, hoping his editor wouldn't think about him too much. A hotel bill at this point would have been all Harry needed to put Nick on the next plane home.

Nick was in for a lot of surprises when he arrived at the pink villa for dinner that night. He was floored that Angela turned out to be a good cook. A houseboy in a white jacket did the serving and cleaning up, but she cooked herself—made something that wasn't half bad out of wilted lettuce and rice and stuff she'd picked up at the local market. Nick also was stunned by the sense that Angela lived here. He knew they were having an affair, but he'd never thought much beyond that. The villa was cozy-chic, sliding glass doors in the dining room overlooking the walled garden with a lily pond. It was strange to see her in a kitchen, stranger to see her in a skirt. Nick had never thought of her before as a nest-maker, and it hit him like a bolt that perhaps it wasn't so weird that Curtis saw her differently than the rest of her pals did.

Curtis had been in Korea, Algeria, Cyprus, the Mideast: Vietnam had him up to his eyeballs with combat. He'd suggested himself, early in the evening, that maybe he was just getting too old for war.

"It's a young man's game, we all know that," he said.

"Or woman's," said Angela, who had just sat back down at the table after a quick trip to the kitchen to check on the dessert.

# EXTRA
## Los Angeles Times
**MONDAY FINAL**

VOL. LXXXVII — FIVE PARTS—PART ONE — MONDAY MORNING, APRIL 1, 1968 — 114 PAGES — DAILY 10¢

### Won't Run — De-escalates
# LBJ BOMBSHELL

## President Halts Bombing of Most North Vietnamese Areas
## Withdrawal Announcement Catches Nation by Surprise

### Johnson Believed Hoping to Become Viet Peacemaker

### Voluntary Withholding of Tax on Incomes Urged by Reagan
*Governor Proposes Plan for Money to Be Deducted From Paychecks and Saved Until Time to Meet State Levy*

### Johnson's Decision Won't Alter U.S. Vietnam Policy, Rusk Says

### 'COMPLETELY IRREVOCABLE'
### Turning Point for Decision Came in Westmoreland Talk

"Or woman's," repeated Curtis, hardly skipping a beat.

"This is *politics*," he went on, biting down hard on the word, "and needs to be covered as politics. I'm too old and, frankly, too experienced for this kind of assignment. Chopper-hopping from one firefight to another is like covering the cop shop on a Saturday night in Detroit or Los Angeles: Checking the police blotter to see how many knifings there were in Watts doesn't give you much insight into the underlying causes of summer riots."

The houseboy took away their dinner plates, and poured more wine. It was clear to Nick that Curtis was just warming up, and that he wasn't overjoyed to have Nick there. Several martinis before dinner had definitely greased Curtis' skids.

"Well, gee, Ford," Nick said, "you don't have to stay."

Curtis continued, as though he hadn't noticed the interruption, or the ever so slight baiting suggestion in Nick's tone. "Some of my contemporaries here complain about the lack of patriotism in the younger correspondents. I must admit I was inclined to agree with them when I first got in-country. But this is the most disillusioning tour I've ever done: the senseless killing, the lack of a front and decisive battles, the folly of rotating men in and out individually instead of letting them build up the camaraderie and morale that comes from fighting as a unit. I was never one to run from a fight, but I don't know what this fight is about any more. No other war was ever like this, and I just want to get the hell out. Drugs and rock music and crazed frenzy seem to have taken over, a psychedelic nightmare. The grunts talk about the 'real world' as someplace other than this, and in that I agree one hundred percent."

"But, Ford," Nick said, "it's here. It's happening. Someone's got to cover it."

"Then let's describe what's happening," he shot back. "Let's describe the random violence that's dehumanizing an entire generation of Americans." His voice began to rise. "What are these GIs going to be fit for when this war is over? They wear ears on a string around their necks, they take pictures of themselves triumphant with their foot on the chest of a dead man, or worse yet a young woman with her pants off and her legs in the air, they sever heads and stick lighted cigarettes between the lips. They call them *gooks* and *slant eyes* and *dinks* and blow them away as though they were animals—man, woman or child—not seeming to care whether they're Cong or South Viets, and who the hell can know for sure, anyway, which side they're on?"

Curtis voice had risen steadily. He abruptly stopped speaking, shook his head as though to clear it, put his hand to his forehead, rubbed his fingers across his eyes as though they ached. Angela poured coffee from a silver pot, and nodded to the houseboy who moved around the table serving each of them fragile crystal dishes that contained what looked like chocolate pudding. Nick frowned. He was pondering something that struck him as odd. Ford's kind of an emotional guy, he thought, for someone who's been around as much as he has. I saw him cry when Angela was in Khe Sanh. He's obviously pissed at me right now, but too polite to say so. And he's pretty hepped up over talking about the war. Other correspondents that I know don't seem to get so wrought up. We're all kind of detached. I wonder if it has to do with Ford's age, seen too many wars, or if it's his bent for analysis? Hard to figure, he decided. I guess I'll never know. This was all strange, unchartered territory for Nick.

Curtis shook his head again, and went on in a quieter, almost melancholy voice. "We're all getting like the GIs, numb to the most ordinary of human sensibilities. The changes I see, Nick, in both you and Angela are extraordinary—a hardness, a cynicism. If you don't both get out of here soon, there will be no turning back. I've seen it happen once in a while to police-beat reporters, on occasion to a war correspondent, but here it's all-pervasive. Everyone's soul is being tainted by the unprecedented brutality of this war."

"Ford," Nick said, "you're forgetting how often most of us have been sandbagged by the military and by our own editors when we try to tell the story. That's our front line, our battleground, trying to get the message through. But that's our job. We've got to stay here and keep trying to write the story."

Angela joined in. "Unfortunately for Ford, he's not forgetting anything. He's the one whose head has been turned around more than anyone else's by this war. I don't think the brutality is making any of us any more cynical than the awful realization of just how difficult it is to try to tell it like it is."

"I repeat," said Curtis, "this is *politics,* and the story's back home, not here."

"Ford, that's one thing you're wrong about," Nick said. "The decisions may ultimately be made in Washington, but without some of us here to paint a true picture instead of parroting the body counts given to us in press releases, there wouldn't be much of a story to write back home."

Angela piped in, "We're just different kinds of reporters, Ford, you and I, that's all."

"Or maybe I'm just older," he said with a sudden and baleful weariness. "I can't tell the good guys from the bad anymore. I can't pontificate and feel superior. And I've had the awful realization that perhaps those qualities of ego and self-righteousness are necessary to keep a reporter running for deadline; the mere act of stopping to take stock and look closely at yourself or the grisly way you earn your living may mean you have already lost your nerve—like a race driver who hesitates at the turn.

"It's time for me to be rotated home," he said. "I've got combat fatigue."

The bottle of fine French wine they had started out with had a weathered, worn-looking label and a smoky, almost hollow, weightless taste. (Curtis was funny: with the greatest solemnity he actually did the swirling, smelling, tasting number with the first sip that the houseboy poured.) Who knows what they ended up drinking that night, although Nick had a vague recollection of their sitting in the garden and passing around a jug that they were all swilling from.

The shouting brought him back from a very far place. It took him several seconds to figure out where he was. At the first moment he thought it was the Cong again, the same terror of that awakening in the UPI apartment with the hole blown in the wall.

Angela's voice: "No, damn it! No."

Nick sat up with a start. As his eyes adjusted to the darkness, and his hands groped for the feel of where he was, he found the contours of the couch in Curtis' living room. Curtis' voice now, the words almost a grunt, only partially decipherable. But the accompanying moans and sounds of flesh on flesh made it unmistakably clear that the nature of his importunings posed no great threat of any intrusion other than sexual.

In fact, as a foggy consciousness and slight mental facility began to glimmer through Nick's haze of sleep and drunkenness, he realized that the echoes of anger and shouting that had awakened him had either been imagined as part of a dream or had been replaced by the randy callings of desire. Then suddenly Angela's voice again, clear and emphatic: "I won't, Ford, I won't. I can't leave now."

Her voice became increasingly frantic and seemed to move around the room as "I won't" repeated and resounded through the house like a mantra bouncing off the walls. Then the groans and thuds took over, the rhythmic slap of hot sticky flesh meeting, followed by the suction whack of momentary parting. It's amazing, thought Nick, how pornographic lovemaking sounds when you aren't between the sheets, so to speak, yourself. He had to get out of here, it was too embarrassing to listen to. Besides, he was getting a hard on. As nearly as he could tell, the door to their bedroom was wide open, they obviously were as drunk as he and had totally forgotten about their houseguest. Nick decided to inch his way out, crawling along the floor, and pray that the sounds of their passion would obliterate the noise of his departure.

His journey to the door seemed interminable. Unsophisticated or as unkinky as it might be, he realized at that moment that he'd never before been witness to any passion not of his own making, other than on celluloid. He felt mortified, thrust into this role of voyeur. He didn't know which embarrassed him more, the sex or the emotional tug of war.

Their argument resumed, but its pitch was passion and agony, not anger. Hearing it made him feel as though his belly were being worked on by the jagged edge of an old-fashioned up-and-down can opener.

Angela was pleading. "I'll only be a few more months. I promise, I promise! Please go ahead without me."

Nick could barely hear Ford's response, his voice was strangled. It sounded like "I can't." As Nick made it to the door and started running down the walk, their anguished voices trailed behind hanging in the oppressive night air.

# 56

# Nick Among the Rhododendrons

Nick plopped himself under a rhododendron bush alongside a villa wall. With the curfew still on and all sorts of roving crazies in uniforms of various hues, he didn't dare take the chance of going far, especially in the half drunken state he was in. With the first light of day, he dragged himself up despite his desire to just burrow in and sleep on. This was a swanky neighborhood, well-patrolled, including MPs keeping an eye over the residences of American dignitaries, so the morning could have exposed him to some awkward explanations.

The Reuters office seemed like the nearest place where he could clean up a little and get a cup of coffee to quell the boozy shakes. He couldn't go back to Ford's place and face Angela this way. He would have to give her some story about spending the night with a girlfriend. He could never let her suspect he'd heard any of that mess last night. He hoofed a while, then got a lift the rest of the way with some MPs who happened along. The two sitting in the front of the Jeep just laughed when Nick explained his appearance by saying he'd been rolled by a B-girl he'd picked up the night before.

But a ferret-faced kid in the back with an oversized white helmet said, "I remember this guy's face someplace from before, I don't think he's legit. I think we ought to run him in." It was the asshole from the Tet explosion at the UPI office. Nick reminded the MP that he was a newsman named Clark Kent. The kid finally recognized Nick, but didn't laugh.

After stalling at Reuters as long as he could, Nick took a taxi back to Ford's. He heard Gerry Mulligan's sax moaning "My Funny Valentine" as soon as he opened the big gate to the pink villa. He wondered why it struck him as such an odd choice of record to be playing at this hour.

*Is your figure less than Greek,*
*Is your mouth a little weak*
*When you open it to speak*
*Are you smart?*

It was about 10 in the morning. Angela was a mess. Her eyes were red, her face was puffy. Harper's Bazaar would not have been pleased. She held up through her first cup of coffee, but as she started to dunk a rice cake into her second, she broke down. It was the second time Nick had seen her cry. Harry of the tough lip hadn't made her cry, nor the Viet Cong. Now she just laid her head down on Ford's red Formica kitchen table and sobbed.

Nick got up and walked out of the room, that can opener working on his belly again. He couldn't bear to see her in such pain. I don't know what the fuck to do, he thought. I feel like putting my fist through a wall, but in this fucking country the fucking walls are probably made of fucking rice paper and I'll probably fucking fall right through. That image made him laugh (what a weird sense of humor, he thought), but it would be just my luck to take my rage out on a wall thinking I'd only break my hand, and instead I'd break my neck falling through a wall that I'd expected to resist, but didn't. Just like the Vietnamese, like smoke, like putty, malleable, no resistance, but they get you in the end.

He found some kind of rough paper in the bathroom and took it to Angela for her to blow her nose. She was quieted down by now, and so was he. They were a cute pair, he thought, she's crying and I'm laughing. For a minute, he thought they were going to reverse, he would cry and she would laugh, but they both calmed down, wrung out and flat.

"Ford is right, he's a good and wise man," she finally said. "This place is ruining us, Nick. We're not going to be good for anything but covering wars when this is over. But I can't leave, not yet. In the meantime, Ford's going to get fed up with waiting. I know he will."

"You've got to do what's right for you, Angie."

"Yeah. But it's probably a mistake. I know this sounds awful, but this is my first war, and no one's going to take it away from me. I can't leave, but I can't bear to lose him. I'll be staring into the dark in lonely hotel rooms for the rest of my life, wondering why I didn't have the strength or wisdom to make this come out differently."

# 57

# Angela Gets the Runaround

ANGELA THREW down the magazine she'd been staring at without seeing. She got a new cigarette going off the old and tried again to sort out how she would begin if they ever finally let her into the general's office.

She had been trying to get this interview for three weeks. Now here she was in command headquarters of northern I Corps, surrounded by color-coded pin-dot maps, and she hadn't a clue what she should say.

It wasn't easy, the task she had set for herself: a single reporter with no backup help and few if any well-placed sources.

But she was determined.

Determined to nail down that the Army was flying its Chinooks knowing full well they were flawed.

She had tried everything she could think of, but she was stymied at every turn. The days had dragged into weeks. Tramping from one battalion headquarters to the next, racing to crash sites. She had talked to so many mechanics at Da Nang that MPs started running her out of repair hangars.

So she was more then hyped to tackle the commanding general at Bien Hoa Air Base, just north of Saigon.

"OK, miss, you're on," said the young airman, rising from behind his desk where he'd been banging away at an old Royal typewriter.

As she followed him down the short corridor to the general's office, she flashed for a moment on Nantucket Bay. Searching for the memory, she studied the airman's straight, military back in his short-sleeved, blue-trimmed khakis. She grinned. His rigidly starched, perfectly creased pants sounded with every step like the luffing of racing sails tacking into a breeze.

The general, who stood up as she entered, had the short barrel-chested body of a hawk, a warrior, and a small head with the quick owlish eyes of a scholar. Without a word, he nodded his head and waved her to a chair across from his broad, uncluttered desk.

She bent to take a notebook and pen from her canvas bag, straightened and smiled.

"Yes?" the general said.

Frontal attack was her only hope.

"I have personal knowledge, sir," she said, taking the plunge, "that at least two Chinook crashes have been blamed on small arms fire when, in fact, their own rotors banged into each other."

It was a long shot, but surprise didn't work. The general seemed unperturbed. He asked no details, he didn't inquire how she came by such startling information, nor did he appear to be stalling for time. He simply said, "That's very interesting. Something I've heard nothing about. When you can pin that down further, let me know." He rose from behind his desk in dismissal.

So much for that. Angela gave the general a small, you-win grin, shut her notebook, and stood up to leave. As she leaned to shake his hand across the desk she said, "Since your command stretches to the border, would it be safe to assume that secret incursions into Cambodia are originating here?"

"I wouldn't make that assumption, if I were you," he said, jerking his head up slightly, his owl eyes squinting smaller. "I think I'd be the first to know something like that. And I haven't heard a word."

"General, sir, I was with a search-and-destroy patrol that not only was in Cambodia, but was part of a coordinated effort."

"Really? That's very interesting," he replied with a faint smile. "You certainly get around. Well, it's been nice talking to you. Let me know when I can be of further help."

"By all means," she said.


A FEW nights later, she thought she was finally on to something when she spotted a kid whom she thought she had seen at Bien Hoa. She was having dinner with two women cable clerks from the Embassy who had been helpful on other stories, but seemed to either know nothing, or wouldn't tell anything, about the Chinooks. They were eating in Jimmy's Kitchen, a French/American restaurant a few doors up the Tu Do from her hotel.

"Excuse me for a moment, I see someone I think I know," Angela said to the women, and approached the kid sitting at the bar. He was a long skinny drink of water with black frizzy hair and John Lennon glasses, wearing civvies—chino pants and a dark denim shirt. She made some small talk right away, but did identify herself as a reporter. He said he was a Spec 4 from California. Finally she popped the question. "Have you heard this thing about the Chinooks' problems with their gearboxes?"

"Oh sure, it's common knowledge," the kid replied. "They're having a bitch of a time with those choppers." He was a third-year mechanical engineering student from Berkeley who'd gotten drafted because he hadn't made his grades. He rambled on for half an hour about vectors and gear ratios, all the while sketching projections on a damp paper napkin. As the evening wore on, she realized that from a news standpoint it all boiled down to less than zilch—she couldn't use him or his information in print. She thanked him and returned to her friends.

Nick laughed when he found out later she'd even bothered to keep the napkin.

"For Christ sake, the kid's a clerk in the quartermaster's office," Nick said. "He doesn't have enough authority to place an order for GI underwear."

When she'd first started her search, she hadn't bothered with press information officers, figuring they wouldn't know anything and certainly wouldn't tell it if they did. But as she got more and more desperate, she started making those rounds.

About the 10th time she used her frontal assault, it worked. Bingo. A slight rent in the know-nothing canvas.

"I hear they're planning to ground the Chinook for rotor gearbox problems," Angela had announced with no preamble as she walked into a refrigerated military assistance office that resembled a library, with its rows of wooden shelves filled with files behind a long Formica counter. "Is that effective immediately, or do they plan to stall around?"

The young PIO captain looked flabbergasted.

"Well, I don't know. I ah . . . I thought that was all over. I'll have to get back to you on that one."

Angela was more stunned than the PIO. Her heart was thumping so loud, she was afraid he'd hear it.

But she managed to keep her voice even and her face straight as she said as matter of factly as she could manage, "Fine. I'll just wait. My story's already written and I've got to file. It would be good, though, to have the Army's response that they plan to act immediately."

The PIO looked startled again. "That's funny, I was thinking it was the Marines, not the Army."

While he went off to search through the file stacks and make some phone calls, she retreated to the hall to try to calm down, chain-smoking, pacing the corridors of the high-ceilinged, ornate colonial building the French Army had occupied before the Americans.

"I was right," the captain said when she got back. "It was the Marines. And it was their Sea Knight, the CH-46. But it's back in action. Everything's fine now. They grounded it last September, but it resumed flying several months later. February, to be exact."

Angela's heart stopped its thudding. Shit. Two months ago!

"But that's the Marines," she said. "What about the Chinook?"

"No problems there. Not that I know of," the young captain replied.

"They're basically the same ship," she said. "Both made by Boeing. Both with double rotors on top. You can't tell them apart in the air."

"The Sea Knight was also grounded for a couple of months in 1966. That's everything I know," the PIO said.

"What was the Sea Knight's flaw?" Angela persisted.

The captain picked the file folder back up from the counter and leafed through its pages.

"Reduced power and compressor stall in '66," he read. "Caused from dirt and junk stirred up by the rotors getting in the engine," he explained. "Last time, it was something structurally wrong with the rear pylon."

Pylon! Her heart resumed its thumping. She finally knew for sure she was on the right track. Pylon was the word George had used. And she knew from her own study that something called the "combining gearbox" was housed in that rear pylon.

It was enough for a spot story, the first thing she'd done in a couple of weeks. But it was no big deal. The information on the Sea Knight was old, the problem had been solved, or so the military said. The real advantage to the story was that it would alert reporters and politicians that there was a potential problem. Cause them to keep their eyes open a bit. What the story ideally would have been was her being able to say that *somebody*, almost anybody with some authority or expertise, had warned that the Chinook had the same problems, or the same potential for problems.

But she couldn't write that because no one had said it. No one except her and a dead pilot and a third-year mechanical engineering student who worked in the quartermaster's office. The best she could do was simply say that the Sea Knight was the Marine version of the Chinook. That was fact. Let readers make their own inference.

She and Nick wracked their brains for some way to somehow get more. Harry, of course, pounced instantly when she finally filed the story. "If the goddamned Sea Knights are so similar to the Chinooks, why haven't they grounded them? How many of them are crashing? Why the hell are you sending me a story with a hole in it big enough to drive a truck through?"

When Nick replied that Angela was stumped on the Chinook, even though she was certain the rotors were hitting each other, Harry's comment was so outraged and unprintable that Nick blanched to the color of bread dough. Angela, watching, knowing that Nick's usual color for emotion was some shade of red, got a pretty good idea of just how bad it was.

When Harry calmed down after a few days, he conceded it was a story that begged for a whole team of reporters. He put his staffer covering the Pentagon to check there, and sent someone to Seattle to see what he could learn at Boeing. The onus, somehow, was still on Angela. But Harry refused to cut Nick loose to see what he could dig up in Nam.

"We got to fill this paper every day," Harry had screamed from halfway around the world. "I can't have you out farting around."

When Harry's regulars ultimately turned up nothing, the foreign editor claimed the whole thing existed only in Angela's head. "Just like a broad," he pronounced. "Fucking dreaming."

Finally, in a totally foolhardy move, Angela marched one afternoon into Kevin Leahey's office at the Embassy.

"To what do I owe this singular pleasure?" Kevin asked with his usual smarmy inflection as his secretary ushered Angela into his large, comfortable office.

"I expected more surprise than that, Kevin," Angela said, matching his unctuous tone. "For all you know, I'm dead after you gave Braeford Curtis a phony list of pacified villages. We both were nearly killed, you know."

"I was really sorry to hear you had a problem," Kevin said, sounding terribly sincere. "But that's the way war is, you know. The pacification program has been highly successful, but now and again the Cong slip in under the cover of night."

"You're a spook, Kevin, and everyone knows it. You don't give a damn about helping the peasants. But the one thing the goddamned Central Intelligence Agency should have is some intelligence about which villages are friendly and which aren't."

"I'm a USAID adviser, Angela. The *Agency for International Development.*" Kevin used his most condescending tone. "Is this supposed to be a joke? We're doing a lot of good in the countryside, with the farmers, the peasants. The Cong are terrorists, it isn't easy to make inroads against fear and intimidation. But pacification is working."

"Pacification, bullshit!" Angela exploded. "It's the program that's a joke. It consists of either showing USIA propaganda films, handing out toothbrushes or putting an entire village behind barbed wire with the bizarre notion that the Viet Cong can't get through."

"You peaceniks are all alike, aren't you," he said not bothering to hide his sneer.

"I'm not a peacenik, Kevin," Angela said quietly. "I'm a reporter whose job is to report accurately what I see with my own eyes and let someone else decide the issues of war and peace. You're so obsessive in your myopic vision of the world that you're willing to lie and cheat to enforce your personal opinions and politics."

"Perhaps it's your own myopia," he snapped back, "that causes your failure to recognize the truth when it's handed to you."

"Fair enough," Angela said. "Here's two questions of truth or falsehood for you: I personally have been in Cambodia with a search-and-destroy patrol. And I've seen two Chinook crashes that I suspect, but can't prove, were caused by a gear malfunction that banged the overhead rotors into each other. Why do I keep getting stonewalled on both those issues?"

"My expertise is agriculture," Kevin replied.

"You know President Johnson ordered that Cambodia's neutrality is to be respected," Angela persisted. "He even ruled out crossing the border in hot pursuit of Cong retreating into sanctuary there."

"Lyndon Johnson's a lame duck," said Kevin. "Or don't you keep up with the news? He's stopped the bombing in the north and he's stepping down. You peaceniks ran him out."

"He's still the president," Angela said, all but yelling as she struggled to keep her voice down. "There won't be another for nine months. And he said we're not supposed to be in Cambodia. Doesn't that mean anything to you?"

"Why should it? We've got a war to fight, and just as you said, you leave the issues of war and peace to others, I leave the fighting to the military."

"The CIA may leave the fighting and dying to someone else, but it sure doesn't have a hands-off policy on strategic planning. It was the CIA that decided this very small place was the spot for us to take a stand against communism."

"This conversation seems less than pointless," he said.

"Kevin, that Chinook that took Ford and me into your so-called pacified village was not brought down by small arms fire. Two crewmen were killed. You may think that Asian lives are expendable, but surely you don't want to see Americans killed needlessly."

"Angela, I really must ask you to leave. I've got work to do. We'll talk another day . . . when you're calmer."

"God, Kevin, can't you get SOMEBODY to do something? The hell with whether I get a story. People are being killed because of this, and you know it."

Kevin just laughed.

# 58

# R&R

Nick lay on the fine white sand slathered in oil, putting a burn on top the burn he'd gotten the day before. The sun was scorching, but with the breeze off the water the heat felt good. A real tropical paradise, he thought, as he half-dozed. Blue, blue sky and water, striped beach balls and canvas umbrellas and chairs, broads in skimpy bikinis—and 2,000 warplanes a day taking off and landing overhead.

But what the hell, a vacation's a vacation, he was grateful for that. Plus Da Nang had the added advantage that Harry would think he was still working. He smiled to himself, lying on his stomach, head on his crossed arms, under the glaring sun. Actually, in a way he *was* working. Editors try to implant the notion that if you aren't banging away at the typewriter or poised, pen in hand taking notes, you're off the job. But everyone knows that's malarkey. Shooting the shit and hanging out are ways reporters sort out what we've experienced and seen. It's also a source of tips and story ideas.

This little R&R was Angela's idea. Tense with Ford, pissed with Harry and ready to kill Kevin, she told Nick she had to get away to clear her head. He was more than happy to volunteer for escort duty. They were staying at the press center at Da Nang, which was conveniently located near China Beach on the South China Sea. Neither of them could afford the time or the dough for an honest-to-God R&R in Hong Kong or Bangkok, so they took what you might call a busman's holiday. But that suited them just fine. Newsmen are funny, Nick thought, half dozing—weird might be a better word—their idea of entertainment almost invariably is sitting around talking shop. That, and of course drinking, was just about all they had been doing. Even lying on the beach, they had been talking about the war, although it would be hard not to, the war was going on all around them. Now Angela and little John Simenson were in battle over behind Nick somewhere, playing a pick-me-up volleyball game pitting the press against the military. She had called over for Nick to join, trying to rouse him from his slumber. The press was outnumbered, she had yelled. He didn't bother to respond, "So what else is new?" He just waved her away, without moving his head from his folded arms, although he knew he was missing a great opportunity. Some of the gamesters were those bikini-clad nurses he had spied earlier; he could tell from the high pitched screeches drifting over. But hell, he was already pretty sick of hearing Angela giggle at corn pone from that flyboy Mac Wheeler, who had organized the game. This was the first time Nick had ever met him, the 1st Cav pilot who had given Angela the hop into Phu Bai that had landed her in all that shit with the Cong. Wheeler had been trying to monopolize Angela's time ever since they ran into him the night before at the officers club bar.

Who cares, Nick thought, this press center vacation isn't half bad. It might not seem like a resort to someone in the real world, but it seems like pretty good digs to me after the moldiness of the UPI apartment. It was absolute heaven if you were just coming in from Hue or Khe Sanh, Quang Tri or Con Thien—places they'd all been at one time or another. Da Nang was the central link between Saigon—or any place else for that matter—and the rest of I corps north to the DMZ and the North Vietnam border.

Because of the air base's strategic location for newsmen, the Marines had set up a complete facility for them in an old one-story, white stucco and tile building overlooking the river and just upstream from the town. They had a wire-and-phone room, hot showers, American food, and an air-conditioned bunkhouse for early arrivals, and more cots without air-conditioning if the place was booked up. A lot of the best bunks were rented on a permanent basis by the networks, wire services and big papers. They had run into John Simenson when they first arrived, and he had used his connections to get Nick and Angela a couple of spots in the barracks that was air-conditioned. She even drew one of the cots with mosquito netting.

Yesterday, they had played basketball, eaten steaks, and watched a movie on the riverside terrace at dusk. They'd even taken a little afternoon drive in the white AP Jeep. They were beginning to feel almost like real people. The plan was to party for three solid nights, then lie on the beach every day to burn out the effects of the night before.

There was a lot of laughing and screeching from the volleyball players. That and thirst finally pulled Nick up on an elbow to take a look their way. Everything was a blur. The glare of the sun and the sand, the shimmering water—the sky and the sea were the same bright blue. He finally was able to focus enough to make out the net. Spots, polka dots and rainbows bounced on one side. On the other, three stick mirages: two squat, and a tall, thin greenish streak.

Nick rummaged around, found his sunglasses, and hauled his sticky body up off his beach towel, the hot sand burning his feet. The players and the volleyball net were coming into blurry focus. A strong wave was breaking just beyond them, as a skinny, pale-chested guy who was obviously a grunt threw himself with a belly flop into the sea. His face and hands were telltale bronze from the sun.

"How about a beer?" Nick yelled at Angela, who materialized from the thin green streak, as she punched a drop shot over the net. He looked hard at her in her one-piece aqua suit. She was still wearing Wheeler's wide-brimmed, bush hat—a lot of the 1st Cav cowboys wore them. Today she said it was to shade her face from the sun, but she'd had it on in the bar the night before. When Nick had mentioned it then, she said, "It beats a helmet." Just behind her, and back-pedaling like crazy to catch the returning ball, was a stumpy little runt with fireplug legs. Nick couldn't believe his eyes! "Jesus Christ," he yelled, "Bullet!"

As the guy turned at Nick's voice, a volleyball hit him square on the side of the head.

"You're a hell of a lot of help," Angela yelled at Nick, but he and Bullet were already racing toward each other for a bear-hug embrace.

Bullet, a friend of Nick's from j-school, was one of those guys people always describe as being able to find three stories just standing on a street corner. Nick couldn't remember why he was called Bullet, because that's the last thing he resembled. He was slung low to the ground and square, just like a bulldog—and tenacious as one—but friendly as a pup, little guy with a big raspy voice and an enormous talent. He and Nick had worked together for the city news service for a short while after they got out of school, but hadn't seen each other since.

After five minutes of how-the-hell-ya-beens, and what-the-hell-'ve-ya-been up tos, Nick introduced Bullet to his volleyball teammates. Little John, it turned out, had seen Bullet hanging around the press room, so asked him to fill out their slender team. They'd all just started playing with no more than a "hi."

Bullet suddenly turned to Angela. "You're not, by any chance, Angela Andrews, are you?"

"Yeah, how'd you know my family name?"

Nick was as surprised as she. "Yeah, Jesus, Bull, how the hell did you know that?" he asked.

"Well, Christ," Bullet said to Nick, "You remember. Her stuff from old copies of The Daily was held up by old Prof Higgins as great enterprise—finding an off-beat idea and then writing the shit out of it."

People outside the business generally don't know what's meant by "enterprise" stories, but it's pretty much the same definition as the dictionary, using your wit and your ingenuity—in other words, getting three story ideas just standing on a street corner. If somebody plants a bomb in the men's john in city hall, you don't have to be a hell of a reporter to figure out that's a story and trot over there to cover it, even if the city desk doesn't tell you to, which, of course, they will. But newspapers would run a lot of blank pages, and the TV guys would have even less of any consequence to say than they do now, if reporters just sat around waiting for something to happen so they could report it.

Bullet could spot stories in anything. A gasoline tanker truck has an accident and everyone else reports the accident and forgets it. Bullet starts sniffing around, finds a couple of other minor accidents too insignificant to have made the papers, and first thing you know they have a statewide probe into those rolling gas bombs. The little bastard was always on target, Nick thought, remembering with awe that investigative series Bullet did when they were first out of school. Those mothers were ticking flamemobiles.

Angela glowed over Bullet's remarks and so did Nick. He suddenly realized that he really was proud of her, as though he had discovered her or something. He'd watched her develop, and he knew how hard she'd worked and how much of herself she put into what she did. A lot of men like bimbos, but he never could stand ditsy dames. They always seemed like a waste of time, too much trouble for so little reward. Unless you could move in and out awful fast, they always had some number to lay on you, something they wanted that had nothing to do with what a normal person would want. Just something they wanted 'cause they wanted it, sort of like they were testing you, or playing power, letting you know you owe 'em.

But the flyboy, Mac Wheeler, completely misunderstood what Bullet had said about Angela. It's a pretty common misconception about us, Nick thought. That's why we like to keep to ourselves, people always seem to be in a snit about how reporters do their work.

Wheeler took it like Bullet meant Angela made stuff up. "So that's what they teach you guys in school: how to invent stories, or blow them out of all proportion." He laughed after he said it, but none of the rest of them did.

"Some reporter do a bum number on you, Mac?" Angela drawled in a wonderful imitation of his Texas accent. She looked him up and down with a sultry, lascivious leer. "Seems to me the 1st Cav has gotten unusually good press, at least as far as making all you cowboys look macho. That's what you want, isn't it?"

"Whoa, little lady, no offense." He had a crazy grin that spread across the whole right side of his face, sort of up and down. Lopsided, they call it. "Sorry, just trying to make a little joke."

"Well, it wasn't very goddamned funny," piped up Simenson, who usually didn't have a lot to say, but once you got the little guy started, it was hard to stop him. "I get pretty damned tired of you guys going around shooting up this whole country and napalming women and children and then blaming the whole thing on us 'cause we write it down. Whadda ya think, asshole, that if it's not reported, you can pretend it didn't happen? You guys make me sick."

"Hey, Sime, slack off. Come on, guy, it's OK," Nick said as he grabbed Simenson by the shoulder and gave him a little shake. The kid was young, Jesus. "We're all on the same side, come on."

Wheeler's face was absolutely drained of blood, you could see he felt awful. "Cripes, I'm sorry. I didn't mean anything. I guess we forget you guys sometimes see as much combat as we do."

"Sometimes more," snapped Simenson who had just come in that morning from a B-52 bombing raid in the A-Shau Valley. "You're the guy, aren't you, who dumped Angela off at Phu Bai air base and left her to make her way as best she could into Hue? She ended up spending 10 days with the fucking Cong, you know."

"Hey, wait a minute, sweetie." Angela was patting Simenson's cheek and being very gentle. It was suddenly quite apparent just how wrecked and strung out he was. The kid had seen some serious shit in the last couple of months, especially in Hue, and a couple of guys who bunked with him pretty regularly said he'd been doing a lot of talking and yelling in his sleep. "Mac was doing me a hell of a favor on that one, Johnny, babe. If it hadn't been for him, I wouldn't have gotten all those terrific stories."

"That's the real bottom line, isn't it? That's all you guys care about is stories," said a Cav pal of Mac who'd been playing volleyball with the military team. He grabbed up his beach gear, motioned for the two bikini-clad nurses to follow, and did an imitation of stomping off, which isn't easy when you're walking in hot sand.

Just another example of the divisions this war is causing among Americans, Nick thought. Vietnam vets were already getting the same crap back home, drunks in bars trying to blame them for the war. But for here and now, it was the military trying to blame the press.

"Come on, Nick," yelled Angela. "Let's have a race. I've got to find something I can beat these guys at."

Nick looked around and grinned to himself. Altogether, they were a funny-looking bunch, two Mutts and three Jeffs. Simenson was such a little bit of a thing, scrawny on top of being short. At least Bullet, short as he was, had a bunch of weight on him. Angela and Wheeler and Nick stacked on top of one another could have reached to the moon.

Nick would have liked Wheeler OK, if he hadn't seemed so sweet on Angela. He was a bright guy and a high-ranker for as young as he looked—a major. Nick also noticed that Mac was smart enough not to talk down to Angela. He treated her like a person, not like some piece of fluff, or just ass. Laconic-acting guy, slouched like a son-of-a-gun. Everyone had kidded that his was hardly a military bearing, but he said he'd started scrunching in his vertebrae to pass his entrance physical. He was right on the edge of being too tall to get into flight school, but they'd kind of looked the other way because he was already an experienced pilot. He'd done some barnstorming in West Texas, where he was from. He had the drawl. Everything about him was slow except his eyes, which didn't seem to miss anything, and made him look like he was smiling all the time because of his heavy crow's feet lines from squinting into that West Texas sun.

He was the only guy Nick ran into in Nam who wasn't bitching all the time about the heat. "This is just about the way it is down home," he'd say, "except the durn humidity is turned up kinda high."

"This is the first time in my life I ever felt like short stuff," Angela said, standing between Nick and Wheeler with her toe on the mark of a line drawn in the sand as they readied to race for the water and take a plunge. With high heels, she could damn near look Nick in the eye, but now in bare feet she barely came to the top of Wheeler's shoulder. Someone hollered, "Get set, go," and they all took off. Bullet fell or tripped, or something, then the little bastard grabbed Nick's ankle on his way down, and next thing Nick knew the two of them were rolling around in the blazing sand, laughing and wrastlin' like idiots, oily sand grains grinding his flesh. From down there, they had a view of Simenson's scrawny little toothpick legs chugging by, laps behind Angela and Wheeler. Mac hit the water just a little ahead of Angela, although he didn't look like he was running with his throttle wide open. Once in, he grabbed Angela, carefully took his hat off her head and put it on his own, then dunked her and got her hair all wet. She was hollering and screaming and splashing water at him—what an American scene: the Norman Rockwell prototype of every Fourth of July picnic since the inception of the Republic, except for the distant backdrop of acrid smoke hanging in the muggy air.

"She's some looker, and it looks like the flyboy has noticed," Bullet said, watching Nick staring.

"Sea green becomes her, don't you think?" Nick replied. Her satiny-looking one-piece suit was at the light side of jade. And she was even picking up a little tan.

"Huh?" said Bullet, giving Nick a what-the-fuck-has-come-over-you look.

"Jesus, Bull," Nick said, trying to cover his embarrassment, "it's no wonder you never get any place with women. You need to notice shit like that, like what colors they're wearing and stuff."

"Who says I never get any place with women, you asshole? What kind of scores are you making that are such hot shit?"

Simenson had finally made it to the water and leaped into the midst of the playfulness between Angela and Wheeler. Bullet and Nick picked themselves up and ran down and dove in.

# 59

# Drunk in Da Nang

"What's a green kitchen?" Nick blurted out, slurred out was probably more like it, drunk as he was, on their second night there. As soon as he'd said it, he wondered why he had asked Angela that, then, sitting in the officers club bar in Da Nang, in front of these other three people. Maybe he wanted to remind her of Curtis (gee, that would be perverse, wouldn't it?), Mac Wheeler sitting there vacantly grinning at her, she, half on the nod, again wearing Mac's hat.

"What?" She looked startled, as did Bullet and John Simenson.

"A green kitchen. You called Curtis that one night when you were real drunk."

Angela frowned, as though she was searching for the answer but couldn't quite remember it.

"Well?"

She laughed. "Oh, it's just a symbol for me of women getting stuck."

"Stuck?" Nick asked.

"Stuck in domesticity, a woman trapped in an avocado green kitchen, refrigerator and stove to match." She laughed again, it had a self-deprecating ring. "Not a very popular stance with the women I went to school with. They've all settled in quite nicely."

"I can see you not liking kitchens, but green?" said Nick.

She told them all a story about those ticky-tacky houses, little boxes on a hillside, when she was at university. The spot was just south of San Francisco where once there were rolling hills and artichoke patches and the Silver Saddle bar and horse stables right where the coast highway begins its meander down to Half Moon Bay. Following a Cal-Stanford game, she and some friends from Berkeley dropped by to see a married guy who had been a fraternity brother of her friends. He couldn't have been more than two or three years older than they, but he was getting a pot belly and had slouched around drinking beer watching the game on TV, wearing a Cal windbreaker—his two-year-old kid, runny nose and diapers, had on a Cal cap—doing the college bit like he was a hundred years old and his life was over. The wife talked about nothing but how Her Old Blue still hadn't kept his promise to replace their prosaic white stove with a green one to match her magnificent new avocado green fridge. The tacky little pink one or green one or yellow one was like every other house as far as the eye could stretch, a little stucco prison cell, the same as every other cell up and down the street, block after block, mile after mile of those ugly little things.

Drunk, the four of them minus Wheeler, burst into a couple of verses of "Little Boxes," a folk song that had been in fashion not long before most of them had come to Nam.

There's a green one and a pink one and a blue one and a yellow one and they're all made out of ticky tacky and they all look just the same.

And the people in the houses all went to the university where they were put in little boxes and they came out all the same.

A chorus of "shut ups" and "can its" soon drowned them out. Folk songs smacked of peace movements, and a Marine base wasn't an appropriate place for such singing.

So, with shrugs that said "what the hell," the five of them ordered another round of drinks. After the waiter had walked away, Angela confided to her friends in a mock whisper, "I was so unnerved by the green kitchen I broke up with the boy from Berkeley before he even got me back to the Stanford campus." She paused, then muttered almost to herself, "That's funny, I broke up with Jackson later because we didn't have a proper home life." Then more loudly, too loudly, as a matter of fact, she announced emphatically to those assembled at the table, "But I broke up first because I was frightened by a green kitchen."

"Buried alive in a green kitchen," quipped Bullet. "I can see the headline now."

"Jesus, Angela, that's morbid," Nick blurted out.

"Like something out of Edgar Alan Poe?" she asked, raising her glass to him in a mock salute.

"Yeah," he said, returning the salute with his beer.

"Exactly," she said in a cocky tone that implied she had won her point. "Walled up alive in a prefab box with less to show for yourself than a cask of good wine."

Jeez! Her fear of being tied down is awesome, Nick thought, almost worse than my own. But he noticed that Wheeler, drunk as he was, was smarter than the rest of them. Wheeler's quick eyes caught the impact right away, although he clearly chose not to be shocked, chose not to challenge her views on marriage. Instead, with his slow voice he acted out the role of the dumb ole boy from Texas, which it was becoming increasingly obvious to Nick he certainly was not.

"That's just the way we feel in Texas, Love." Wheeler leaned toward Angela and put his arm around the back of her chair. "We hate being penned in. But what were you doing at Stanford? I thought these turkeys said you went to Northwestern with them?"

"Command performance," she replied, smiling at Wheeler. Mother went to medical school at Stanford, so I was enrolled in pre-med there practically before I was born. But as you've pointed out, I turned out to be a wastrel, no-count journalist instead. Much, I might add, to my family's horror."

"So," Wheeler said, tightening the space between his face and Angela's, and moving his hand from her chair's rim to her shoulder, "your mother the doctor decided not to be penned in, either."

"Her father was a surgeon," Angela replied. "It apparently never crossed his mind or hers that she wouldn't be a surgeon, too.

"When she and my father met during his last year at Harvard med, the deal they cut was that he would intern at Stanford—one of the few medical schools that would admit a woman in 1928—but then they'd settle down in his home in Chapel Hill." Turning her head, Angela looked directly into Wheeler's eyes. "Mother always considered North Carolina an outpost. I suppose I'd feel that same way about Texas."

Simenson suddenly came to. It wasn't clear what had penetrated the stupor.

"Whaddid ya mean," Simenson growled at Wheeler, "when you said there were too many reporters here trying to make a name for themselves and not enough covering the war?" Simenson had toughened up a lot in the last few months, but he still got teased about being such a kid. He had even grown a mustache, trying to head off the razzing.

"Listen, fella," said Wheeler, clearly making an effort to keep his voice even, "I'm not looking to pick a fight. But, since you brought it up and with all due respect to present company, seems like a lot of your compatriots spend most of their time in Saigon."

"Plenty of action there, lately," said Simenson, suddenly standing up and belligerently wobbling around the table to where Mac was sitting between Nick and Angela. Looking at Little John's scraggly mustache, it was all Nick could do to keep from laughing. Christ, he thought, this kid's no match for the flyboy.

Wheeler appeared to be thinking the same thing, as he seemed to suck on his front teeth, clearly suppressing a grin.

"Ah, Johnny, you know part of what Mac says is true," said Angela. "There's nearly 650 people that MACV credentialed to cover this war, and not more than 50 or 60 of us really working. That's why the guys made it so rough on me at first, figuring I was just one more of the ragtag bunch looking for thrills or cheap grass."

"Yeah, but that's not what he really meant," Simenson said, turning to Angela. "He's trying to sidestep the issue, 'cause he's hot for you and doesn't want to make you mad. But he thinks like the rest of 'em that we're ghouls over here looking for blood just to make a name for ourselves, while they're over here getting themselves shot up to make the world safe for democracy. They figure they got to destroy this country so they can save it."

"Shit, Simen, slack off. You're goddamned drunk," Nick said. But he knew, and so did the rest of them, that John was speaking a drunk's truth, and even the flyboy knew it. There were bad divisions and hard feelings in just about any direction you looked in this war.

But the press/military schism played a small role in the outcome of Angela's story. At least that's the way Nick figured it.

# 60

# Mac and Maggie

ANGELA WASN'T under the mosquito netting that night in Da Nang that Simenson mixed it up with Mac Wheeler. Nick, desperate for a drink of water, stumbled down the rows of metal cots in the press quarters near dawn, and noticed her empty bunk.

He had fitful dreams during what was left of the night. As new arrivals flipped on the barracks lights, dumped their gear and fell on top of their cots, their jungle boots still on, the neon lights flashed on and off in variations of Nick's Raymond Chandler movie: A woman on the next cot in the dirty wrapper was his stepmother, the man in the blue and white striped boxer shorts—his member bulging erect through the flap—was Nick's father. The slide, click, slide, click, was Uncle Dennis taking pictures through the transom with his Speed Graphic. The woman in the white shroud with her eyes closed was Maggie, Nick's mother. The smell of flowers and incense was overpowering as Nick, a gangly kid of 12 with black curls and violet eyes, knelt to touch her cold forehead. Those fuckers couldn't even wait 'til she was in the ground!

Nick woke up sticky, in a clammy sweat. His pillow was on the floor, the covers tangled around his left leg. He looked at his watch: 10 a.m.! Shit, what was his assignment today? Was he missing a press conference? His feet hit the floor before he remembered that he and Angela were supposed to be on vacation.

Some vacation, he thought, thanks to Mac Wheeler. The flyboy and

Angela seemed to have turned this into some goddammed little mini honeymoon. Nick lay back down. He had the place to himself, no sense in rushing out of bed to go watch the two of them frolic some more on the beach. He lay on his back, put his hands behind his head, watching the ceiling fan do its slow turns. With this place air conditioned, the fans were turned low to a laconic, pro forma whirl that targeted cigarette smoke instead of heat.

Might as well give the fan some work, he smiled to himself. We can't all be on vacation. He found a butt and a light in the pocket of his jeans, thrown over the foot of his cot. Floor for an ashtray was fine. This may be high class compared to the other bunkhouses, but it wasn't the Ritz. He wasn't usually into pondering Angela and her intentions—didn't do any good to try to worry over that kind of shit—but he had a heavy-duty hangover and it was hard to even think, much less control the places his mind wandered. So what, a fling? Didn't make any difference. Angela was in love with Curtis. Wheeler'd figure that out soon enough, just like Nick himself had. But who knows when Angela will finally figure out that she's always going to be fighting with Curtis? I should quit looking at that fan, Nick thought, it's making me dizzy. Wheeler won't last long, his snipes about the press aren't doing him any good with her.

Nick remembered her telling him once that she'd never had any interest in any man who wasn't in the business, except Jackson. "And Jackson was when I was young." They had looked at each other then, and started laughing. They were sitting down by the Saigon River at the time, watching the sky suddenly light up with tracers. "Yeah," she had said with a grin, nodding her head in the direction of what had just been a direct hit on what was probably an ammo dump, "everything pre-Nam was like kindergarten. Except Jackson. He was practically born playing the sax. Maybe that's what made him savvy and wise." He had understood her restless side, she said. "One more river, he would say to me, and laugh." She credited him with giving her the courage to defy her parents and leave pre-med and Stanford and eventually go to journalism school.

"Most men just never seem to know what I'm talking about, or why my hours are so screwy," Angela had said.

"Amen," Nick had replied, "but it's a lot tougher for men than women. There's just not that many broads in the business to choose from."

That made her laugh. "My God, I guess I'm a lot more of a hot commodity than I realized."

ONE MORNING, after they'd been in Da Nang for several days, Nick found her just after sunup sitting on the terrace staring out over the Da Nang River. The sky was red in shades from magenta to watermelon as streaks of yellow wove in and out of petite cloud puffs. Angela, in cutoff jeans and flip flops, her hair in a single braid down her back, was rolling a Styrofoam cup of coffee back and forth in her hands, holding it up to her nose and inhaling the aromatic steam from the hot brew.

"I wonder what's across the river," she said.

"Another war," Nick replied, wasting no time getting directly to the point. "While you were out screwing around, Martin Luther King was killed."

"What?" Cup on the way to her mouth, Angela nearly spilled hot coffee as she jerked her head up. "You're kidding."

Nick just stared, with barely a nod of his head.

"You're acting like it's my fault," Angela said, frowning.

"That's what happens when you're not on the job." This time Nick's face took on some life—a distinctive smirk.

"Jesus, what happened? Klan types?"

"Details are sketchy at this point. He was in Memphis to lead a march, and someone picked him off his motel balcony. Cops are looking for some white guy who dropped a rifle and escaped in a blue car." The percussion of a B-52 taking off enveloped them for a moment in a vacuum, then stirred the air slightly, before settling them back down to earth.

"Memphis, jeez," Nick said softly. "I thought I knew heat down there, but this place puts it to shame." The sun was up, the red streaks were gone. The sky was a clear crystal blue, and another hot, humid day had begun.

Angela pulled the front of her yellow T-shirt back and forth in a fan like motion. It was already beginning to stick to her skin. "You interviewed King once, didn't you?"

Nick laughed. "Naw, not really. In March '65, I was with a herd of reporters slogging through the rain for five days marching from Selma to Montgomery."

"Yeah, while I sat in upstate Illinois and edited recipes," she replied in a melancholy, self-deprecating tone.

"You got to keep your eye on the prize, kiddo." Nick was smirking again.

She looked across the muddy water that ultimately would make its way into the China Sea. "I'm trying," she said with a soft smile.

She turned again toward the river, a furrow deepening in her brow. She was squinting as though there were something far away that she couldn't quite see.

She thought about how she'd gone from one job to another following her husband's career. First, she gave up her internship at the Tribune because Peter was offered a better job as city editor at a small paper in upstate Illinois. The managing editor had made a spot on the women's page for her, because they were eager to hire her husband. At Peter's next move, the paper had a rule against hiring both a husband and wife, and there was only one paper in town. She had finally landed something about 75 miles away. The commute was bearable, but she had worked nights and Peter was working days. He used to laugh that neither the bed nor the car ever got cold. She'd drive in just about the time he was ready to drive out. They would have time for a cup of coffee together, then he would hop in the car and she would fall in bed. We might still be together, she thought, if we had both had jobs at the same place. She smiled to herself. But probably not. Peter was content, and I always have another river to cross.

Angela broke the silence. "I envy you Selma. The one job I could get was writing about weddings and flower arrangements. Coming here and working freelance was the only way I could make my bones. I'm not about to throw all that away to get involved with someone like Mac who doesn't have a clue about what we do, or why."

"Amen," Nick said with a grin.

She took a sip of the coffee, lukewarm now, and stared again across the river. They sat that way for a long time.

"I'm going back to Ford," she finally said, "and try. I need him. I need a family. I'm in love with him. And unlike the rest of us, he's sane. I'm going to tell him about the rotor blade story to see if *he* can dig up anything. I've been too wary of him, anticipating that he would be too much like my past. Thanks, Nick, for coming on this trip with me, you've been a good friend."

# 61

# Stuff Happens

THE CONG made a new assault on Saigon in early May and had taken some of the outlying areas and parts of Cholon—the Chinese section—with the same kind of house-to-house fighting they had used in Hue. The situation changed literally from hour to hour, a street that had been in the hands of friendlies at 3 p.m. might be enemy territory by 4. But Nick joked that this latest "war front" had its advantages. No early morning flights to get to a battle zone, and you could go to work in the morning and know you could be back at the Continental in time for cocktails in the afternoon.

A banging on his door woke Nick, but before he could yell, "It's open," Ray Corrigan burst in. The Reuters correspondent's face was ashen, ghostly, not a drop of color behind the drooping walrus mustache. Nick was out of bed and on his feet before Corrigan had time to move the gray slit in his colorless skin. "What the hell is wrong?" Nick demanded.

"A Jeepload of correspondents has been ambushed in Cholon."

"What? That doesn't make sense, it's too early in the morning." Nick knew he was the one not making sense, but he couldn't seem to comprehend. "Are you sure?"

"Yeah."

"Where are they? Who, for Christ sake? Were they killed?"

"That's what I wanted to tell you."

"What?"

"Max saw Angela having coffee on the terrace with two of 'em about 8:30 this morning."

"Angela? What do you mean Angela?" His brain just wasn't functioning, he kept feeling like he was still asleep. He knew there was something he should be trying to think about, but he couldn't think what it was.

Corrigan was still talking. Nick could see the gray lips moving, but he couldn't seem to figure out what Ray was saying. God, it was a funny feeling . . . they gave him Demerol in the hospital once after surgery when he wracked up his knee playing football. First, there was a rush up through your nose, then the front part of your head felt spacey. It made it hard to focus. Corrigan's slit was still opening and closing and Nick stared at it real hard to see if he could figure out what he was saying by reading his lips like a deaf person. Corrigan took Nick by the arm and led him over to the big chair where he had to sleep sometimes when someone with more seniority got his bed. As Nick sat down, he heard Corrigan say, "The reports are there's only one survivor, and it isn't a woman."

"Tell me again, what's this got to do with Angela?" Nick said, furrowing his brow and frowning hard at Corrigan.

"None of the bodies has been identified yet, but Max saw her this morning having coffee with two of the guys we think were in there. I called her room before I even came by to tell you, but there was no answer. She could be any place, Nick, but I thought you'd want to know. It's a pretty good guess she was in the Jeep."

Curtis was right, this war had done something to him. He felt completely numb, as though he didn't even care whether or not Angela was in that Jeep. But maybe that was what shock felt like, sort of detached, like his head was off in one corner of the room watching his body put on his pants.

"What do you think I ought to do?" Nick asked Corrigan.

"I dunno."

"Putting on my pants is a good start, I guess."

That made Corrigan laugh. It was the first time he had appeared human instead of like a skull with a slit in it. He laughed in spite of himself, then turned mean. "What the fuck's the matter with you, fella? Can't you be serious about anything?"

People were always saying things like that to him, Nick thought. But shit, if you were serious in this place the top of your head might just blow off from the pressure.

"Is the injured guy at Grall or Saigon Hospital?"

"Grall."

"I'll start there," Nick said. "You coming?"

"Yeah, I need details. The guys downstairs put out a bulletin, and so has the AP, but no one knows much. I'll file from the hospital. They'll have some kind of useable line."

"Me, too. If bulletins are out, Harry'll wonder what the fuck is holding me up. I'll call UPI or Reuters from there and maybe they'll pass it on through."

They decided to hoof it up the Tu Do, faster than a pedicab in the always clogged streets. People coming and going, hawking their wares, eating their *pho* in open-sided, street-front buildings. It shocked Nick that things looked perfectly normal. He felt like a robot, mechanical, as though his arms and legs were making the jerky motions of a windup toy. He expected people on the street to make a move, then freeze, stop action with an arm extended, a leg caught in mid-motion, suspended over the sidewalk. But life was fluid, molten, running past him.

It didn't take them much time to get to the hospital. It was just off Hai Ba Trung about a block from the Embassy. This war was getting convenient as hell, you didn't have to go far at all to find fighting, or the wounded or the dead.

From several hundred yards away, they could tell they'd found the right place. There was an NBC Jeep at the curb and they spotted a couple of guys they recognized walking up the steps to the hospital.

Nick was hoping those guys would still be milling around when he and Corrigan got to the reception desk, but no luck. Nick was dreading going through the inevitable minuet with some Viet cluck who couldn't spell in English and would slowly search through sheets of chicken scrawl looking for he knew not what: perhaps the number of the morgue slab that held the body with a tag on its big toe of a stunning American woman who was very much alive and laughing yesterday? At least here she probably wouldn't be in a green plastic body bag with flies swarming on it like the grunts who died in a paddy. They couldn't ask for the room number of the person who had survived because they didn't have a name. Nick gave the clerk Angela's name, spelled it, then wrote the letters out for him. The clerk went through his sheets of paper, then shook his head. Nick didn't want to think about what that might mean, so he tried *"bao chi,"* Vietnamese for journalist, and the clerk's face lit up immediately. He gave Nick a ward number on the second floor.

Nick took the steps two at a time and didn't even have to slow down when he got to the floor because the ward was immediately identifiable: An NBC crewman he recognized was lounging outside the door. Several press guys were standing over a bed halfway down the ward, saying nothing, just staring at its occupant. The covers at the foot of the bed were raised up about three feet, elevated by some sort of arched contraption underneath, which blocked Nick's view of the head. It wasn't until he got right up to the bed that he saw it was Angela. He figured she must be alive or they would have had her in the morgue. Her face was swollen and covered with bruises and dried blood. Her eyes were closed and she didn't appear to be breathing until Nick got up right in her face, and could finally detect a faint throb in her temple—her pulse must have been practically zero. He could see a piece of scalp about the size of a half dollar where her hair was completely gone, like the spot on a calf's rump singed by a circular branding iron.

Someone got Nick a chair and he sat there for a long time, holding her hand, hunched over with his face close to hers so he'd know instantly if she stopped breathing or anything. A lot of guys came and went—he didn't remember much about it, he didn't know how much time passed. His mind was just a blank. The first thing he really remembered was Parks showing up. When Parks started asking questions, it jolted Nick out of the dream state he'd been in. It was only then that he realized he didn't know what had happened, he didn't know what was wrong with her, he didn't know if anyone had gone to look for Curtis—and he had totally forgotten to call Harry! Parks volunteered to go get Nick a cup of coffee and to go look for Curtis, in that order, and the coffee helped. Jesus, here it was past lunchtime, and he hadn't even brushed his teeth. When a doctor finally came by on rounds, Nick had collected his wits enough to ask some questions.

The doctor spoke good English, thank God. His name was Pang, said he'd done his undergrad at Michigan State, and medicine at the Sorbonne. He said Angela had a leg that was pretty badly banged up, and most likely a broken kneecap. That was the reason for the tent-like structure over the foot of her bed, they hadn't done anything to the leg but keep it immobile for the time being. There were a number of those funny scraped burn places like the one on her scalp on the rest of her body, he said, and he wasn't sure what they were from. Maybe she'd been thrown from the Jeep and skidded on the pavement. They were kind of like the sidewalk burns you'd get as a kid when you'd fall and scrape your knee, but circular and much deeper. She was sedated now, the doctor said, because the pain in her leg was pretty bad.

Parks had worked fast. He found Curtis in no time, and brought him back on his scooter—fast pick-up and delivery service, another advantage of keeping the war right at home. Curtis looked simply berserk, his hair was standing straight up from the wild ride with Parks. Damn, Nick almost laughed, conjuring the sight of ole Braeford Curtis "the third" riding on the seat behind Parks, arms clasped around the rocker's waist, hanging on for dear life. Fate is certainly a mean bitch, no one escapes her comeuppance.

Parks also came back with the information that Sweet John Simenson had been in that Jeep.

Nick jumped up and gave Curtis his chair, then looked around and found an abandoned wicker rocker on a tree-shaded verandah outside the ward. He hauled it in to the other side near the foot of the bed. Curtis sat just as Nick had in the chair by her head, intent, holding her hand, waiting. He seemed a totally different person, even the contours of his body seemed changed or somehow rearranged: He was no longer inflated. The skin was at rest, not taut like a puffed tight balloon. There was a softness, a gentleness, as he periodically touched her brow, or ran a finger along her cheek, or perhaps kissed the inside of her palm.

When she finally opened her eyes in the late afternoon, his face was a few inches from hers.

You could watch her face and read her memory coming back. First, a blankness, with almost simultaneous loving recognition of Curtis, then the furrowed brow of wonder, the strain of recall, then terror and pain all within seconds.

"He fell on me. My leg," she whispered as her face stiffened against the pain.

"Take it easy, baby, don't think about it now." Curtis' voice and hands were a hum of soothing reassurance.

She tried to raise up to look at the foot of the bed and apparently was frightened by the sight of the contraption under the covers. "My leg, did I lose my leg? My foot feels gone. I've lost my foot like Spike!"

"You're going to be fine," Curtis crooned, his hand cradling her face. "Just stay calm, darling, and take deep breaths, that will help the pain. We're going to get you the best doctors available, even if we have to charter a flight back to New York."

"They just started shooting," she said. "They stopped us, we told them who we were, and they opened up on us with automatics. Back and forth, back and forth, spraying across the Jeep."

"It's OK, sweetie, it's OK. We'll talk about it later."

"Johnny's dead. They're all dead. Aren't they?"

"Yes," said Curtis. "But, darling, please, don't try to talk about it now. You've been through so much."

"Johnny threw himself on me. I was pinned on the floorboard, my leg twisted under..."

Her voice was rising and in her agitation she tried to raise herself up, but Curtis held her shoulders down against the pillow, trying to quiet her. "Please, baby, please. Don't worry about it now."

The restraint calmed her. When she spoke again her voice was barely a whisper, confiding in Curtis, explaining, as though she were unsure she had done the right thing. "I didn't dare move, they were still there, walking around the Jeep. It was excruciating, but I didn't dare move, lying there, Johnny's blood dripping all over me—his body was like a sieve, I was soaked."

She stopped. There wasn't a sound. No one was breathing. Nick strained, trying to hear breathing. It was steaming in here—Saigon was always steaming—and for a flash Nick thought he was in a diving bell in an underwater movie. He looked around at the faces of the other correspondents ringing the bed and they all looked like fish seen through glass; not one of them was breathing, not one of them had any expression. There was one guy Nick didn't even know with water streaming down his face. Nick guessed it was coming from his eyes, but maybe it was just the heat. Nick found himself wondering if a guy could cry without breathing and with absolutely no expression on his face. If they're all breathing through their gills there should be bubbles...

Angela stirred, interrupting Nick's thoughts, and the guys all around him took audible deep breaths.

She turned her head on the pillow, her bruised face away from the cradle of Curtis' hand. Nick saw her jaw line harden.

He never heard her mention Cholon again.

The doctor came by shortly and sedated her. Curtis took a break to get a cup of coffee and call his bureau with notes on the story he'd been working when Parks found him. After he finished dictating, everyone all over the hall could hear him yell: "And tell those bastards in New York to rotate me the hell back home."

# 62

# The Cost of Doing Business

FOUR CORRESPONDENTS died in the Jeep that day, May 5, 1968. Four more were killed and about a dozen wounded within the next two or three weeks of the May offensive. Everyone had the jitters, a real change in their outlook. For a brief period, it made Nick stop and think about attitudes he'd never questioned before. Reporters always feel invincible. He'd seen a lot of them, even back home, himself included, go into dangerous situations like walking into inner city shooting galleries to get a feature story on a day in the life of an addict, or, just on a tip, meeting with some mobster who was into breaking kneecaps or with some play-for-keeps union type. You don't worry, you figure you're neutral, have a magic shield around you, like the guy in the glass booth. But no more.

"These suckers are playing for keeps," he said to Corrigan one night, when the two of them stopped for a drink after leaving the hospital together. "They're gunning for us. Cholon was no accident. Those mothers opened fire *after* the guys in the Jeep identified themselves as journalists in both Vietnamese and English."

Meanwhile, the doctors had decided that Angela's kneecap wasn't broken, but that the long bone in her leg had been shattered in several places. They had to repair it surgically and put some kind of metal rod in through from her hip that would help hold the whole thing together. An intermedulary pin, they called it. They said with therapy she might eventually be able to walk without a limp, but it would be a long, slow process. In those early days, she was in and out of surgery and doped up or feeling just plain sick most of the time. So Curtis and Nick didn't see a lot of the May offensive. And you might say Angela missed it altogether, after her own early and explosive participation.

Curtis and Nick kept working, after a fashion. Nick did pick up one great interview with an Air Force pilot who had rescued three ground personnel accidentally left stranded when the U.S. abandoned a Special Forces camp on May 10. The camp, at Kham Duc on the Laos border, was surrounded by NVA. The pilot, a Korean War vet named Joe Jackson, had managed through some very tricky maneuvers to land in the midst of the occupied field and was on the ground less than one minute. The feat was likely to get him nominated for a Medal of Honor.

Otherwise, Nick and Curtis did cursory work, not much more. They even stooped to going to the Follies. Other reporters helped them a bit by giving them an occasional lead. The people in Curtis' bureau were especially good about it, handing things off to him, so he'd have something to file. He and Nick took turns sitting with Angela; the one out drumming up a story would share at least the general outlines of it with the one back at the hospital. But when Angela had to be in surgery, or have some grueling test, or some other diabolical hospital procedure, they'd both stay, sitting out on a verandah or pacing up and down a connecting corridor like a couple of expectant fathers. That's when the other guys were particularly good about giving them a hand with something to file. Harry figured what was going on, but he was pretty decent, too. There were several times during those first few weeks that he had to patch and fill what Nick sent him with wire copy, but he only bellowed mildly, he didn't really come down hard. From Harry, that was something.

# 63

# Praise the Lord

IT WAS mixed up, like a strange dream you knew was a dream while you dreamed it. The blood dripping, the stickiness, but she was awake then—she knew it was Johnny bleeding to death on top of her. She knew not to moan, not to move, try not to even breathe. They were still there, the Cong who had stopped them, sprayed the Jeep. How would she know when they were gone? Put your mind in another place, think of swaying palm trees, or body surfing, surfing pound, pounding surf, that's it. Maybe that would cover up the pounding sound of her own heart. She was holding her breath because the noise was so loud, but that was making the air stop up in her chest, she would have to heave out a breath or she would burst. If she could think of pounding surf, maybe she could relax against the sound and breathe more shallowly so it wouldn't show. If she could only faint. God, if she could only sleep to get away from the pain in her knee . . . her feet, her feet hurt, blisters. She had walked all day. The little man ahead of her on the trail hadn't looked back in what seemed like five minutes or more, but who knows, maybe it was a few seconds or an hour. They had taken her watch away, but she knew the man behind carried an M-14, it was trained on her last time she looked. How long ago was that? Maybe yesterday. Heat stroke, maybe that was it. Letting your mind wander was good, drift and float, drift, don't be frightened. Pain isn't if you don't acknowledge it, don't fight against it, flow with it, flow, don't fight, flow, drift. But she was a reporter, she should be observing. What if she got out of here, tried to escape, then couldn't describe where she'd been, what she'd seen . . . She knew she'd crossed another river, Jackson told her that. But how did he tell her? Hadn't seen him in a long time. A letter, that was it, tucked in with a reel of tape, a recording he'd made. Dear Valentine, Glad to hear you didn't get killed in that Jeep, he'd said. You can toss out Mulligan's rendition, I've recorded my own "Funny Valentine," dedicated to you . . . The nurse said she was tired of hearing it over and over . . . don't change a hair for me . . . There was another song, Jackson said, at the end of the reel, the Cal Marching Band playing "One More River." No need to listen, no more rivers. Please, God, no more rivers, I am so tired . . . But I must concentrate, focus. Try to come to. They're talking to me, they want me back. Try. Ignore the pain, come back to where they are, focus and come back to where they are . . . She swung higher, up out of their reach. The nun tried to make her come back down to earth. The nun with the white habit and black veil, a Dominican, nervously twisted her long rosary beads in her hands, she was going to tell Angela's father of her defiance. "Praise the Lord and Pass the Ammunition, and we'll all stay free." Angela kept singing as the swing went higher and higher out of the little nun's reach. Don't call on the Lord for killing. Angela knew her father wouldn't punish her, anything she did was fine with him. Her mother just laughed. "Stick to your guns," she said, no pun intended. "You must always be your own person, no matter what the cost."

Angela opened her eyes and a nun was there, but the habit was different from those of her childhood: nurse white. And there was Nick and Ford, and her father.

The first operation, they said, was over.

# 64

# Father Andrews

THEY STAYED—ALL of them, Angela's three men—well into the sultry night. They sat by her bedside, saying little, each in his own scavenged chair squeezed in between Angela's bed and the ones on each side. The sweet smell of flowers was everywhere, almost funereal. Get-well notes dangled from vases and bunches of flowers that were on the windowsill, the bedside table, and lined up along the floor.

Angela, her leg held high and immobile in a Rube Goldberg contraption attached to the foot of her bed, alternately mumbled, then babbled, all the while clutching her father's hand. The doctors had ordered her kept awake and off sedatives until the effects of the anesthetic had completely worn off, so she seemed to be in quite a lot of pain. But her main concern appeared to be the belt around her waist, anchoring her to the bed. She frequently tore at the thing, then would raise up slightly to inspect it, trying to unlock the mystery of how to disengage it. Each time her father would patiently explain that it was there to keep her from tossing in her sleep and undoing the effects of the surgery. "But I'm not asleep," she would counter, her voice stern despite the drugged slur of her words. "I talk to you. Can't you see? I'm a prisoner."

Nick would periodically feel so angry—it didn't occur to him to wonder at what—that he would get up and pace the room, or go outside to smoke a cigarette. After, he'd settle down a bit and report back to his station—that's the way he viewed it, his duty post, his fate-worse-than-death, obligatory chair of pain, watching Angela suffer—he'd wonder at the other men's calm.

Dr. Andrews, Angela's father, had arrived just before the surgery, directly from the airport, carrying his suitcase. Nick marveled that instead of looking bushed and rumpled, he seemed composed, almost serene compared to the rest of them. In contrast, Curtis looked gray and gaunt, evasive, his eyes didn't seem to connect to any of them, not to the doctors or nuns, certainly not to Nick or Angela's father.

Dr. Andrews was tall, and fit, wearing a blue and white seersucker suit. He had shed his striped tie, but despite the unrelenting heat, in all these hours, he had not removed his jacket. Easy to tell, Nick thought, where Angela got her height, but not her green eyes. The doctor's were a vivid blue. Guessing about her red hair, Nick decided Dr. Andrews was probably the source, certainly his smattering of sandy freckles suggested so, despite the steel gray of his closely trimmed crop.

His neat, almost military cut, contrasted sharply with Curtis' longish hair, cut in the British style of the day. Nothing hippy, of course, but it did almost brush the collar of Curtis' blue, short-sleeved cotton shirt. Nick realized with a start that there didn't seem to be much difference in age between Curtis and Andrews. Of course! He frowned at the thought, what a dunce I am. Curtis has got to be ill at ease, feel jealous, maybe. It's her father's hand Angela is holding, not Curtis'. Maybe Angela's got some kind of father fixation! That would explain her stupid attachment to Curtis, Nick thought, with more than a little malice. Nick felt left out, wanted to be the one to hold Angela's hand. Curtis must be feeling the same, in spades. Did anyone, even Angela, understand her priorities? A nurse came by and took her temperature. An orderly brought fresh water, and held her head up while she took a sip. The pages of a letter on her bedside table, fluttered then rested, fluttered then rested, with the rotations of an overhead fan.

Nick found himself daydreaming, as he sat there in the subdued to-and-fro of the hospital ward, Angela moaning, drifting in and out. In his mind, he saw her sit up brightly, unwrap the bandages from around her head, and turn a questioning eye on her father, who promptly delivered a stern parental lecture on the folly of hooking up with a codger as old as himself. "Our knees are creaky, our wind is short." He smiled and patted his daughter's hand. Yeah, Nick grinned ruefully to himself, Andrews said he was a tennis player, he can probably outrun me.

Finally, well past visiting hours and with Angela fast asleep, a nun in white shooed the three men out to a hall, where they stood and awkwardly shifted around. Curtis pulled out his pipe and became very engaged in packing the tobacco, Nick patted around at each of his pockets until he found and lighted a Gauloise. Nothing was said beyond a few mumbled platitudes until Angela's father finally broke the uncomfortable silence. "Can I buy you gentlemen a drink?"

Nick tried to excuse himself, but Curtis immediately insisted, his eyes pleading.

"Dr. Andrews just arrived, Nick. I'm sure he's going to want to talk to as many of Angela's friends as possible to get a clear picture of what's going on here."

Why not, thought Nick. The poor bastard's never laid eyes on Angela's father before. Besides, again his malice made him all but chuckle, I'm curious how this little encounter is going to play out. He didn't at all dislike Curtis, he just wished he'd go home to his wife.

Dr. Andrews was staying in Angela's room at the Continental. They decided to go there so he could dump his suitcase. The first problem they faced was how to get all three tall men into the ubiquitous beetle VWs that were Saigon's version of the yellow cab.

The Volkswagens, their top-half painted white, their bottom a dark royal blue, were distinctive, easy to spot, but not so easy to climb into. As one pulled up at their hail, the three men let the stress of their day explode in giant guffaws as the driver pushed back the passenger seat, beckoning them to get in.

"We'd have to be Indian rubber men," Dr. Andrews said through his laughter.

"I've got the ticket," Ford said to Nick, "let's put the good doctor here, into a cyclo. Might as well give him a taste of native life."

"No, thanks," Andrews replied with a grin. "Coming in from the airport, I thought Saigon traffic was the most frightening thing I'd ever seen. People on bicycles, rickshaws, scooters, running with those poles over their shoulders. I'm a bit too tired tonight to take my life in my hands."

The ice was broken. The three companions found a Mercedes taxi and headed for the hotel.

Before they were five minutes into the ride, Andrews and Curtis discovered they'd both gone to Harvard, although the doctor was well into medical school by the time Curtis arrived.

Nick had been looking forward to a few sparks between these two, but it didn't look like that would materialize.

Nick and Curtis settled on the terrace to order drinks, while Andrews was checking in and depositing his suitcase in Angela's room.

"So what do you think of Angela's father?" Nick tried to prime the pump.

"Great guy," Ford said.

"It's a shame Angela's mother didn't come," Nick persisted.

"You heard what Andrews said." Ford's voice was sharp. "She had surgery of her own to perform."

Nick remembered well. When the doctor had spoken about his wife's absence, he'd said in a teasing voice that he was the only person she would trust to carry her instructions to the doctors who were going to operate on Angela.

Nick settled back in his wicker terrace chair, planning on a slow, uninformative evening.

When the doctor returned from checking into the hotel, he had a quick drink with them on the terrace, then excused himself, pleading exhaustion from his long flight and harrowing day at the hospital. Nick hailed Corrigan and Marbles at a table across the terrace, made his excuses to Ford, and moved on to join the others.

# 65

# Mother Courage

ANGELA SAT in a rocking chair on a side verandah of the hospital, waiting for her father. He was checking on a problem with his ticket. This somehow felt to her like home, the South. The heat so early in the day. Sitting on a porch, rocking, praying for a breeze. The heavy sweetness of flowers. She grinned to herself. Anything would feel homey, good, just to be out of that ward, that bed, away from the antiseptic smells, the sense of helplessness. It was her first day of freedom since the surgery. The doctors had finally put on a walking cast, and with a great deal of effort and support from a nurse and a cleaning woman who happened to be working nearby, she had made it to this second-floor outdoor porch.

The South and flowers. "Clinging vines," her mother loved to call Southern women. She used to say they weren't good for anything, they even were rotten cooks. "Everyone needs to be useful for something," she'd say. She reasoned that if they couldn't take out a spleen, they at least ought to be able "to make a sauce out of something other than Velveeta cheese."

Thoughts of home are nice. Maybe. Maybe not. Mother forever in her silver frame sitting on her polo pony, assured, self-confident. But Johnny's dead. All the others riddled with bullets. Do I have the courage to stay here? Do I want to? I want to be with Ford, but I also need to finish what I started. Perhaps I am my mother's daughter more than I think.

Lifting her plaster cast with both hands, she shifted with some difficulty in the old-fashioned wicker porch rocker to keep her face out of the sun that had moved higher overhead. The plaster should be a relief, it made her mobile at least, but the damned thing was sweaty and confining. She'd seen friends in the past trying to scratch inside their casts with bent coat hangers, or any other long thin object at hand, but at least hers was fresh enough that her skin hadn't started flaking off inside the thing yet.

Taking deep breaths, trying to clear her head, she looked about her at the lush grounds. It was a tropical garden, a green oasis. More like an expensive resort than a hospital. Palm trees. Two-story, verandah-type rooms circling a garden that had barbeque pits! The only odd touch was laundry hanging from balcony railings drying in the sun.

Thoughts of home, that's funny. Ford feels more like family than anything I ever felt in childhood.

Below the verandah, a tiny Vietnamese woman, wearing a bright blue *ao dai* with elaborate white embroidery, walked beside a young man, guiding him along one of the pathways through the thick greenery. She's probably his mother, Angela guessed, from the tenderness the woman showed as she touched his arm, giving gentle direction through her light fingers. The youth, dressed in Ho Chi Minh sandals and a long flowing, dark cotton garment, had white gauze wrapped around his head covering his eyes, and his left arm was in a sling.

God, this war! I've got to get out of here—go to New York with Ford and build a home *and* a career. New York is the perfect place, plenty of newspapers there. Even Nick, who knows so little about emotional participation, who basically shut down at age 12—the day his mother left without telling him by dying—has had to keep pointing out how suspicious I've been about my feelings for Ford. Perhaps it's not the war causing trouble between Ford and me, it's me against myself. Mother moved to North Carolina and had home and career. Did she have to sacrifice a lot to do that?

She followed Pops to Chapel Hill, the same way Ford wants me to follow him. She could have been a surgeon anywhere. But maybe . . . I'd never thought of this before . . . she could have had a more distinguished career somewhere else, a more prestigious hospital. But she's a professor, for Christ sake, in Chapel Hill. She made a bargain with the devil— not my father, but with life. Is that what I have to do, to have a good marriage? It never occurred to me before that Mother had to struggle with anything, everything came easy. She sailed through medical school, surgery residence, childbirth, grammar school—I never heard of anything that was difficult for Mother. If she could help me now, what would she say?

A nurse came and took Angela's temperature, popped a pill in her mouth. She smiled to herself. It feels a hundred and sixteen degrees out here, even with my rocker in the shade, how can one's body temperature stay normal in this heat? Question for a doctor. I guess I have a lot of questions for my mother. Mainly, Mom, what should I do with my life? If I compromise about the place to practice my career, like you did, will I have a joyous marriage, like yours? But was my father attached to your soul from the moment you met? And did I try to repeat with Peter, and perhaps Ford, what you *did,* instead of understanding what you *felt*?

I always figured you'd learned early on to play down as much as possible the fact that you weren't one of the boys. But maybe you had it a lot tougher than you let on. Did you stagger under the weight of parental expectations, too, or was it as easy for you as it always appeared to me? Besides Pops, I thought your only weakness was floozy shoes: closets full of spike heels with bows and sling straps and ankle straps and sequins. But I usually saw you in white oxfords. They always had rust-colored stains, where you'd scrubbed off the spattered blood. Angela sat there, in her rocking chair, and looked at the well-kept grounds and marveled at the sounds of traffic and war beyond the garden walls. She chuckled to herself and thought, this is like no hospital my mother ever saw.

Anything you can do, I can do better; the song lyric ran through her head. Good grief. Why am I sitting here talking to my mother? Johnny died, bleeding to death on top of me, I've got a busted-up leg that's going to need serious rehab, I've got to decide what's next in my life, and I'm having an imaginary conversation with my mother, a woman I rarely ever talk to except in my head. But I've never dared ask her for help with much of anything, even when I was a child. She wasn't critical, just seemed to assume there wasn't anything I didn't know how to do. Didn't leave me much room for either fear or failure. No nonsense. Sent me to the convent school because . . . Angela cocked her head, pursed her lips, and in a poor mimic of her mother's Boston accent silently mouthed her mother's words: *The antidote for papal hokum is easier to provide than warding off the clinging-vine mentality of Southern womanhood.*

Angela was startled from her reverie to see her father come through the metal grillwork gate to the hospital grounds. The image in the silver frame of her mother on her polo pony, Angela's grandfather grinning at her side, was so vivid in Angela's mind that it was disorienting to see her own father walk into the black and white photo that had always stood on her mother's desk.

Dr. Andrews stepped onto the verandah and took the vacant rocker next to Angela. "I brought you some fresh pineapple that I had the hotel chef wrap up for you. And some of your favorite candy bars I brought from home. But I'm afraid they've melted several times over, and will be pretty gooey to unwrap."

"So, Pumpkin," he said to Angela, taking her hand, "my plane is set. I hate it, but I'm afraid I'm going to have to leave you tomorrow."

Angela's face clouded over, the jade eyes took on a shine. Without a word, she raised to her lips the hand that was holding hers, then rubbed the back of it against her cheek.

Angela and her father sat silent for a while, gently rocking, fanning themselves for a breeze.

Dr. Andrews broke the stillness. "Why did you come here, to Vietnam, putting your life at risk?"

"One turns to work when it is the only love you can find," she replied softly. "Mother was lucky, she had both. She had you, and she had work. But it didn't leave much room for me."

Her father cleared his throat. "I always worried about that."

"I know you did."

"Your mother is a remarkable woman."

"Yeah, she's a great surgeon." Angela's tone was measured. She paused for a beat. "But a child needs a mother, not a role model."

"Angela," her father said, his voice skirting anger, but patting her hand, in a doctor-to-patient tone of the pediatrician that he was, "you've been through such an awful time. One harrowing experience after another, and now this—months of rehabilitation after surgery. This is not the time to be deciding your future, nor do I want to be arguing your mother's virtues *or* her shortcomings."

"I got lucky, and ended up with a trail-blazing Madame Curie." The surly, teenaged response bubbled up, along with the resentment of those years.

"Angela, please." Her father's pain was clear, his tone a plea. "Don't take this too far."

His distress seemed to give her permission to say what the child had never said. "Typical. It was you, not her, who showed up here when I was hurt."

"Oh, my baby." Her father appeared stricken.

"She tried to teach me to hate cooking. I don't know how to keep house. Peter did those things for me, and we saw how that worked out. This is where I really belong—with work and servants."

"Pumpkin, you're much more like her than you realize. The same stubbornness, the same perseverance. She's not disappointed you're not a doctor. She just wants to make sure you're on track with yourself. She's more a role model than you want to give her credit for. I know she's been tough on you, but she knows it, too. That's the way she is, and you're very much her daughter."

"Oh, God, Pops, don't tell me that," Angela's voice was nearly a wail. "She's so unreachable, for everyone but you."

"Are you in love with Mr. Curtis?" her father countered.

"Yes," she said, without a moment's hesitation. "He feels like a home. But I'm afraid of ending up in his shadow. I've tried to resist him because I'm afraid I'll lose myself in him."

"Surely, you've established yourself enough by now. Can't you go home, whether it's with him or not, and leave this awful war?"

"I don't know, Pops, I just don't know. I'm still kind of lost."

"Oh, baby," he leaned over and took her in his arms. "What can I do to help? Is it still about Peter?"

"It's about me, I guess," she said softly. "I need to be a success like mother, but I need to have a *you*, like she did."

## 66

# The Easter Chick

As June approached, a quiet settled over Saigon, and Angela began to emerge from her eggshell. The swaddlings of bandages slowly diminished and colors began to appear, not of the bruise variety. One day she had on lipstick, the next a ribbon in her hair. The day she finally had the energy to swap her white hospital sackcloth for a frilly yellow number Curtis had brought, she looked to Nick like an Easter chick busting out.

Curtis said a kind of strange thing that night when he and Nick were leaving the hospital together. "It's awful to say this," he said, "but it's an enormous relief to know where she is. When I go in there in the morning, I know she'll be there. It gives me a kind of contentment. Sounds demented, doesn't it?"

"Not really," replied Nick. "You've kept expecting something awful. Now you know what the worst is."

"Beyond that, I know *where* she is. That woman's like smoke. But this is a definable situation."

They walked on in silence for a while. It was dusk and in the side streets around the hospital there were summer smells of tropical flowers, the city was silent of the sounds of war, although the rat-a-tat-tat of traffic and clouds of exhaust billowing from scooters and chugging ancient Peugots were a war unto themselves.

Curtis broke into the stillness with a question that he seemed to expel rather than say, as though he had been wanting to ask it for a long while. "Who the hell is George?"

"A chopper jockey," replied Nick. "The one whose head blew off in Angela's lap."

"Oh, good Lord," gasped Curtis. "She used to whimper his name in her sleep, and I was fool enough to be jealous."

They walked on, enveloped by another silence. Nick didn't know what to say at this point to console Curtis. That chopper incident had been two months ago, Angela obviously had never told Curtis the full story. Not surprising, considering how he constantly worried about her safety. But she had said in Da Nang that she was going to ask Curtis to see what he could find out about the rotor blade story. She probably hadn't had time before she was hurt. But, Nick wondered, was it up to him to fill Curtis in?

Curtis stopped by a street lantern to light his pipe. It seemed to Nick that he was taking unusual care as he poked at the tobacco, packing it down. But Ford Curtis was a deliberate man. It was that very deliberation that radiated the serenity, even to Nick at times, that caused Angela to call him "my anchor, a safe harbor." Curtis took a hard draw on his pipe and said, "Angela cares for you a great deal, and I think she feels that you understand her better than I."

Oh, hell, thought Nick, now what?

"I'm sorry to always be starting these conversations that embarrass you," Curtis went on after a moment, still looking at the tobacco instead of Nick, "but I'm tired of constantly being cast in the role of the heavy. Angela loves me, I know, and yet she actually views me as some sort of enemy."

Nick blurted it out before he'd had a chance to make up his mind what he should do. "Help her with a story that's extremely important to her."

"Like what?" Curtis' head shot up, he glowered at Nick.

"Well," Nick began, "it has to do with that crash you and Angela were in, and that's why she was so frantically trying to find George."

# 67

# The Lonesome Cowboy

ANGELA WAS up and moving around on a walker a few days after her second operation. She and Nick were making their way slowly around the hospital's interior courtyard, Nick along to make sure she didn't fall. She felt so unsteady, she was afraid she'd break something else. But it was so good to be outside, out of that damned bed, away from waking nightmares, she felt burbly, almost giddy. Downright giddy, she thought. This almost-wellness is a new kind of high.

"Hard to believe we're in a hospital," she said. "Palms, banana trees. It's like a jungle." Several large barbecue pits with open, palm frond roofs were dotted around the grounds where relatives came to cook patients' meals. Laundry drying in the sun hung over the balcony rails of the hospital's second-floor porches.

It was shortly after a rain that had left the humidity so high there were visible steam and water vapors rising from the tropical plants and even the lawn. Smoke curled up from one of the cooking pits that had been used at lunch. The mugginess accentuated the sweet smell of flowers and honeysuckle, a nice contrast to the odors of gangrene and antiseptic she had endured for weeks.

She was wearing a pair of shoes she'd had Ford pick up at a local market. They were just the thing for her present gait. She'd seen old Chinese women mince along in them, funky, black fabric, little girl shoes. She needed the Mary-Jane strap across the instep because she didn't have enough mobility to hold anything else on her feet. She was shuffling along sliding one foot in front of the other, just like she'd seen the Chinese do, trying to learn to use arm strength to guide the walker and keep her going, when she looked up and let out a little yip of joy.

"Durned if this place isn't really hotter than West Texas," drawled Mac Wheeler, his arms loaded with presents.

As Angela threw her arms wide in a welcoming embrace, Nick leaped to steady the walker and Mac grabbed Angela in a bear hug that left them standing in a growing pile of tapes, candy and brightly colored silk scarves. A rain of get-well cards in their white envelopes slowly fluttered to the damp lawn.

"It looks like chopper jocks have raided PXs from Da Nang to Cam Ranh Bay," Nick said. There was even a bush hat and a bright yellow 1st Cav neckerchief on top of the pile.

"I don't exactly know how word got around that you'd durn near done yourself in. But I'd get to talkin' to fellas one place and another and was amazed at how many got a little glint in their eye whenever your name came up," Wheeler said to Angela with a glint in his own. "I'm afraid I dishonored your profession when last we met, with suggestions that some of y'all spend a little too much time on your duffs. Judging from all the pilots who claim to have carried you in or out of a firebase, I'd say that you've brought the national average for trips per man way up."

Angela beamed, hearing Mac's honeyed words. He *is* a charmer, she thought. In another life, or in a time before she met Ford, she would have grooved on the idea of a barnstorming adventure with him. Learning to fly, really getting good at it, making a small plane do dips and turns and pinpoint landings. She loved the hot dog stunts, the low-level flying of the chopper pilots. She was amazed by their mastery, their skill. Being shot at was another matter. The thrills of peace-time soaring, living in the clouds, would be quite enough for her. But there was just never time in life to have all the adventures one would like. To get really good at anything, you had to stick, had to take a stand, you sometimes had to fight. One can't just blow around like a tumbleweed.

"You guys are doing one hell of a job," Angela replied, matching his easy palaver with some of her own, knowing that talk of tumbleweeds would just make them both sad. "You're saving lives like crazy, dipping in and getting guys out and to MASH units seconds after they're hit. It's awesome."

"Hot damn! That kinda sweet talk's obviously gotten you any place you set your pretty little head to go," Mac said, that lopsided grin taking over his face.

"You better believe it," Nick quipped. "The correspondents with a pilot on their side are the lucky ones getting out and the ones with the competitive edge going in."

"Well, Petunia," said Wheeler, "you really stuck your foot in it this time, didn't you?"

"Yeah, literally. I'll have a bad leg for a long time, maybe forever."

"Have to start calling you gimpy, I guess."

"Thanks a lot! You sure know how to cheer a girl up!"

"I'm from Texas, ma'am. We just call 'em right out, down there. Didn't you ever hear of Deaf Smith County?"

"Lord, no! Are you serious?" she sputtered out before she broke up laughing. Wheeler had a good effect on her, he could always make her laugh. "So does that mean from now on I'll be known as Gimpy Martinelli, or Martinelli the Gimp?"

"I'm not crazy about either," said Wheeler. "Seems to me Petunia the Gimp, or maybe Gimpy Short Stuff has a much better ring. What do you think, Nick?"

Nick, looking startled to be included, stammered as he made his move to go. "Sounds like the Mafia. But, your call. I'm outta here. I got stories to file and some drinking to do and all sorts of other serious matters to attend to." He started to cross the lawn, then turned back. "I'm not sure about the petunia part, though. This kid behaves more like a cactus."

"You guys are wonderful hospital companions," Angela said with a grin, "just one cheery word after another."

"Are you planning to marry Curtis?" Mac asked in an abrupt change of both subject and mood.

"Oh, shit," Nick said under his breath as he hurried out of the courtyard.

"Yes, I am," Angela replied.

"Well, if you ever get around to thinking you could stand West Texas . . ." Mac's voice trailed off.

Angela balanced herself with one hand on her walker and reached out and patted his cheek: "I couldn't work there, Mac," she said, hoping that would take some of the sting from the rejection.

"I know," he said. "And I couldn't work any place else."

"I know," she said.

"Trains passing in the night. It was fun," he said. "See you around, pretty lady."

"See you around," she said. And he was gone.

Angela tied the yellow scarf around the crown of her new bush hat and started wearing it around the hospital all the time.

Finally, Nick snapped one day in an exasperated voice: "Whatever happened to the seaweed hair? Anything would be an improvement over that fucking cowboy's hat."

"It's something fun to do," Angela said with a laugh. "I need all the help I can get to keep me cheered up until I can get out of this hospital."

# 68

# War Lovers

ANGELA HAD graduated from the walker to a cane and wore a yellow hibiscus in her hair. She and Nick were in the hospital courtyard again, sitting on a tree bench, shaded from the hot noonday sun. They were talking about war, a subject ever on their minds. But this was different, more philosophical, about their childhoods, and how they landed up in Vietnam.

"Staying here has to be some form of insanity," Nick said.

"Yes," said Angela. "What are you going to do?"

"I don't know," Nick replied. "Harry's got another bug up his ass."

His foreign editor was starting to put pressure on him to come home, and Nick had been using every stall imaginable to resist. Admittedly, he hadn't been coming up with any good enterprise, the spot stories he'd filed the first couple of weeks of Angela's recovery were definitely routine. But in the last week or so, he had borne down and come up with some better stuff. It wasn't all that difficult. With the stepped-up fighting in May, roughly two thousand U.S. troops were killed—the highest body count of any month since the war began. Still, Harry was pressing. Things were heating up like crazy at home. Bobby Kennedy had been assassinated in early June; civil rights protests and anti-war demonstrations continued; and with Johnson having declared himself out of the running, the Democratic National Convention to nominate a presidential candidate—slated for Chicago in August—was expected to be a mess.

"Do you think I'm weird, or sicko, or what?" Nick asked. His feelings about the war were a muddle.

Angela started laughing.

"No, seriously," Nick said. "Maybe it's like prison, or something: After a while you can't imagine what life would be like or how you could survive on the outside."

And suddenly, he began reminiscing. It was the first time since Angela had known him that Nick had seemed to be speculating on his own motives about anything. He remembered that when he was a kid, he secretly didn't want World War II to end. Without the war, he couldn't imagine what H. V. Kaltenborn would have to say on the radio news, or what his family would talk about at the dinner table. The war had given him this big sense of purpose. He'd saved his pennies to buy war stamps and pasted them in his savings book. He took his wagon out every Saturday around the neighborhood to collect old newspapers and bacon grease and fat that the housewives saved in their kitchens for recycling for the war effort. He sat through "Thirty Seconds Over Tokyo" seven times.

"I knew it was bad to want the war to keep going, but I couldn't image life without it," he told Angela, as they sat there in that tropical garden with its war going on outside.

"So, I don't know. Does that make me a sicko?"

She didn't laugh this time, but admitted to somewhat similar childhood experiences. She recalled swinging on the playground when she was in the first or second grade and pumping higher and higher out of reach of her favorite nun who was trying to stop her from singing, "Praise the Lord and Pass the Ammunition."

"That little nun really had me pissed over that song. She'd been singing it herself the week before. Now here she was suddenly being downright unpatriotic. As I swung higher and higher out of her reach, I demanded to know why she'd changed her tune, so to speak. Poor thing, she was so distressed she blurted out that Mother Superior didn't think it appropriate for nuns to be invoking the Lord to supply arms to the Allies. I won the battle by making her give me an answer. But I lost that war. I wasn't her favorite anymore."

"I guess war's a really big thing to little kids," Nick mused aloud.

"Judging from the two of us, big ones too," she said.

Wisps of smoke curled up from the ashes of cooking pits. Lunch hour was over, mothers and wives who had come to feed patients had left, little stirred on the hospital grounds. No breeze, no people. It was quiet time in the wards, where they at least had ceiling fans.

"Let's walk," Angela said, grabbing her cane. "It's so sticky, maybe moving will give us a breath of relief."

They shuffled along in a few moments of silence, Angela leaning hard on her cane. With no lead in, Nick said into the quiet, "It's hard to be patriotic or unpatriotic about this mess, it's just a dirty job." But it also was the Big Story. It was easy to resent guys like Curtis who got broken in on earlier, more clear-cut wars. It was the civilian involvement here that blurred things so. A kid riding a bike having an arm blown off, a grandmother decapitated as she bent to weed her garden.

They talked a lot about the war in those weeks that Angela lived in a hospital.

They talked about the charge that they were some kind of glory hounds, willing to put up with anything to build professional reputations. That, they decided, was sappy. In any other profession people are complimented for working hard and doing a good job, especially under difficult conditions. But reporters get accused of being headline hungry, self-important.

"Deadline pressure, the need to get the story first, doesn't make sense to readers," Nick said, as they slowly made their way through the hospital gardens.

"Yeah," said Angela, "but if you didn't have the competition, you'd end up with someone leisurely putting out a white paper when they feel like it. And guess what? That would end up being the government. You'd get nothing more than tonnage of bombs dropped, or body counts."

"Or worse," laughed Nick, "nothing but fucking propaganda like the North Viets dish out."

Angela especially fretted over the differences between emotional distance and the ethical restraints of a reporter's detachment. Was Curtis right that she and Nick were getting jaded? Or did the work nourish a jaundice whose seed was already planted?

"Or were we once truly young?" Angela said, in a nearly inaudible voice, her jade eyes suddenly vacant.

Neither looked at the other in the ensuing silence. Angela limped to the next bench and sat, slightly out of breath.

Nick, still standing, stuck his hands in his pockets and looked down at her with a frown. "Hell, all this talk is just a waste of time. We'll never figure it out."

"So what's going to happen when you go back?" asked Angela, sitting straighter, and putting on a bright, cheerful voice. She reached behind her, and tore an unidentifiable blue flower from its bush. "Marry that girl?"

"Mary Alice Ordinary?"

"Nick, you're terrible. Surely she has a last name. You're always referring to her that way."

"Moriarty."

"I don't understand you at all," Angela said with impatience. "Do you love her?"

"She's OK. I just felt sort of roped into the deal. She's not my type. She aspires to a green kitchen. Maybe we should get her and Ford together."

Angela laughed. "You've got it wrong. He's not the green kitchen type. He's just well-grounded, orderly."

"Yeah, he's been orderly about moving your stuff from the Continental to his place, while you're stuck in here. He's been orderly about being rotated home right after you get discharged."

"That's fine with me. You already know that, thanks to *you*, Ford got them to put together a team that's just about got the rotor blade thing nailed. They've put their Pentagon guy on it, and someone from the Seattle bureau is dealing with Boeing. My name will be on the story as a contributor."

"Jesus, a contributor. What a rip off."

"Yeah, I was crushed, at first, but at least it's getting done. And it means that I won't have any trouble finding a job in New York. He's already found us an apartment."

"While his wife stays in Boston?" Nick fairly screeched. He sat down hard. He had sensed *something* was coming; Ford had been looking fairly smug lately. But definite plans to move to New York!

"His wife's filed for divorce," Angela's retort was quick and sharp. "She's the one who refused to come here, wants to '*do her own thing.*'" This last was delivered with hand on hip, an imperious toss of her head, shaking loose the hibiscus, which fell to her lap to join the mysterious blue. "I'm not some kind of home wrecker, for Christ sake."

"Curtis seems to have a problem with do-your-own-thing women," Nick said dryly.

"That's ridiculous," Angela replied. "He just doesn't want me to get killed, or spend the rest of my life limping like this," she threw her arms wide, shaking her cane in the air, "around a hospital."

Nick persisted. "Don't leave with him!" He jumped to his feet in his agitation. "Let's put him with Mary Alice, and you and I can go off into the sunset together."

Angela laughed, but her tone was gentle, her voice held a smile. "Yeah, and live off beer and canned beans and TV dinners the rest of our lives?"

"What's wrong with that? Now you're sounding like Ford."

"Someone has to provide the stability. Even you know that much. I'm sure that's why you picked someone like Mary Alice to get engaged to."

"I told you, I didn't get engaged to her. She and her mother just decided that without much consultation with me."

Angela grinned. "Well, sweetie, I guess you're beginning to catch on that's the way women are supposed to operate. It keeps the world going round."

"How about you?"

"If all the women were like me, we wouldn't have any homefront to come home to," she replied with a distinct edge of sadness in her voice.

# 69

# Saying Goodbye

The night before they were to leave, Angela and Curtis had a huge party. The pink villa was bare as a barn; most of their personal things already had been shipped out. Curtis' house boy, Kim Chi, had brought in what appeared to be his entire family—mother, father, several younger siblings—and put them to work serving up drinks and little bites of things. There also was a table laden with obvious PX purchases—potato chips, pretzels, Ritz and Nabisco crackers, Oreo cookies and Lipton's onion soup dip.

It seemed to Nick that every correspondent in the country had shown up, even guys who'd been out in the field and had to make a special effort to get back. There were several military press officers, and Oscar Brown and Jive Knees, who had gotten Angela out of Cambodia, and some cowboys from the 1st Cav, including Mac Wheeler. She wore that bush hat Mac had given her through the whole evening, although she was otherwise demure in a long cream-colored hostess skirt, which had the added advantage of helping to hide her limp.

When Nick first arrived, he spotted a cute little blonde with a turned-up nose surrounded by a gaggle of guys. Single women were a rare commodity and always had an entourage. Undaunted by the competition, Nick sauntered over to check out the goods.

"I think it's great she's getting out of here," the woman was saying to her circle, as Nick joined them.

"How come you're hanging in?" was Nick's opening gambit.

"I made the mistake of enlisting," she responded in a little girl voice that belied the grown-up nature of her words. "And I've got two months, four days, and," she checked her watch, "and 14 hours." The woman was an Army nurse, named Mary Lou.

"Angela's been through one horror after another," Mary Lou continued. "She loves Curtis and she's going home to a good life. We should all be so lucky."

"Amen," said Curtis, the smiling host, welcoming Nick to the party and joining the group.

Parks came bobbing by, stoned and drunk, and mimicked Curtis. "Amen. Amen," Parks said again. "We got to get to Cambodia."

"Don't remind me," Nick said. It was a bad night for a party as far as he was concerned—he, Parks and Corrigan were headed north early in the morning because of continuing reports of incursions into Cambodia. Crazy Parks said he'd just stay up all night. Nick was planning to at least pass out somewhere for an hour or so, or he knew he'd be too wrecked to function.

The evening was a swirl. There were toasts and a big cake, and booze that ran like rain. Curtis told anyone who groused about Angela's leaving that he had put out feelers at several New York papers about finding her a job. And, he pointed out, the Chinook rotor blade story was set to run within a couple of days. Angela was being credited for initiating the investigation, and what she had run into with the Army's stonewalling was being attributed to her.

"The Army and Boeing were aware of the problem all along," Curtis said. "A timing mechanism would apparently just suddenly go haywire, and they couldn't figure out what was causing it. They're not quite sure if they have yet. That's why they didn't want press near the downed planes. It's a hell of a good story."

Nick laughed. "It sure is. None of us could believe Angela, at first. But she was right."

"Indeed she was," Ford replied with something akin to a proud-papa grin.

The pink villa was wall-to-wall people for a while, but at a reasonable hour the more sensible types said their goodbyes and left. The old standards—Cole Porter and Frank Sinatra—that had started out the evening on the record player morphed into The Doors and James Brown, which had to compete with ever-louder dissertations on

Johnson, General Giap, print versus TV, Buddhist immolations and, as always, the Boston Red Sox. A few folks, who were too drunk to do so with any focus, were attempting to dance. Throughout the raucous chaos, Curtis appeared to be gliding, wearing a beneficent, placid smile. It seemed to Nick that Brown's belting, "I Feel Goo od," expressed the old fart's sentiments exactly. What a switch, Nick thought in wonderment—no more objections, no world-weary pronouncements on the climate of assassination. Just that goddamned, stupid, fucking cat-that-ate-the-canary, shit-eating glide. Everything finally became a blur for him, and around 1 a.m., Nick found a couch that was being left behind and curled up for a snooze.

Someone finally shook him awake, and as he and Parks were leaving with the last diehards about 3 a.m., Parks told Angela they'd pick her up in a couple of hours and give her a lift to the airport. Angela leapt at the idea, saying that way she wouldn't have to say goodbye yet. Curtis already had arranged for a car to pick the two of them up, but he said he would go ahead in the morning and she could ride to the airport with the guys.

WHEN NICK, Parks and Corrigan arrived at 5:30, Angela was standing out in front of the villa holding her cane and a lightweight duffel bag.

Nick wasn't surprised to see her carrying her bush hat by a cord instead of the big picture hat she had been traveling with the first day she'd arrived in-country, but he was startled to see her wearing jungle boots with her jeans.

"She's dressed for work," Parks yelled. He jumped out of the Jeep and started doing a crazy kind of Indian war whoop, making a little circling dance around the duffel she'd tossed to the ground as she climbed with difficulty into the Jeep because of her gimpy leg.

She laughed and said, "You're nuts," to Parks as he threw her bag into the Jeep and climbed in the back with Corrigan, but she hardly said three more words all the way to Tan Son Nhut. She said she felt like "death warmed over" from the effects of the party, and since no one else but crazy Parks felt any better, they made the trip in grim silence.

When they got to the airport parking lot, Corrigan got out of the backseat and helped her down and picked up her bag to carry to the reception area. She leaned in and hugged Parks, then limped around to Nick on the driver's side. His hands were frozen to the wheel; he couldn't look at her. She reached over and turned his face toward her and kind of shook it. "Chin up, Buckaroo, I'll see you in New York in two months. This man's war is almost over, and before you know it, you'll be back in Chicago covering grass fires."

Corrigan gave her his arm and she took it. It was the first time Nick had ever seen her lean on anyone. Just before they got to the door of the terminal reception area, she turned and reached for her duffel bag. Parks and Nick could see by his body language that Corrigan was reluctant to give it up. They talked for a second, she took the bag and pushed open the glass door.

# 70

# Each Time We Say Goodbye, I Cry a Little

Angela finally caught a glimpse of Ford in the swirling mélange of sweating, shouting, shoving transients who seemed forever milling through the steam-room atmosphere in the unairconditioned, barracks-like main passenger terminal of Tan Son Nhut. This hot box and the people in it never seemed to change—not their faces nor their piles of luggage, some rope-tied, some with designer labels. She wondered if a hidden conveyer belt didn't endlessly rotate the same Hades-shackled souls in and out, round and round like painted wooden figures on a carnival merry-go-round. The circus image probably came from the calliope beat of her own racing heart, her breath coming in short, harsh gasps tooting in her ears.

There he stood, that wonderful serene shelter of a man calmly puffing on his pipe, surrounded by parcels and bundles and bags, looking just like someone who was in the orderly process of relocating his household. And he had the birdcage. That damned bamboo birdcage, Christ, she was afraid she was going to cry. She knew the lace tablecloth they had bought during the three-day holiday in Bangkok and the crystal candlesticks were stuffed in with his shaving gear in his overnighter. The notes she'd finally had the courage to make on the ambush in Cholon were in the beige suede satchel under his foot. She and Peter had bought that bag after agonizing over its expense on their honeymoon in Cordoba. She'd always wanted a cordovan leather suitcase, but the one she ended up with was a light-colored suede that showed the dirt, and it was under Ford's foot. There he stood, her life neatly wrapped in tidy bundles at his feet, with a cage for a bird balanced precariously on the top of the heap.

H E   S A W  *her* the instant she pushed through the door. One of the lesser advantages of being tall, you could always see who was coming at you. Christ knows, he could hardly have missed her, he'd had his eyes riveted on that door for the last 20 minutes as he absently rolled between his fingers like Captain Queeg her only jewelry—jade earrings and a string of pearls—knotted into the end of a silk scarf and stuck for safekeeping into the right-hand pocket of his bush jacket. He hadn't really believed she wouldn't show up, but still . . . And he could hardly lose her in the crowd now as she moved toward him, her rolling, stiff-legged gait was as easy to track as a bobbing surfboard, crisscrossing as it angled its way through the waves toward a beach. As tall as he was, he also saw the shadow cross her face at the very moment she got near enough for him to feel the familiar impact of the sea-green depth of the jade eyes. That goddamned birdcage, he thought. He should have chucked it, but he didn't have the heart—they'd been so happy the day they'd bought those lovebirds.

"I'm sorry," she said. "But *please* understand. I can't go with you. Not yet. I hope you'll wait in New York for me, not go back to Boston."

"DAMMIT . . . don't." The first word came out hot, but cooled fast to despair. He felt hope run down like a depleting wind-up toy.

"Please, let me come in my own time." Her voice was pleading. "I've got to find out what's going on in Cambodia."

He reached over and gently touched her hair. "In this business, my darling, there is *always* another Cambodia."

"L E T ' S   G E T moving," Nick yelled at Corrigan from the Jeep, its motor still running.

The old Reuters guy just kept standing there, rooted, staring at the door Angela had pushed through to enter the terminal.

"He's acting like some dummy. It's bloody hot just sitting in the bloody sun," Parks complained from the backseat.

Nick yelled again and started honking. They had work to do, and Nick wanted to get the fuck out of here.

"For Christ sake," Nick grumbled and shifted into gear, as Corrigan finally came back to the Jeep. He got into the front seat, then started to climb over it into the back.

"So what's happening, man?" Parks asked him.

With the same quizzical expression in his voice that he had on his face, Corrigan said, "She said maybe we should wait."

Nick looked up and she was coming through the glass door, leaning heavily on the cane in her left hand as she rolled along, making a wide swing with her stiff right leg. They all just sat there, staring. Even Parks was quiet. She used part of the roll of her gait to give her the momentum to toss her duffel bag in the back. As she jammed the bush hat on her head, heaved herself into the front passenger seat and pulled her stiff leg in behind her, she said, "Let's go."

The Jeep was already in gear and Nick shot out of there like a bull out of a rodeo chute.

He kept his head straight on the road and didn't say a word, but watched from the corner of his eye as she pulled a pair of wraparound shades out of the breast pocket of her khaki shirt; the white tag sewn on the flap said "Martinelli, *bao chi*." When Nick finally turned to look, he couldn't see her eyes or read any expression behind the big sunglasses, but there was a faint streak of white marking a line of washed-away rouge down her cheek. It was the third time he'd seen her cry.

—30—

# Reading Group Discussion Questions:

1. To what does the title refer: *The Five O'Clock Follies*? What does this name coined by the war correspondents suggest about their perceptions of the military bureaucracy? As you progress through the novel, do you feel the name to be appropriate? Why or why not?
2. What first impression does Angela make on Nick O'Brien and Bo Parks when she steps off the plane in Saigon? What impression does she make at the first military briefing? What problems face an unknown freelancer in a war zone? What problems face an attractive woman beginning a freelancing career in a war zone? Is gender bias currently a problem in the United States? With help, Angela evolves as a war correspondent. How do opportunity and acceptance happen for her? How is Nick instrumental in her success? How does her story-seeking nature contribute?
3. Some characters seriously influence Angela's opportunities and perceptions as she begins her career as a correspondent in Saigon. How and why do some characters go out of their way to help her? Consider Bo Parks, Mac Wheeler, John Simenson, George, the Medevac pilot. Does Ford Curtis fit into this category as a "helper"? Why or why not?
4. Angela observes late in the novel that Nick "lacks emotional participation." Do you agree? Do you receive some insights about why this may be true of him? How does this "flaw" manifest itself? Do you see Nick growing emotionally as the novel progresses? What does his behavior after Cholon suggest about Nick? What does his acceptance of Curtis as her romantic choice suggest about him?

5. Explain the trauma Angela experiences during the Medevac expedition and at Khe Sanh. How does Nick's sensitivity bring Angela and him closer emotionally? Explain. They had begun to trust each other early in the novel and actually admitted to being "best friends" previously. What events with the "White Mice" and Tet offensive led to this trust and friendship?
6. Angela seems conflicted about love. How might her childhood have triggered this? Describe the dilemma she feels, the needs that she has. How has her life seemed to reflect this confusion? Consider Jackson's challenge . . . "another river to cross" . . . Peter as a safety net that failed. How does the phrase that pops up repeatedly . . . *a green kitchen* . . . epitomize her fears? How does her father help her deal with her insecurities, to see her mother in another light as she recovers from her Cholon injuries?
7. This conflict seems to confuse her feelings for Ford Curtis. Why is she afraid of him? Why is she so attracted to him? What leads to the emotional blow ups they have, one in Curtis' home in front of guests, the other in the hotel among other correspondents. Are her physical attraction and her feelings when she's with him sufficient reasons for a long-term commitment? What future do you foresee for Angela if she marries Curtis and returns to the States? Is it possible that she and Nick might have a future? What's the symbolism of the bird cage?
8. Angela has a need to prove herself. How do her war zone decisions and forays reflect this need? Consider Hue. Was this a wise choice? Was it a successful choice? Why? What motives does the military brass ascribe to her experiences as a prisoner of the Cong and her politically charged stories? What other danger does she seek out in order to find "enterprise" stories? Consider her Medevac foray and Khe Sanh. Also she challenges authority with her observations about the Chinook's mechanical failure. Explain.
9. A conflict that crops up repeatedly in the novel is the military's and the public's view of reporters, their motives, their competitiveness. Angela voices their importance when she states: "Reporters can freeze the event, lift it up for a moment and put it on stage . . . we represent society's support and sympathy. Our very presence means this is horrendous, we're going to record it for all time, put it in the newspaper." Can you agree? Why or why not? The

bureaucracy would like the press to subscribe to the "official" line. What discrepancy in official information almost kills Angela and Curtis? How does withholding important information contribute to tragedy in the novel?
10. Why have the wars in Vietnam, Iraq, and Afghanistan been divisive for our country? Has public acceptance of Vietnam changed over time? Explain. Compare the public view of these later wars with World War II.

THEASA TUOHY has worked for five daily newspapers and the Associated Press. She is co-book author of **Scandalous: The Musical,** an award winning show about the life of DH Lawrence, and has written a memoir about renovating her home in France. She is currently working on a mystery set in Paris. She lives in Manhattan.